S
Through Dark Clouds

1870 - 1871

Book # 15 in The Bregdan Chronicles
Sequel to Misty Shadows of Hope

Ginny Dye

Shining Through Dark Clouds

1870 - 1871

Published by Bregdan Publishing
Bellingham, WA 98229

www.BregdanChronicles.net

www.GinnyDye.com

www.BregdanPublishing.com

ISBN# 9781093497069

Printed in the United States of America

For Linda Baumgarten

Friends create the magic of life. We have traveled many roads together, tackled challenges, and been fierce Scrabble competitors. You are a gift to me!

A Note from the Author

My great hope is that *Shining Through Dark Clouds* will both entertain, challenge you, and give you courage to face all the seasons of your life. I hope you will learn as much as I did during the months of research it took to write this book. Once again, I couldn't make it through an entire year, because there was just too much happening. As I move forward in the series, it seems there is so much going on in so many arenas, and I simply don't want to gloss over them. As a reader, you deserve to know all the things that created the world you live in now.

When I ended the Civil War in The Last, Long Night, I knew virtually nothing about Reconstruction. I have been shocked and mesmerized by all I have learned – not just about the North and the South – but now about the West.

I grew up in the South and lived for eleven years in Richmond, VA. I spent countless hours exploring the plantations that still line the banks of the James River and became fascinated by the history.

But you know, it's not the events that fascinate me so much – it's the people. That's all history is, you know. History is the story of people's lives. History reflects the consequences of their choices and actions – both good and bad. History is what has given you the world you live in today – both good and bad.

This truth is why I named this series The Bregdan Chronicles. Bregdan is a Gaelic term for weaving: Braiding. Every life that has been lived until today is a part of the woven braid of life. It takes every person's story to create history. Your life will help determine the course of history. You may think you don't have much of an impact. You do. Every action you take will reflect in someone else's life. Someone else's decisions. Someone else's future. Both good and bad. That is the **Bregdan Principle**...

Every life that has been lived until today is a part of the woven braid of life.
It takes every person's story to create history.
Your life will help determine the course of history.
You may think you don't have much of an impact.
You do.
Every action you take will reflect in someone else's life.
Someone else's decisions.
Someone else's future.
Both good and bad.

My great hope as you read this book, and all that will follow, is that you will acknowledge the power you have, every day, to change the world around you by your decisions and actions. Then I will know the research and writing were all worthwhile.

Oh, and I hope you enjoy every moment of it and learn to love the characters as much as I do!

I'm constantly asked how many books will be in this series. I guess that depends on how long I live! My intention is to release two books a year – continuing to weave the lives of my characters into the times they lived. I hate to end a good book as much as anyone – always feeling so sad that I must leave the characters. You shouldn't have to be sad for a long time!

You are now reading the 15th book - # 16 will be released in early Fall 2019. If you like what you read, you'll want to make sure you're on my mailing list at <u>www.BregdanChronicles.net</u>. I'll let you know each time a new one comes out so that you can take advantage of all my fun launch events, and you can enjoy my BLOG in between books!

Many more are coming!

Sincerely,
Ginny Dye

<u>Chapter One</u>
September 1870

Carrie stared down into the depths of her luggage, determined not to listen to the whinnies and calls of the horses cavorting through the plantation pastures. Early September in Virginia was always hot, but this day promised to be hotter than normal. Closing the window to block out the sounds pulling at her heart would only make the heat in her and Anthony's bedroom even more unbearable. She shoved back the strands of black, curly hair escaping her travel bun and reached for another dress to fold.

"We'll be back before you know it," Anthony said encouragingly.

Carrie sighed, not surprised her perceptive husband had picked up on her discontent. "I know. It's just so hard to leave," she lamented, immediately suffused with guilt. "I want to go home to Frances, and I'm eager to finish my internship..." Her voice trailed off as she thought of her beautiful daughter whom she hadn't seen in almost a month. Frances had chosen to stay behind in Philadelphia for this trip, eager to stay with Jeremy and Marietta to help with the twins, but her last letter had revealed how much she missed her mother and father.

"But every time you leave the plantation, it feels like a piece of your heart is ripped out."

Carrie gazed into Anthony's green eyes, which were so like her own, as he finished her sentence. "Yes." Despite her determination, she stepped to the open window to look out over the fields. There had been just enough rain to keep the grass a verdant green, but the trees were drooping from the heat. A bank of clouds on the far horizon promised relief by late afternoon, but it also made her realize they needed to hurry if they hoped to reach Richmond before the storm hit. Summer storms made carriage travel not only miserable, but dangerous. She took a deep breath and turned back to her luggage. Delaying her departure would not change the inevitable outcome.

"I'll be just as glad as you to put Philadelphia behind us once and for all," Anthony murmured as he folded a shirt a bit haphazardly.

Carrie knew how true that was. Anthony had been amazingly supportive during this past year, and had encouraged her to do her surgical internship with Dr. Wild, but she knew his heart was here on the plantation, and also in Richmond with River City Carriages.

"Three and a half more months," she said firmly. "Three and a half months, and then we'll be home for good." That knowledge gave her the strength she needed to finish folding her dress and place it in her luggage.

Anthony joined in the game. "Three and a half more months before you and Janie return to start your practice in Richmond with Elizabeth and Florence."

Carrie smiled. "Three and a half more months before I'll never have to tell Granite good-bye again." She sobered quickly at the thought of leaving her beautiful Thoroughbred, who was showing his advanced age. She believed he would be waiting for her when she returned, but that didn't make it easier to be separated from him again.

"Annie said she would have breakfast ready for all of us in ten minutes." Anthony eyed the grandfather clock in the corner of their room.

Carrie nodded. "Matthew and Janie are probably already waiting downstairs."

Anthony grimaced. "Which means Matthew will have already attacked the cinnamon rolls Annie promised to make."

Carrie smiled, knowing he was trying to distract her. "Annie will have made enough for ten people."

"As long as they came out of the stove *after* Moses left for the fields, that will be true."

Carrie laughed. "You're right that Moses can eat as much as six men. If John was with him, then there may not be *any* left." Moses' six-year-old son was quickly growing to his father's imposing size.

Anthony stuffed his last shirt in his luggage, then latched it securely and hefted it into his hand. "I would stay to commiserate with you, but the lure of cinnamon rolls is too great. If there are only two left, I'm afraid you'll be out of luck." His eyes twinkled as he headed for the door.

"Not a chance!" Carrie retorted. Pushing aside all pretense of careful packing, she threw in her comfortable pants, secured her luggage and whirled to beat him to the door.

A firm knock stopped both of them in their tracks.

"Miss Carrie? Mr. Anthony?"

Carrie frowned at the frantic note in Annie's voice.

Anthony stepped forward immediately to open the door. "What's wrong, Annie?"

Annie's dark eyes were wide with concern, her round, ebony face creased with worry. "It's Miss Janie. She's done gone into labor."

Carrie gasped, dropped her luggage and reached for her medical bag. "It's too early."

"Seems like somebody forgot to tell whatever little one be in there wantin' out," Annie snapped as she turned to hurry back down the hallway.

Carrie and Anthony were right on her heels as she entered Matthew and Janie's bedroom. Matthew, his blue eyes crinkled with concern beneath his red hair, looked relieved when they entered the room.

Carrie hurried to Janie's side. "This couldn't wait until we got to Philadelphia?" she asked lightly. She understood the stark fear on Janie's face. Her friend's first pregnancy had nearly ended in disaster. If it hadn't been for Carrie's ability to perform a Cesarean section on her, little Robert wouldn't be with them. Janie would very likely have died, as well. She glanced around the room for their rambunctious son.

Annie read her mind. "Robert is playing with Mr. Thomas downstairs. Your father knows what be going on."

Carrie nodded and turned back to Janie "Tell *me* what's going on."

Janie gazed into her eyes, obviously searching for strength and courage. "The contractions started about fifteen minutes ago. I thought it was false labor, but they're getting stronger." She reached out to grab Carrie's hands. "It's too soon," she whispered, her voice vibrating with the fear imprinted in her soft, blue eyes. "Is it happening again, Carrie?"

Carrie squeezed her hands but didn't bother to give her false assurances. She glanced up at Anthony and

Matthew. "I need to examine my patient," she said smoothly. "Please send for Polly." Having an experienced midwife to assist her, no matter what happened, would be wise.

"I'll get her," Anthony said quickly.

"And me and Mr. Matthew gonna get some hot water ready," Annie announced.

Carrie, grateful Annie would keep Matthew busy, turned back to Janie as the room emptied. "Tell me what you're feeling."

"Terrified," Janie managed.

"I understand," Carrie soothed, "but there is every reason to think this is just an early birth." She pushed aside the haunting memory of the umbilical cord wrapped around Robert's neck during Janie's first birth.

"Or a repeat of Robert," Janie said bluntly, though fear laced her words. "You know that's a real possibility. Do you have what you need to perform another Cesarean section if necessary?"

Carrie took a deep breath. "Yes." Her mind raced through the procedure. As soon as Polly arrived, she would send her to the clinic to get all the needed supplies. "However, we're getting way ahead of ourselves," she said as she pulled back the bedcovers. "Let me do an exam and figure out what's going on."

She used her stethoscope to check Janie's vitals, listened carefully to the baby's movements, and then did a more thorough examination. A few minutes later, she looked up with a smile. "The contractions have started, but you're dilated only a tiny bit. Your baby isn't exhibiting any symptoms of distress. This is probably false labor. I don't think your time is here yet, Janie."

Relief suffused Janie's face, but then she frowned. "I can't travel in this condition."

"That's true," Carrie said calmly. "I'll let you out of bed in a couple of days, but you're not going anywhere."

Janie shook her head. "I have to get back to Philadelphia so I can finish medical school."

"You're not going anywhere." This time Carrie's voice was firm. "There's no reason to believe this child's birth will be as difficult as Robert's, but I don't suspect you want to experience birth of any kind on a train."

Janie grimaced and collapsed back against the pillows. "I suppose you have a point."

"You're here on the plantation until this little one decides to enter the world," Carrie said calmly, even while her mind raced. She couldn't leave Janie today, but she and Anthony might be able to catch the train tomorrow. A sound in the hallway jolted her from her thoughts. Moments later, Matthew and Annie arrived with tubs of hot water.

"I don't think we'll be needing those right now," Carrie announced. "This little one is eager, but I don't think it's ready to make its entrance just yet."

Matthew sagged with relief. "Janie is all right?"

"I'm fine," Janie assured him. "Of course, if you could lower the temperature in the room a little bit, I would be grateful."

Matthew smiled. "I can't do that, but I can at least fan you." He reached over for the large fan sitting on the nightstand and began to wave it.

Janie closed her eyes as the air cooled her flushed skin. "Thank you."

Matthew locked eyes with Carrie as he continued to fan. "You can't leave, Carrie." His face tightened. "What if something goes wrong?"

Carrie stared into his eyes. She had asked herself the same question.

Janie reached up to grab her hand again. "I know it's asking a lot to have you stay, Carrie..." Her voice trailed off, but her eyes spoke the rest of her message.

Anthony walked into the room just as Janie made her beseeching request. "Polly is on the way."

"Thank you, dear." Carrie was glad to have a moment before she had to answer. It could still be weeks before Janie delivered her child. While it was true she didn't want to leave the plantation and return to Philadelphia, she had a daughter who needed her and an internship to finish. How did she weigh that against her special friend who obviously needed her as well?

Anthony saved her. "I'll go to Philadelphia and bring Frances back. She'll be thrilled." He met Carrie's eyes. "I'll also speak to Dr. Wild. I'm certain he'll understand."

Carrie relaxed as Anthony offered her the solutions she needed. "Thank you," she said fervently.

"You're sure?" Janie asked tentatively, hope lighting her eyes.

"Absolutely," Carrie said. "Frances will be delighted to come to the plantation for a while. I have to warn you though; she'll probably be hoping your delivery will be overdue so she can stay longer."

Janie groaned. "I don't want this little one born too early, but I also don't want it to go a day longer than necessary. God should have figured out a way for babies not to be born during a Virginia summer."

Matthew waved the fan harder. "Just focus on how wonderful it is to have a devoted servant to fulfill your every whim."

Janie smiled, her eyes glowing with love. "I'm glad you're back on your feet and able to be my servant," she teased.

Carrie echoed her sentiments. Matthew had come far too close to death during the collapse of the Capitol in May. Months of both legs encased in plaster had weakened him, but six weeks of lengthening walks had almost restored him to his usual strength. "Don't even think of slacking off on that fanning," she warned. "It was your legs that were broken, not your arms. You have no excuses."

Matthew shook his head as he exchanged an amused look with Anthony. "How did we end up being married to such hard-hearted women?"

Abby smiled as Carrie settled down into a rocking chair on the porch. "I love it when everyone gets what they want."

Carrie remained silent until the dust disappeared after Anthony's carriage took the curve in the long driveway, and turned to her stepmother. "I can do nothing but agree with you," she replied. "I don't have to go back to Philadelphia and leave all of you, Frances will be here in a few days, and I can keep an eye on Janie."

"Will prolonging your visit mean you'll also have to prolong your internship?" Abby asked. "As happy as I am for you to stay longer, I know how eager you are to return to Virginia for good once you've fulfilled your obligations in Philadelphia."

Carrie shrugged. "I've learned to not cross bridges until I get to them. I hope I can work hard enough when I return to make an extension unnecessary, but I'll do what I must. It feels right to be here longer." When she looked up and caught Abby's amused gray eyes, she blushed and laughed. "Perhaps I've learned to not cross bridges *sometimes*," she admitted. "It's probably something I'll always battle with."

Abby chuckled. "I just wanted to make sure you haven't accomplished something at age twenty-nine, that I still struggle with at age fifty-seven."

"I imagine I'll fight it all my life," Carrie said ruefully. "The good thing," she added, "is that it doesn't seem to be quite as big of a struggle. Staying here with Janie is the right thing to do. Everything else will have to work itself out." She settled back against her chair as she reached for the glass of cold lemonade that Annie had brought her.

"You're learning how to trust," Abby said quietly.

Carrie stared out over the treetops, praying the storm building on the horizon would hold long enough for Anthony to get to Richmond. Thankfully, it was blowing in from the east. It would hit the plantation before it reached the city. "I suppose so," she finally murmured. "At least on some days. It seems a lifetime ago that I was eighteen and longing to leave the plantation. So much has happened..." A sudden breeze ruffled the leaves of the trees, exposing their silvery undersides, making them gleam like diamonds. She took a deep breath, pulling in the beauty of her home. "I've lost so much. But I've also gained so much." She turned to look into Abby's wise eyes. "Is life always like that?"

"As far as I can tell," Abby responded, her face shining with compassion. "It seems to be a total mix of joy and sorrows, blending in with what seems to be boring times." She reached over to take Carrie's hand. "The boring times have come to be more and more appealing to me," she said dryly.

Carrie smiled. "Is it wrong for me to agree with that when I'm not quite thirty years old?"

"Hardly. The amount of living you've been forced to do in the last decade would make anyone long for boring times."

Carrie relaxed. "There's nothing I want more than to just be here on the plantation, ride Granite, and be with the people I love."

Abby returned her smile, but her eyes grew serious. "Are you regretting your decision to open a medical practice in Richmond?"

Carrie considered the question carefully. It was, after all, one she'd been asking herself daily in the last couple of weeks. It was no surprise that it was Abby forcing her to take a closer look. Carrie loved running the plantation clinic. Her patients needed and depended on her. Between her practice and the money from the successful horse stables she co-owned with Susan Justin, not to mention Anthony's income, she could afford to stay on the plantation. Why complicate her life when she didn't have to?

Abby rocked gently, giving her time to answer.

Carrie stared out over the fields, watching Granite graze contentedly, his head lifting every few minutes to see if she was still on the porch. Amber was hard at work in one of the round pens, training a six-month-old colt born on the plantation that spring. The girl's dark skin and hair glistened in the sun as the colt circled her at the end of a long lunge rope, his bay coat gleaming with good health. It was no surprise Cromwell Stables' horses were in high demand. As she continued to watch, Susan walked out leading one of the new brood mares she had bought the week before.

"You love it here," Abby said, finally breaking the long silence.

"I do," Carrie agreed instantly. "I love being on the plantation with all my heart, but living life isn't only about what *I* want." She hesitated as Abby remained silent, giving her time to formulate her thoughts. "So many miraculous things have happened that have kept me moving toward becoming a doctor, and now being a certified surgeon. I can't ignore that."

"You're doing that here on the plantation," Abby replied.

"Yes," Carrie murmured. She looked at Abby closely. "Are you saying I should stay here? Not start the practice in Richmond?"

Abby smiled as she shook her head. "I simply asked if you were regretting your decision to start the practice."

Carrie returned the smile, recognizing the tactic that had defined their relationship for a decade. "I know you better than to think you would influence my decision."

Abby's smile turned to a chuckle. "Well, I'm not above influencing my beloved daughter's mind so that I can spend more time with her, but I learned a long time ago that you'll make the decisions you believe you're supposed to make. I can't possibly know what you're meant to do.

Any suggestion I have would only make you feel guilty if you choose something different. I never want to do that."

Carrie's heart swelled with love. "Thank you." Her voice thickened. "It would be easy to stay, but I'm meant to do more. I don't know where all the roads will lead me, but I do believe I'm supposed to help start the practice in Richmond. I've met so many incredible women who have been forced to do things that society deems unacceptable. It's because of their courage that I've been able to do the things I've done. I want to honor their courage," she said thoughtfully. "I also want to pass the gift along to Frances and her generation."

"Thank you," Abby said softly.

"You were the first woman I ever met who had the courage to go against society," Carrie reminded her. "You believed in my dreams and encouraged me, even when no one else did. I want to do that for other girls and women."

"What do you think it will be like?" Abby asked.

Carrie met her eyes. "Four women opening a medical practice in Richmond, Virginia?" Considering the struggles she knew they would face, it was remarkably easy to laugh. "I think it will make the memories of going to medical school in Philadelphia seem quite easy." She would never forget the verbal taunts and cruel abuse she and her friends had experienced on their way to and from school, but she had learned to ignore them because she was doing the right thing. Carrie knew she would have to pull from those lessons when they dared to open a female medical practice in a city that had long been the seat of Southern aristocracy.

"You can do it."

"Yes," Carrie agreed, suddenly certain that they could, and would. "So, no, I'm not regretting my decision. I'm just not ready to leave the plantation today. Janie needs me."

Carrie relaxed as Granite settled into an easy trot. Their days of wild runs were over because of his advanced age, but both of them found complete joy in simply being together. She laid her hand on his iron-gray coat gleaming beneath the moon and breathed a prayer of gratitude.

"It's a beautiful night," Abby said softly. Rocky, the sorrel gelding Susan had asked her to ride, was relaxed as he fell into place beside Granite.

"I'm glad the rainstorm cleared the air of that horrible humidity," Rose replied. Her honey-colored mare, Ginger, looked to be just as grateful.

Carrie looked over at her best friend, not missing the strain in her eyes. "Annie told me Felicia is coming home in a few weeks."

"We got the letter this morning," Rose answered. "We can hardly wait to see her!"

"Then why the stressed look?" Abby asked, speaking the words in Carrie's heart.

Rose sighed. "I thought the dark would hide it."

Carrie chuckled. "Since when have we ever been able to hide anything from each other? What's wrong?"

"I don't know. Perhaps nothing." Rose hesitated. "I don't have a reason to think anything is wrong."

"But you do," Abby said perceptively. "You have a gift for knowing things before they happen."

"It's not always a gift," Rose said wryly.

"Perhaps not, but you become more like your mama every single day," Carrie responded.

Rose sighed again. "Once again, I'm not sure that's a gift."

"Nonsense," Carrie said crisply. "Your mama was an absolute saint."

"Who carried a lot of people's burdens," Rose retorted.

"Oh, for heaven's sake," Abby said in an exasperated voice. "We can debate whether or not it's a gift another time. Right now, I just want to know why you're worried."

Rose smiled, and then shook her head helplessly. "It's just a feeling. The letter said she loves school but is missing us terribly, so she's coming home."

"For how long?" Carrie asked.

Rose met her eyes. "Until Christmas."

Carrie whistled, understanding why Rose was concerned. "Felicia is leaving college for an entire term because she misses her family?"

"That's not so unreasonable," Abby interjected.

Carrie and Rose turned to stare at her at the same time.

"Perhaps a little out of character for Felicia," Abby added weakly.

"That's all she said?" Carrie demanded.

Rose nodded. "We have to wait until she gets home before we find out what's really going on. She won't tell us in a letter." Her expression tightened. "She's also not likely to tell us in person if she doesn't want us to know. She's good at hiding her feelings."

"She had to be that way," Abby said gently. "It's the only way she survived losing her parents in that riot."

Carrie knew Abby was right. It had been four and a half years since the terrible riot in Memphis, Tennessee. Carrie's own adopted daughter, Frances, had lost both her parents to illness, but the knowledge that Felicia had watched her parents be murdered was beyond Carrie's comprehension. "She'll tell you what's going on when she's ready."

"I hope so," Rose whispered. She shook her head. "There's nothing we can do about it tonight, however." She turned her attention to Carrie. "Will Janie have to stay in bed until her baby is born?"

"No. I want her to be careful the next two days, but after that she can continue regular activity. Well," Carrie amended, "*most* regular activities. Horseback riding is not included in that. I told Matthew they could go on walks, but I don't want them too far from the main house. She doesn't want to go into labor out in the fields," she added with a smile.

"Keeping up with Robert will be all the regular activity she'll need," Abby observed. "I swear, that little boy never stops. He is like a little ray of sunshine that never quits beaming. Carrie, your father is thrilled that *all* of you can't leave, but he thinks the sun rises and sets on that little boy."

"I wish Robert could have known him," Carrie said wistfully. She loved Anthony with all her heart, but part of her would always belong to Robert. He would have been so thrilled that Matthew had named his son after him.

Abby and Rose remained silent, but each rode close enough to reach out a hand to touch her. They rode that way for several minutes, giving Carrie time to process her feelings.

Carrie took a deep breath and decided to change the subject. "Did y'all hear about Louisa Swan?"

"A friend of yours?" Abby asked.

Carrie chuckled. "No. I only wish I could know her."

"Who is she?" Rose demanded.

Carrie smiled. "Louisa Swan is the first woman to cast a vote in an open and public election in America," she announced. "It happened last week."

"How do you know about this?" Rose asked in astonishment.

"The same man who delivered your letter this morning also delivered some of Father's newspapers. Father was too busy with Robert to read them, so I had Annie bring them up to Janie's room while she napped."

"Where was this?" Excitement radiated in Abby's voice.

"Laramie, Wyoming. The Wyoming Territorial Legislature granted women the right to vote last year."

"Wyoming was the first government in the world to grant women that right," Abby interjected. "They haven't been granted statehood, but they already recognize the power and ability women have to make America better."

"Did the newspaper article say anything about her? She must be quite a woman," Rose said admiringly.

"I agree," Carrie replied. "Louisa Swan is sixty-nine years old. She grew up here in Virginia, in Norfolk. She was raised as a Quaker. She and her husband have only been in Wyoming for a year; they went there to be near their son and his family after they moved there." Carrie smiled as she thought about the thrill of casting a vote. "The article said she rose early, put on her apron, shawl and bonnet, and walked downtown. She arrived at the polling place before it opened. The officials saw her there, invited her in, and Louisa cast her ballot."

"Walking right into the history books," Abby murmured.

"She was in Norfolk when I was there teaching at the internment camps," Rose said, a touch of awe in her voice.

"She probably fought for abolition for years, and then moved on to fighting for women's right to vote," Abby added. "I don't know how long it will be before we all have the right to vote, but this shows us what is possible."

"We'll never give up," Rose said. "Change only comes when enough people are willing to pay whatever price is necessary to make it happen."

"You're so right," Abby agreed.

"Speaking of which," Carrie said, "when are you going to run more Bregdan Women meetings?"

"I was going to tell you girls about that tonight. I got a letter of my own this morning from a friend in Baltimore. She's invited me to host a meeting there next spring. I'm to let her know what dates will work best. Thomas has agreed to join me. In the meantime, I'll continue holding meetings for the local women."

Carrie laughed with delight. "And so it begins. You weren't happy with retirement, anyway."

Abby nodded. "You're so right. Your story about Louisa Swan has given me even more motivation to keep going— to keep fighting for women in America. I love being on the plantation, but I need something more." Her voice grew thoughtful. "You said something to me earlier, Carrie. You said it would be easy to stay on the plantation, but you're meant to do more." She pulled her horse to a stop, waited for Carrie and Rose to do the same, and reached out to grasp their hands. "I'm meant to do more, too. Thomas and I still have a lot to give this country. We're going to do it for as long as we're able."

"So will I," Rose vowed, stretching across Granite's neck to take hold of Carrie's hand, forming a circle.

"As will I," Carrie said firmly, feeling the solemnity of the moment.

Glancing at the moon, she knew it was getting late. "It's time to head back. I don't want to be too far away from Janie in case she needs me. After all, if it weren't for her little one threatening to come early, I would just be disembarking the train in Philadelphia!"

As Carrie rode through the lush tobacco crop, she thought about the vows they had all taken. In the back of her mind, she knew that such vows usually preceded challenging times and struggles, but they would face whatever was coming together.

Chapter Two

"Mama!"

Carrie laughed with delight as her daughter sprang from the carriage and leapt into her arms. "Frances! I'm so happy you're here. I've missed you terribly." She hugged her tightly, inhaling the aroma of her hair.

"I've missed you too, Mama." Frances' brown eyes gleamed beneath light brown hair pulled back into a braid.

Carrie greeted Anthony with a warm kiss and then turned back to her excited daughter, who was almost dancing in place. "Peaches is waiting for you. Susan has her ready in the barn."

A wide grin threatened to split her daughter's face. "Really?"

"Really," Carrie assured her. "Run in and give your greetings to everyone. I have a special treat planned for you."

Frances nodded vigorously and turned to dash up the stairs to the house. Moments later, they heard the screen door slam shut.

"I done told all of you to not slam that—" Annie's scold ended abruptly. "Miss Frances! It's about time you got here, girl. I just pulled some molasses cookies out of the oven for your picnic."

Carrie shook her head. She had wanted to keep the picnic a surprise, but she had forgotten to inform Annie of that little fact.

"A picnic?" Frances squealed. "But, can't I have a cookie now, Miss Annie?"

Carrie shook her head again. She knew Annie would never turn down that sweet, beseeching voice. She didn't need to be in the kitchen to envision Frances' eyes gazing up at Annie with heartfelt yearning.

"Just one," Annie complied. "You gonna get me in trouble with that mama of yours. You get on outta here. You'll get more cookies soon."

"Yes, ma'am," Frances said. Her mumbled answer, floating to them from the kitchen window, revealed her mouth was full.

"A picnic?" Anthony asked with a raised brow.

"I want to do something special with her on her first day on the plantation. Just the two of us. I hope you don't mind."

"Not at all. I've had her all to myself the last few days. She'll love it," Anthony assured her as he gave her another kiss. "I'm going in to find your father and Matthew, but first, how is Janie?"

"She's fine," Carrie answered. "There have been no more contractions."

"Was it a mistake to stay?" Anthony asked.

"A mistake to stay longer on the plantation?" Carrie asked with a smug smile. "Never. Now that I've decided to stay, I'm not in a hurry for Janie to deliver her child. The longer she waits, the more time I have at home." Her smile faded as another thought entered her mind. "I only hope Michael…"

"Dr. Michael Wild told me to not waste a single thought on delaying your return for your internship. You and Janie are very special to him. All he cares about is Janie having a healthy baby," Anthony said warmly. "You can relish staying on the plantation without a thought of guilt."

"I hope my patients feel the same way," Carrie murmured.

"Michael is treating all the amputee veterans with the Hypericum. I suspect he would certify you as a surgeon even if you didn't return to Philadelphia," he said ruefully. "He told me your time at his practice has changed so many things for the better."

Carrie smiled. "I'll certainly return, but it's nice to not feel pressured."

She felt, even before she heard, Frances explode from the house.

"I'm ready, Mama!"

"I can see that," Carrie said with a laugh, and then lowered her voice to murmur to Anthony. "It's probably a good thing my mother died before she met her granddaughter. If she thought I was uncontrollable, she certainly wouldn't have known what to do with Frances." Her eyes danced with laughter as she watched her slim daughter run down the stairs and head to the barn.

"Come on, Mama! I'm ready for my surprise picnic!"

Shaking her head, Carrie followed her daughter as Anthony's laughter filled the air. She had a feeling she would be shaking her head a lot during the years to come, while her heart was also bursting with pride.

The late afternoon heat wrapped around them like a thick blanket as Granite and Peaches walked steadily down the road sharply carved through the tobacco fields.

"It's hot, Mama," Frances complained.

"Hotter than Philadelphia?"

Frances considered the question and then shook her head. "It's a different hot. At least the air moves around some down here. Up in Philadelphia it seems to get stuck in between all the buildings. Sometimes I think the hot air will suffocate me."

"I understand how you feel," Carrie said sympathetically. "Do you want to go back to the house now?"

Frances' eyes widened. "Go back? We haven't had our surprise picnic yet!"

"I thought perhaps you were too hot for a picnic," Carrie teased. "Besides, when did I say that a picnic was the surprise?"

Frances stared at her. "It's *not* the surprise?"

Carrie shook her head but said no more. Keeping her daughter in suspense was half the fun.

"What's the surprise, Mama? You have to tell me."

Carrie chuckled. "The point of a surprise is that you don't know what it is until the person is ready to give it to you."

"But I want it now!" Frances demanded.

"If I were you, I would focus on the moment." Seconds later they broke out onto the banks of the James River. "Look at the hawks circling above the water searching for a meal. You can tell by the ripples and rings on the river that there are fish feeding just beneath the surface."

"Not realizing they're about to become a hawk's next meal," Frances observed, her neck craned as she watched the circling predators. For at least that moment, her mind was off the surprise. Seconds later, she gave a quiet squeal. "Here comes one!"

Carrie and Frances watched with rapt attention as a hawk tucked its wings and dove. Just before hitting the water, it pulled up, expertly plucking a squirming fish from the river. Seconds later it was airborne, the unlucky prey shining in the sunlight.

"Look, Mama! That hawk grabbed the fish with its feet."

"Talons," Carrie corrected. "A hawk is considered a raptor. Its feet are actually claws that are called talons."

Frances stared at her. "How do you know that?"

"Father taught me when I was about your age. We used to come riding down to the river, too."

"Did you have Granite then?"

"I had just gotten him," Carrie replied, her mind flooding with memories as she reached down to caress his neck. "I couldn't believe I had such a magnificent horse all my own."

"I feel that way about Peaches," Frances replied as she gazed longingly at the river. "I bet that water feels good."

"That's what we're going to find out," Carrie answered. She pulled Granite to a stop and dismounted.

"What do you mean?"

"You've never been swimming in the river," Carrie replied. "It's time to change that."

Frances' face split into a wide smile as she slipped off her beautiful Palomino mare.

"Go ahead and take Peaches' bridle and saddle off."

"Without tying her up?" Frances' voice was disbelieving.

"She won't go anywhere without Granite," Carrie promised. She quickly pulled off Granite's tack, including the saddlebags that contained their picnic, and then turned him loose to munch on the sweet grass in a nearby clearing.

Frances followed her lead and then stared at the glistening water. "I don't know how to swim, Mama," she said a little nervously.

"That's not a problem," Carrie said soothingly. "The water is quite shallow at this point in the river. There's a sandbar not too far from the shore that we can go to." Carrie thought quickly. "I'll bring you out every day during this visit. By the time we return to Philadelphia, you'll be swimming like a fish."

Frances' face flooded with delight. "You promise?"

"Promise," Carrie said solemnly.

Frances looked at the water again, and then down at her clothes. "Do we swim in our riding clothes?"

Carrie shook her head and began to unbutton her shirt. She laughed when Frances' eyes widened. "It's no fun to swim with clothes on. We're going to swim in our underwear."

Frances' gasped. "Really?" Then her eyes glistened with anticipation. "I bet the water is going to feel wonderful!" Quickly, she began to follow Carrie's example. When she was down to her underwear, she lifted her arms above her head and lifted her face to the sun. "I've never been outside in my underwear," she confessed. "I had no idea it would feel so good."

Carrie sighed with contentment as the sun warmed her skin. Why was this the first time she had been swimming this summer? Clearly, she needed her daughter to remind her of the fun things in life. "Wait until you feel the water!"

Frances walked carefully to the edge of the river. "Why don't we go to the beaches near Philadelphia? I heard some women talking one time about going swimming at the beach."

Carrie shrugged. "Only if you want to call it that."

"What do you mean?"

"I grew up swimming here in the river," Carrie explained. "Not that my mother ever knew about it, though," she said ruefully. "She would have died of shame and dismay if she knew Rose and I used to slip down to the river to swim. Sam brought us here in the beginning, but then we would come on our own when we could get away with it."

"Really?" Frances breathed. "She never knew?"

"Not even my father knew," Carrie revealed, realizing it was something they'd never talked about.

"Would he have been mad?"

Carrie considered the question. "I don't know. Probably not, but he kept so many secrets from my mother about me that I thought it best to not add another one."

"Who was Sam?"

Carrie smiled softly. "I'm pretty sure he was an angel in the shape of the plantation butler. He lived here for many years."

"What happened to him?"

"He died of old age here on the plantation," Carrie said sadly. "The same night Hope was born."

Frances frowned. "Was he a slave? I thought all the slaves were free by then."

"He was free," Carrie agreed. "He didn't want to leave the plantation, though. He loved it here. In the end, he was simply part of our family. I loved him very much."

Frances absorbed that news. "I'm glad he had a family," she replied, and then returned to the original subject. "I still don't know why we don't go to the beaches around Philadelphia."

Carrie snorted. "Because women have to wear a ridiculous amount of clothing. There are rules about not letting the sunlight touch your skin," she said disdainfully. "Women wear long black stockings and lace-up bathing slippers that are often knee high." Her lips curled as she thought about it. "They have to wear long dresses and fancy caps to go to the beach. And corsets!"

Frances gasped. "I know you hate wearing dresses in Philadelphia. I can't imagine you putting all that on to go to the beach. No wonder we don't go." She gazed around as a soft breeze caressed their faces, and then stepped forward to let her feet touch the water.

"I suspect it will change in time, but for now, I'm going to take my daughter swimming in a far better way."

"What if someone sees us?" Frances asked.

"Then we might give someone a heart attack," Carrie said soberly, her eyes dancing with fun. "We're safe, though. No one ever comes to this part of the plantation. Rose and I found it many years ago."

Frances chuckled, but her eyes were serious. "It seems awful silly to have to hide, Mama. When is life going to be easier for girls like me?"

Carrie met her eyes. "When enough girls like you keep fighting to make things easier, Frances. My generation is doing all they can, but there will still be a battle for you to fight."

"Like the battle we're fighting to get children out of the factories?"

"Exactly like that," Carrie answered, and then shook her head. "Enough serious talk for now, young lady. It's time to get my daughter wet." She grabbed her hand and walked into the water, not stopping until they were up to their waists.

"Mama!" Frances cried. "It feels wonderful!" Without warning, she released Carrie's hand and collapsed backward into the water. Moments later she came up sputtering, her face creased with a wide grin. "This is the best thing I've ever done!" she cried.

Carrie laughed, not surprised Frances had reacted to the water with no fear. She plunged backward, luxuriating as the cool, silky water swallowed her body. The heat of the day was forgotten as the river did its magic. When she stood again, Frances was dancing around in the water, her arms raised high above her head, her face tilted to the sun.

"I want to come swimming every day!" Frances called.

"First you have to learn how to have a water fight," Carrie called back. When Frances turned around with a curious look, Carrie splashed water in her direction, covering her daughter with a shower of glistening drops. The shocked expression on Frances' face disappeared almost as soon as it appeared.

Moments later, water was flying in both directions, their laughter pealing through the late afternoon.

One week later, everyone was gathered on the front porch to enjoy a perfect late summer evening. The sun had just slipped beneath the horizon, sending out glorious rays of light that turned clouds into puffs of orange, red and purple. An artist would have tried in vain to capture the magnificent hues on a canvas.

Clouds of fireflies had begun to rise from their nesting places on the forest floor, their flickering bodies creating a miracle of lights throughout the dark woods. An early afternoon storm had cleared the air and pulled forth a sweet perfume that competed with the aroma of Annie's Irish oatmeal cookies fresh from the oven.

"There is no more beautiful place on earth than Cromwell Plantation," Janie said with a contented sigh.

"I couldn't agree with you more," Moses said, his deep voice radiating with satisfaction.

"You have every right to sound so satisfied," Thomas observed, the remaining rays of sunlight illuminating his silvery hair and bringing his blue eyes to life. Robert was perched on his lap, the little boy's head snuggled against his broad chest. "Abby and I rode through the fields this afternoon. The tobacco crop is going to be a good one."

"Best one yet," Moses agreed. "Clearing those extra acres over the winter is paying off, but it's more than that. The fields were getting tired from constant crops. Covering them with rye grass this winter helped restore them."

"As well as adding the marl," Thomas observed. "It has certainly created astounding results. I've never seen such healthy plants. They're going to go for a premium."

"I believe so." Moses' eyes shone with pride. "The men have worked hard. Plans are already being made for what they'll do with their share of the profits."

"Slavery was such a waste. Owning people and forcing them to work could never create the same results as giving them partial ownership of the fruit of their labor. I wish more plantation owners understood that." Thomas shook his head. "I wish I could blame their resistance on ignorance, but even after sharing the results we're getting, they're determined to keep their workers as sharecroppers."

Moses snorted. "Barely allowing them to survive," he said angrily. "I turn away men begging for a job every single day. I wish I could hire them all, but it's not possible. I ache when I see the look of frustration and helplessness on their faces. All they want to do is use their skills to provide for their families."

"You should be proud of all your men," Thomas replied. "I've never seen men work so hard, nor so cheerfully."

"They know they're building a life they can count on," Moses said. "Only two of them who received land from you haven't built homes yet, but that will be taken care of this fall when they get their share of this year's profits. Livestock is being purchased, and bigger gardens are going in."

"Will you clear more land this winter?" Anthony asked as he reached for a cookie.

"Yes, but it won't increase next year's crop. There are a couple fields that need more renewal. We'll plant the newly cleared land but keep the other fields under a cover crop to fertilize the soil. It will create better results two years down the road, making up for not planting them next year."

"Smart," Anthony said admiringly.

"When do you plan to harvest?" Matthew asked.

"In less than two weeks. I always hate to see the fields bare, but I love what shows up in everyone's account, so I've learned to deal with it." Moses' eyes glimmered with amusement.

Carrie listened to the easy conversation flowing between the people she loved. She was attuned to what was being said, but she was happy to sit back and let the air wash over her. As promised, she had been taking Frances swimming every day. Her daughter's confidence in the water grew daily, but Carrie was careful to not let her out in the deep water where the current might easily become stronger than she could handle. The long hours in the river, finishing up with a picnic every afternoon, had increased their closeness and communication. She knew this was a time that would forever be a treasured memory.

Talk turned to Matthew and Harold's newest book.

"I hear it's doing well," Anthony said.

Matthew shrugged, but Janie was eager to answer for him. "It's doing fabulously," she said. "In fact, the publisher sent a letter a couple days ago saying it is now a bestseller."

"What?" Carrie sat up straighter and stared at her friends. "A bestseller? You didn't think this was news you should have shared as soon as you received it?" she asked indignantly.

Matthew shrugged again. "We're very fortunate," he said modestly.

"You're very *good*," Janie said firmly. "You and Harold have written a book that's giving people hope. Amid all the horrible news, you're telling stories about people who are doing good things and making a difference. Our country needs your book right now."

"I completely agree," Anthony replied. "Congratulations on your bestseller status!"

His sentiments echoed around the porch as everyone chimed in.

"Does your publisher want another one?" Thomas asked.

Matthew nodded, but it was Janie who filled in the details again. "They're eager for another one as soon as possible."

"It will take me being able to travel again," Matthew acknowledged. "My legs are getting stronger every day, but I can't envision a long trip quite yet."

"Not to mention the fact that your wife is about to have a child," Abby observed.

Rose had remained silent, seemingly content to rock Hope against her chest as she listened to the conversation. "You'll be ready when the time is right, Matthew. There will always be more stories to tell."

"That's what I figure. I'm finally free from the casts, walking every day, and waiting for our newest one to decide to come into the world. I'm not in a hurry to do anything else for a while. The money coming in from the books is nice because it means I have the freedom to make the decision to stay with my family. I know I'm a lucky man."

"That you are," Thomas agreed, shifting Robert who had fallen fast asleep on his lap.

"I wrote something." Frances' announcement was made in a voice that revealed her nervousness.

"Is that right?" Matthew asked, all his attention turned on the girl. "What did you write about?"

Frances straightened her shoulders and met his eyes. "What we talked about in the spring, Matthew. I wrote about children I know who work in the factories."

Matthew continued to gaze at her. "How do you know them?"

"Through my best friend, Minnie. Even though she doesn't have to work there anymore because her mama cooks for my mama and daddy, she still knows kids that do. When I go to her place, I get to talk to them." Frances' eyes darkened. "Not that they talk much. They're too tired from working all day in those terrible places." She frowned. "I wish I could bring all of them to the plantation."

Carrie's heart softened and filled with pride as she watched her daughter's compassionate face. Frances knew that if she hadn't been rescued from the orphanage, she would probably be working in one of those same factories.

"Can I read it?" Matthew asked.

Frances looked startled. "Read it?"

"Read what you wrote?" Matthew pressed. "Do you have it with you?"

Frances hesitated. "Yes."

Carrie supposed that if Frances had brought it with her, it was because she wanted it to be read, but wanting something and having the courage to make it happen were two different things. It would be up to her.

A long silence stretched on the porch as Frances wrestled with her decision.

Abby finally broke the quiet. "It would mean a lot to us to hear what you have to say. You talked earlier this year about wanting to help make a difference. Is that why you wrote something?"

Frances turned to gaze at her grandmother. "Yes." Her lips trembled with uncertainty.

"It can't make a difference if no one ever reads it," Abby said gently.

Frances locked eyes with her, and then slowly nodded. "All right," she conceded, and then swung around to look at Matthew again. "But just you. If it's terrible, I don't want everyone else to hear it." Her voice tightened with stubbornness. "That's the only way I'll do it."

"Deal," Matthew said solemnly.

Frances turned quickly, as if she knew she might change her mind, and disappeared into the house. When she emerged a few minutes later, she was carrying a sheaf of papers that she thrust at Matthew. Then, as if regretting her decision, she turned and entered the house again, closing the door quietly as if she didn't want to draw any more attention.

Matthew watched her go. "It takes a lot of courage to let people read what you write," he said thoughtfully. He stared at the pages in his hand for a long moment and then looked up. "Normally, I would wait to read this until I'm alone. I know Frances is afraid I won't like it and she couldn't bear to hear that. I have a feeling, though, that Frances has a gift. Do you all mind if I read it now?"

"Please do," Carrie and Abby said in unison.

Matthew straightened the papers, read for a few moments and looked up with a smile. "I already love it. It's only fair to read it to all of you." He cleared his throat and began.

It may seem odd to read an article about child labor written by a thirteen-year-old girl, but I actually believe I'm the very best person to tell you what is going on in Philadelphia. The first thing you should know is that I used to be an orphan. Both my parents died from the flu a few years ago. I was only a few months from being old enough to go to work in one of the factories near my orphanage when my new mother adopted me and gave me a wonderful life.

I'm one of the lucky ones.

I know many of the ones that aren't so lucky. My best friend, Minnie, almost died in a factory accident before I met her. Her hair got caught in one of the machines and almost ripped her scalp off. Instead of helping her, the boss hit her for being careless and made her keep working until the end of the day. She's told me what horrible pain she was in, but she knew her mama needed the little bit of money she made, so she kept working.

My own mother, who is a doctor, fixed her scalp. We became best friends after that. Because of her, I've met many more children my age who work in the factories. Well, not all of them are like me. Many of them are far younger.

I met a young boy last week who is only seven years old. Not that he looks seven. I thought he was much older, even though he's little. He's been working in the factories for almost two years now. He starts at six o'clock in the morning and works until eight o'clock at night. He's very pale and skinny, and he coughs all the time. He told me he's afraid he is going to die, like one of his friends who worked there with him.

I met a girl my age who worked in a factory for four years. She can't work there anymore because her arm got caught in a machine. They had to amputate it to save her life. All seven of her brothers and sisters work in the factories, but her family still doesn't get enough to eat because they're paid so little. She feels guilty because she can't work. She never learned how to read and write so I'm helping her.

Minnie took me to have dinner with a family that lives near her. The father used to work in the factory for seven dollars a week. It was hard, but they managed to get by. Then the factory fired him. The crazy thing is that they hired his five children for just one dollar a week each. I suppose they decided five children working for almost nothing was better than one man working hard to take care of his family.

I don't understand any of this. From what I can tell, America has done nothing but create a different kind of slavery. I know all about the war we finished fighting just a few years ago. I know that all the slaves were set free. Except... that they weren't. I'm really glad all the slaves in *the South were freed, but the children of Philadelphia are also slaves.*

I suspect it is going on all around the country.

I don't know a lot about business, but I do know about greed. It's not right for children to suffer so that factory owners can make more money. I've seen some of the huge mansions they live in. I've been in the tiny little rooms without heat that my friends live in with their whole family.

I hear adults talk about leaving their country to come to America so they could have a better life. They didn't know they were coming to a country that would make their children into slaves. I remember how sad my mama was during the war when she couldn't feed us because my daddy was off fighting for freedom. My daddy came back, but there still wasn't enough money to feed us because he lost an arm during one of those battles for freedom.

The problem is that I don't see many people living in freedom right now. Especially the children of Philadelphia who are slaves in the factories just so other people can make money.

I hope my writing this will help change things. I'll keep telling stories as long as people want to read them.

Matthew lowered the pages and took a deep breath. Carrie joined Abby, Rose, Janie, and Annie in wiping away their tears, while the men cleared their throats.

"Well..." Abby finally murmured, obviously searching for words.

Matthew stared at the pages again for a few moments. "She went straight to the core of the issue," he said gruffly. "I suspected she would have a gift for writing, but what she has written is more than that. It's *important*."

Carrie and Anthony locked eyes and exchanged an unspoken message. She had long been impressed with her daughter's passionate heart, but she had had no idea she could write like that.

Matthew gazed at her. "Did you know she could write?"

Carrie shook her head, not certain she could form words to express her feelings.

"Will you publish it?" Janie asked, her voice thick with emotion.

"Definitely. I'm sending this to my editor at the *Philadelphia Inquirer* tomorrow. If Frances will let me, of course."

"I'll let you." Frances pushed through the door and appeared on the porch, her eyes wide in her face. "You really believe it's all right?"

Carrie found her voice. "It's much more than *all right*, Frances. I'm so proud of you I could explode."

"As am I," Anthony said, standing to pull her into a hug.

"And me," Annie said gruffly, her eyes shining with pride. "I ain't too good with words, but I know something good when I hear it. I reckon I'll have to make you another batch of cookies."

Rose reached out to grab one of Frances' hands. "You've written some good things in my class, but I had no idea you could write like that. It was well-written and very powerful."

Frances ducked her head for a moment. "I guess I never had anything I cared about enough to take the time to really write about it." She hesitated. "Marietta helped me make sure all the spelling was right. She only had to help me with two words, though."

Matthew lifted the pages. "Your mama is correct. This is much more than just *all right*, Frances. The purpose of writing is to be able to change how people feel about things. A lot of people can write the facts about something, but it's a gift to be able to write something that will engage their emotions. You've done that," he said warmly. "I hope you meant what you said about writing more of the children's stories. The movement to change child labor laws in Pennsylvania is growing. Your stories will help immensely."

Frances blushed, but met his eyes squarely. "I'll do anything I can to help." Then she looked at Carrie. "It's a good thing you're not done with your internship yet, Mama. I've got more work to do in Philadelphia before we come home."

Carrie chuckled. "I suppose we do, my dear." She opened her mouth to say something else but was interrupted by a sharp gasp from Janie.

Chapter Three

"What is it?" Matthew dropped the pages and turned to his wife.

"I believe it's time," Janie's face twisted with pain as she exchanged a look with Carrie.

The look told Carrie that Janie's water had broken.

Annie stood immediately. "I'll get the hot water going."

"I'll go get Polly," Anthony announced as he pushed from his chair and hurried down the stairs toward the barn.

Miles was just leaving the barn after a long day of work. It took only one look at Anthony's face to tell him what was needed. "I'll have a horse saddled lickety-split," he called. Then he looked at his wife. "Annie, I'll be up for some of your lemonade as soon as I get Mr. Anthony on his way." His eyes swung to Janie. "It's time?"

"It's time," Janie agreed with a smile.

Abby stood. "I'll get your medical bag, Carrie."

Rose headed for the door. "I'll put Hope and John to bed so that I can do whatever you need. It won't take me long to join you."

"You go on up," Moses said quickly. "I'll take care of our little ones."

"I'll put Robert to bed," Thomas added.

Carrie took Janie's hand and helped her stand. "You and I are going upstairs to your room."

Matthew stared at everyone, his mouth agape. "Seeing this is like watching a well-trained army. Everyone knows their place. What am I supposed to do?"

Thomas laughed. "You're supposed to do what every father does. You're going to sit in the parlor and worry until Carrie comes to tell you about your new child."

Matthew managed a chuckle, but the worried glint in his eyes revealed the truth.

Carrie understood his fear. After Robert's difficult birth, Matthew had reason to be concerned. She took one of his hands. "I'll give you news as soon as I can," she promised. Then she led Janie into the house and up the stairs.

Carrie was talking quietly with Janie when Polly pushed through the door thirty minutes later. The experienced midwife's dark face was serene, but Carrie didn't miss the tight worry in her eyes. Everyone knew the story of Robert's birth.

"How are things in here?" Polly asked calmly as she walked over to push Janie's soft brown hair off her forehead. "You picked a beautiful night to have a baby, Miss Janie."

Janie gritted her teeth as another contraction struck.

Polly raised a brow as she looked at Carrie.

"Everything is progressing smoothly," Carrie assured her. "I suspect it will be quite late, or early tomorrow morning, when this little one decides to make an appearance, but my examination doesn't reveal any distress on the part of the baby."

"And Janie?"

"She's doing well also."

"What is *well?*" Janie demanded as she breathed through the contraction. "Does having your insides feel as though they're being pushed out count as *well?*"

Polly chuckled and grasped her hand.

Carrie could imagine what Janie was feeling, but the fact that she didn't actually *know* was a painful truth she pushed away. Carrie's own baby, Bridget, was stillborn when she collapsed after her first husband's death. She had never felt a contraction...never held her child. She forced a smile and gave Janie all her attention. "It's better than the terrible pain you felt with Robert, isn't it?"

The gentle question was all that was needed to give Janie perspective. She smiled weakly. "So this is what every woman feels when they're giving birth?"

"Yep," Polly replied. "This is why men don't have babies. They ain't tough enough to handle it."

The three women were laughing when Abby and Rose entered the room.

"Are you having a party in here?" Rose asked.

"For as long as we can," Carrie assured her. A knock at the door revealed Moses with a worried expression.

"What can I tell Matthew? He's about to drive us all crazy."

Carrie smiled with sympathy. "Tell him there's no reason for concern, but that Janie is doing this on her own timetable. I suspect it will be, at the very least, several more hours. I promise to let him know immediately if there is reason for him to worry."

Moses snorted. "As if that will help the poor man."

"Perhaps a game of cards?" Janie said. "If you get him involved in a good game of poker, it will make life easier for all of you."

"Now that's an idea I can get behind," Moses said with a grin before he turned and disappeared.

Dawn was kissing the horizon with its rosy glow when Carrie walked downstairs stifling a yawn.

"Carrie!" Matthew jumped up, joined immediately by Thomas, Anthony, Moses and Miles.

"Who won the poker game?" Carrie asked lightly.

Matthew stared at her. "You're asking us about a poker game?"

Carrie laughed. "Which should be your first clue that all went well with Janie. I came down to tell you that y'all are now the parents of a beautiful little girl."

Matthew sank back down into his chair. "We have a daughter?" His weary eyes suddenly brightened with joy and excitement.

"You certainly do," Carrie said happily. "Your little girl wasn't in a hurry, but everything went off without a hitch. Except, that you have a very tired wife." She took Matthew's arm. "A wife who would like to see her husband and introduce you to his daughter before she gets some much needed sleep."

Matthew turned and ran up the stairs, his laughter echoing behind him.

Carrie watched him go, noting the double miracle. Just months ago, it was doubtful that Matthew would ever walk again. To see him running up the stairs gave her as much joy as the new child nestled against her mother's chest. Polly could have easily handled Janie's delivery on her own, but Carrie had no regrets about her extra ten days on the plantation.

Frances stumbled into the parlor, rubbing sleep from her eyes. "How is Janie?"

"Janie is now the mother of *two* children," Carrie announced. "And Robert is a big brother to an adorable little sister."

Frances grinned. "That's great!" Her eyes turned to the kitchen. "I'm not usually awake so early. Do you think there's food to eat?"

Anthony wrapped an arm around her shoulder. "I'm sure we can find something. After a night of beating Matthew at poker, I'm starving."

Thomas stood to join them. "After a night of beating *you* at poker, I suppose I should get first choice of whatever is left from yesterday," he teased. "Seems only fair."

Annie appeared through the front door, tying the apron around her ample waist as she entered. "There are some extra biscuits wrapped up in a towel on the counter," she said with amusement, and then turned to Carrie. "How many am I cooking for this morning?" she asked keenly.

"One more than last night." Carrie smiled through her yawn. "Janie's daughter won't be eating your cooking, but I'm sure Janie will be hungry enough for two when she wakes. Of course, I suspect she'll be wanting lunch at that point."

Annie clapped her hands joyfully. "Now, that's right good news. I be awful glad there weren't no problems. Miss Janie was real worried." She looked toward the stairs. "Can I send something up for her?"

Carrie shook her head. "She's exhausted. I gave her a glass of milk before I came down, but all she really wants to do is go to sleep as soon as she introduces Matthew to his daughter."

Matthew cradled his daughter in his arms and gazed at her rosy, puckered, tiny face. "She's beautiful," he breathed. He leaned down and kissed Janie gently. "How are you?"

"Happy," Janie said softly. "And exhausted."

"I can only imagine."

"You're right about that," Polly said. "Ain't a man I know who could give birth to a child."

"You'll get no argument from me." Matthew smiled down at his wife. "Thank you for being strong enough to give me two children."

"You're welcome," Janie whispered, her eyelids drooping as she struggled to stay awake.

Matthew gazed down at his daughter again. "Did anything happen to make you change your mind about her name?"

Janie shook her head. "No." Her voice was a little stronger. "You are holding Annabelle Marie Justin."

Matthew's eyes misted over. "My mother would have loved to meet her namesake," he said hoarsely.

Harold walked into the room at that moment. "I got back from a trip late last night or I would have been here playing poker with you, twin brother. Miles came to let me know the good news." He touched Annabelle's hand lightly. "You did well, Janie. She's beautiful."

"I suspect your brother had something to do with it," Janie replied.

"Perhaps a little," Harold said dismissively, a playful glint in his eyes. Then he met Matthew's eyes squarely. "Mama would have loved Annabelle and Robert. I hope that somehow she knows you named this little one after her."

"Me too," Matthew said quietly as he cuddled his daughter a few moments longer. "Let me give you back to your mama, little girl."

"I'll take her," Polly said quickly. "Janie is already sound asleep. She did the hard part, now she gets to rest. I'll clean Annabelle up a little more and then let her sleep with her mama."

Matthew's eyes softened as he leaned down to kiss Janie on the forehead. "Sleep well, my love."

Chapter Four
September 10, 1870

Florence gazed around the crowded docks of Le Havre, France as she joined the throngs of passengers disembarking from the steamship tied securely to the wooden pilings. She had loved being at sea, and was thankful their trip had gone so smoothly, but the feel of solid ground was wonderful. At least, her mind told her she was on solid ground. Her body felt as if it were still swaying, rocking and bobbing on the ocean swells. She paused for a moment, less concerned about the crush of people around her than she was about the odd sensation she was feeling.

"It will pass."

Florence looked at her father, the angular body, red hair and blue eyes so like her own. "Are you feeling it, too?"

"I imagine everyone is," Dr. Robinson assured her. "Your body adjusted to the motion of the ship over the last month."

"For which I will always be eternally grateful," Florence said fervently. "The first three days were horrible. If I'd been ill like that the entire month, I probably would have jumped overboard to stop the agony of being seasick."

"I know you were miserable when the voyage began," her father said sympathetically. "I promise what you're feeling now will disappear in a day or two. Your body will adjust very quickly to being on land."

Florence was discomfited by the feeling of being mildly seasick while standing on the dock, but she was much more intrigued by the resilience and adaptability of the human body. As a newly minted medical doctor, she hoped she would always feel that way. "It still amazes me that you weren't sick like I was."

Dr. Robinson shrugged. "Months on a merchant ship when I came over from Ireland gave me sea legs. We were traveling in the lap of luxury compared to how I arrived in America as a lad," he said with a chuckle. "I'm grateful you weren't huddled in the dank hull of a wooden ship while you were sick."

"Me too," Florence said emphatically. She had heard the story of her father's emigration from Ireland many times, but it never ceased to amaze her that the successful, distinguished man in front of her had once been a starving refugee. Suddenly, she frowned. "Why does everyone look so unhappy, Father?"

Dr. Robinson swung his head around to follow her gaze. His eyes narrowed as he scanned the people who had stopped at the end of the dock and were now gathered in little knots, their faces tight with anxiety.

"I suppose we should find out, daughter darling."

Florence looked at him sharply. His voice was casual, but she didn't miss the ridge on his forehead that always stood out when he was concerned or worried. She increased her speed to match his lengthened stride.

"War?"

"The Prussians are attacking France?"

"What will happen to us?"

Voices floated to Florence and her father as they approached the groups. Worried looks had taken on a specter of fear, and many passengers were looking back at the ship hopefully.

"I want to go back to America!" one woman cried.

"War?" Florence asked. "What are they talking about?"

"I don't know," her father said grimly. "There was no talk of war before we left America a month ago."

"The Prussians are winning the war!" A woman's hysterical voice floated to them on the still air.

"Napoleon has been captured!" another man shouted. "The Battle of Sedan was a disaster. The Emperor has been captured, along with large numbers of his troops. France is doomed!"

"What disaster have we sailed into?" a portly woman wailed. "I want back on that boat!"

Florence listened with growing dismay. For a moment, she wished all these people were speaking in French, so that she wouldn't know what they were saying. During their month at sea, she had met many bilingual travelers. She knew getting back on the steamship, no matter how much they might want to, wasn't possible. There were long queues of people waiting to board as soon as they were granted entry. Eager faces behind the dock gates revealed how glad they were to be leaving. Based on what she was hearing, Florence understood their eagerness.

"Dr. Robinson!"

Florence and her father turned at the same time.

A slightly built man with thin, balding hair hurried up to them. "You're Dr. Robinson?"

"Yes," Florence's father answered, "and this is my daughter, Dr. Florence Robinson."

"It's a pleasure to meet both of you," the man said, his darting eyes revealing he was in a rush. "My name is Victor Reille. Minister Washburne sent me to meet you."

Dr. Robinson looked startled. "I thought we were to connect with Minister Washburne when we arrived in Paris on the train? I was to telegraph him when we knew our arrival time."

Victor looked uncomfortable. "The situation has changed in France, Dr. Robinson. Minister Washburne was concerned about what you would hear, and he wanted to be sure you made it to Paris safely."

Dr. Robinson glanced around at the throngs of people. "Is Paris safe right now?"

If possible, Victor looked even more uncomfortable. "I wish I could tell you that anywhere in France is safe right now. Unfortunately, I can't." He glanced back in the direction he'd come. "I have tickets purchased for the next train. Please, let's go. I will give you more information when we are en route." He looked at the trunks resting beside them. "Is this all your baggage?"

"It is..." Dr. Robinson frowned with concern. "Monsieur Reille, I have my daughter with me. I don't want to take her into an unsafe situation."

Victor smiled sympathetically. "I understand, Dr. Robinson. If it had been possible to send a message to sea, we would have had your steamship turn around and return to America. Unfortunately, you are now here, and it's not possible for you to return on the same boat. Every ship is fully booked for weeks." His voice deepened with passion. "Minister Washburne is committed to your safety and believes that will be best provided in Paris."

Florence listened closely. She knew Minister Washburne had been friends with her father when they were students at Harvard. They'd not been in the same course of study, but the students of medicine and law had become close friends. Though it had been years since they'd last seen each other, their communication had been steady. Her father had reached out to his old friend when he decided to give her a trip to France as her graduation gift. Minister Washburne had responded with a brief telegram saying he would be honored if they stayed with him while they were in Paris.

Dr. Robinson still hesitated, glancing over his shoulder at the ship. "You're certain we can't obtain passage?"

"I'm afraid it's not possible," Victor repeated in a strained voice, as he looked behind him. "Please, come with me. The train will be leaving shortly."

Dr. Robinson locked eyes with Florence.

She understood his quandary. As grateful as she was to be on dry land, suddenly the steamship seemed much more appealing. After four years of war in America, she was appalled by the idea of war in France, but what choice did they have? She could only hope his friendship with the American Minister to France would offer them some protection, and that Paris would not become a target for the Prussians. She looked at her father and nodded once before turning back toward the gleaming water that stretched to the horizon.

How long would it be before they could return to America?

Dr. Robinson turned to Victor. "We will come with you."

Florence, despite the harsh reality of the situation they were in, was delighted with Paris as they rolled the final few miles to the train station. Tree-lined streets awash with blooms stretched out in every direction. She wished with all her heart that she and her father had arrived at a different time.

"Paris is the largest city in continental Europe," Victor said proudly. "There are now two million people here." His eyes glowed with pride. "Emperor Napoleon has done so much for our city. When he took office eighteen years ago, Paris had beautiful buildings, but it wasn't a beautiful city. The Emperor has changed all of that. Paris is now the most beautiful city in all of Europe."

"I hope we'll have a chance to explore it," Dr. Robinson said quietly. "From everything you've told us, the future of Paris seems rather tenuous."

"Nonsense," Victor said with a snort. His pride in his city seemed to have made him forget all he had told them on the long train ride from Le Havre – including the fact that Napoleon had been defeated, and was no longer the Emperor. "The Prussians would never try to take the Jewel of Europe. Our forts and our army will keep them out."

Florence remained silent. The one thing she had learned from the war in America was that war was impossible to predict. All people could do was deal with the consequences of the choices their leaders made.

"Washburne! Being the Minister to France suits you, my friend."

Elihu Washburne, a tall, broad-shouldered man with graying hair and light gray eyes laughed as he reached out his hand. "Robinson! I can't believe it's been twenty years since we last saw each other. Welcome to Paris."

He turned his piercing eyes to Florence. "This must be the brilliant daughter you told me about. Welcome to Paris, Dr. Robinson, and congratulations on your graduation." His smile widened. "It's quite impressive to have two doctors in one family. Are you planning on giving your father some competition?"

"That she is," her father confirmed. "We had talked about going into practice together, but she has decided to move to Richmond, Virginia and start a new practice with three other women doctors that she went to medical school with."

Washburne's eyes widened. "An all-women medical practice in Richmond, Virginia?" He shook his head as he eyed her closely. "Do you think the South is ready for that?"

"Probably not," Florence replied with a chuckle. "They'll have to *get* ready, however, because we have quite made up our mind."

"And when does this practice open?"

"I'm supposed to be in Richmond the first week of January." She frowned and met the minister's eyes squarely. "Assuming, of course, that we'll be able to leave France to return home. Our steamer is due to leave on October fifteenth, giving us five weeks here in your lovely city."

Washburne's eyes clouded as he took a deep breath. "What has Monsieur Reille told you?"

Florence's father was the one to answer. "That depends on what part of the conversation you're referring to. For most of the journey, he informed us of the staggering losses the French army has suffered since hostilities began the first week of August. As we got closer to the city, however, he assured us no one would ever consider attacking the Jewel of Europe." He paused. "Which version should we believe?"

Washburne took a deep breath. "Let's go into the parlor, Robinson." He turned to Florence. "I'm sure you're exhausted. Would you like to be seen to your room to freshen up before dinner?"

Florence shook her head, pushing any weariness aside. "Thank you, Minister, but no. I would much prefer to know the truth about the situation we find ourselves in."

Washburne hesitated and sought her father's eyes. What he saw there made him nod graciously and offer his arm to escort her into the parlor.

Dr. Robinson spoke as soon as they were seated in front of the large bay window that looked over splendid gardens lush with summer green and blooming flowers. "Is the situation as dire as Monsiur Reille led us to believe?"

Washburne chuckled. "You haven't changed, Robinson. You never were one to beat around the bush."

Florence watched as her father met his friend's eyes but remained silent. She suspected, as she assumed her father did, that Washburne would try to diminish the seriousness of what was going on.

He surprised them both.

"Yes, it is dire," he said. "The French started a war I don't believe they have any hope of winning. Some say Prussian Chancellor Otto von Bismarck deliberately provoked the French into declaring war. I'm not certain that's true, but I do believe he is exploiting the circumstances as they unfold."

"Exploiting how?" Florence asked keenly. Before they landed in France, she wasn't sure she had ever heard of Prussia, but Monsieur Reille had given them quite an education.

"I believe Bismarck recognizes the potential for new German alliances," Washburne answered. "His goal all along has been the unification of Germany. Four years ago, after the Austro-Prussian War, Prussia annexed several territories and formed the North German Confederation."

"Which evidently wasn't enough," Dr. Robinson said wryly.

"Of course not," Washburne replied. "It did, however, make the rest of Europe quite nervous because it destabilized the balance of power. Napoleon tried to secure France's strategic position by laying claim to some of the territory Prussia had annexed, but Bismarck flatly refused. What he did, instead, was turn his attention toward the south of Germany where he sought to incorporate the southern German kingdoms. France was adamantly opposed."

"Did France's opposition matter?" Florence asked. She was becoming increasingly aware of how little she knew about Europe. When France was just a country somewhere across the ocean, it had seemed to have no importance to her. Now that she was obviously trapped in a country caught in political turmoil and war, it was quite important to understand the situation.

Washburne looked at her with approval. "Good question, Dr. Robinson."

Florence smiled. "Please call me Florence. Two Dr. Robinsons can be quite confusing."

"You're right." Washburne agreed. "To answer your question, Florence, yes. Regardless of the actions Prussia took after the war, France still has great influence. Bismarck is smart enough to know that the rest of Europe would not respond well if Prussia was the aggressor.

France has had great power, and has helped maintain the balance of power so that things have been relatively peaceful in Europe."

"So what caused this war?" Robinson asked.

Washburne scowled. "I suppose the immediate cause was the candidacy of a Prussian prince to the throne of Spain. France feared encirclement by an alliance between Prussia and Spain. They exerted enough diplomatic pressure to have the candidacy withdrawn, but Bismarck responded with communication that made it seem as if the prince gaining the Spanish throne could happen again in the future. The way he did so was said to be quite demeaning, which, of course, inflamed public opinion here in France." He shrugged. "The French are quite a proud people."

"Monsieur Reille is certainly proud of his country," Florence responded.

"As he should be," Washburne said quickly. "France is a magnificent country full of wonderful people. Paris is a city that has no equal."

Dr. Robinson examined his friend. "You like it here."

"I love it here," Washburne corrected. "My travels brought me here before, but when President Grant gave me the job of Minister to France, it took me a very short time to realize how special a place it is." He frowned. "Which makes this current situation even more untenable." He shook his head heavily. "When France declared war and started hostilities, Bismarck got his wish for further German unification. All the southern kingdoms threw their support to Prussia. It also gave him an army that is unbeatable. France has sustained terrible losses, including the imprisonment of Emperor Napoleon."

"Monsieur Reille told us the government has undergone a change," Dr. Robinson said.

"He was correct. When Napoleon was captured at the Battle of Sedan, his army was decisively defeated. When that happened, his government was overthrown by a popular uprising here in Paris that resulted in the Government of National Defense."

"How long ago was this?" Florence asked.

Washburne grimaced. "Six days."

A stunned silence fell on the room.

"Six days?" Robinson repeated.

"Six days. The whole thing is a chaotic mess. After the German victory at Sedan, most of the remaining French army is either under siege at a place called Metz, or they're prisoners of the Germans. I think Bismarck planned on demanding peace after the Battle of Sedan, but there is no longer a legitimate French authority to negotiate with. The Government of National Defense has no real electoral mandate, the emperor is a captive, and the empress is in exile."

Robinson shook his head. "And I thought the *American* war was a mess. What's going to happen now?"

Washburne shook his head ruefully. "Four days ago, the new government took a hard stand and renewed their declaration of war. They've called for recruits from all over France and pledged to drive the Germans out of the country."

"Which means Germany has to continue the war," Robinson observed with a frown.

"Unfortunately, the bulk of the remaining French armies are digging in near Paris. My guess is that the German leaders will put pressure on France by attacking Paris," he said reluctantly, his expression apologetic.

"When?" Florence asked bluntly.

Washburne looked at her sadly. "No one knows, but..." His voice trailed off into a prolonged silence.

"But what?" Florence said persistently. "I would much prefer to know the truth, Minister Washburne. I would appreciate it if you not try to hide reality from us. Being prepared is much better than being taken by surprise." She hoped he wouldn't be offended by her assertiveness, but she didn't really care how he felt about her. There were much more important matters at stake.

"You're right," Washburne said. Then he spread his hands. "Still, I simply don't know. There are many factors to consider before attacking a city of two million people, but I believe it will happen. How long it will take to consider all the factors and then take action is still an unknown."

"And yet you had Monsieur Reille bring us here," Robinson said, a mixture of frustration and anger in his voice.

"I understand what you're feeling, old friend. If I could have sent you back to America, I would have," Washburne replied. "I've not given up hope of finding a private boat that can take you across the channel to England, but all conveyances are in high demand right now. Many reasonable people are choosing to leave the country until this conflict has been resolved."

Florence flushed with anger. "Except the millions of reasonable people who don't have the luxury to leave. They're stuck here to see what happens while leaders play with their lives."

"You're right," Washburne agreed again. "Just as countless millions suffered in America during our recent war, so too will millions of the French suffer." His expression darkened with his own feelings of anger and despair. "My job is to make life bearable for as many people as possible."

"Why?" Florence's father asked. "Surely you could leave until this is over."

"I could," Washburne agreed. "I was actually in a lovely little spa town in the Czech Kingdom when I received word about the war. I could have stayed for my vacation, and then traveled on to America until the war ends, but I returned. France is now my home. I've fallen in love with the country and with the people. I believe I can help." He smiled. "I suspect I'll need the hot springs of the Czech Kingdom even more when all this is over."

"How will you help?" Robinson probed.

Washburne met his eyes. "Both Germany and France have appointed protecting powers. I was Germany's choice."

"A protecting power?" Florence asked. "I'm afraid I don't know what that is."

"It's a new thing," Washburne assured her. "A protecting power is a country that represents another sovereign state in a country where it lacks diplomatic representation, especially during a conflict. I know that sounds confusing, but it's meant to make war more humanitarian – if that's possible," he said ruefully. "Since the United States has been named Germany's protecting power, I am responsible for looking after Germany's diplomatic property and all German citizens in France. It is also my job to look into the welfare of German prisoners of war."

Florence stared at him. "Your job is to take care of the Germans who are destroying France?" she asked with disbelief.

"If only it were that simple," Washburne mused. "I suspect that if the Germans really do attack Paris, I will be the only diplomat left from a major power. The Germans who live in Paris have nothing to do with the decisions their government has made, but they'll suffer greatly. I'll do all I can to help the Germans, the Parisians, and also the Americans who are here in Paris." He gazed out the window for several long moments before he turned back to them, a slightly overwhelmed look on his face. "I will do what I can with the resources I have access to."

"Are there many Americans in Paris?" Florence asked.

"At least a thousand," Washburne replied. "Not everyone can get out, though I've helped provide transport for as many as possible in the last month."

"Which is why we can't get passage on a ship," Florence remarked.

"That would be the crux of it," Washburne answered. "If I'd been certain of your arrival date, I could have made arrangements, but I had no way of knowing when you would actually reach France." He smiled. "If nothing else, my position as the German protecting power will ensure your safety while you're here."

Florence thought through all he had said. "What can we do to help?"

Washburne was momentarily struck dumb. "Help?" he finally asked.

Florence nodded impatiently. "Two of my new business partners lived in Richmond, Virginia during the American war. They've told me many stories of how horrible it was. If Father and I are to be stuck here, I would prefer to know we're making a difference however we can."

Washburne's eyes shone with admiration. "Thank you, Florence. I, too, lived through our recent war in America.

I'm holding onto hope that the Germans won't attack Paris, but if it comes to that, I'll take you up on your offer. I'm sure there are ways you and your father can be of assistance." He turned his eyes to her father. "You've raised a remarkable daughter."

"Her mother and I are very proud of her," Robinson agreed.

Washburne stood abruptly. "For now, Paris is not under attack. Which means you must avail yourselves of as much of this lovely city as you can. The French have a love of life that is quite contagious. Napoleon transformed this city into a remarkable oasis of the world. I will have Monsieur Reille escort you for as long as possible."

Robinson shook his head. "Thank you for the generous offer, but I suspect he has more important things to do than escort tourists around Paris. We'll explore the city on our own for as long as it's safe."

Washburne opened his mouth to protest but closed it again. "You're right that he has important matters he can attend to for me. However, don't hesitate to ask me for anything." He rose and laid his hand on Robinson's shoulder. "Florence, I owe your father a debt of gratitude. When I was young, I got into a bit of trouble at Harvard Law that had the potential to get me expelled. He never told me how he did it but somehow, he intervened and made it all go away. Without him, I wouldn't have had the career I've had. It's my honor to host you while you're here."

Florence gazed around with delight as their carriage approached the city center of Paris. Their approach down the Rue de Rivoli, one of the four intersecting boulevards that created a huge cross through the city, had filled her with awe. "Oh my!" she gasped. "I've never seen a city so beautiful."

Their hired driver looked back at her with a face filled with pride. "The Emperor changed our city," he told her in heavily accented English. "He was the one who conceived the four avenues that intersect, and built many more to make transportation easier. He wanted to open the city to more air and sunshine. He had more than one hundred thousand trees planted along the new avenues, and added wonderful squares, fountains and parks. Everywhere you look, there is beauty."

"The architecture is lovely, as well," her father observed.

"There are quite strict architectural standards for every building along the new avenues," the driver responded, evidently quite practiced in his job as tour guide. "All the buildings have to be the same height, follow a similar design, and be faced with the same cream-hued stone."

"It's quite distinctive," Robinson said admiringly.

Florence noted the brilliant flowers decorating every building. Window boxes laden with brightly colored blooms painted the creamy sameness with vibrancy and life. When she turned her eyes away from the buildings, however, she couldn't miss the worry and uncertainty etched on the face of every person walking or riding down the roads.

"I hate that this magnificent city is being threatened by war," she murmured to her father.

"If the Germans bring it to our city, we will fight," the driver vowed. "This is Paris," he said fiercely. "We will not give up our beloved city."

Florence thought about all the stories Carrie had told her of the endless attacks on Richmond. She knew it would do no good to focus on mere possibilities, but from what Minister Washburne had told her, it wasn't really *if* an attack would come, it was *when* it would come. She let her eyes rest on the horizon, wondering if the Germans were gathering troops at that very moment on the outskirts of the city.

"Washburne has gotten us tickets for the opera tonight," her father said brightly.

Florence knew he was trying to take her mind off their situation by doing the best he could to give her the wonderful graduation gift he had planned. The least she could do was swallow her worry and play along. "That's wonderful!" she said enthusiastically.

The driver continued their education. "Napoleon demolished the old theater district that was known as the *'Boulevard du Crime.'* It was a blight on Paris for a very long time. He replaced it with five new theaters and commissioned a new opera house." He pointed off into the distance. "You'll be going to the Palais Garnier, the home of the Paris Opera. I've never been there for a performance, but the outside is quite magnificent. They've been building it for the last nine years, but the work will continue for years to come. It will seat almost two thousand people. The most famous operas in the world have all been performed there."

He cast a dark look toward the north. "The Germans are at our doorstep. You must take advantage of every moment you have here in Paris."

Florence felt as if her head would spin from her shoulders as she tried to take in the splendor of Palais Garnier. Interweaving corridors, stairwells, alcoves and landings allowed smooth movement of the two thousand who had bought tickets for the night's performance. If there was fear of an attack, you would never suspect it by looking at the faces of the eager attendees.

The whole opera house was rich with velvet and gold leaf. Cherubim and nymphs peered down at them from everywhere.

"Father, look!"

Dr. Robinson smiled, tucked Florence's hand through his elbow, and led her up the grand staircase made of white marble with a balustrade of red and green marble.

Florence felt like a queen as she swept up the staircase, her beautiful new gown floating around her. She had brought few dresses with her on the cruise because her father had insisted on replenishing her wardrobe with Parisian fashion. In their first three days, since an attack could be imminent, he had insisted on taking her to the finest shops.

Her eyes widened as she gazed up at the ceiling adorned by beautiful paintings. "Magnificent!" She was thankful her father was leading her so that she could continue to look upward.

When they reached the grand foyer, she was rendered speechless.

"The grand foyer was designed to act as a drawing room for Paris society," her father informed her. "The paintings on the ceiling represent moments in the history of music."

"I've never even imagined something so beautiful," Florence whispered. "The chandeliers themselves are a work of art. The glow they cast is magical." She continued to look upward as her father steered her through the massive doors that opened to the auditorium. When she looked forward, she was once again speechless. She had been to theaters in America, but nothing could even begin to compare to the Palais Garnier.

"Their stage is the largest in Europe," her father said. "It can accommodate as many as four hundred and fifty artists."

"The chandelier!" Florence gasped. She had never seen anything so beautiful. She could only imagine what it took to clean the massive light that glittered like a jewel. The interior of the theater was as extravagant and sumptuous as the rest of the building.

The evening passed in a haze of enjoyment as the drama of *Das Rheingold*, an opera by Wagner, unfolded on the stage.

Florence and her father were seated at a charming café three days later, sipping coffee and enjoying a pastry, when they heard sounds in the distance. As the tensions in the city had increased over the last few days, Minister Washburne had warned them it would be best if they didn't stray too far from his residence.

Dr. Robinson stood immediately. "The attack has begun," he said quietly, the ridge bulging on his forehead as he spoke. "We must return to the house."

Trying to swallow her fear, Florence took his arm and retraced their steps to the minister's residence.

War had come to Paris.

Chapter Five
Late September, 1870

Matthew and Janie were already up and gone when Carrie rapped lightly on their bedroom door a few days later. She smiled, knowing where she would find them.

Matthew was walking from the kitchen with a tray full of steaming coffee cups and fluffy biscuits stuffed with slices of Virginia ham. He smiled and handed her the tray when she descended the stairs. "Go on out and join Janie on the porch. I'll get another cup of coffee."

Carrie accepted his offer with a grateful smile. "Another short night?" she asked as she stepped onto the porch.

Janie looked up with a tired smile. "Annabelle seems to believe sleeping is only for daylight hours. She was restless all night. Look at her now." She pulled back the thin blanket wrapped around her daughter to reveal a soundly sleeping baby, dark lashes resting peacefully on creamy cheeks. "As soon as I give up and come outside, she goes to sleep. But only if the sun is ready to rise," she complained. "Matthew brought her out a few hours ago while it was still dark, but she just thought it was nighttime playtime! He finally decided he could at least be in bed beside me while we were wide awake."

"She's not crying or in pain?"

"Not a bit," Janie assured her. "She just seems to like night better than day. Her schedule may kill her parents, but she seems to be completely content."

Carrie smiled. "She'll adjust in time."

"And you know that *how*?" Janie asked. "I happen to be a doctor, too. I don't remember reading anything about this."

Carrie laughed. "Let's go with the fact that I'm choosing hope. I really have no idea whether she'll adjust or not, but I certainly hope she does before you and Matthew collapse."

Janie groaned and reached for her cup of coffee. "At least this helps to make it a little more bearable." She smiled softly. "I'm tired to the bone, but also completely happy."

"Focus on that."

"You're still leaving tomorrow?" Janie asked.

"Yes. It's time to go back to Philadelphia. I'm going to see some final patients at the clinic today, and then we'll ride into Richmond tomorrow. We'll get there in time to meet Felicia and her teacher-companion at the train station and take them to the house. Jeb will bring them to the plantation the next day, while we catch the train. Micah and May will be thrilled to have us at the house for an afternoon and night."

"Matthew and I are going to stay another three weeks before we head back to Philadelphia," Janie revealed. "Annie tried to convince me to take this term off, but after missing the last term to care for Matthew, I'm eager to finish my degree."

"Annie could be right," Carrie said thoughtfully. "It's going to be hard to go to school while Annabelle is so little."

"I only have a few classes left," Janie protested. "I'll have to study a lot at home, but I'll be right there with her. Matthew will take care of Robert and Annabelle while I'm in class." She shook her head. "I know medical school isn't going anywhere, and I know they would let me miss another term, but I'm eager to come back to Richmond. I want to start our practice together, just like we planned."

"I want that, too," Carrie assured her. "But—" she started the sentence with her sternest voice.

"But if I find it's too much, I'll finish school during the next term," Janie promised.

Carrie had to be satisfied with that. She reached for her cup of coffee, inhaling the rich aroma before she took her first, grateful sip. Leaning back in the rocker, she breathed in the early morning air that carried a hint of the fall season that lurked just beyond the horizon. It was certainly not cool, but the cloying heat of high summer had finally departed.

Matthew appeared on the porch. "Look what I found on the table in the foyer," he announced. "It must have gotten lost in the shuffle of all the mail that arrived yesterday."

Carrie glanced at the letter in his hand, not wanting real life to interrupt the peaceful morning. "Who is it from?"

"Florence Robinson."

Carrie sat up straighter and reached for the letter. She knew Janie would have claimed it if her arms weren't full of her sleeping daughter. "Give it to me," she commanded.

Matthew complied, then sank down into his own rocker and raised a coffee cup to his lips. "Annie is making pancakes and bacon this morning," he said happily.

Carrie was too busy opening the envelope to pay much attention to him, though she did register that her stomach was soon to be very happy. She pulled out a single page of lined paper, along with another envelope, and began to read. "Oh my…"

"What?" Janie asked. "Is something wrong? Did something happen to Florence?"

"No," Carrie assured her. "I'll read it to you." She held up the single sheet of paper first.

Dear Carrie and Janie,

I'm so sorry for the late delivery of this letter. Florence asked me to send it over a month ago, just as she and her father were leaving. In the rush of their departure, I set it aside and neglected to send it. Here it is now. Please accept my apologies.

Sincerely,
Matilda Robinson

"Where did Florence go with her father?" Janie asked with surprise. "I thought she was going to work with him at his practice in Philadelphia this fall before she came down to join us."

Carrie shook her head. "My mind-reading skills appear to be a bit rusty," she teased as she quickly undid the seal on the enclosed envelope and pulled out another sheet of paper.

Dear Carrie and Janie,

I have wonderful news! My father is taking me to Paris, France! We have talked about taking a trip like this for years. He decided to give me the trip as a gift for graduating from medical school. It will take us four to six weeks to cross the ocean, but the trip to get there has been another dream of mine for a long time. We're going to stay for five weeks, but I will be back in plenty of time to make it to Richmond by January. I'm as excited as ever to work with you two, along with Elizabeth, in our new practice.

Sincerely,

Florence

"Paris, France?" Janie exclaimed. "How wonderful!"

Carrie tried to shake off the feeling of dread that had suffused her when she read the letter. Florence was going on the trip of a lifetime. There was no reason for her concern.

"What's wrong?" Janie asked as she eyed her closely.

Carrie shrugged. "Nothing, I'm sure. Florence will have a fabulous time and return to America with stories that will keep us enthralled for hours."

Janie stared at her for a long moment with narrowed eyes, but only nodded.

Carrie's determined answer did nothing, however, to shake her feeling of uneasiness.

Carrie was finishing up with her last patient when the sound of approaching hoofbeats made her swallow a sigh. She was tired and hungry, but since this was her last time in the clinic until she returned in December, she didn't want to turn anyone away.

"I can take care of whoever it is," Polly said, straightening up from where she was stocking the new supplies that had arrived the day before from Richmond, as well as the herbal remedies she created from the recipes passed down from Old Sarah.

"I know," Carrie acknowledged, "but you're going to be carrying the full load once I'm gone. Go on home. I'll take care of it."

Polly hesitated only a moment before she opened the back door with a grateful smile. "I'll come by the house to see you off in the morning," she called over her shoulder.

Carrie stepped out onto the front porch to welcome her newest patient. "Hank!" she said with surprise.

"Hello, Dr. Wallington."

Carrie eyed him closely. His clear eyes revealed he was still winning his battle against alcohol, and his pain-free face said the Hypericum was still working to relieve the torment from his amputated arm, a relic of Gettysburg. "It's good to see you, Hank," she said warmly. "How are you doing?"

"I'm doing real good," Hank assured her, although he looked around nervously.

Carrie felt a surge of unease. "What's wrong?"

Hank shook his head. "Can we go inside?"

Carrie's throat tightened with the knowledge that he didn't want to be seen at the clinic, but she kept her voice calm. "Take your horse around back. You can come in the rear entrance."

His face flooded with gratitude as he led his horse where it couldn't be detected from the road.

"Who are you hiding from?" Carrie asked when Hank entered her office.

"I wish I knew for sure," Hank mumbled, meeting her eyes. "It may be nothing at all, but me and Newton been hearing a lot of talk, Dr. Wallington."

Newton, Hank's friend, had been the first veteran patient she had seen. He'd been convinced to bring Hank to see her, and then the multitude of veterans she treated on a regular basis had followed. Carrie didn't need to ask Hank what kind of talk, but she knew she should get all the information possible. She sat quietly while he told what he had come to tell her.

All the children were sleeping soundly in their beds before Carrie broached the subject she'd been holding close all night. "Hank came to see me today."

Rose eyed her closely. "From the sound of your voice, he didn't bring good news."

Carrie shook her head. "I'm afraid he didn't." All conversation on the porch ceased as everyone turned their attention to her. "Hank and Newton hear a lot of talk."

"Are they still making liquor in the woods?" Rose asked indignantly.

"No," Carrie said quickly. "They've both sworn off moonshine. They know they can't make it and stay sober, so they shut down the still. Men continue to get together there, however, and there's a lot of talk."

"What have they heard?" Abby asked.

Carrie had thought about different ways to soften the impact of her news, but there was no point. All of them had been forced to deal with violence in the past, and none of them believed it was over. The lengthy respite had been welcomed, but it hadn't made them drop their guard. Moses still had men posted at the entrance to Cromwell, and there were armed men posted around the school and clinic every day.

"There's talk about another attack on the plantation," Carrie informed them.

"When?" Moses asked sharply.

"They don't know," Carrie admitted. "They're doing all they can to get more information, but if a date has been decided, they aren't aware of it. Hank promised that the minute he had solid information, he would come here and let all of you know."

"I thought the men you were helping promised there would be no more violence?" Rose protested, her eyes shooting toward the bedroom where her children slept peacefully.

"They're not from around here," Carrie explained. "Hank says all the men I'm helping have made sure no more violence happens from anyone locally, but as things heat up in the South, the KKK and other vigilante groups are sending men into areas they deem to be especially troublesome."

"And Cromwell Plantation is at the top of the list because we treat our workers fairly," Moses said bitterly.

Carrie didn't bother to respond to the obvious truth. She understood Moses' bitterness.

"He didn't tell you anything else?" Thomas pressed.

Carrie shook her head with regret. "I could tell he was terrified to be there. He suspects he's being watched because of his connection with me. It took quite a bit of courage for him to come see me today."

"It won't change anything we're doing," Moses said, his face set in grim lines that made him look older. "We've already got guards watching during the day. We double that number at night, and the school and clinic are always being watched."

"The men must be so exhausted," Abby murmured. "They work all day in the fields, and then have to stand guard at night?"

"They all know the consequences of a surprise attack," Moses said bluntly. "They do what they have to do to protect their families and the crop they're counting on. No one complains."

Carrie knew he was right. She also knew Annie often baked late into the night in order to send hot food out to the men.

Moses stood and walked to the edge of the porch, his massive shoulders outlined like blocks of granite as he stared out over the plantation. Rose joined him and reached down to take his hand.

Tears came to Carrie's eyes as she watched them, their figures silhouetted against the deepening dusk. These two whom she loved so dearly had been forced to endure far too much simply because they were black. She hoped it would end someday, but she was aware it wouldn't happen any day soon. Emotions were still running too high in the South. She turned her eyes to her father and Abby. They were in equal danger because of their agreement with what was happening on the plantation. Carrie's heart burst with pride for all of them, but that didn't diminish the worry and fear.

Her father read her mind.

"Carrie, y'all are going back to Philadelphia in the morning," Thomas said firmly. "You might as well stop what you're thinking."

"Your father is right," Anthony said gently. "There's no way of knowing when an attack will take place, or *if* it will take place. We've all learned we can't live our lives based on fear."

While he may have been right, Carrie couldn't imagine riding away from the plantation when an attack was most likely imminent.

Rose turned to gaze at her. "You can't come home for good until you finish your internship," she said. "I hate seeing you leave the plantation every single time, but this time I know that when you return, it will be for good. Your practice in Richmond will take you away at times, but it's not like being in Philadelphia. You have to go finish what you started, Carrie. We'll take care of things here."

Carrie's eyes filled with tears. Knowing her best friend was right didn't make it any easier to leave.

When Carrie turned in the carriage to wave good-bye to everyone the next morning, she swallowed the fear that someone she loved may not be waiting for her when she returned to the plantation. Granite, his massive head hanging over the fence, watched until they rounded the last curve. His whinny carried to them on the breeze even when he was out of sight. Anthony took her hand and squeezed it tightly. Carrie clung to it, drawing the strength she needed to leave.

Frances smiled up at her through her own lingering tears of good-bye. "We have to go back to Philadelphia, Mama," she reminded her. "We both still have work to do there."

They were on the outskirts of Richmond before Carrie's heart settled enough to anticipate what awaited them. It seemed the city had become even more congested during their weeks on the plantation. Now that the war was over, the Virginia capital was growing explosively. Eager to put the destruction and poverty of the war behind them, Richmonders were rebuilding their city and bringing as much new business to it as possible.

The growing wealth meant the streets were even more crowded.

Carrie gazed around. "It's almost as chaotic as Philadelphia," she murmured.

Frances heard her low comment. "Are you sure you want to have a practice here, Mama? Aren't you going to hate leaving the plantation?"

The last two weeks on the plantation with Frances had been such a delight. Daily swims... Long rides... Working together in the clinic... Watching sunrises and sunsets over the beautiful Virginia countryside... "I hate leaving the plantation every single time," Carrie admitted, "but—"

"But there is still work to be done," Frances finished, her voice a combination of sadness and resolution. "And Daddy will be here, too, running River City Carriages."

Carrie nodded. "Yes." She looked at Frances' face more closely. "Will being here in the city sometimes make *you* unhappy?" She was appalled to suddenly realize she had not thoroughly contemplated that possibility.

Frances considered the question carefully. "I miss the plantation every time I leave it, too, Mama, but I want to be with you and Daddy. Staying in Philadelphia with Jeremy and Marietta was fun, and I liked being with the twins, but I missed you and Daddy the whole time. Besides, if I'm going to be a doctor like you, I need to learn as much from you as I can." She paused thoughtfully. "I heard you talking with Grandma last week about running a women's medical practice in Richmond. I know it's going to be real hard. You told me that girls my age will have their own battle to fight for women's rights. I figure I can learn a lot from watching you and Janie run the clinic."

Carrie stared at her, amazed at her growing maturity. Frances had been forced to grow up quickly through the hardships of the war, watching her family die, and living through the deprivations of the orphanage. This was different, however. Carrie knew she was watching the transformation of a girl into a budding woman. She liked what she saw.

"I'm glad your mama is going to have you with her," Anthony said gently. "I figure the two of you together can accomplish anything."

Frances grinned. "I believe you're right, Daddy!"

Micah was waiting on the porch when the carriage rolled up to her father and Abby's home on Church Hill. The butler's face was creased with concern as he hurried out to meet them.

"What is it, Micah?" Anthony asked. "Is May all right?"

"May is just fine," Micah responded. "She's in there cooking up a feast for you right now, but I doubt you're gonna get to eat much of it, Mr. Anthony."

Anthony waited for him to explain.

"There was a real big storm up there in the mountains last night," Micah said. "Mr. Peter sent a telegram that got here a little bit ago. The James River done turned into a real lion. It's real bad," he said somberly. "The flood is headed this way."

Anthony turned to look at Carrie. "What will happen in Richmond if the flood is big enough to reach us?"

Carrie frowned. "The last big flood was a hundred years ago, but my father has told me the stories passed down through our family. Shockhoe Bottom will flood terribly."

Anthony tensed. "Which means River City Carriages is right in the path of the flood."

"That's the truth, Mr. Anthony," Micah agreed. "I done told Marcus and Willard that I would let you know as soon as you got here."

Carrie listened with growing concern. Marcus and Willard were capable managers and employees, but it would take everyone working together to rescue the horses and equipment from the destructive floodwaters if they reached the city. It was possible the danger would pass, but they couldn't rely on that. If they waited until the river started rising to act, it would be too late. "Have they started evacuating the horses?"

"I don't rightly know, Miss Carrie," Micah answered. "I don't reckon any of them boys know what will happen when the river floods."

Anthony turned to her with questioning eyes.

"Once the river starts to rise, it will rise quickly," Carrie told him. "I've heard the stories. It's important that we get all the horses and equipment out as quickly as possible."

Anthony turned to Frances. "I want you to go inside and stay with May. Eat enough fried chicken for me."

"I want to come help, Daddy," Frances protested.

"I know you do, sweetie. I appreciate your desire, but I can't worry about you while I'm worrying about the horses. It will be a big help to me if you will stay here."

Frances frowned, but nodded reluctantly. "What about Mama?"

"She's coming with me," Anthony replied. "We both know I could never convince her to stay here."

"That's true," Frances agreed.

Carrie chuckled; grateful Anthony knew her well enough not to attempt to keep her from helping.

Micah reached for their baggage and began to haul it out onto the walkway.

At that same moment, May bustled out onto the porch, carrying a large basket. "Y'all ain't going down to fight floodwaters without some food," she called.

Carrie jumped down from the carriage and gave the elderly servant a hug. "Thank you, May. We'll return as soon as we can. Thanks for watching after Frances."

"It's always a pleasure, Miss Carrie." May turned to the young girl. "The first apples of the season just came in, Miss Frances. How about you and me fix an apple pie while we're waiting?"

Frances grinned. "Just one? How about if we fix two of them so that we can take one on the train tomorrow?"

May chuckled, her dark eyes flashing with amusement. "Two it is, child. Now hop down out of that carriage so your mama and daddy can get going."

Carrie kissed Frances on the cheek before she stepped from the carriage. "I love you, honey. We'll be back as soon as we can." Then she turned to May. "Watch this one. She has been known to eat all the apples before they have a chance to get into the pie."

May raised a brow. "And just how would you know that? You ain't never cooked an apple pie in your life, Miss Carrie."

Carrie smiled good-naturedly. "Deirdre warned me." Her Irish cook in Philadelphia had saved her family from Carrie's poor cooking skills.

May shrugged nonchalantly. "We got plenty. Micah brought a whole big box just this morning. What Miss Frances doesn't eat, and what we don't put in the pies, will get canned for later this year."

Carrie nodded, her thoughts turning to River City Carriages. As the last bag was lifted down to the sidewalk, she looked at Anthony. "Let's go," she said urgently.

Chapter Six

Carrie's mind was racing as they wove their way through the traffic as quickly as possible. She was certain most people hadn't received news of the impending flood, but it would spread quickly. She turned to Anthony. "It's going to take all the drivers to get the horses and carriages to safety. When will they be coming in from the morning shift to switch out the horses?"

Anthony pulled out his pocket watch. "They'll be coming back within the hour," he reported.

Carrie nodded. "That's good, but we have another problem. We have to stable the horses somewhere until the waters recede."

"How long should that take?"

"I have no idea. I remember my father saying that after the last big flood it took about a week for the waters to go all the way down. Fortunately, River City Carriages isn't down at river level, so it shouldn't take as long to recede. The biggest job will be digging out all the mud and debris that the river will leave behind."

Carrie forced herself to remember everything her father had told her about the flood of 1771, which had devastated the plantation when her great-grandparents had just arrived in Virginia. The destruction had killed one hundred and fifty people, as well as wiping out most of the buildings within reach of the river in Richmond. The water had reached a flood stage of forty-five feet above normal. She tensed as she thought of the plantation, but there was nothing she could do from here. All her focus had to go toward Anthony's business.

"How soon could the flood get here?" Anthony asked, his face tight with anxiety.

"I don't know," Carrie answered honestly. "All we can do is be as ready as possible."

Anthony nodded, his eyes fixed on the road ahead as he maneuvered through traffic. "We're in trouble if all the feed and hay is destroyed," he muttered.

"As every driver comes in, we'll have them load the carriages with as much as they can haul."

"We just had four tons of grain delivered two weeks ago," Anthony said grimly. "Along with several wagons of freshly cut hay."

"We'll simply do the best we can," Carrie said soothingly. "I would imagine we have several hours before the waters start to rise, and then it will take longer before it climbs high enough to reach the stables—*if* it does," she added. "We have to prepare for the worst, but it might not happen."

Marcus met them at the front door, his ebony eyes flashing his concern. "I'm real glad to see you, Anthony. I hear trouble is coming." He nodded at Carrie. "I'm glad to see you, too," he said warmly.

"Good to see you, Marcus," Anthony said. "The news is that a heavy storm in the mountains is going to cause flooding here in Richmond. The stables could be right in the path of it if history is repeated."

The concern in Marcus' eyes deepened. "What are we gonna do?"

"We have to get all the horses out," Anthony said urgently. "That is our first priority. How many are in the stables?"

"Twenty-four," Marcus answered. "There be another twenty-four out working, but they'll be back pretty soon to switch out."

Anthony thought quickly. "I want you to send out word to as many men as you can in the Quarters. Tell them I'll pay them for a day's work if they'll come help us. They'll have to lead the horses to safety while the drivers load their carriages with all the extra harnesses and as much feed as they can."

Willard, the other River City Carriages manager, walked around the corner just then. "Grace just got here with some lunch. I'll send her to spread the alarm. The Quarters is high enough to not worry about flooding. We'll have men here quickly. How many should she ask for?"

"Forty, if we can get them. They can help lead horses out and load up the carriages."

Willard nodded. "A few of the men I know have big wagons. I'll get them to carry out as much of the grain and hay as they can."

"I would tell as many men as possible to come down here," Carrie said quickly. "We can't use them all, but the other business owners are going to need as much help as we do in order to save their inventory."

Willard disappeared. Moments later, the sound of running feet told them his wife, Grace, was on her way to spread the alarm. After months of loneliness when the couple had first arrived, the Quarters had finally embraced the white veteran and his black wife. Anthony's willingness to hire Willard as one of his managers, along with Willard's close friendship with Marcus, a resident of the Quarters, had opened the doors to the young couple. White Richmonders still turned up their nose at the biracial couple, but they had found their place in the black community.

Anthony looked around, his mind racing. "Carrie, will you pack up everything in the office? I don't want to lose all the business records. There are wooden crates in the storage area. Once you fill them up, I'll have men come and carry them out for you."

"I'll take care of it," she promised as she turned and disappeared down the hallway.

Anthony locked eyes with Marcus. "We're going to start pulling harnesses and tack out of the tack room. All the grooming equipment as well."

"I figure we're gonna take everything we possibly can," Marcus replied. "We don't want to have to replace nothing we don't have to."

The three men went to work. It wasn't long before they all were glistening with sweat, but no one slowed down.

"The first boxes are ready," Carrie called about thirty minutes later.

"I'll get them," Willard announced. A few minutes later, four wooden boxes joined the growing pile outside the stables.

They had just pulled the final harnesses from the tack room when they heard the clatter of wagon wheels approaching.

Anthony met the first driver at the entrance. "Hello, Paul."

"Hello, Mr. Anthony," Paul called. "It's real good to see you." He looked over at the large pile of harnesses quizzically. "What's going on?"

Anthony explained quickly.

Paul whistled. "The James River gone wild? I done heard stories of how bad it can be."

Anthony didn't have time to hear any more history. "I need you to load your carriage with all these boxes, and then as many harnesses as you can."

"Sho'nuff," Paul responded. "What do I do with all of it once I got it loaded?"

Anthony paused. He still hadn't come up with a solution to that part of the problem.

Carrie appeared at his side. "Take your carriage up to my father's house on Church Hill. Do you know where it is?"

"Yes ma'am, Dr. Wallington. It's a pleasure to see you." Paul's face was bright with a smile.

Anthony knew the people in the Quarters loved his wife. She had saved many of them from illness and injuries over the years.

"It's good to see you, too, Paul," Carrie replied. "When you get up to the house, put your horse into the stable and leave the carriage in the backyard. There's only one stall, but you can put all the harnesses and the boxes in the tack area. They'll be safe there. You'll have to walk back, but we'll probably still need your help here."

"You know I'll do whatever needs to be done," Paul assured her. He began to help Willard and Marcus load harnesses into the carriage.

Carrie turned to Anthony. "The rest of the records are loaded into two more boxes. I'll water Paul's horse before he leaves." She hurried away to fill a pail with fresh water.

Anthony watched his wife for a moment, grateful for her clearheaded thinking and calm actions, before he turned away to speak with the next drivers who had arrived. It only took three carriages to contain all the tack and harnesses. As more drivers arrived for their horse switch, he directed them to load bags of grain into their carriages, being careful to not overload them.

Minutes later, a stream of men began to arrive from the Quarters.

"I hear you need some help, Mr. Anthony," one of the men called.

Anthony recognized Clarence, a friend of Marcus'. "I do," Anthony confirmed, relief surging through him. "Thank you for coming."

"I gots ten men with me, and there be a lot more coming," Clarence said cheerfully. "You tell me what you need done. We'll get it done."

Anthony managed a smile. "We've got to get all the horses to safety. That's our highest priority. I need a man to lead each horse to higher ground."

"And then what?" Clarence asked. "Where we gonna take the horses?"

Once again, Anthony was faced with the question he didn't know the answer to. There were other stables in town, but none that could accommodate forty-eight horses. His face must have shown his dilemma.

"Tell you what," Clarence said thoughtfully. "We'll take them horses up to the big lot behind the church building. When I got word about the river, I suspected you might not have nowhere to take them. The pastor is a friend of your wife. He said we can bring the horses up there. We can put up some hitching posts real quick. That will give you time to figure out where you gonna keep them until the waters go down."

"Thank you," Anthony said gratefully. "Please make sure they all get water and food. I'll have one of the drivers take up grain and hay for them, along with their water pails."

Clarence nodded. "You ain't got nothing to worry about, Mr. Anthony. I'm real good friends with horses. When I was a slave, I done took care of all the horses on the plantation. I hated slavery, but I sure did like those horses. These here animals gonna be just fine."

Anthony's smile was less forced this time. "That's wonderful, Clarence. I appreciate your help more than you can know."

Clarence returned his smile. "It ain't no problem. We all like you just fine, Mr. Anthony, but I don't know anybody in the Quarters who wouldn't do anything possible for your wife. We owe her a lot."

"A fact for which I'm very grateful," Anthony admitted with a grin.

Yelling from down by the river caught his attention. He turned to look, but already knew he couldn't see anything through all the buildings. A man running by the stables answered his question.

"The river is rising!" the man hollered. "It's rushing faster than I've ever seen, and is rising quickly. Prepare for a flood!"

Anthony became all business again. "Thank you, Clarence. I'll come to the church when everything is taken care of here."

Willard appeared beside him, his green eyes flashing with intensity under his thick thatch of brown hair. "The wagons are almost here, Anthony."

"How much grain and hay are left?"

"The drivers have been able to load about a third of it."

Anthony cast a look at the sky. The storm that had created the flood could very likely descend on them next, and he suddenly realized he hadn't told his drivers where to take the feed.

Willard read his mind. "The pastor of the church in the Quarters where Clarence is taking the horses said we could put all the feed in the church building."

Anthony stared at him. "In the church building?" He didn't know any pastor that would let his sanctuary become home to tons of grain and huge stacks of hay.

Willard shrugged, his eyes glistening with appreciation as he looked toward the office. "Once they found out it was you..."

"They're doing it for Carrie," Anthony said with wonder.

"Yep," Willard agreed cheerfully. "She ran her hospital for the Black Quarters at this church during the war, when Jeremy's father was the pastor, before he died. The pastor who took his place told us to fill it up if we needed to." He turned away when the first wagon rounded the curve. A swarm of men appeared from within the stables and began to load feed into the wooden conveyance pulled by a strong team of horses.

Everywhere Anthony looked, men and women were moving down the sloped road toward the river, determined to save what could be saved. When you lived in a river town, you had to be prepared for rising water at any time. Wagons rumbled along with wares of all kinds, while hundreds of people trudged past, carrying whatever they could.

Anthony caught the eye of one of the men, bowed under the weight of several boxes. "How fast is the water rising?"

"The first buildings along the river have water in them," the man said in a labored voice. "It's going to be a bad one. There are huge trees bobbing along like they're saplings. I saw one take out the side of one of the tobacco warehouses."

Anthony scowled. Farmers had already begun to harvest tobacco. They'd been paid, but the tobacco brokers were going to sustain a tremendous loss. Then his thoughts flew to the plantation. Moses was planning on harvesting the following week. How badly would the flood damage the tobacco crop?

He turned back to the stables. He had to put his entire attention on saving all he could. Both his livelihood, and all the men who counted on him for a job, were at stake. He dashed in and began to heave sacks of grain.

When the first wagon was full, the second one pulled into place. Anthony worked tirelessly, while Carrie delivered pitchers of water to all the men who had come to help.

When the third wagon pulled away with the final bags of grain and the last bales of hay, along with the wooden rolltop desks they had saved from the office, Anthony joined everyone in a lusty cheer.

The cheer died away when the sound of rushing water close enough to be heard told them the river was rising rapidly. Cries of dismay sounded below as more and more people appeared with all they could carry. Many faces were full of hopeless despair. Just five years after watching most of the buildings along the waterfront burn at the end of the war, they were now suffering a new type of destruction.

Anthony exchanged a look with Willard and Marcus, and then turned to all the men who had gathered. "They need our help."

The men all started running in the direction of the flood. Whatever racial animosity that existed in Richmond was forgotten as crisis demanded the best in every person present.

Carrie joined Anthony. Together, they forged into a store that was close to the river. They knew it would be underwater soon. They grabbed everything they could and carried it out of the building. Bending under the weight, they plodded up the hill to a point they were sure was high enough. Crudely written signs identified the businesses that were in danger of flooding. They located a sign that said *Isenberg Clothing*, and added their armfuls to the pile of inventory. Grim-faced police stood guard to protect from looting.

Unencumbered, they ran back down the hill and gathered more clothing. People were working frantically everywhere Carrie and Anthony looked. One glance at the river told them the store would be inaccessible when they returned.

"These poor people!" Carrie cried.

Anthony was newly appreciative of the outpouring of help and support that had allowed them to save every belonging in River City Carriages. "They will rebuild!" He had to shout above the sound of the raging river.

 He stopped for a moment, mesmerized by the sheer power of the torrent gushing past below them. Rooftops and small sheds were being swept along as if they were nothing. There was no way to tell whether they were from nearby, or the result of demolished homes far above them in the mountains. He could identify pieces of furniture and mattresses. He shuddered at the thought of families washed from their homes. Then he turned and moved rapidly up the hill again. He would help until there was nothing more to be done.

Anthony and Carrie were collapsed on the porch swing far above the raging river when a carriage turned onto their street several blocks away. They glanced at it but didn't pay much attention. They weren't expecting company. Exhausted and hungry, they had just finished the big plate of fried chicken, biscuits, corn, and apple pie that May had saved for them.

Frances, tired from a long day, was already sound asleep when they had arrived home. Loath to wake her, they had tiptoed in, kissed her on the forehead, and then crept back out quietly.

They had eaten silently, their hearts and minds heavy with the ramifications of the flood. They had stayed long enough to see the flood overtake River City Carriages, but the water had not been deep in the stables when the darkness drove them home. There was nothing more they could do, but at least they had the satisfaction of knowing they had done all they could.

Clarence had come back to assure them the horses were all doing well at the church. In the morning, they would go about finding more suitable stabling for them until they could get them back into the River City Carriages stables. There was nothing more that could be done that night.

"Thank you," Anthony said quietly.

"For?" Carrie asked. "We both worked equally hard."

"Yes," Anthony acknowledged, "but we wouldn't have gotten everything out of there if it hadn't been for the relationships you've built with the people of the Quarters."

Carrie smiled. "They were magnificent, weren't they?"

"Everyone I thanked told me they would do *anything* for Dr. Carrie," Anthony said with an amused glint in his eyes. Then his face grew serious. "You've done so much for the black people in the Quarters. When most people didn't care, you went out of your way to help them. In the middle of the war, you gave of your time to run a hospital for them."

Carrie sobered. "Abby told me long ago that I would never be able to out give God. Today is more proof that she was right. It meant so much to see all those people coming to help us at a moment's notice." She gazed toward the river thoughtfully. "I don't think about what I'm going to get in return when I give to my patients, but today was very special."

"Even if we lose the stables, we'll be able to rebuild," Anthony said. "We have all the horses, the carriages, the tack and all the feed. Not to mention the business records you saved. It would have been a tremendous loss if they'd been destroyed. We're very lucky. I know most businesses down by the river can't say the same thing. The warning didn't come in time for them to save all their inventory and equipment."

"Hello!"

Carrie looked up, startled. The carriage they'd seen turn the corner was now in front of the house. The darkness made it impossible to see the passenger hailing them, but she knew she recognized the strong New York accent. She forced her tired brain to identify it. Suddenly, her eyes widened. "Peter? Peter Wilcher?"

"It's me," the voice confirmed. Moments later, Peter appeared on the porch.

Carrie could tell, even in the dark, that his tall, muscular body sagged with fatigue. She and Anthony jumped up at the same time.

"It's good to see you, Peter," Anthony said warmly. "To what do we owe the pleasure?"

The door to the house swung open as Peter slumped into a rocking chair on the porch. "Hello, Mr. Peter!" May called. "What a nice surprise! You hungry for some of my fried chicken? I got just enough left to feed a starving man."

Peter's face, illuminated by the oil lantern, brightened with a smile. "Hello, May. That's the best offer I've had in a while. I would appreciate it greatly."

"I'll have it right out to you." The door slapped shut as May disappeared into the house.

"Where are you traveling in from?" Carrie asked, concerned by the deep fatigue she saw etched not only on Peter's face, but also in his eyes. She recognized the same look she had seen on Matthew's face many times when he had covered a particularly disturbing story. Being a news reporter in America during this turbulent time had to be very difficult.

Peter frowned. "I caught the train in from the Shenandoah Valley," he said wearily. "I hear the flood has reached Richmond. How is River City Carriages?"

Anthony shrugged. "It was taking on water when we left, but we saved everything else. A tremendous outpouring of help from the Black Quarters made it possible." He reached over and put a hand on Peter's arm. "Their help, and the telegram you sent. If we hadn't had warning, it would have turned out much differently. Thank you."

"That's good news," Peter replied. "I was hoping the telegram would make a difference."

"Not everyone was as lucky as we were," Anthony admitted, "but thanks to you, everyone was able to save at least a portion of their inventory." He glanced west. "How bad was it in the mountains?"

Peter's face darkened. "Terrible," he said flatly. His voice deepened with emotion. "I don't know how much more those poor people can take. The entire valley was devastated by the war. The Union Army cut and burned everything they could, turning it into a wasteland."

Carrie winced, remembering all Robert had told her. She knew Peter was right.

"I was in Lynchburg covering another story when it started to rain. At first, the rain was welcomed after the long, dry summer. When it kept coming down in torrents, we realized there would be trouble. There were fifteen inches of rain in two days, but most of it fell within a few hours." He shook his head. "The valley didn't stand a chance. The soil is depleted. The forests are gone. Almost all vegetation was stripped during the war. They've worked hard to restore the land, but they haven't been able to accomplish enough." He scowled. "Now they're going to have to start over. When the rains fell, there was nothing to prevent runoff and erosion, and nothing to slow down the massive amounts of water going into the James River."

Carrie and Anthony listened quietly, hearing the agony in his voice.

"When the sun finally came up, we realized how destructive the rains had been. Entire towns were completely ravaged," he said heavily. "Landslides buried many homes, killing everyone inside."

Carrie gasped as tears filled her eyes. Losing the contents of a business was one thing; losing everything you owned, and watching families lose their lives was another. Her heart ached for the people who had endured so much during the war. They had worked hard to rebuild, but their suffering had begun anew.

"Tens of thousands have lost their homes all up and down the river," Peter said. "Entire communities had rebuilt on old floodplains, not realizing the danger they were in. They've been wiped out. Those who escaped with their lives have lost everything else," he muttered, his eyes shadowed with the memories of what he'd seen. "Houses were overturned. Boats were swept away." He shook his head. "Everything..." His voice broke off as May stepped out onto the porch.

"Some hot food will help you, Mr. Peter," May said sympathetically. "I whipped up some mashed potatoes, and there's a big piece of the apple pie that me and Miss Frances baked this afternoon."

"Thank you," Peter said gratefully as he reached for the plate. "My stomach is telling me how long it's been since my last meal."

"Eat," Anthony commanded. "You can tell us more when you're done."

Peter complied willingly.

All of Richmond seemed to have gone quiet in deference of the flood. The only sound on the porch as Peter ate was the lingering chirp of summer crickets. The hint of a cool breeze revealed their song would soon be finished for the season. The honk of geese overhead said the fall migration was underway. The final blooms had withered on the magnolia tree, and the sheltering oak leaves carried a slight hint of yellow, a harbinger of the fall colors that would soon encompass the city.

Carrie leaned back against the swing, grateful for Anthony's solid strength beside her. It was almost impossible to believe they'd left the plantation just that morning. It seemed they'd been in Richmond for days. The idea of catching the train for Philadelphia the next morning was almost more than she could bear.

Peter took a final swig of tea and wiped his mouth with a napkin. The expression on his face said May's food had worked its magic. He didn't look peaceful, but the agony wasn't as intense. Until he spoke again...

"It will take as long to recover from this flood as it took to recover from the war – not that they've completely recovered yet," Peter began. "Businesses all up and down the river have been completely washed away. Entire inventories of lumber, wheat, flour, tobacco, corn, oats and many other crops have been lost to the floodwaters. What wasn't washed away has been ruined."

"What about the mills and foundries?" Anthony asked. "There are so many up there."

"Destroyed," Peter replied. "People who were barely surviving before have lost all means of support now. Even when the waters recede, there's going to be nothing but thick mud to deal with. Crops can't be replanted until spring. Those people are already impoverished. I'm afraid starvation is going to be inevitable this winter for many." His voice thickened again. "I've talked with many of the mill and warehouse owners. For the first time since the war, they were actually going to be able to pay their taxes. Now, they will most likely lose their businesses."

"Surely the government will help," Carrie said, her heart breaking for the people who were suffering, and what they would have to endure in the months to come. She thought about all the cities along the river. "How did Harpers Ferry fare?"

Peter scowled. "I talked to a fellow on the train who had just come from there. The town is located at the confluence of the Shenandoah and Potomac Rivers, which means they received double the amount of floodwaters. The destruction they sustained from the battle during the war was nothing compared to what the flood has left behind. Waterpower built that town, but it's also the power of water that destroyed it."

Anthony looked startled. "Is it truly destroyed?"

Peter nodded. "I'm afraid so. They may rebuild, but it will never fully recover. Many of the people, like the fellow I talked to on the train who left Harpers Ferry during the war, had returned, hopeful they could rebuild their lives. This man watched everything he owned wash away, including one of his children who was caught up in the flood."

Carrie held a hand to her mouth. "That's terrible," she breathed.

"The man I spoke to was traveling with his wife and his daughter, who survived. They were headed north, *never* to return to Harpers Ferry. As bad as this flood was, there are certainly more to follow. It's going to take decades to return forestation and vegetation to the Shenandoah Valley. He was taking his family away from the inevitable."

Anthony looked deeply troubled. "I wonder if the Union had any idea what the long-term repercussions of their actions would be when they were burning and destroying the valley in order to win the war."

Peter's lips narrowed. "I daresay it wouldn't have mattered. They believed the only way to win the war was to completely crush the spirit of the South. They did it with Sherman's March through Georgia. They accomplished the same thing in the Shenandoah Valley campaign." His eyes flashed angrily. "I would like to think someone considered what it would really mean when they actually won the war, but I no longer believe they did. The cost has been excruciatingly high. It's going to be excruciatingly high for a very long time."

Carrie looked at him, saddened by the defeated look she saw on his face. Again, she recognized the same expression she had seen on Matthew's face many times. Peter had been traveling tirelessly, going from one crisis to the next as the country struggled to recover from the war that had decimated so many people's lives. Matthew, because of his book, had been able to step back from the daily grind of reporting. Peter had not had that luxury.

She was also completely aware that the North was not wholly responsible for the devastation. They had done what they believed was necessary to end a war that the South had begun. Hot heads on both sides of the recent war were responsible for all the repercussions that would take generations to overcome.

Peter took a deep breath. "Cromwell Plantation is going to be underwater," he said. "There will be flooding all the way down to the Atlantic Ocean."

Carrie and Anthony exchanged a long look. She nodded in response to the question in his eyes.

"Carrie is going back to the plantation tomorrow," Anthony announced in a firm voice. "I have to stay in the city until we're able to reopen the stables, but we can't leave until we know what's happening on the plantation. You need a break, my friend. Go with her."

Peter shook his head. "I can't. I have to..."

"You have to have a reprieve," Carrie said sternly. "I know there are more stories to cover, Peter. There is one right here in Richmond, but you also must take care of yourself. You're on the verge of a breakdown if you don't give yourself some time." Her voice softened when she saw the stubborn glint in his eyes. "There's a limit to what the human spirit can endure, Peter. You pour your heart and soul into every story you cover, and into every article you write. At some point, the well runs dry. I've seen Matthew come to the same place I see you in right now."

Peter met her eyes, obviously deep in thought. "How long will you be on the plantation?"

"For as long as I'm needed," Carrie answered. "I don't know how long that will be, but we can't get on the train to Philadelphia when we know the flood is inundating the plantation, as well as impacting many of my patients." She tried to push away the thoughts of Granite and the other horses. It was certain some of the tobacco crop would be destroyed, but surely they would be able to move all the horses further inland to escape the waters.

Peter started to shake his head again, but then paused. "Where are Matthew and Janie?"

Carrie understood the question. Only Matthew could truly understand what Peter was feeling. "On the plantation," she said, thrilled she could tell him that. "In the midst of everything, I haven't been able to tell you that Matthew and Janie are the proud parents of a beautiful little girl. Her name is Annabelle Marie. She was born less than two weeks ago. They decided to delay their return to Philadelphia for a month."

"I'll come with you," Peter said reluctantly, his face revealing the battle he was fighting over his decision. "What time do we leave in the morning?"

Carrie wanted to leave at the crack of dawn but knew that wasn't possible. "I'm meeting Felicia tomorrow morning at nine o'clock. She and her teacher-companion were going to stay in the city for a day before leaving again, but we'll depart right away. Jeb was coming in from the plantation to drive them back, but that won't be necessary now."

"Who is going to drive you out?" Peter asked.

Carrie smiled. "It may come as a surprise to you, but I am perfectly capable of driving a carriage."

Peter chuckled, the first sound of amusement he'd made since his arrival. "Trust me, I'm not surprised. Merely impressed."

"I'm happy to have one of my men drive you out," Anthony told her, his expression indicating that he knew the offer was futile, but felt he must make it anyway.

Carrie looked at him lovingly. "You need every one of your men working here to take care of the stables, my dear. Besides, we'll have Peter with us now. I can assure you that we'll be just fine."

Chapter Seven

Dawn was lighting the sky when Anthony pulled the carriage to a stop a block away from the flooding river. Barriers had been erected to keep carriages from venturing too close. He exchanged an anxious glance with Carrie and Peter, and then stepped down. A messenger had come by earlier to let them know the river had stopped rising. It was time to see how much damage had been done.

All three of them stopped at the top of the hill leading down to the Shockhoe Bottom business district. The lower two streets lined with businesses and warehouses were completely submerged by rushing brown water, still thick with debris. It was impossible to know if any of the buildings were still there, or if they had all been washed away with the flood.

Further down the road, where the elevation was a bit higher, rooftops were barely visible. As the road climbed above the torrents, evidence of more structures and buildings could be seen.

Anthony held his breath as he walked to a spot where he could see down to where River City Carriages should be. "It's still there," he whispered, relief surging through him. It was true that six feet of water swirled through the stables, but the structure itself was still standing. He thought about his decision two years earlier to build the stables in its current location. He'd had the opportunity to buy land closer to the river. At the time, he feared he was making a mistake. Now, he was profoundly grateful.

Peter clapped him on the back. "Congratulations. You'll have quite a cleanup ahead of you, but when the waters recede in a day or two, you'll be able to start clearing out the mud and debris. It will take some time for everything to dry out, but it won't be that long before you can move the horses back in." He cocked his head. "Where are they now?"

"Twenty-four of them are once more traveling the roads of Richmond, pulling passengers through the city," Anthony said proudly. "My men only missed an afternoon of work. The other twenty-four are tied at one of the churches in the Quarters. My job this morning is to find more permanent stabling for them until I can bring them back here." He patted his pocket. "Carrie made a list of people in the city who have stalls behind their homes. All of them are Thomas' friends. We're hopeful they'll allow us to rent them out for a few days."

"You have your work cut out for you," Peter observed.

"It could have been so much worse." Anthony understood when Peter's expression darkened with grief and frustration. He pulled his watch from his pocket and glanced down. "It's time to go back to the house. May will have breakfast waiting, and then all of you have to leave for the train station."

Moses pounded up the stairs to the plantation house, taking a moment to savor the towering white columns soaring to three stories before he flung open the door.

"Land sakes, son! What in the world be the matter with you?" Annie demanded, her eyes wide with alarm when she came rushing from the kitchen, her apron and face smeared with flour. "You making enough noise to raise the dead. And," she continued without taking a breath, "what you doing out so early? I barely got started in on the breakfast biscuits."

"I'm sorry, Mama, but the river is rising. Fast."

He turned and rushed to the foot of the stairs. He didn't have time to go from room to room. "Everybody up!" he hollered, his deep voice reverberating through the house.

Moments later, Rose stumbled to the top of the stairs. "What's going on, Moses?"

Thomas and Abby appeared behind her, their bedclothes and hair rumpled and awry.

"What's wrong?" Thomas asked sharply.

"The river is rising," Moses said. "It's already into one of the tobacco fields, and it's moving fast."

Thomas frowned. "It's flooding. There must have been storms in the mountains."

"I've seen some fast waters on the river in my life," Moses said, "but nothing like this, Thomas."

Thomas nodded quickly, then turned and disappeared.

Moses knew he was going to get dressed. He looked up at his wife who was now staring at him with fear. "You need to get the children up, Rose."

"Where do I take them?"

Moses thought quickly. "The school. I believe it's far enough from the river that the water won't reach it." He wasn't actually confident of that, but there would be time to move everyone farther away if the waters reached that far inland.

"I'll wake Matthew and Janie," Abby said. "They're far enough back in the house that they probably didn't hear you. I'll have Janie take the children to the school, as well." She glanced at Rose. "You can all go together."

Miles pushed in through the door. "I could hear you hollering all the way out in the barn. What's going on?"

Moses explained quickly.

Miles scowled as he nodded. "I'll start moving the horses. I heard stories about the flood back a hundred years ago. It came all the way up into the house and barn. Weren't much here then, but the river took it all away."

"Where are you taking the horses?" Moses asked.

"Two miles back to the mares' pasture," Miles answered. "The waters won't reach that far. I'm gonna need some of the men to help. And I need someone to go fetch Susan and Amber. They'll be able to keep the horses calm."

"I'll send you twenty men as quickly as I can."

Miles peered at him more closely. "What you doin' up so early?"

Moses shrugged. "We're supposed to harvest in a few days. I woke up early and decided to ride through the fields one more time."

Miles eyed him sharply. "How bad is it?"

Moses' gut tightened. "Bad." That was all he needed to say for now. He wouldn't know how bad it was until the river stopped rising and began to recede. He was sickly aware that a large portion of the crop would be destroyed, but for now he needed to focus on protecting everything he could. There was nothing he could do for the tobacco crop.

Susan Justin rushed into the barn, her long blond hair haphazardly pulled back into a ponytail instead of its usual careful braid. Breeches, boots and a buttoned-up shirt completed her attire. "Harold will be here in a minute," she said, and then turned to look toward the river. "How bad is it?" she snapped.

"Won't know until we know," Miles answered, barely looking up as he pulled horses from their stalls. "The only thing we can do now is get all the horses where they be safe."

"The mares' pasture?" Susan asked.

"Yep," Miles agreed. "Except for Eclipse. He's done bred all the mares he's gonna breed for one season."

Susan thought quickly. "Jeb had a small pen built at the school so his horse can be loose while he guards the school during the day. I'll have Amber take Eclipse there."

Amber walked in as Susan spoke her name. "What's wrong?" she cried. "Is the river going to come into the barn?" Her voice was shrill with alarm.

Susan knew Amber's fear would infuse the horses if she couldn't control it. "Amber," she said calmly, "the river is flooding, but we don't know if it will make it this far or not. We're just being careful." She laid a hand on the young girl's shoulder. "The yearlings trust you and your brother the most because you spend the most time with them." She looked over the girl's shoulder. "Where is Clint?"

"He's right behind me," Amber said quickly.

Seconds later, her strong, muscular brother strode through the door. "The river is flooding?" he asked keenly.

Susan relaxed a little when she saw the calm expression on her barn manager's face. "Have you been through something like this before?"

"Nope," Clint said easily. "I read about it, though."

Susan's heart swelled with gratitude that Clint was such a voracious reader. All that he'd learned about horses had helped them create one of the most renowned stables in the South in less than five years. His easy manner helped her relax more.

"What are we going to do, Clint?" Amber demanded, her eyes still full of anxiety. "What if something happens to All My Heart? Or to Eclipse? Or to Pegasus? Or to the other horses?"

"We're going to move them," Clint said cheerfully. "Nothing is going to happen to them, Amber. The river may rise, but it can't go on forever." He turned to Miles. "I assume we're moving them all to the mares' pasture, but what about Eclipse?"

"I reckon he gonna be okay in that pen behind the school," Miles answered. "We'll leave one of Moses' men there to keep an eye on him until we can bring him back."

Susan's insides tightened again. Eclipse, the Cromwell Stables' stud, was immensely valuable. "I would prefer if there were two armed men with him," she said uneasily. "We can't afford for anything to happen to him."

Moses walked into the barn, overhearing the last of the conversation. "Two armed men it will be," he agreed. "Gabe is out sounding the alarm to all the men. They were due to work in less than an hour, but we'll have them here in a few minutes."

Susan smiled her thanks . "We'll move all that we can now. Miles, you stay here to direct everyone." She looked at Moses. "We'll need to move all the tack, as well. I suppose the best place for it is the school and clinic."

"Miles and I will take care of things," Moses promised. He watched as Rose emerged from the house with John and Hope, her arms full of clothing. Janie followed closely, her arms full of her infant daughter. Robert toddled his way down the stairs carefully. Moses wanted to go to his wife, but knew he was needed in the stables. It was enough to know his family would be safe. He turned away, but then swung back around. "Where is Mama?" he hollered across the yard.

Rose shot him a frustrated look. "She won't come with me," she called. "She says she isn't leaving until the water is lapping at the door."

Moses gritted his teeth, but before he could start toward the house, Miles clapped a hand on his shoulder.

"Don't bother, Moses. Annie ain't gonna do nothing she ain't ready to do. You known your mama a lot longer than I have, but I been married to her long enough to know *that*," he said with a chuckle. "Don't you worry none. I'll get your mama out of here if need be."

Moses nodded hesitantly. Miles was right. His mama had survived trauma after trauma by being stubborn and strong-willed. "Go on!" he called to Rose. "We'll take care of Mama."

Rose nodded, stepped into the carriage Jeb had pulled in front of the house, and waved her hand.

"I'll see you soon!" Moses called as the first group of his men dashed up from behind the barn.

Franklin, his assistant, was at the front of the line. "What do you need us to do?"

Moses knew all the men were desperate for information about the tobacco crop, but there was no time to fill them in on the situation. It could wait until the horses were all safe.

Thomas appeared on the porch. "Can you afford two men to help here in the house?" he yelled.

Moses could see more men coming, and Harold Justin had just ridden up. He calculated quickly, and then pointed to two of the men who had arrived with the first group. "Please go do whatever needs to be done in the house," he said crisply, and then turned to Harold. "I'm sure Thomas and Matthew can use your help, too." He waited for Harold's nod and then entered the barn to start moving tack. It was imperative everyone act quickly.

Thomas gazed around the house that had been home his entire life.

Abby stood beside him. "Will the river come this high, my dear?"

Thomas took her hand. "I don't know, but I don't want to regret not taking action. The river has flooded while I've been alive, but never badly. I remember the stories my father heard from his parents when they arrived a hundred years ago. The flood back in 1771 covered almost the entire plantation. It was their first year in America. Back then, the house and barn were small and simple, but they were completely submerged. When the waters receded, everything was gone."

Abby's face went white, but she spoke calmly. "What do we need to do?"

"The best we can do is move everything to the second floor. If the waters come this far, I don't believe they'll reach that high." The clomp of boots on the stairs told him the help he'd asked for had arrived.

Matthew appeared beside them. "Tell me what needs to be done."

Harold walked in with two of the plantation men. "We're here to do whatever you need."

Annie appeared at the door to the kitchen. "I'm already packin' up the kitchen things," she announced. "You can send them men in here at any time. I'm just gonna keep workin'." She turned and disappeared back into her domain, her face set in determined lines.

Abby gazed after her. "I'll go help Annie," she announced. "You men can handle the heavy things."

Thomas kissed her lightly. "Thank you." Tightening his lips, he went to work. He couldn't control the river, but he could lessen the impact if the waters made it to the house.

Carrie's eyes scanned the crowded platform at the train station. Passengers were disembarking the train, everyone eager to have reached their destination. She was eager to retrieve Felicia and her traveling companion so they could depart. They would be tired after traveling for two days, but it was urgent they get to the plantation. They would be able to rest when they got there. Finally, she spotted the girl's head in the crowd. "Felicia!"

Felicia waved and quickly began to weave her way through the throngs of people.

Even from a distance, Carrie could tell the girl was angry and upset, her face set in mutinous lines. She was followed by a slender young woman with blond hair covered by a red bonnet who evidently was the teacher chosen by Oberlin College to be her traveling companion.

Each time Felicia returned home, a teacher accompanied her who would spend the time teaching with Rose at her school. It was a situation that worked well for everyone, but a closer inspection of the teacher's face revealed she was upset as well. What had happened?

Carrie caught Felicia in a tight embrace when she reached her, taking note of the sparks flying from the girl's eyes. "Honey, what's wrong?"

"I want to get out of here!" Felicia hissed.

Carrie was alarmed as she caught the eye of the other woman. "Hello. My name is Carrie Wallington."

"Phoebe Waterston," the young women replied. She cast a concerned look at Felicia but shook her head slightly at Carrie's inquiring look.

Carrie took Felicia's hand but didn't ask any more questions. She had been forced to park the carriage almost a block away. "How much baggage do you have?"

"Two trunks," Phoebe replied.

Carrie felt a jolt of surprise. Felicia had never returned for a visit with more than a large satchel. She managed a smile and nod while she tried to figure out how to get their trunks to the carriage. The question of why there was so much baggage would have to wait.

"Dr. Wallington!"

Carrie turned her head as her name was called, quickly identifying one of Anthony's drivers who was there to provide transportation for the disembarking passengers. "Hello, Smitty. I want to thank you again for all your help yesterday."

"Weren't no problem, ma'am," Smitty assured her, his narrow face lit with a smile. "Mr. Anthony said you might need some help down here. I was just comin' to check."

Carrie smiled with relief. "I do. We have two trunks that need to be taken to our carriage a block away."

"I'll take care of that for you," Smitty assured her.

Felicia gazed around, confusion momentarily replacing the anger. "Why aren't we going to take one of the carriages right here?"

"Because we're not staying in the city tonight. We're going out to the plantation," Carrie answered.

Felicia stared at her. "Why? And why are *you* going to the plantation? The telegram I received before leaving school said you would meet me before you left for Philadelphia on the next train. We're supposed to be going to Thomas' house."

Carrie could feel the girl's agitation, but still had no reason for it. She kept her voice steady, not wanting to add to the unidentified angst. "There's a terrible flood happening right now. All of Shockhoe Bottom has been affected." She continued quickly, recognizing the alarm in Felicia's eyes. "River City Carriages is under water, but all the horses and equipment were saved. The flood will have reached the plantation by now. Anthony is staying here in town to handle things, but I couldn't leave until I know everyone on the plantation is safe."

Felicia nodded immediately, the anger dissipated by the news. "Mama and Daddy are in the way of the flood? John? Hope?"

Carrie wanted to assure her that everyone was fine, but she wouldn't lie. Felicia was far too intelligent to not see through any attempted subterfuge. "That's what we're going to find out," she said quietly.

They were outside the city limits before Carrie broached the subject she had been avoiding since meeting Felicia at the train station. She had deliberately asked the girl to sit beside her on the driver's seat. "You were upset when you arrived, Felicia. What happened?"

Felicia's eyes darkened with anger, but she cast a look backwards toward Frances.

"Oh, for goodness sakes," Frances burst out in an exasperated voice. "Do you think I can't see that look? I may not be in college like you, but I can certainly tell when someone is angry and upset. I know the world can be a horrible place, Felicia. I'm your friend. Whatever you say won't come as a surprise to me."

Carrie gazed at her daughter, once again impressed by her perception. Her time in Philadelphia talking to the factory children had done more for her than she realized. Pushing aside that realization until she had more time to focus on it, she turned her attention back to Felicia. "Honey, what happened?" She had loved the girl since the day she arrived home with Moses after the riot in Memphis almost four and a half years earlier. If someone had hurt her, Carrie wanted to know about it.

Felicia hesitated and then snapped. "I'm sick of being treated like there's something wrong with me!" Her face tensed. "Life in Oberlin is wonderful. I'm treated with respect. No one seems to care that I'm black, or even that I'm younger than any of the other college students."

Carrie waited quietly, giving her time to express her feelings. She noticed Peter watching Felicia carefully. He, too, cared about her deeply. He had been in Memphis during the riot that had killed her parents.

Frances wasn't so patient. "Someone treated you badly for being black while you were on the way here?"

Felicia turned to her friend. "Yes," she spat. "All I was doing was standing on the platform yesterday waiting for the next train. Phoebe had gone to the restroom, so I was alone." Her face tightened even more as she remembered. She looked away from Frances to stare straight ahead down the road as she relived the experience. Her entire body was rigid with fury. "A lady walking by me jostled me rather roughly. Instead of apologizing, she glared at me and told me I should be more careful where I was standing."

Felicia's eyes flashed fire when she turned her head to stare at Carrie. "I told her she should be more careful where she was walking, and that I had every right to stand on the platform."

Carrie stifled her groan. She completely agreed with her, but also knew that outside the safe confines of Oberlin, words like that could have put Felicia in grave danger. The fire in Felicia's eyes dimmed as fear crept in. Carrie's stomach tightened. "What happened, Felicia?"

Felicia swallowed hard. "Two very big white men came up to me and told me if I didn't want to know what it felt like to swing at the end of a noose, that I should learn how to respect white people. One of them said I might not be a slave anymore, but that didn't mean I should think I could ever possibly be equal to a white person." Her voice trembled as she spoke the final words.

Tears filled Carrie's eyes at the look of helpless rage, fear and pain on the girl's face. She turned to look at Phoebe, but Felicia wasn't done.

"I didn't know what to do," she admitted softly, a trapped expression in her eyes. "Phoebe came back from the bathroom then. She heard what they said, so she told the men I was with her." Her eyes flashed again. "They told her that she should teach her *help* how to behave around white people!"

Carrie reached over to grasp the girl's hand, transferring the reins into her other hand. "Felicia, I'm so sorry that happened to you." She knew Phoebe had done the right thing to protect Felicia, but she understood Felicia's reaction, as well.

"I wish I'd been there to take care of those two men," Peter growled.

"Me, too," Felicia said, her voice cracking as she vacillated between fear and fury. She shook her head, defeat creeping into her voice. "Is it always going to be like this, Carrie? I feel smart and powerful when I'm at Oberlin, but is the rest of the country terrible? Will I always have to watch every word I say just because I'm black?"

Carrie searched for the right answer, once again knowing that truth was the only option. "There are other places in the country as wonderful as Oberlin, but there are many more places where people are like the ones you dealt with today, Felicia." The fact that Carrie had to speak those words made her feel sick inside. Felicia was far more intelligent than any of those white people who had treated her with disdain, but all they saw was the color of her skin.

Felicia frowned, a trapped look reappearing on her face. "But it's not right."

Carrie ached at the little girl sound in Felicia's voice. This brilliant young woman, attending college at a younger age than anyone before in the history of Oberlin College, had been reduced to fear simply because of people's ignorance and hatred. Her own heart surged with anger, but she knew expressing it wouldn't help the situation. "You're correct that it's not right," she said firmly. "There are many of us who know that, and we're doing everything we can to change it."

"But *can* you?" Felicia demanded. "Can you really change it?"

Frances was the one who answered. "Mama told me that women like her and your mama are doing all they can to change things, but that there will still be a battle for us to fight because it's going to take a long time."

Felicia opened her mouth to respond, but closed it again and sagged against the carriage seat, a defeated look creeping into her eyes.

Carrie's heart ached as she looked at the young woman's face, but Frances' answer had been completely true. The most important question was why Felicia was so defeated. This was not the young lady who'd been accepted as a college student at Oberlin, determined to stay behind when her parents returned to the plantation. That young lady had been strong and confident. What had happened? Not knowing what to say, Carrie held Felicia's hand more tightly and prayed the long ride out to the plantation would give the girl some respite from the trauma of the previous day.

Carrie held her breath with anticipation as the carriage rolled onto Cromwell Plantation. She was relieved water hadn't made it to the gate, but she couldn't know what they would see as they rounded the curves down the long driveway. How far had the river raged inland?

The entire carriage was silent as all of them stared ahead.

Each curve brought a breath of relief as nothing but green stretched out before them.

Carrie tightened her hands on the reins and forced herself to relax as they rounded the final bend. She sagged against the seatback when she saw the house glimmering in the sunlight.

"Mama! The flood didn't make it to the house!" Frances cried.

Carrie's eyes shot toward the barn. If the flood hadn't reached the house, it wasn't likely it had reached the barn, but she had to see for herself. Her eyes filled with tears of happiness when she saw the stables were safe, as well.

"What is that noise?" Felicia asked, her forehead creased with puzzlement.

Peter frowned. "That's the river."

Carrie stiffened again. Normally, the river was too far from the house to be heard. "Just how close is it?" she muttered. Now that she knew the house and barn were safe, her mind turned to the tobacco crop. The sound of rushing water so close to the house could only spell disaster for the crop that was to be harvested in a week. Her heart pounded as she thought what that would mean for the men who had worked so hard.

Moments later, Annie stepped out onto the porch, her eyes shielded against the sun. "Land sakes, Miss Carrie. What you be doing back here?" She shook her head and rushed down the porch stairs. "Felicia, darlin', you are a sight for sore eyes. Welcome home!"

Felicia clambered from the wagon and fell into her grandmother's arms. "Hello, Grandma!" She took a deep breath and gazed around. "It's so good to be home. I'm glad the flood didn't get this far."

Annie looked at Carrie over the girl's head. "Is that why you're back here?"

"I couldn't leave until I knew everything was all right," Carrie answered. "Frances and I will just leave for Philadelphia a little later than we planned."

Frances leapt from the carriage and raced up the stairs. "I'm going to find Grandma and tell her we're back!"

Annie smiled and then looked back at Carrie intently. "How are things in Richmond?"

"Shockhoe Bottom is severely flooded. River City Carriages is full of water, but we were able to save all the horses, tack and equipment." She glanced back. "Peter sent a telegram that gave us enough warning so we could gather help to save everything."

Annie turned quickly. "Mr. Peter!" she exclaimed. "My eyes were so set on Miss Carrie and my grandbaby that I didn't see you there. Welcome back to the plantation! Thank you for helpin' out." Then her eyes narrowed. "You don't look so good, son."

Peter managed a smile. "I'm doing better now that I'm at the plantation," he assured her.

Annie continued to scrutinize him. "Uh-huh... I seen that look more than once. You done covered some story that messed with your mind and heart, didn't you?"

Peter shrugged but didn't deny it. "Nothing some of your cooking won't take care of, Annie."

Annie planted her fists on her hips and stared at him with piercing eyes. "Going to take more than my cookin'," she announced. "Still, I reckon it's a good place to start.

The men emptied everything from the first floor of the house this morning when we didn't know what was going to happen, but they's putting it all back. I'll be able to cook again pretty soon."

Finally, she turned to Phoebe. "I reckon you're the teacher Oberlin College sent down with my granddaughter. I appreciate you keepin' her safe. I'm Annie."

"It's a pleasure to meet you, Annie. My name is Phoebe Waterston. Cromwell Plantation is incredibly beautiful. Felicia has told me all about it, but hearing about it and actually seeing it are two different things."

"Yep. It be a right nice place to call home," Annie agreed. "Welcome, Miss Phoebe. Do you like Virginia ham?"

Phoebe smiled. "This Yankee has never *had* Virginia ham, but Felicia assures me that you're the best cook in the world, so I'm sure I'll love it."

Annie pulled Felicia into a tighter hug. "I reckon my granddaughter tells the truth."

Carrie watched Felicia, not missing the look of sheer relief on her face as her grandmother pulled her close. Felicia had always been happy to visit, but this was the first time she had ever indicated that she *needed* to be home. Rose had told Carrie that Felicia was missing home, but her instincts told her it was something more. Only time would tell.

Felicia looked toward the house. "Where's Mama?"

"She's out ridin' the fields with your daddy and Mr. Thomas. They left just a little bit ago."

Carrie watched Annie closely. She could tell by the grim expression in her eyes that the flooding must be devastating. "Is Abby with them?"

"Nope. She be inside watchin' after all the little ones while I put the kitchen back together."

Janie appeared on the porch then, Annabelle cradled in her arms. Her eyes widened with surprise. "Carrie!" Then her eyes grew wider. "Peter? What are you doing here?"

"I had to come see your new daughter for myself," Peter said easily. "Let me have a look at her." He climbed the stairs and bowed his head to look down at the swaddled bundle. "She's as beautiful as her mother. Congratulations."

Janie met Carrie's eyes over the top of Peter's dark head. "It's bad in Richmond?"

"Not as bad as up in the mountains," Carrie responded, nodding slightly toward Peter. Since Janie was married to a newspaper reporter, she would understand what Carrie wasn't saying.

Janie glanced down at Peter tenderly. "Come on inside, Peter. Matthew has been working all day to save furniture from the flood. He's resting his legs now. He's going to be thrilled to see you."

As the two disappeared into the house, Felicia looked up at Carrie. "Can we ride out to find Mama and Daddy?"

"Of course," Carrie answered. She was eager to ascertain for herself just how badly the flooding had impacted the plantation.

"Do you mind if I join you?" Phoebe asked tentatively.

"Do you ride?" Carrie didn't want to take a rank amateur into what could still become a dangerous situation.

Phoebe smiled. "I've never had Virginia ham, but I've ridden since I was old enough to walk."

Carrie laughed with delight. "Then you're going to love it here on Cromwell Plantation." She turned toward the stables. "There are breeches for all of us in the tack room." She hesitated. "If they weren't moved out of the way of the flood."

"They were, but your trunk made it back only a few minutes ago."

Carrie turned when she heard Miles' voice. "Hello, Miles!"

"Hello, Carrie girl. I'm not surprised you came back to check on things. Everything all right in the city?"

Carrie updated him quickly and introduced him to Phoebe. "I'm assuming you moved all the horses. Have any been brought back? We'd like to ride out into the fields. Felicia is eager to see her parents."

"We moved them, but the river done quit rising, so I got the fellas moving them back. Granite is already here, and I got a couple of geldings you two ladies can ride. Some other men are hauling back all the tack and gear. Give me a minute and I'll have them ready for you."

Carrie opened her mouth to offer help but was interrupted by Abby's voice.

"Welcome back, dear." Abby looked down at them from the porch. She had Robert perched on her hip and was holding Hope by the hand.

Carrie could scarcely believe it was little more than twenty-four hours since they'd said their good-byes, expecting to not see each other until she finished her internship in December. She grinned. "It's good to be back," she called. "There's someone I want you to meet."

Abby walked down the stairs and made her way across the yard to where everyone was standing, an anxious look in her eyes.

"What's wrong?" Carrie asked sharply. Phoebe's introduction could wait.

"Is John out here?" Abby asked, her eyes turned toward the barn.

Miles appeared. "John ain't here. I thought he was in the house with you."

"He was," Abby said in a worried voice. "I had to change Robert's pants. When I got back, he was gone." Her distressed look deepened. "I assumed he was in the barn with you."

"Nope. I ain't seen him."

Abby frowned. "Is Rascal here?"

"He is," Miles responded. "He came back with the first batch of horses."

"Will you check?" Abby said insistently.

Miles' frown matched hers now. "I will, but that boy done promised me he wouldn't go out on his own."

"Please check," Abby repeated, a frantic note creeping into her voice.

Carrie could tell Abby was battling fear. John, Rose and Moses' son, was seven years old. He was an excellent rider, but he was just a boy. Everyone had secured a promise from him that he would never ride on his own.

Miles disappeared into the barn, reappearing a moment later. "Rascal is gone," he reported, both his voice and eyes grim with concern.

Chapter Eight

"I can't believe that boy broke his promise to me." Miles' voice was thick with frustration and concern.

Carrie spun and looked down the road. She could still hear the river. She ran into the barn and quickly saddled Granite.

"I'm going, too," Felicia announced, appearing beside her to throw a saddle and bridle on the bay gelding Miles had chosen for her. "He's my brother."

Carrie didn't argue. She would have felt the same way.

Phoebe quickly saddled and bridled the remaining sorrel gelding, her practiced efficiency revealing that she was indeed comfortable around horses. "I may be able to help," she said quietly.

Carrie didn't know this young lady, but she liked the shine of confidence in her eyes. "Go ahead and change into breeches. We'll be much better equipped to handle whatever we find if we're out of these dresses."

A few minutes later, Carrie led them out of the barn at a swift trot.

"Wait!" Miles called. He ducked back into the barn and reappeared moments later. He thrust a long coil of rope toward Carrie. "Take this."

Carrie took the rope, praying there wouldn't be a need for it.

"Bring John back," Abby called.

Carrie hated the fear she heard in Abby's voice, but she wouldn't make a promise she didn't know she could keep. She merely waved and kept riding.

Moses fought the sick feeling in his stomach. Two days ago, tobacco fields had stretched as far as the eye could see. The lush, thick leaves had promised an extremely profitable crop. Now, all he could see was swirling, muddy water. He had expected flooding, but nothing could have prepared him for the destruction he was viewing. He could think of nothing to say.

Thomas and Rose were equally speechless.

The roar of the river beat at their hearts as cruelly as it was beating at the Virginia countryside.

Moses thought of all the men who had counted on the profits from the crop. They'd already been paid for the work they'd done, but it was the additional money from a share of the profits that made working at Cromwell so attractive. Plans were going to have to be put aside, and he knew some of the men and their families would suffer without the additional income to get them through the winter. His brain spun as he thought of what this disaster was going to cost the plantation.

"I'd say eighty percent of the crop is gone," Thomas said loudly enough to be heard over the river.

Moses nodded, still unable to form words.

"It happens, Moses."

Moses swung in the saddle to stare at Thomas. How could his business partner sound so calm and matter-of-fact? They were looking at almost total destruction.

Thomas smiled slightly. "The only thing you can be certain of with farming is that there's no such thing as certainty. I've had drought destroy crops. Once it was a massive hailstorm. The year I was born, back in 1816, was known as the year without a summer. My father told me about it. Farther north was hardest hit, but we had frosts here in August that year that killed off a lot of the crop and stunted the growth of much more of it." He shrugged. "No one has ever discovered how to control Mother Nature. I doubt they ever will." He looked out over the boiling waters. "This time it's a flood. It's impossible to know at the beginning of every growing season whether your efforts will pay off in the end." He paused. "It's not going to pay off this year."

"We've still got to pay our costs," Moses reminded him.

"Yes," Thomas agreed, his voice still calm. "But we've prepared for something like this. We've set aside money from the last four years. We've been more fortunate than most since the war ended. There's enough money to tide us over until the next crop." His eyes darkened. "I'm afraid I can't say the same for our neighbors up and down the river."

Moses scowled, thinking of the freed slaves who were working as sharecroppers. In a world where they were barely getting by, the destruction of the crop would mean total devastation for far too many families struggling to build a life after years of slavery.

"Our workers are going to be fine," Thomas said quietly.

"But so many of them had plans for the extra money from a successful crop," Moses protested. His thoughts spun. Jeb was planning to put an addition on his house for his growing family. Jarden was buying a wagon and a team of horses so he could increase his own farming production. Davis' oldest was planning on heading north to college, an extraordinary accomplishment for a young lady who had not known how to read before the end of the war. He met Rose's eyes and knew she was thinking the same thing.

"Everyone who makes a living from farming has to learn to accept the good with the bad," Thomas said philosophically. "I used to rant and rave at failed crops, but it never changed the outcome."

Moses gritted his teeth. "So I'm supposed to smile and accept it?"

"Well, I didn't say anything about smiling," Thomas replied, his eyes soft with compassion. "But, acceptance surely can't hurt you."

Rose reached over to take Moses' hand. "My brother is right, you know."

Moses sighed loudly enough to be heard over the water. "He also sounds like your mama."

"I was going to mention that, but I'm not sure he's ready to be told he sounds like a woman who used to be his slave," Rose said lightly, her eyes dancing with amusement.

Moses shook his head, distracted momentarily from what he was witnessing. He'd grown accustomed to co-owning the plantation with his wife's half-brother, but even in his wildest dreams during all his years as a slave, he couldn't have imagined joking about racial issues with a white man.

Thomas laughed. "From everything I've been told about your mama, I'm nothing but honored. I knew who she was during all the years she lived here, but I wasn't smart enough at the time to take advantage of her wisdom." He shook his head. "I wish I had been."

Suddenly, the smile on Rose's lips died and she cried out in alarm. "John!"

Moses whipped his head in the direction she was looking. What he saw made his blood freeze. John, riding bareback on Rascal, was edging toward the river, fascinated by the rampaging waters. "John!" he hollered, praying his voice would be heard above the noise.

John continued to edge Rascal forward. The towering black gelding obeyed him, but tossed his head in protest.

"Look!" Rose screamed as she pointed upriver from Rascal and her son.

Moses saw the impending danger at the same moment as his wife. A huge tree was barreling down the river, headed straight toward their son. "John!" he hollered again. Desperate to reach him in time, Moses sent up a frantic prayer as Champ leapt forward, seeming to sense the danger.

"John!" Moses' voice boomed through the air, finally breaking through his son's intense concentration.

John looked up, his face a mixture of delight and worry—worry because he knew he was breaking every promise he'd made to the adults on the plantation.

Moses knew the allure of the river had been too much for his son to resist. He would probably feel anger later, but right now anger couldn't surface above the raw fear that gripped him. "Back away!"

John, suddenly aware he was going to be in deep trouble, pulled back on the reins to follow the shouted order. The sun gleamed down on his black curls and glistened off his dark skin.

Moses had a moment to notice how beautiful his son was just as the tree trunk veered toward the shore, tossed by the currents of the river. Rascal, frightened by the specter looming in front of him, shied back, rearing as he tried to dodge the obstacle.

Moses wanted to close his eyes to block out the inevitable, but all he could do was watch in horror as the tree trunk crashed into the shore, knocking Rascal's legs from beneath him. The horse went down with a scream, and John shot off him like a cannonball.

Moses vaguely registered Rose's screams behind him as John was caught up by the river and swirled downstream, his choked cries ripping at Moses' heart.

Moses vaulted off Champ before the horse came to a stop. Without a thought, he plunged into the churning water, his eyes focused on John's head and wildly waving arms. His son knew how to swim, but he didn't have a chance against the strong currents. Putting all his strength into the effort, Moses fought to catch up with him. Never had he felt anything like the power of the water roaring around him.

Moses watched in horror as John was pulled farther out to the center of the river where the current was the strongest. His mind raced as he considered the options. He refused to acknowledge that John could drown. He *had* to save him.

He knew he didn't have much time.

Feeling movement to the right, he glanced over in time to dodge a massive limb surging past him. Moments later, a bobbing rooftop, its metal shingles glittering in the sun, swept by.

Gritting his teeth, Moses continued to stroke as hard as he could. He wanted to cheer when he realized he was gaining on his son, but he merely pushed harder, his muscles screaming as they fought the flood.

John's head stayed above the surface, but Moses knew his son had to be tired. He would soon weaken and be unable to fight. "Save him, God," he pleaded. "Please, save my boy."

Another stroke brought him within a few feet of his son. "John!"

"Daddy!" John cried, his words ending in a choking sound as water swirled into his mouth.

Moses' heart split when he saw the terror in his eyes. "Hold on!" He groaned with the effort as he pulled his arms through the water.

"Daddy!" John screamed again. His head dipped below the surface but came back up, his arms flailing wildly.

One final stroke brought Moses to his son's side. He reached out an arm and pulled John into his body. "Hold on!"

"Daddy!" John clung to him, his body shaking with terror.

"I've got you," Moses said tenderly. He knew, however, that they were still in grave danger. They could still drown, only now they would drown together. He steeled himself against the thought. He would *not* let Rose watch her husband and son be swallowed by the flood. His job now was to keep them both above water until he could find a solution.

Carrie's screams joined with Rose's as she watched John be sucked into the river. "No!" Urging Granite into a gallop, she raced down the waterline, determined to keep John's head in view. She registered Moses plunging into the water, but her focus was on the boy. She gave Granite his head, knowing he understood the crisis they were watching unfold.   She prayed he would have the endurance to do what was necessary.

Her mind raced as she thought about how to save John, and now Moses. As strong as he was, he would be no match for the river if he was forced to fight it for long. As she stared out over the water, she realized they were racing along one of the roads that bordered the tobacco fields. It wouldn't be long before the field ended at the edge of some thick woods. Her throat tightened as she thought about what that meant.

Granite wouldn't be able to follow the river once they entered the woods. It also meant, however, that there would likely be treetops sticking above the water that would offer a way for Moses to pull himself and John to safety.

Moses could feel himself growing weak. John was only seven, but he was a very big seven-year-old. Holding his son left Moses with only one arm to swim. He was kicking ferociously, but they were being pulled along by the current. The shore was still impossibly far away.

"Daddy! Watch out!"

Moses managed to lurch away from another bobbing tree trunk, but the effort cost him. How long would he be able to keep them above water?

Dark shapes far ahead presented the solution.

Moses realized he was looking at the top of the trees bordering the tobacco field they'd been inspecting. If he could get close enough to one, he could haul them into the branches.

Another rooftop roared past. Moses managed to reach out his free arm to push off of it before it smashed into them, but the movement thrust both he and John below the water. He forced their bodies up, gasping and choking as he fought for air.

The reality that they probably wouldn't make it crashed into his soul, but he tightened his lips and kept moving. He might die, but he would die fighting until his last breath.

Summoning all his ebbing strength, Moses kicked even harder and stroked furiously with his one arm. He was forced to lie on one side in order to keep John's head above water. He groaned when he realized John's body was limp. He didn't know if John was too exhausted to move, or if he had swallowed too much water when they'd been submerged. As much as Moses wanted to look at his son's face, he knew the only hope for their survival was to get them out of the water.

As they approached the trees, Moses prayed even harder. In the midst of kicking, he felt a shift in the current that pulled him inland. Watching the trees roar toward him, he continued to press forward, his eyes on the closest branches. Another shift in the current swept him toward a large oak that seemed to be only fifty feet or so from shore.

Calling on his dwindling power, Moses reached out his good arm as the trunk loomed in front of him. He felt limbs crashing into his body, threatening to rip John from his arms, but his focus remained on the trunk. He groaned as they smashed into the tree, but he was able to wrap his arm around it, and then his legs. He grunted with gratitude when he realized his body had taken the brunt of the collision, but John remained ominously still.

Moses somehow managed to push back far enough to pull John into the gap between himself and the tree. Pinned against the oak by the force of the river, he angled his body so he could peer down into his son's slack face. "John! John!"

Moses' heart sank when his son didn't respond. What if he had failed despite his best effort? "No!" he yelled. "No!"

He refused to believe John was dead.

Carrie barely gave herself a moment to feel relief when she saw Moses grab hold of the tree. He and John were far from danger. The water could snatch them away from the tree at any moment.

"Give me that rope!"

Carrie whirled around to discover Franklin, the plantation manager, beside her. His narrow face was tight with concentration. She had no idea how he'd gotten there, but it didn't matter. "What are you going to do?"

"Bring them to land!" Franklin growled. His eyes raked the waters between their position and Moses' in the tree. He held the rope up as he calculated the distance.

"What do I need to do?" Carrie asked.

Franklin leapt from his horse. "Nothing, I hope. I'm going to wrap the rope around this tree." He quickly tied it, double-checking the security of the knot. "More of the men are close behind. Miles sent us."

Carrie felt her confidence growing with this realization. Surely, all of them working together could save Moses and John.

"I'm going to tie the other end of the rope around my waist." Franklin worked as he talked. "Then I'm going out into the water to where Moses and John are. If I can't make it, the rope will catch me. I may have to stop along the way, but I believe I can make it."

"I believe Moses and I can pull us back in with the rope, but the other men are right behind me," Franklin reminded her. "If I have to wait a while for them to pull us in, that'll be all right."

With those words, Franklin turned and plunged into the water.

Moses watched, hope building in his heart, as Franklin headed toward them. He could see the rope tied around his waist. "Hang in there, John," he murmured. He was afraid to let go of the tree to stroke his son's face, but he hoped John could hear his voice. "Help is on the way, John. Help is on the way."

Franklin gritted his teeth against the pain as his body was pushed into trees he couldn't see below the surface. He tried to keep his long body parallel in the water to protect his legs from being broken, grabbing onto limbs above the surface to pull himself forward. He grunted as debris slammed into him, but he refused to concede defeat. Moses and John wouldn't make it if he couldn't get them out of the river. Inch by inch, he fought the current, spitting out torrents of muddy water that pushed into his mouth. Occasionally, he reached down to touch the rope secured around his waist. He pushed aside the thought that he didn't know how to swim. The men would pull him back to shore if he and Moses couldn't make it. He had no idea how badly Moses might be injured. What if he had to pull them all back? He was already tiring.

He prayed the other men would arrive soon.

It felt like an eternity, but Moses knew he had watched Franklin battle the river for only a few minutes. As he watched, the river current shifted, threatening to pull him away from the tree that was his only lifeline. Moses gripped harder. The rough bark bit into his legs and arms but there was nothing that would make him loosen his grip.

"Help is on the way, John. Help is on the way."

Moses fought the waves of desolation roaring through his soul, stronger even than the waves of the flooding James River. Everything in him said John was dead, but he refused to accept it. He might have to accept the destruction of the crops, but he refused to accept the death of his only son. "I love you, son. I love you!"

He managed a weak smile as Franklin finally floated toward the tree Moses clung to. "You are a sight for sore eyes." He was astonished how weak his voice sounded.

"We're going to get you out of here," Franklin promised.

"We?"

Franklin nodded his head toward shore.

Moses bit back a cheer as a group of his men rode up. "What's the plan?" He and Franklin had been in plenty of bad situations during the war. This one was unusual, but Franklin's appearance, and the arrival of more men, had renewed his hope.

"How's John?"

Franklin's question sent Moses' hope crashing again. He shook his head. "I don't know," he admitted hoarsely. He wasn't going to voice the fear that he was holding his son's dead body. He had seen Carrie ride up on Granite. He had no idea why she was back on the plantation, but surely she would know what to do if they could get John back to land. "We have to get him to shore," he grunted.

"That's what we're going to do," Franklin said calmly.

The pitying look in his friend's eyes told Moses that Franklin suspected he was holding a dead child, but the words would not be spoken.

Franklin grabbed hold of the tree, wrapped his legs around it tightly, and carefully untied the rope from his waist. "Tie this around you," he commanded.

Moses stared at him. "What are *you* going to do?"

Franklin shrugged nonchalantly, but his eyes couldn't hide his fear. "I'm going to wait until someone comes out to get me."

Moses thought about the current that had almost pulled him from the tree. "No," he said firmly. "Franklin, you don't know how to swim."

"A small detail," Franklin scoffed.

"No," Moses repeated. "We'll go together."

"How?" Franklin demanded.

Moses thought quickly. "I'll tie the rope around my waist first, but leave enough so you can tie it around yours." He eyed the group of men on shore. "There are enough men to pull us back to shore at the same time."

Franklin shook his head stubbornly. "You've got to get John to shore. You need to go now. I'll be fine."

"We'll get there faster if you quit arguing," Moses responded. Everything in him shouted to take John to safety, but he wasn't going to leave the friend who had risked his life to save him. "We all go together."

Franklin finally nodded.

Moses had to loosen his grip on the tree to tie the knot, wedging John against the branches to hold him in place. He tied the rope around his waist securely, gripping the rough bark with his legs with more strength than he knew he had. His legs were being chewed up, but he barely registered the pain as the current threatened to dislodge him.

When the knot was finally secure, he nodded to his friend. "Your turn."

Franklin wrapped the rope around his waist and knotted it tightly. "I'm ready." He looked toward shore and waved his arm to indicate the men could pull them in.

Moses sucked in his breath as he and John floated free from the tree. He had no strength left to help move them toward shore. The best he could do was keep their heads above water. He was going to have to rely on his men.

Rose rode up with Thomas, Felicia and Phoebe in time to watch as the plantation men hauled Moses, John and

Franklin to shore, their muscles bulging as they fought the river's current. Their grunts sounded above the raging water, intermingled with their shouts of encouragement to the men they were working to save.

Her heart ached at the sight of pain and weariness etched on her husband's face, but terror ripped at her heart when she realized John wasn't moving.

Rose urged her mare forward and slid off next to where Carrie was standing beside Granite. "Carrie?" All she could manage was a single agonized whisper that she wasn't sure could be heard above the torrent.

Carrie's eyes brimmed with compassion and concern as she wrapped her arms around Rose. "They'll be here soon. Hold on."

"Mama?"

Rose had been so intent on the drama unfolding in the water that she hadn't even realized her daughter was there until her frightened cry sounded behind her. "Felicia!" Tears choked her voice as she pulled Felicia into a fierce embrace. John had been swept away before she had had a chance to greet her.

"Mama! Is John all right? Why isn't he moving?"

"I don't know," Rose managed, once again glued to the sight of her husband and son being pulled closer to shore.

Felicia turned to Carrie. "Why isn't John moving, Carrie? Shouldn't he be moving?" she asked frantically.

Rose wanted to tell her to be quiet. She wanted to insist that John was going to be fine, that he was merely resting in his father's arms. She tightened her lips against what she knew could be lies.

All any of them could do was wait.

Carrie heaved a sigh of relief when Moses finally reached shore, but she had to bite back a cry of dismay when he stumbled from the water, John clasped in his arms. His clothes hung from his body in shreds. She could see blood oozing from his powerful arms and legs, but she knew care of his wounds must wait.

The men who had donated their shirts to make a pad for John gathered round silently as Moses gently lay his motionless son on the wad of clothing.

Carrie's heart sank when she gazed down into John's face. His body had open cuts too, but his face was peaceful.

Too peaceful.

Was John dead? She leaned down close to his mouth but couldn't detect any breath. Her heart pounding, she laid her fingers across his pulse point to determine if he was still alive. In all her experience, she had never dealt with a drowning victim. She racked her brain as she tried to remember if she had read about it. There had to be a way to help her best friend's son.

"I can help!"

Carrie whipped her head around to stare at Phoebe. "What?"

Phoebe knelt next to her, her blond hair gleaming in the sun. "I can explain later. Right now, we just have to get John breathing again."

"You know how?" The look in Phoebe's eyes told her the teacher did. There was no time to waste. "Tell me what I can do," she said as she moved to the side.

Phoebe quickly rolled John onto his back. First, she turned his head and opened his mouth, probing to make sure there was nothing lodged there. When she found no obstruction, she straightened his head again, knelt behind him, and raised both of his limp arms upward and back. Her face tight with concentration, she gave a firm tug. Then she lowered his arms, folded them across his chest and applied several firm compressions.

Everyone watching stayed completely silent, their eyes all focused on John's lifeless body.

Phoebe repeated the motions. Once...twice...three times...four times.

After the fourth time, she jumped up so she could turn John's head again, checking to see if anything had been dispelled that needed to be removed. Finding nothing, she resumed her position at his head and continued to manipulate his arms.

Carrie held her own breath as she watched and prayed. She was vaguely aware of Rose's death grip on her shoulder, but her entire focus was on John.

Phoebe continued her motions, her lips narrow with determination. "Come on, John," she muttered. "Come on...breathe!"

Carrie lost count of how many times Phoebe had lifted the boy's arms and compressed his chest. It seemed like hours, but she knew that fewer than two minutes had passed. How long could John survive without air? Were Phoebe's actions forcing air into his lungs until she could bring him back?

"Breathe!" Rose cried, her commanding voice sounding like a bugle call ripping through the air. "Breathe, John!"

Suddenly, as if in response to his mother's plea, John gave a soft gasp.

Phoebe turned him on his side just as a stream of water came gushing from his mouth.

Carrie stared, knowing the fluid had been released from his lungs. She also knew she had just witnessed a miracle.

"Breathe!" Moses said hoarsely. "Breathe, son!"

John gasped again, his chest expanding as fresh air filled it. Phoebe jumped behind him, pulling his body up to rest against her chest. "Breathe," she urged. "Breathe, John."

John took a shuddering breath that ended in a cough. More water dribbled out.

Another breath.

Another cough.

More dribbles of water.

Carrie took John's hand as the boy fought for air. "You've got this, John. Nice and easy breaths," she said soothingly. "Nice and easy breaths." She kept her attention focused on his closed eyes, willing him to come back to them.

After what seemed an eternity, John's breath settled into a steady rhythm. Finally, he opened eyes that were clouded with confusion. Moses and Rose knelt in front of him, tears rolling down their cheeks.

"Hello, son," Moses said tenderly.

"Daddy?" John's eyes floated to Rose's face as the word came out weakly. "Mama?" He frowned. "What happened? Why are you crying?"

Carrie sagged with relief. John was breathing. He was talking. He was asking questions. She knew he was going to be all right.

"You gave us a scare, John," Rose said in a broken voice. "We're so glad you're all right."

"Hi, John."

John's face lit with a weak smile when Felicia knelt to join them. "Fe-Fe. You're home."

Carrie grinned. No matter how old these two got, she doubted John would ever call Felicia anything but the nickname he had given her when his young tongue couldn't form her name.

"I'm home," Felicia confirmed, her face still tense. "You scared me!"

John stared at her, his eyes still confused, and then glanced toward the water. His body went rigid with fear. "I was in the water," he stuttered. He gazed at the muddy river, and then his eyes shifted to Moses. "You saved me, Daddy."

"And then Franklin and the other men saved us both," Moses said roughly. He caught John's face between his scraped and bloody hands. "How about you promise me you never go swimming in a flooded river again?"

John's eyes filled with sadness. "I'm sorry, Daddy. I broke my promise about Rascal."

"You did," Moses agreed, "but for now I'm just glad you're safe."

John's body stiffened again as distress replaced the sadness. He looked around wildly. "Rascal! Where is Rascal?"

Chapter Nine

An uncomfortable silence fell over the assembled group.

John whipped his head around to stare at them. "Rascal! Where is Rascal?" His voice was frantic.

Carrie had a sick feeling she knew the answer to the question, but her entire focus had been on saving Moses and John. She had seen Rascal go down, and had heard his scream, but she knew nothing more.

John's eyes grew even more frantic. "Daddy! What happened to Rascal?"

Moses shook his head, looking around to see if anyone knew the answer.

It was Miles who finally stepped forward.

Carrie's heart broke when she saw the grief etched on his face. He didn't have to say a word for her to know what had happened.

John looked up at him. "Grandpa? Where is Rascal?"

Miles slowly lowered his aging body to the ground so he could be at face level with his grandson. "John, I'm real sorry to tell you that Rascal didn't make it."

John's confused eyes grew even wider as he stared into his grandfather's face. "What do you mean? What happened to Rascal?"

Carrie knew Miles was searching for a way to break the news to the little boy who had come so close to death. She stepped in to help. "John, the reason you were thrown into the river is because a big tree came on shore and hit Rascal very hard," she said gently. The brief memory of

Rascal rearing as the tree slammed into him made her eyes fill with tears. It wasn't necessary to have been there to know the result.

Carrie took a deep breath and gripped John's hands. "Rascal was hurt badly, John. The tree broke his legs."

John stared at her and shook his head. "Can't you fix them, Carrie? You're a doctor! Can't you fix his legs?"

Carrie's eyes flooded with more tears. "Doctors can't fix everything, John," she said sadly. "Rascal was hurt too badly. He was in a lot of pain and there was nothing anyone could do to make it better." She had already guessed the humane action Miles had been forced to take, but there was no way she was going to leave in John's mind the image of Rascal being shot to release him from his agony.

"So what happened?" John cried as he reached out to grab her hand.

Carrie took a deep breath. There was no easy way to say what needed to be said. "John, they couldn't save Rascal." She searched for the right words, but there was no way to make the truth any more bearable. "Rascal is dead, honey." Her throat spasmed as she forced the words out.

Vivid memories of John and Rascal raced through her mind. They had shared such a special bond from the very moment Miles and Anthony had brought him to the plantation. The huge black horse would have done anything for John. She pushed aside the realization that his willingness was ultimately what led to his death. Under normal circumstances a horse wouldn't have approached a raging river. Rascal was simply giving John what he wanted.

"No!" John screamed, his voice faltering as fresh coughs shook his weakened body. "No," he whimpered. "No..." Silent sobs shuddered through him as the truth settled into his soul.

There was not a dry eye as Moses silently picked up his son and carried him to where Champ waited. He was too exhausted to lift John into the saddle, however. He mounted, waited for Franklin to lift John to him, and then cradled his son's body into his chest. Rose mounted and rode to join him. Felicia followed suit.

"We're taking him home," Moses said somberly. "Thank you all."

Carrie watched him closely. She knew the agony on his face was a combination of John's distress and his own battered body. "I'll be there soon," she promised. "I'll treat you at the house."

"I'll be fine," Moses said gruffly as he turned and rode away.

A long silence followed their departure.

The miracle of John's survival had been swallowed by his soul-wrenching grief.

Rose gazed up at Moses as they gently laid John in his bed. The little boy had cried all the way back to the house. Moses had carried him upstairs and sat with him in the rocker, holding him close until he'd fallen asleep in his father's arms. Sleep was the best thing for him now.

"Thank you for saving our son." She blinked back the tears that threatened anew.

Moses met her eyes but remained silent. His eyes revealed the terror and the pain of the rescue.

Rose reached up to stroke his cheek. "I was terrified I was going to lose you both." Her voice caught as the memories assailed her. She blinked hard, knowing Moses needed her to be strong. "You're exhausted, Moses. You need some rest, too."

Moses turned back to gaze at John. "I thought he was dead," he finally managed. "I thought we'd lost him, Rose."

Rose had shared all the same fears, but she hadn't been in the flooded river fighting to save their son. "He's alive because of you, my love. You saved him."

Moses stared at her, but his eyes were strained with fatigue and sorrow. "He's going to blame himself for Rascal's death. It's going to break his heart."

Rose took a deep breath. Her heart had already broken over the truth of his statement. "Some lessons are learned in a terrible way," she said sadly. She would have done anything to save her son from the lesson he was facing, but she couldn't undo what had happened.

Moses flinched. "You blame him?"

Rose shook her head. "It's not a matter of blame," she said gently. "That doesn't change the fact, however, that Rascal is dead because John took him down by a raging river. Rascal loved him enough to do whatever he asked. Ultimately, it led to his death. You and John could have died, as well. I wish none of that were true, but it doesn't change the facts."

Moses' eyes flashed with anger. He opened his mouth to protest, but then closed it again. Reluctantly, he nodded his head. "You're right," he admitted slowly. He turned back to stare down at his sleeping son. He could only imagine what dreams and nightmares would assault him in the days and months to come. "What are we going to tell him?"

"He doesn't need us to tell him it's his fault," Rose said. "He already knows. All we can do is love him hard enough to get him through it. Both of us have made mistakes we'll regret for the rest of our lives. This is one John will regret for the rest of his life, but it doesn't have to ruin his future."

"We have to help him learn how to forgive himself," Moses replied quietly.

"That's all we can do," Rose agreed. She leaned down and kissed her sleeping son's cheek tenderly. "Now it's time to get you taken care of, dear husband. You were a hero today, but even heroes feel pain."

It was dark when Carrie and Rose walked into the parlor where Abby and Phoebe were talking.

"How is Moses?" Abby asked anxiously. "He looked terrible when he got back to the plantation after saving John."

"He's asleep," Rose answered. "He's exhausted, and he's going to be in pain for a long time, but Carrie and Janie took care of him. Janie is with Annabelle now."

Carrie sank down into one of the chairs facing the cold fireplace. "I lost count of all the cuts and gashes. It took a while to clean everything. The cuts are bad, but the real danger is infection from the dirty river. There's no telling what contaminants the river is carrying from all the businesses that were flooded upstream. I pretty much covered his entire body with honey, and a mashed onions and garlic paste. It will take care of any infection, but he isn't going to smell pleasant for a while," she said with a weary smile. "I don't care what the medical field comes up with as a replacement; there will never be a better answer to infection than those ingredients."

"He's also going to be sore from being battered against the trees, and from fighting the river," Rose added. "I don't believe I've ever seen him so exhausted."

"Moses is strong," Abby said encouragingly. "He survived that terrible wound during the war. He'll come back from this quickly."

Rose nodded, but remained silent.

Abby looked at her closely. "You're worried," she said quietly.

When Rose hesitated, Phoebe stood. "I'll leave you ladies to talk."

"No," Rose protested. "Please stay, Phoebe. This wasn't how I imagined your first day on the plantation would be, but if it weren't for you, my son would have died. I'm not hesitating because of you... I simply don't know what to say."

Phoebe nodded and sank back into her chair.

Carrie was aware just how correct Rose was about how close John had come to dying. She had questions for Phoebe, but they would wait.

Rose took a deep breath and met Abby's eyes. "Moses' and John's bodies will heal from almost drowning, but I'm worried about my son."

"Why?" Abby's voice was tender.

Carrie watched the exchange silently. She was certain Abby was aware of why Rose was worried, but Abby would do nothing except ask questions. It was one of the things Carrie loved most about her mother.

"Because he's going to blame himself for Rascal's death," Rose answered. "He loved that horse with every fiber of his being. Knowing he was responsible for his death is going to be very hard."

"Do you believe he's responsible?"

Rose turned to gaze out the window at the darkness for several moments before she answered. "There's not a child who ever lived that didn't make a mistake or make a decision they're sorry for. John doesn't have a mean bone in his body. His curiosity to see the river while it was flooding produced a very bad consequence." She sighed heavily. "All of us make mistakes, but not all of us are forced to deal with such horrible consequences." She shook her head heavily. "I know I have to help him move past the grief and guilt, but the combination of the two is a very heavy load for a child not yet eight years old."

"It's a heavy load for anyone to bear," Carrie said quietly.

Rose eyed her closely. "I know there was a time when you felt responsible for Bridget's death," she said, "even though you weren't. No one will ever know if her death was a result of your ride to be with Robert. You were simply trying to reach your husband who was dying."

Carrie smiled. It had taken her a long time to come to grips with Bridget's death, and she would always grieve, but she had finally released the guilt. "And John was simply following the instincts of a seven-year-old boy," she said carefully.

"Instincts that had grave consequences," Rose replied.

"No one is denying that," Abby agreed. "Can you think of a time you made a decision at that age that had grave consequences, Rose?"

Rose fell silent as she pondered the question.

The other women sat quietly, letting her process her memories.

"Yes. I was seven when I was made to move into the Big House," she said slowly. "I cried myself to sleep every night because I missed my mama so much. I'd been told I could only to go to the slave quarters on Sunday to see her. Sam told me that being a slave in the Big House was my job now. He said if I ever went down to the slave quarters on a day I wasn't supposed to, that he would get in real bad trouble."

Carrie felt a piercing pain as the words came from the lips of her best friend. She had never heard whatever story Rose was about to reveal, but the pain shimmering in her eyes said it was going to be bad. Even with their closeness, she knew there were things Rose had never revealed to her because she knew how hard it would be for Carrie to hear them.

Rose continued slowly, the words almost wrenched from her. "One night I had a very scary dream. When I woke up, all I wanted was my mama. I don't really remember leaving the house, but I do remember my mama holding me while I cried for a long time. She took me back real early, but..." She hesitated and glanced at Carrie.

"Go ahead," Carrie encouraged her. She already knew the story was going to be painful to hear, but if it helped Rose with John, then it needed to be told.

Rose continued in a halting voice. "Mama took me back real early...but Carrie's mother must have been looking out her window. She...saw us." She swallowed hard. "Sam didn't even know I'd left the house, but he got in trouble."

Carrie's gut clenched, but she had to know the truth. "What kind of trouble, Rose?"

"It doesn't matter now," Rose replied with averted eyes. "It was a long time ago."

Carrie wasn't sure *why* she needed to know the truth, but suddenly it was vitally important. "What kind of trouble?" she repeated. "Please, Rose, I need to know."

Rose still hesitated, looking to Abby for help.

"Hiding the truth never helped anything," Abby said. "Carrie already knows she isn't going to like what you have to say, but she evidently needs to hear it."

Rose turned and met Carrie's eyes, her own full of apology and pain. "Your mama had Sam whipped three times for letting me leave the house."

Carrie drew back in shock. "No!" she cried. "My mother wouldn't have done that. She wasn't like that." Her mind raced as she struggled to deny what she had heard. "She knew my father didn't allow the slaves to be whipped."

Rose took a deep breath. "It happened, Carrie. She made me watch so that I wouldn't make the same mistake again." Her eyes filled with tears. "I don't believe your father ever knew. Your mother could be like that sometimes. I don't think she liked doing it, but your mama was a very fearful woman. She handled being afraid of the slaves by showing power when she could."

Carrie stared at Rose wildly, trying to figure out a way to disprove her story. She sagged against the chair when she finally accepted the fact that Rose had no reason to make something like that up. "I'm so sorry," she whispered. "I never knew."

Rose managed a pained smile. "We were both six years old," she said softly.

Carrie shuddered at the thought of Sam feeling the lash of a whip. "Poor Sam," she murmured as she envisioned his kind, wise face. She knew her mother had been beleaguered by fear for her whole life, but she never would have imagined that fear would make her do such a terrible thing.

Silence filled the room for several minutes as Carrie and Rose struggled with their feelings.

"I understand now," Rose said. "I wasn't able to understand the possible consequences of my actions when I was only six years old. I needed my mama, and I went to her." She glanced toward the stairs leading to John's bedroom. "John was intensely curious about the flood. He did what any young boy would do. He went to see it. He could never have known the consequences."

"Any more than you could have," Carrie replied. "I know Sam was never angry at you."

Rose nodded. "You're right. Sam was my daddy for most of my life—until you found my real father and brought him back. Sam never did anything but love me."

Another silence filled the room, the faint sound of an owl hooting in the distance flowing in through the window.

"Do you forgive me?" Abby asked suddenly.

Rose stared at her. "What?"

"Do you forgive me?" Abby repeated, her eyes glittering with regret. "You left John in my care. It was up to me to make sure he stayed in the house. I failed."

Rose stood immediately and crossed the room to kneel in front of her. "I've never had one thought of blame toward you, Abby. I know my son. When he has something in his head, he's hard to stop. With all the chaos over the flood, and with all the children to take care of, it would have been easy for him to slip away. Please don't feel bad," she implored as she took Abby's hands and squeezed them tightly. "Does Miles feel guilty, too?"

Abby nodded. "He can't believe he didn't hear John leave the stables with Rascal."

Rose managed a smile. "My resourceful son can be sneaky. He knew that if he rode bareback it would take him only a minute or so to run into the stable, climb the slats of Rascal's stall, jump onto Rascal and take off. No one was thinking about watching for him. Everyone was focused on the flood and working to save everything we could." She looked in the direction of the barn. "I'll talk to Miles."

"He's afraid you blame him," Abby said gently. "I think probably everyone feels a little of the blame," she said, "but John is going to feel the burden of it."

Rose laid her head in Abby's lap for a moment. "Thank you," she said softly. "While it's true that John's actions created the consequence of Rascal's death, he was simply being a young child. Just like I was so long ago."

Abby stroked her head. "Tell him your story when you think it's the right time. Guilt is a terrible burden to carry around for a lifetime."

"Can I interest you ladies in some hot tea and cookies?"

Carrie looked up at Annie as she appeared in the doorway. Abby and Rose had gone to bed, leaving her alone with Phoebe. "That sounds wonderful," she said gratefully. "But, Annie, what are you still doing in the house? You should be with Miles."

Annie looked at her keenly. "I just finished puttin' my kitchen back right. Ain't no way I was gonna end this day with things all messed up."

Phoebe raised a brow. "You had time to make cookies?"

"Ain't nothin' some good, hot cookies can't fix, Miss Phoebe," Annie declared with a smile.

"Then you should take some to Miles," Carrie said.

Annie had turned to leave the room but swung back when Carrie spoke. "What you talkin' about, Miss Carrie? What needs fixin' with that husband of mine?" she demanded.

Carrie wasn't sure she should say anything, but the thought of Miles carrying the guilt for John's near drowning and Rascal's death made her reveal what she knew. "He blames himself for what happened today, Annie."

Annie stared at her with disbelief. "Why?"

"Because he thinks he should have caught John before he left the barn."

Annie snorted as she shook her head. "That old fool. He never coulda kept my grandson from takin' off on that horse any more than Miss Abby and I could have kept him in the house. If that boy be intent on doin' something, he gonna figure out a way to make it happen. He's just like his daddy was at that age. Moses didn't get in as much trouble 'cause he was a slave workin' out in the fields, but he was always a sneaky one."

"It might help Miles to hear that," Carrie said gently.

Annie's flashing eyes softened. She turned to look out toward the apartment above the barn that she and Miles shared. "You mind gettin' your own tea and cookies, Miss Carrie? I reckon I should go check on my man."

"Go," Carrie urged. "I'll get anything we might want. I may be a lousy cook, but I can handle hot tea."

Annie winked at Phoebe. "There's already a kettle gettin' hot on the stove. Keep an eye on this one, Miss Phoebe. Carrie may be a real good surgeon, but she's right dangerous in the kitchen."

Phoebe chuckled. "I'll make sure nothing happens, Annie, but I have to warn you that I'm probably not any better in a kitchen than she is."

Annie rolled her eyes. "You two just be sure I have a kitchen to come back to in the morning."

Carrie laughed and pointed her finger toward the front door. "Get out of here," she ordered. "You have better things to do than harangue us."

Annie scowled, but her eyes were twinkling when she turned away and walked out the door.

Carrie glanced at Phoebe. "Are you sure you want some tea and cookies? You must be exhausted after the day we've had. Not to mention the fact that you were traveling on the train for two days before you arrived."

"It's hard to believe it was only three days ago that we left Ohio," Phoebe agreed. "If you don't mind, though, I would enjoy some tea. I need time at night to unwind when I've had a stressful day."

Carrie busied herself making two cups of tea, while Phoebe arranged cookies on a plate.

Returning to the parlor, Carrie sank down in the chair closest to the window and laid her head back with a sigh. "It won't be long before we can't have the windows open at night. I'm going to savor it as long as I can." She drew in deep breaths of the bolstering air.

"I can feel fall coming," Phoebe said, "but it's far warmer here than it was in Oberlin when Felicia and I left. I suspect we'll have a frost this week."

Carrie frowned. "I know I have to go back to Philadelphia, but I'm not looking forward to another Philadelphia winter. At least I'll miss the worst months of January and February."

Phoebe eyed her. "Felicia said you're finishing up your surgical internship in December. That's quite impressive."

Carrie saw the opening she had been waiting for. "Thank you, but what you did today was astounding. I'm afraid John would have died if you hadn't been here. I've saved a lot of people, but I've never had a drowning victim. Can you please tell me what you did, and how you knew how to do it?"

"My father is a doctor. I never had a desire to follow in his footsteps, but I learned so much from being around him. He never minded me coming to his clinic, so I got to see a lot. That's where I met Dr. Silvester."

"Dr. Silvester?" Carrie had never heard of him.

"Yes. Dr. Henry Robert Silvester. How familiar are you with methods of artificial respiration?"

"Not at all," Carrie admitted. "I'm appalled at that realization, and eager to learn if you have the energy to teach me."

Phoebe shrugged. "There isn't much to teach. The first method of artificial respiration was created by a London physician named Marshall Hall in 1856. In essence, his method involved alternate rotation of the victim's body from a prone position to the side in order to get them breathing again."

"That's all he did?" Carrie asked. "Did it work?"

"It worked on some," Phoebe answered. "Too many others still died, however. Two years later, Dr. Silvester used Hall's method on a stillborn male infant without success. He decided to change the position of the baby. He put him on his back and raised both arms upward to cause expansion of the chest in order to pull air in. Then he folded the arms on his chest and applied pressure to expel the air. He kept doing those same movements until the child took his first breath."

"He was creating breath for the baby," Carrie said with astonishment. "Artificial respiration."

"Yes," Phoebe agreed, and then looked at her more closely. "Why do you suddenly look so sad?" As soon as the question escaped her lips, she grimaced. "I'm sorry. I don't know you well enough to ask probing questions."

"It's fine," Carrie assured her. "My daughter was stillborn several years ago. I can't help but wonder if this technique would have saved her."

"I'm so sorry," Phoebe exclaimed, compassion flooding her face.

Carrie took a deep breath and shook her head, forcing images of Bridget from her mind. "I can never know the answer to that question. Now all I can do is learn as much as possible so I can save others." Her forehead creased in thought. "Silvester's method can save drowning victims, but it must also help people whose hearts have stopped beating for some other reason."

"Not in all cases, but many have been saved," Phoebe confirmed. "My father has used the technique several times to save patients." She took a sip of tea and then continued. "Silvester believes his method is much closer to being an imitation of natural deep respiration."

Carrie thought about what she was hearing in relation to all she had learned about the human body. "It makes sense," she said thoughtfully. "When we breathe, we lift our ribs and sternum in order to inflate our lungs. You did that when you raised John's arms." Her eyes widened with understanding. "You created a vacuum in order to inflate his lungs."

"Yes," Phoebe answered.

"Crossing John's arms and pressing his chest expelled the air." Carrie's mind raced. "Every time you repeated the process, you were breathing for him."

"That's right. In John's case, the procedure also helped force the water he'd swallowed out of his lungs. Once they were empty, he could breathe on his own again."

"Fascinating," Carrie murmured. "I'm so grateful you saved John. I'm also thrilled to learn a new medical technique."

Phoebe gazed at her thoughtfully. "You love being a doctor, don't you?"

"I do," Carrie replied. "It's all I've ever wanted to do."

"And you worked in the hospitals in Richmond during the war?"

Carrie frowned. She wished the memories would go away, but she was sure she would be forced to live with them for the rest of her life. "I did," she said simply. It wasn't a topic she wanted to discuss.

Phoebe just nodded and took a bite of her cookie.

Carrie's liking for the young woman increased. She wasn't afraid to ask hard questions, but she was comfortable with not getting an answer. She drank some more of her tea, enjoying the feel of the refreshing air washing over her face. Now that the drama of the day had passed, her thoughts returned to Felicia. "What's wrong with Felicia? She seems quite different than when I last saw her."

Phoebe's eyes shuttered closed. "I'm sorry, but that's something I should talk with Rose about first."

"Of course," Carrie replied, her heart growing heavy with the realization that something was indeed wrong. She had hoped her suspicions were incorrect. A throng of questions sprang to her mind, but she forced herself to remain silent.

Chapter Ten

Moses finished the remainder of his breakfast and pushed back from the table. "I'll be back later," he announced.

Thomas frowned. "Talking to the men can wait, Moses. Carrie told me it would be best if you took it easy for at least two more days. She's concerned about infection."

Moses shook his head. "The men have worked hard all year. They deserve to hear the news from me."

Thomas eyed him. "You're not going to tell them anything they don't know. You can't harvest a crop that was washed away by a flood," he said matter-of-factly.

Rose knew Thomas was right. The James River was finally confined to its banks again, but almost all evidence of the lush crop was gone. Its legacy was a thick layer of mud that would take a long time to dry, and hordes of trees and limbs that had been left behind when the water retreated.

Moses shook his head again. "Still, they need to hear it from me..." His voice trailed away.

"You want to leave them with hope that the plantation will recover, and next year will be better," Rose finished for him.

Moses looked at her with gratitude. "Yes."

Rose looked at him lovingly. Only she knew that the last three nights had been full of nightmares for both Moses and John. She had spent the long nights holding them in turn, praying for a release of their fears and memories. Amid utter powerlessness, talking to his men about the crop was something Moses could take a modicum of control over.

Thomas' eyes filled with understanding. "I'm sure it will go well, Moses. Let me know if there's anything I can do."

Moses took a final sip of his coffee, then stood and walked out into the morning.

Rose watched him go before she pushed back her chair. "I'll be in the library," she announced. "Phoebe, will you join me?"

"Certainly," Phoebe replied.

Rose turned to Carrie next. "Are you heading to the clinic this morning?"

Carrie shook her head. "No. Polly is taking care of the clinic now. This is my final day on the plantation before we leave, so I'd like to spend it with all of you."

Rose smiled, nodded her head toward the library, and turned to Abby. She needed Bregdan women around her. "Abby? Can you join us?"

"Certainly," Abby replied, only the spark in her eyes revealing her curiosity.

Rose turned to Janie next. "I know Annabelle is taking most of your time, but..."

Matthew reached over and plucked his daughter from Janie's arms. "I'll take care of our recalcitrant daughter," he said quickly. "Mama could use a break, anyway."

"Thank you, dear," Janie said gratefully.

Rose knew all the women present were aware they were being summoned for something important, but they wouldn't ask questions until it was the right moment. She glanced out the window in time to see Susan ride off with Felicia. Rose would have welcomed Susan's input, but it was more important for her to keep Felicia occupied. It was a testament to Susan's persuasive powers that she had talked Felicia into an early morning ride.

Rose closed the door to the library carefully and then turned to gaze at everyone. "Thank you," she said quietly.

"Are we about to find out why we're all here?" Carrie asked, her eyes locked on her friend's face.

"Yes," Rose replied, her heart heavy with the knowledge she carried. "I want to read something to all of you." She pulled a single sheet of paper from her pocket and began to read.

No one sees me.
They see my color.
My black skin shimmering in the light.
My dark eyes staring in defiance.
No one sees me.
They see my skin and they hate.
They see my skin and they attack.
They see my skin and they threaten.
No one sees me.
Will my color be all they ever see?
Will they always hate?
Will they always attack and threaten?
No one sees me.
I have no hope it will ever change.
Do I accept it?
Do I fight back?
No one sees me.
Do I hate with the same hate?

Do I threaten and attack?
Do I make them afraid like I am afraid?
Why does no one see me?

Rose understood the shocked looks on the faces surrounding her. Taking a deep breath, she picked up another sheet of paper and began to read again.

Listen very carefully
To the cry rising from the earth.
Does anyone really love me?
Do I really have any worth?
Does anyone know who I really am?
Does anyone really care?
Is there anyone I can lean on?
Is there anyone with whom to share?
Is there anyone who will see my faults?
Look beyond mistakes within?
See what's beyond the surface things,
See past the color of my skin?
Please! If there is anyone who really cares,
If there is anyone with whom I can share,
If, of my hurt and pain you are aware,
Won't you please let me know you are there?

Rose's voice stumbled on the last words, emotion clogging her throat as she finished the poem and laid the paper down.

"Did Felicia write that?" Carrie asked, her eyes glimmering with concern.

"How did you know?" she asked sharply.

Carrie considered her response carefully. "Felicia had an encounter at one of the train stations on her way home," she answered. "I was going to tell you about it before I left again, but you had all you could handle with Moses and John."

Rose opened her mouth to protest that Carrie should have immediately told her about anything to do with her daughter, but then closed it again. Her best friend was right. Finding the poems in the library had almost undone her. Truth should always be communicated, but the timing of when to communicate it was crucial. "What happened?" she asked.

Carrie glanced across the room. "Phoebe would probably be the best person to explain since she was there."

Rose's eyes widened as she turned to Phoebe. "You were there?"

"I was waiting until things calmed down a little. Felicia seems to be much happier on the plantation, however."

"Happier than what?" Rose demanded. She held up the sheets of paper as evidence for the accusation shooting from her eyes.

"We don't know when she wrote those," Phoebe said softly.

Rose took a deep breath. "Are you saying there are more?"

Phoebe looked around the room hesitantly.

"Anything you have to say can be said in front of these women. They're my family. They love Felicia as much as Moses and I do."

"Felicia told you that she was coming home because she missed all of you terribly," Phoebe began. "I know that's true, but there's more to the story. The Oberlin College administrators decided she needed a break, and that it would be best for her to come home."

Phoebe paused, waiting for Rose's reaction.

Rose felt like she had been punched. She reached behind her for the chair she knew was there and sank down into it. "Felicia was *sent* home?" Her mind spun. "Why? Did she do something wrong?"

"No," Phoebe said quickly. "Felicia is brilliant, but she is still just a child. The administrators feared the pressure of school was becoming too much for her."

When Phoebe stopped speaking, Rose was only more confused. "I don't understand. Were her grades suffering? Was she not doing what was required?"

"It wasn't that," Phoebe assured her, "but..." Her voice trailed off again. She was obviously uncomfortable with the responsibility she had been given to impart the news.

Rose shook her head and gritted her teeth. All she wanted were answers.

Abby spoke into the silence. "It would be best if you're straightforward, Phoebe. I know you're choosing your words carefully, but all Rose really wants is the truth, no matter how difficult it may be to hear."

"Felicia is angry," Phoebe said quickly. "She's been lashing out at people." She took a long breath. "Her teachers... other students. She always feels horribly afterwards, though. Then she cries," she said sadly. "Until the next time she loses her temper. I'm afraid it's been happening often."

"My Felicia?" Rose whispered with disbelief, and then looked down at the papers in her hands. She met Phoebe's eyes, desperate for understanding. "Please tell me what happened at the train station."

Phoebe explained the situation. "I'm sorry I wasn't with her the entire time. If I had been, it wouldn't have happened."

Rose fought to control her own fury—not at Phoebe, but at the whole scenario. Dealing with hatred and prejudice directed at her was one thing, but dealing with it directed at her daughter was another. Rose had no trouble imagining how Moses would respond when he discovered what had happened. She bowed her head and struggled to manage her breathing. "My poor girl," she whispered.

Suddenly, she felt the presence of all the other women in the room. One by one, they placed their hands on her shoulders and back. Their warmth and strength flowed into her, allowing her to breathe normally. "What do I do?" she asked in a broken voice. "What do I do?"

"You love her," Abby said firmly. "Felicia has every right to be angry, Rose. She's seen terrible things. She's been safe here on the plantation, but she hasn't forgotten."

"But she's been so strong," Rose protested, trying to make sense of this new development. "She's in college. She's determined to make a difference in the world because of what happened to her."

"Yes," Abby replied. "All those things are true, but that doesn't change what she has experienced. We don't always react to trauma in our life right away. We choose strength and we continue to move forward, but all the feelings are still there." She paused and leaned down to look into Rose's confused eyes. "At some point the feelings have to come out, honey. Felicia's are coming out."

"The good thing," Janie added, "is that Felicia has the plantation to come home to. She has people around her who will love her unconditionally."

Rose knew that was true, but it didn't make her feel any better. "How do I help her?" she pleaded. Coming home to unconditional love was wonderful, but Felicia had lived in that love before she chose to stay at Oberlin. There had to be something more they could do to help her past her anger.

"Do you remember when you hated me?" Carrie asked.

Rose flinched, ashamed she had ever felt that way about her best friend.

"You had every reason to hate me," Carrie continued. "I had everything you wanted, and you never dreamed you could have it, because you were a slave and because you were black. It made you furious."

"I remember." As Rose thought back to that time, she had a much clearer understanding of how Felicia felt, but the overwhelmed feeling didn't lessen. "John, and now Felicia." She shook her head, almost feeling the raging waters of the James River close over her head. Once again, she found it difficult to breathe.

"You have to give her time," Carrie urged. "There are no magic words you can say to make the anger go away. I was so angry when Robert died. I was grief-stricken, but I was also angry. Angry because I'd been through so much. Losing Robert and Bridget seemed like a cruel joke that God was playing on me."

Rose lifted her eyes to look into her friend's face, drinking in the compassion and love she knew she would find there. "You made it through," she murmured.

"I did," Carrie agreed. "So will Felicia. Being here on the plantation with everyone is the best thing for her. She's so young. She can handle college intellectually, but the pressure is probably making it too hard to handle all her emotions at the same time. She needs time to deal with what happened to her, Rose. Seeing both parents murdered in Memphis was a terrible thing. She just needs time."

"And she needs a safe place to express her emotions," Janie added. "She needs to be angry at times. Keeping all her emotions bottled up has done nothing but create an explosive situation. I remember when I was fifteen. Everything seemed bigger and more dramatic than it actually was. In Felicia's case, what she is dealing with at fifteen is big and dramatic. She needs to be able to let her emotions out, while also dealing with them."

"And she needs her family," Abby added. "She's made herself be so strong and mature. I'll admit I've been in awe of her sometimes. She tried to push away what happened to her, but all the time it's been simmering inside. It's finally forced its way to the surface." Her voice was thick with empathy. "She has so many of us here who love her, Rose. Our love will cushion her while she figures out how to deal with everything she has boiling inside of her." She paused and then reached over to turn Rose's face so she could gaze into her eyes. "We'll do the same thing for John. Every child on this plantation is precious. There's not a single person who gets through life without hardships. We'll just keep loving them. Felicia will be all right, honey. She made the right decision. She came home."

Rose stared at her for a long moment, and then nodded. "You're right,"' she breathed. "*All* of you are right."

Out of the corner of her eye, she saw Susan riding back with Felicia. She hoped sending her out to ride hadn't been a mistake. It must be demoralizing for her daughter to see her beloved plantation under a thick coat of rancid mud. She had come home searching for a haven, but instead she had ridden into more trauma.

She watched as Felicia smiled up at Susan. She could tell from her daughter's relaxed expression that she had had a good time. The ride had been good for her. While the flood had been traumatic, Felicia had also watched her daddy and brother be rescued. She had spent hours reading books to her little brother, and also sitting with Moses.

Rose's friends were speaking the truth. Felicia would be all right.

"Thank you. I feel much better." Rose shook her head. "I can't imagine how other women deal with the hard things in life without friends like you to surround themselves with." She gazed around the room. "We're very lucky."

"We are," the other women echoed.

Rose found John in his room, sitting on the bed as he stared at the wall. It broke her heart to see him that way. "Would you like to go to the barn, son?"

"No," John answered in a hollow voice.

"You sure you don't want to go out to the barn, John?" Rose asked gently. "Grandpa Miles says he wants to show you something."

Wild grief and guilt filled John's eyes. "No," he whispered. He shook his head frantically, refusing to even look in the direction of the barn. "I'm never going out there again, Mama."

"Honey…"

"No!" John yelled, twisting away from the hand she reached out to him. He shrank back against the pillow on his bed. "No! I killed Rascal!" Sorrow flooded his face before he dissolved into a torrent of tears almost as violent as the waters that had nearly killed him.

"Alright, John," Rose said soothingly. "It's alright. You don't have to go. Not until you're ready."

John stopped crying for a moment. "I'll never be ready. I killed my best friend," he whispered. He hunched over, holding his stomach as the sobs racked his body.

Rose sat down on the bed and wrapped her arms around him. He stiffened but didn't pull back. Encouraged, Rose pulled him close against her. "I love you," she whispered. "I love you." She let him cry until he sagged against her with exhaustion.

A look out the window told her evening was claiming the plantation. It was earlier than John's usual bedtime, but he was still exhausted from his ordeal in the river, and his wild emotions were giving him no relief. She pulled back his covers, waited until he had crawled under them, kissed him on his forehead tenderly, and then held his hand until his eyes closed in sleep.

Rose knew she couldn't let John hide away in his room for much longer, but she also had to respect his need to grieve Rascal. She was glad school was starting early this year. Now that the harvest had been destroyed, the children could come back to school instead of helping in the fields. It would keep John away from the plantation and the barn.

She prayed the day would come when he would be able to return to the horses he loved so much. When he was ready, they would find another horse he could love, but she knew that time wouldn't come quickly.

Carrie gazed around the dining room table the next morning. "You would think leaving would get easier, but it doesn't. I'm grateful I got to come back, but I hate the knowledge that I'm leaving all of you with such a mess to clean up."

Moses raised a brow. "Are you saying you would go out into the fields and help clear away all the trees and debris the flood left behind?"

Carrie smiled, not minding the good-natured teasing. She was glad to see the smile in Moses' eyes. His cuts weren't completely healed, but her inspection the night before had convinced her there would be no infection. "No," she answered with a smile, "but I would deliver food to you and the men."

Moses chuckled. "You go on back to Philadelphia. We need a full-fledged certified surgeon around here. You won't get that by staying here and handing out food."

Carrie knew he was right, but it didn't make leaving any easier.

Janie walked into the room with Annabelle wrapped in her arms. "This little girl actually let us sleep a few hours last night," she said with a yawn. "Not enough to recover from all the other sleepless nights, but we still consider it a miracle."

Matthew and Peter walked into the dining room from the library. The two men had spent long hours sequestered in the book-lined room. Whatever they'd talked about, the haunted look was gone from Peter's eyes.

Annie pushed out of the kitchen holding a large basket. "I got enough food for your trip into the city," she announced.

Peter chuckled as he settled into his chair at the table, which groaned under the weight of scrambled eggs, thick slices of Virginia ham, a plate of crispy bacon, mounds of fluffy biscuits and jars full of strawberry, blackberry and grape preserves. "This breakfast alone would fuel us all the way into Richmond." He eyed the basket. "I'm sure that whatever you've packed in there will feed us for several days."

Annie sniffed. "Only if a big man like you has the appetite of a tiny woman," she retorted.

Peter laughed outright. "Not everyone eats like Moses. The rest of us aren't giants. We are mere mortals."

Moses pushed back from the table. "You leave me out of your squabble with my mama. You're going to lose anyway. I don't know why you even try."

"Me either," Peter admitted. He tried to look downcast, but his twinkling eyes made everyone laugh.

"Peter reminds me of Florence," Janie told Carrie. "The two of you used to go at each other like this all the time, too. Neither of you ever won the war of wits, but you certainly kept the rest of us entertained."

"Neither of us ever *won*?" Carrie asked with a disbelieving look. "In my opinion, I always won."

"And you can keep that opinion," Janie assured her. "Florence isn't here to set you right."

Peter cocked his head. "Who is Florence? I don't believe I've heard that name before."

"Florence was one of our housemates during the beginning of medical school," Carrie explained. "She'll be moving down to Richmond in January to start the medical clinic with us. She's a surgeon, as well. And quite the character!" She grinned. "You would like her."

"I'm sure I would," Peter replied. "Does she live in Philadelphia?"

"She does," Janie answered, "but she's on a trip with her father. His graduation gift to her was a vacation to Paris, France."

Peter frowned and leaned forward. "Paris?" he asked sharply. "When did they leave America?"

Carrie felt a twinge of alarm that she saw reflected on Janie's face. "She sent us a letter when they departed. I believe they left in early August. They were scheduled to arrive in Paris during early September, I believe."

Peter's lips tightened. "Have you heard from her?"

"No." Carrie reached out to grasp his arm. "Peter, you're frightening me. What aren't you telling us? Is Florence in danger?"

Peter sighed. "I'm afraid she probably is," he admitted. "I hadn't thought to tell any of you what's going on in France." He paused, his eyes deeply troubled. "France is at war with Prussia. They've has been invaded and things have gone badly. There aren't a lot of communications coming through, but we do know that the Emperor was captured, most of their army are prisoners of war, and Paris is under siege."

Chapter Eleven

Florence gazed around her, astonished at the beauty of Paris in October. A month had passed since she and her father had arrived in the capital of France. The city was under siege, but so far, the Prussian Army was satisfied with simply surrounding the city and cutting off all communications and deliveries. Nothing had happened to mar the beauty of the city she had fallen in love with.

Children played in the streets of the neighborhood she and her father strolled through. The leaves of thousands of trees throughout Paris painted the city with vibrant colors. Their beauty defied the violence and suffering that gripped France in the areas that had experienced battle since the war had begun in August. Blue skies and bright sunshine somehow made the reality of war completely surreal. It also somehow made the reality of war more palatable. She wondered if Carrie had felt some of the same feelings in Richmond during the war, but then remembered how quickly the blockade had made life miserable for the capitol city.

After several weeks confined inside, with the exception of strolls through his private gardens, Minister Washburne had finally acknowledged it was safe to venture farther from the house. He had assured them that, at least for the time being, Prussia had settled on the strategy to simply put Paris under siege. He was confident there would be no attack in the immediate future. The enemy seemed to be content with slowly wearing down the Parisian morale.

Florence watched the throng of children playing in the streets. "What's going to happen to all of them if Prussia attacks the city?" The idea was deeply troubling. It also made her think again of all Carrie had endured in Richmond during the war.

Dr. Robinson frowned. "I'm afraid the future doesn't look good for them whether the Prussians attack or not."

"I don't understand."

"An attack would probably end quickly," Dr. Robinson explained. "France has already lost this war. Most of their armies have been decimated—either killed or captured. I suspect Prussia is holding off an attack because of world opinion, but a long siege will create terrible suffering," he said somberly. "If it doesn't end quickly, there will be much hardship and misery when winter comes. There are already shortages of food, and the prices have gone way up."

Florence scowled as she remembered things Carrie had told her about the Siege of Richmond during the last year of the war. "Are there really shortages, Father? Or are store owners simply gouging customers because of the presumption of shortages?"

Her father shrugged. "It's probably a combination of both," he admitted. "It's true, however, that food is no longer entering a city of two million people. Prussian troops have Paris completely shut off from anyone entering with new supplies. It's probably also true that store owners are holding onto what they had in stock when the siege began. While there may be an abundant supply in storage, no one knows how long the siege will last. No matter how much is held back, at some point the stores will run out."

"While the store owners become wealthy in the meantime," Florence retorted, her eyes flashing angrily. Her father's silence was confirmation. "I haven't noticed any lack of food at Minister Washburne's home," she said.

Dr. Robinson eyed her. "Would you prefer to be going hungry?"

Florence stared at him and then dropped her eyes. "No," she admitted uncomfortably, "but I hurt for those who don't have enough to eat. It's not right."

Her father laid a hand on her shoulder. "There's nothing about war that's right," he said sadly. "You and I both saw that during our Civil War."

"People in the North didn't suffer nearly as much as those in the South," Florence argued.

"It's true that most of the battles happened in the South, but people died on both sides," her father responded. "I'll never forget the hundreds of wounded men I treated during the war. Philadelphia was not under siege, but we took care of tens of thousands of soldiers who had been horribly wounded," he said heavily. "Each one of those men, and their families, suffered greatly. Many still are."

Florence's heart swelled with sympathy. She had seen the burdened, sorrowful look on her father's face when he'd come home each night from the hospital. She had overheard some of the stories he told her mother, but she was aware, even then, that he withheld the most painful ones in order to protect his wife. He hadn't spoken of his experiences since the end of the war. She knew he was trying his best to put it all behind him, just as so many others in America were.

Florence had done what she could as a nurse, but Carrie's stories of the South had convinced her she had never experienced the worst the war had offered. Never once had they been without supplies. Never once had their patients been cold in a hospital. Never once had they writhed in pain because medicine had been denied due to blockades.

"Where are the soldiers who were wounded in battle before they closed off Paris, Father?"

Her father's lips tightened. "They're being cared for around the city. Hospitals are called '*ambulances*' here in Paris."

Florence recognized in his eyes what he wasn't communicating with words. "The conditions are bad," she said flatly.

Dr. Robinson shrugged. "Paris isn't equipped to handle tens of thousands of wounded soldiers. They're doing the best they can."

Again, Florence read the truth on his face. She didn't need him to say more in order to understand how much men were suffering all around this lovely city.

"How can we help?" she asked.

Her father shook his head. "Washburne says it's best if we don't."

"Why?" Florence demanded. "Paris is full of wounded men. We're doctors."

Her father hesitated. "The hospitals in Paris are quite bad," he finally said. "I'm told the French have an aversion to fresh air in medical facilities. They believe it's harmful to the patients." He paused, and then plowed on as if he were determined to say it all. "When men go into the hospitals here...very few of them come back out," he said grimly.

"They're *dying* from gunshot wounds?" Florence was horrified by what she was hearing. She thought back to the hospital in Philadelphia where she had served during the war. "We had to amputate many limbs, but most of the wounded men lived," she protested. "Why are these men dying?"

"They're going septic," Dr. Robinson said sadly.

Florence stared at him. "They're dying from blood infections because of unsanitary conditions in their hospitals? The conditions are really that horrible?"

"Yes." Her father's eyes sparked with both anger and sorrow.

"And we can't help them?" Florence was both horrified and disbelieving. "I don't understand."

"Washburne is afraid for us."

"And he's afraid we'll bring disease into his house," Florence guessed. Her father's expression gave her the answer. Fury coursed through her, even as she recognized the truth of Minister Washburne's fear.

"He is our host in a foreign country," her father replied. "A foreign country that happens to be at war. He feels responsible for our safety. I honestly can't say what I would do in a similar situation."

Florence wanted to protest that surely her father would cast aside concerns to care for the sick, but she remained silent. This wasn't America. They didn't speak the language. If they were hosting people in America during the war, would they let them walk into the same situation? It was easy to say what you would do, but until you were in the exact position, you couldn't really know. On the other hand, she couldn't imagine being trapped in a city under siege, unable to make any difference at all.

Biting back her desire to scream with frustration, she began to walk again.

"Florence..."

"I just want to walk, Father. I *need* to walk."

Dr. Robinson fell into step beside her, tucked her hand into the crook of his arm, and matched her long stride.

Florence was grateful for the silence as they walked, unmindful of where they were going. There was an army perched right outside the city. There were tens of thousands of men dying all around her. She was stranded in a country at war, far from home and far from the future she had so carefully planned, and with no idea when the situation would ever change. She didn't know that she had ever felt so helpless.

Or so useless.

Florence lost track of how long they had walked, and she had absolutely no idea where they were. It hardly mattered. They would find their way back to Minister Washburne's house. In the meantime, the walking had helped to calm her. She still felt powerless and useless, but she no longer wanted to scream.

Looking up, she stopped short. "What is that?"

Her father stopped beside her; his face equally quizzical. "That must be what Washburne was telling me about this morning. I was getting ready to discuss it with you, but you needed to walk."

"What is it?"

"It's the American Ambulance. Washburne told me this morning that if we're determined to provide medical care while we're here, that this was the one place he could support. He had quite complimentary things to say about it."

Florence glanced around for a street sign, and then continued to stare at the collection of canvas buildings situated on *Avenue de l'Impératrice*. "It looks like an American hospital," she muttered.

"That's because it is," Dr. Robinson answered.

"How did an American hospital end up in Paris?" Florence demanded, a horde of questions that needed answering exploding in her mind.

"I'm afraid I don't have the answers," Dr. Robinson said. "Washburne was just beginning an explanation when he was called away to duty."

"Then we have to go find out for ourselves," Florence declared as she walked closer to the buildings. It was easy to tell they were operating as a full medical facility. Several women, obviously nurses, walked from the buildings attired in long dresses complete with long sleeves and aprons.

A dark-haired man with swarthy features stopped them with a raised hand as they approached the hospital. "Bonjour."

"Hello," Florence said.

The man eyed her. "You're from America. I'm sorry, but only medical staff is allowed in the buildings." His accent was clearly American.

Dr. Robinson nodded courteously. "Of course. I am Dr. Robinson. This is my daughter, Dr. Florence Robinson. We came to Paris last month to celebrate my daughter's recent graduation from medical school in Philadelphia."

The man raised a brow. "I'm afraid you had poor timing, Dr. Robinson."

"I wholeheartedly agree with you, but that doesn't change the fact we're here, and captive in this beautiful city."

"Is this really an American hospital?" Florence asked, eager for answers.

The man turned, his eyes seeming to appraise her.

Florence straightened her shoulders and met his eyes evenly. She had learned long ago how to deal with men who believed there was no place for women in medicine.

The man grinned, his smile transforming his features. "Where were you in school, Dr. Robinson?"

"The Women's Medical College of Philadelphia."

"Did you know Dr. Amberton?"

"Of course. She was one of my instructors." Florence was amazed to hear the name of someone she knew so far from home.

"She's my sister," the man revealed. "I'm Dr. Silas Amberton."

"It's a pleasure to meet you," Dr. Robinson said warmly.

Florence managed to close her mouth, which had dropped open with astonishment. "Dr. Amberton was one of my favorite instructors. I can hardly believe you're related."

Dr. Amberton grinned again, his dark eyes lit with merriment. "I hardly think you would reveal if you *hated* her as an instructor now that you know my identity," he teased.

Florence laughed. This was a man she could be friends with. "You're right," she agreed. "I suppose I should be glad I'm telling the truth. You would most certainly ascertain a lie."

"That's probably true," Dr. Amberton agreed. "Now, what are the two of you doing walking around a city under siege?"

"I was quite sure I would go mad if I had to stay inside for even one more day," Florence responded. "My father and I would like to make a difference while we're here. We understand the medical need is quite dire."

"That would be putting it mildly," Dr. Amberton said sardonically. "Disastrous would be a better word." He waved his hand at the collection of canvas buildings. "We save more than ninety-five percent of the patients who come here. Most French hospitals have a sixty percent mortality rate." His voice grew grimmer. "The Grand Hotel, converted into a hospital soon after the war began, has a much higher mortality rate. I've been told that ninety percent of their patients who undergo amputations die from sepsis."

Florence gasped and put a hand to her mouth. "That's horrible," she breathed. "How can they allow that to happen?"

"That's just the beginning," Dr. Amberton continued. "There is scarcely a hospital in Paris that doesn't have appallingly high rates of infection and death. They seem to have no regard for hygiene, and the military doctors are poorly trained. Combine that with the fact that the buildings have almost nonexistent ventilation, and you can see that they're nothing but a breeding ground for infection and disease." He took a breath and waved his hand toward the horizon. "Since the standard hospitals are full, there are scores of private homes all around Paris that have taken in patients. The sentiment is admirable, but they're sorely equipped and untrained for how to care for these gravely injured men. The death rate is staggering."

Florence wanted to block out what she was hearing, but her curiosity required satisfying. "How did this hospital come to be?"

Dr. Amberton laughed. "It's quite a story. I won't go into all the details now, but I can give you the basics. Dr. Thomas Evans, a dentist from America, is responsible for this hospital."

"A dentist?" Dr. Robinson echoed. "That's extraordinary."

"He's an extraordinary man," Dr. Amberton replied. "You may know that the International Exhibition was here in Paris three years ago, in 1867. It was the second World Fair."

Florence wasn't aware of the *existence* of a International Exhibition, but she nodded, catching the amusement in her father's eyes as he watched her. She flushed and looked away, uncomfortably aware she was acting out of character around a complete stranger.

"Anyway," Dr. Amberton continued, "Dr. Evans has quite a commitment to medical hygiene because he's seen the deadly results when it's not a priority. He spent his own money to set up an exhibit of American medicine at the fair. He spent some time in Philadelphia learning current medical procedures, and then he brought over American hospital tents, wagons and all the medical equipment and surgical supplies that he could pull together."

"All the way from America?" Florence asked in astonishment. "That was quite an undertaking."

"That it was," Dr. Amberton agreed. "When the fair was over, he put everything in storage on his property, certain there would come a time when it was needed."

"Sadly, he was right," Dr. Robinson responded, eyeing the hospital with even more respect. His voice turned brisk. "Is there a way we can be of service?"

Dr. Amberton eyed him. "Can you tell me about your medical background?"

"Certainly. I operated a traditional medical practice for many years, serving as a surgeon during the American Civil War. Recently, convinced of its efficacy, I have put most of my focus on homeopathic medicine, but I still perform surgery when needed."

Dr. Amberton turned to Florence. "And you?"

"I've just graduated with my medical degree, with a certification in surgery," Florence answered. "I served as a nurse during the war, and I've been working at a clinic in Philadelphia while I'm in school."

Dr. Amberton eyed her. "What are your plans when you return to the United States?"

Florence wasn't sure how this was related to their possible involvement at the American hospital, but she didn't mind answering. "I'm moving to Richmond, Virginia to open a practice with three of my closest women friends from medical school. If," she said ruefully, "I'm able to leave Paris."

"Oh, the siege can't last forever," Dr. Amberton said cheerfully.

Florence decided to not point out that the Prussians could decide at any moment to end the siege and attack the city. She knew he was simply taking a positive approach to a terrifying scenario.

Dr. Amberton was still watching her. "An all-women practice in Richmond, Virginia," he mused. "Isn't that highly unusual?"

Florence smiled. "Knowing who your sister is, I'm sure you know that women in medicine are highly unusual in *any* situation," she said wryly. "We decided that as long as we're going against the protocols set for us, we might as well make as big of an impact as possible."

Dr. Amberton chuckled. "Very admirable." His manner turned brisk. "I think the both of you would fit into our hospital quite well. We would appreciate all that you can do. You'll be paid, of course."

Dr. Robinson shrugged. "That is of little consequence to us." He looked toward the hospital. "Do we need to meet Dr. Evans?"

"I'm afraid that won't be possible. He's on a mission to sneak the Emperor's wife out of Paris. We have hope he succeeded, but since there is very little communication coming in or out of Paris, we don't know."

Florence was startled. "Dr. Evans is sneaking Emperor Napoleon's wife out of Paris?" She wasn't certain she had heard correctly.

"Yes. When the Emperor was captured at the Battle of Sedan, public sentiment turned against the Second Empire rather quickly. The crowds ripped the Napoleonic eagles off the palace gate and started yelling for the death of his wife, Empress Eugenie, who happens to be a Spaniard." Dr. Amberton waved a hand at a gentleman who passed by and then returned to his story. "Dr. Evans is friends with both the Emperor and Empress, so she came to him late one night asking for help. The last I saw them, he was driving off in a carriage, the Empress disguised as a patient." His voice was amused, but turned serious quickly. "I trust this will stay between us. There are factions in Paris that would be less than happy to know the Empress is on her way out of the country."

"Of course," Florence said quickly. "I'm glad he was able to get her out. Where is he taking them?" She was intrigued by the story.

"His plan is to obtain sanctuary for her in England, but he's also trying to discover whether her son, Lou-Lou, is still alive. He's only fourteen, but already a soldier in the French Army."

Florence shook her head. "I hate war," she said angrily.

"Another thing we have in common," Dr. Amberton assured her. "I'll show you around the hospital. You can let me know when you want to start."

Dr. Robinson exchanged a brief glance with Florence. When she nodded, he spoke quickly. "We'll start tomorrow."

Two weeks later, Florence and her father joined Minister Washburne for dinner. Despite sharing a residence, they rarely saw the minister now that they were working at the hospital. Between their shifts, and Minister Washburne's busy schedule, their paths seldom crossed. There had been a message waiting for them from one of the house staff that morning, requesting they join the minister that evening.

Florence smoothed down the folds of the green silk gown her father had bought her when they had first arrived in Paris. It felt odd to be dressed so elegantly when there was a siege, especially after a day of performing surgery on wounded soldiers, but dinner with the minister seemed to demand it. She gazed around the opulent dining room. Within the confines of his grand residence, no one would ever guess at the citywide distress that grew daily.

"You look lovely, Dr. Robinson."

Florence smiled and dipped her head. "Thank you, Minister Washburne. It's a pleasure to see you."

"The pleasure is mine," he replied graciously. "You and your father are quite busy at the American Ambulance these days."

"That we are," Florence agreed as she eyed the sumptuous meal spread across a white linen-covered table beneath a huge, glowing chandelier. A mass of blooms from the garden graced the center of the table, reflecting in the wall of ornate mirrors that faced her. In other times, she would have enjoyed the beautiful room – now, she couldn't help feeling unsettled.

She thought about her father's question two weeks earlier: *Would you rather be hungry?* The answer had been *no* then, and it was *no* now, but it still made her uncomfortable. Why did the scales have to be so unevenly balanced? Hunger was becoming more prevalent in Paris as the siege wore on. Surely those who had all they needed could share with those less fortunate.

"I'm hoping you can give us an update, Washburne."

Florence forced her thoughts away from the food and turned to hear what the Minister had to say.

"What have you heard?" Washburne asked.

Florence gazed at him more closely as they all sat down. She noticed, for the first time, the weary lines that surrounded the minister's fatigued eyes.

"Not much," Robinson replied. "I'm aware there was another battle outside the city during the last few days. Our wards were already full, but as fast as we release men, the beds are full again. I hear wounded men have poured into the city."

Washburne sighed heavily. "Yes." He nodded his thanks as a servant stepped forward to fill his cut-glass goblet with white wine, took an appreciative sip, and sighed again. "Even though the French don't stand a chance of winning this war, there are factions that are determined to continue the fight. Until two days ago, General Carey de Bellemare commanded the strongest French fortress north of Paris at Saint-Denis. A lack of orders to take action didn't deter him from attacking the Prussian Guard at Le Bourget. Evidently, he was growing restless at the inactivity of the Paris defense so he initiated a battle. He succeeded in taking the city."

Dr. Robinson cocked a brow. "I hear a 'but' in there."

Washburne shrugged. "Parisian citizens were thrilled with the news, but when General de Bellemare asked for reinforcements, General Trochu declined."

Florence was still trying to put all the names to the proper positions. "Does General Trochu have overall command of Paris' defenses?"

"Yes. He was also elected acting President of France when Napoleon was captured and his government overthrown," Washburne replied. "Trochu felt the village offered no strategic advantage and was vulnerable to Prussian artillery." He paused. "My sources tell me the Prussian Guard didn't really care to fight to regain the village, but Crown Prince Albert…"

"The commander of the Prussian Army?" Dr. Robinson asked.

"Yes. The Crown Prince ordered the village retaken yesterday. The Prussian Guard may not have really cared, but they fought well anyway. Le Bourget was retaken. While the French were being driven from the city, twelve hundred soldiers were taken captive." He scowled "You're already seeing the results in the number of wounded."

"What a waste," Florence murmured.

Minister Washburne eyed her. "I completely agree with you. While the Parisians were initially bolstered by news of the victory, they are now more disheartened than before. I believe the reality is sinking in a little more each day that Paris really has no hope of victory." He glanced out the window, seeming to take comfort from the bank of roses just outside. Frost would soon kill them for the season, but for now, their colors were beautifully vibrant.

Finally, he turned back. "Even though Trochu never wanted an attack on the village, and certainly didn't order it, he is, of course, receiving blame for the defeat."

"That hardly seems fair," Florence protested.

"The price of leadership," Washburne replied sardonically.

Dr. Robinson changed the topic of conversation. "Have there been any lines of communication opened?"

Florence knew her father was eager to get word back to her mother. She was equally eager to get word to Carrie, Janie and Elizabeth. Surely, they were aware of the French war. She knew they would be frantic with worry. Even a short telegram would reassure them, at least for the moment. No one knew how any of this would end.

"It all depends on your definition of 'open,'" Washburne replied with a mysterious glint in his eyes.

Florence stared at him. She was aware communication had been totally cut off. The telegraph line running at the bottom of the Seine River had been discovered and cut by Prussian forces. How could he treat any of this lightly?

Washburne smiled slightly at the expression on her face. "I'm sorry, Florence. I'm afraid I'm more than a little weary. I assure you I'm not nonchalant about the affairs in Paris, however."

"Of course," Florence said quickly. "I understand, Minister." In truth, she wasn't certain she did, but she certainly didn't want to offend their host.

Minister Washburne turned to her father. "I am the only head of a diplomatic mission from a major power who has remained in Paris. While I'm in the unique position of having a channel of communication in and out of the city, I'm afraid it's very limited. I've been besieged with requests to get letters in and out of Paris, but it simply isn't possible." He flexed his broad shoulders. "I spend most of my days providing humanitarian relief to foreign nationals, including the ethnic Germans trapped here."

"Do you find that difficult?" Dr. Robinson asked curiously.

"No," Washburne replied quickly. "They had nothing to do with their government's decision to go to war. They're people living in a foreign land who are in a treacherous position because they're surrounded by people who hate them simply for being German. I'm doing my best to provide food, and now heat, for everyone."

Florence frowned as she was reminded of the hunger throughout the city. She remembered a restaurant she had passed on the way home from the hospital that day. "Did I see horse on a restaurant menu today?" Her French was improving daily, but she hadn't been certain of what she was reading.

Washburne nodded. "Ah... *la viande de cheval.* Yes. Paris began to eat horsemeat at the beginning of October. Actually, butchers began to offer horsemeat to poor people four years ago, but it's gained in popularity throughout the city now that meat has become so scarce."

Florence struggled to keep the look of disgust from her face as she glanced down at the meat on her plate.

Washburne chuckled. "You were not served horsemeat tonight," he assured her. "Horse has become quite widely accepted throughout Paris, however. Stark necessity has enabled many to overcome their initial reticence."

Florence shook her head. "I won't judge, but I also won't eat horsemeat," she said firmly. "I would appreciate knowing if it's ever on the menu here. I can do quite well with vegetables and bread."

"Vegetables will become scarcer," Washburne said grimly. "The supply in Paris has run out and nothing can come in from the farms. Butter and milk are already gone from the store shelves."

Florence gazed at the food on the table in front of her. A platter of roast beef was surrounded by tiny potatoes, carrots and beans. "How is this meal possible, then?"

Washburne inclined his head toward the window. "We have a large vegetable garden in the back," he informed her. "The basement has a supply of root crops, and there is a large amount of canned vegetables. It was determined long ago, well before my taking up residence, that this home needed to be prepared for drastic circumstances. The supplies will last for quite a while, but there's no guarantee they won't run out."

"And the butter and cheese?" Dr. Robinson asked.

"I have a friend nearby who keeps two cows in his basement," Washburne revealed with a twinkle in his eyes.

Florence gasped. "His basement?" She wrinkled her nose as she thought of the odors that must come from confined cattle.

"You do what you must do," Washburne said ruefully. "We trade him some of our vegetables in exchange for butter and cheese. At least for now."

Florence fought to control her expression but failed.

Washburne smiled sympathetically. "I understand how you feel, Florence. If it were possible to feed all the hungry in Paris from my house, I would. I can only ensure that those under my roof have the energy to continue to do their jobs and help as many as they can. In the meantime, I work to keep as many people from starving and freezing as possible."

Florence flushed with shame. She realized it wasn't possible to feed everyone in a city of two million. What a burden to be forced to make decisions about who would eat and who would go hungry. "You're right," she said. "Forgive me for not understanding."

"No forgiveness needed," Minister Washburne assured her. "I struggle with it every day."

Silence filled the room for several moments.

"You were rather cryptic in your response about communications," Dr. Robinson said. "May I ask what you meant?"

"It's been an ongoing struggle," Washburne replied. "You already know the telegraph cable was cut at the bottom of the Seine. Couriers who have attempted to breech the lines have been captured. The city has floated message canisters down the river, but all have been intercepted."

Florence felt her hope dying.

"Hot air balloons, however, have been quite effective so far."

Florence and her father both put down their forks and stared at the minister.

"Hot air balloons?" her father asked incredulously.

The minister smiled. "I thought the idea was farfetched at first, but it's been quite successful in delivering mail.

That's part of the reason I wanted to have dinner with you tonight. I've obtained permission for the two of you to send out communications. I know you're quite eager to get mail back to the United States. If you're sending letters, it will obviously take many weeks for them to make it to the port at Le Havre and onto a ship. Very few steamers are coming into France because of the war, but the letters can be sent to England and placed on a steamer there." He held up a hand when Dr. Robinson started to interrupt. "I already know that's not optimal. Your other option is to send a very brief message that can be telegraphed."

"Are the hot air balloons reliable?" Florence asked skeptically.

Minister Washburne shrugged. "Most of them get through, though no one knows exactly where they will land since they're dependent upon the winds. To our knowledge, only a few have been lost."

"Fascinating! How do you know they've made it through?" Dr. Robinson asked keenly.

"Each balloon goes out with a carrier pigeon. They release the pigeon if the balloon landing is successful. It returns with a message relaying the successful journey, as well as the location where it landed."

"Pigeons? I've never heard of such a thing," Dr. Robinson said incredulously.

"The first time they were used was during the inaugural flight made by Jules Duruof, a professional hot air balloon pilot. He carried two hundred and twenty-seven pounds of mail out with him and sent the pigeon back with the news. While he was flying over the Prussian Army, he dropped visiting cards on them," Washburne said with amusement.

Florence chuckled. "They must have been furious." She could well imagine the faces of the Prussian soldiers as they stared up at the balloons far from the reach of their guns. She had another thought. "Are balloons bringing mail back to Paris, as well?"

Washburne shook his head regretfully. "Unfortunately, it's not possible because of the direction of the winds. It's also not possible to steer the balloons, so there is too big of a risk that they would land in enemy territory. "However..." His voice trailed off mysteriously.

"What?" Dr. Robinson demanded. "I well remember your flair for the dramatic, my friend."

Washburne chuckled. "I've learned it serves me well in political service." Then he turned his attention back to Florence's question. "They've started sending out carrier pigeons to bring the mail back."

"Carrier pigeons?" Florence echoed. "How can carrier pigeons deliver mail? I can understand a single message about the safe landing of the balloons, but you said that the first hot air balloon took out over two hundred pounds of mail."

"The pigeons used to carry just one message within a small canister, but they figured out a way to increase the bird's ability. Their method is quite clever," Washburne replied. "Each message being sent to Paris is limited to twenty words. The messages are copied onto sheets of cardboard and photographed, and then reduced to a much smaller size. The photo paper is rolled up and stuffed into the canister attached to the pigeon. Mail has been coming back to the city for several weeks now."

"When can we send messages to America?" Florence asked eagerly.

"Tomorrow," Washburne assured her. "Besides the fact that you and your father are my guests, you're also both performing a valuable service for Paris."

Florence smiled happily. News would shortly be going to her mother and her soon-to-be business partners.

Chapter Twelve
November 1870

Susan basked in a feeling of deep satisfaction as she strolled away from the wooden auction barn in Norfolk, Virginia. She had been grateful for the tip Peter had given her during his visit about a breeding operation in Norfolk that was going under and needed to sell their stock. It had been easy to convince Harold to join her on the buying trip because he was eager to interview a local politician while she was at the auction. She was going to meet her husband for dinner in another hour.

There hadn't been many horses that met the strict criteria for Cromwell breeding stock, but she was thrilled with the four mares she had purchased. She had obtained them at a good price and was confident they would produce valuable offspring.

"Stand still!"

Susan was jolted out of her pleasant thoughts by an angry voice.

"You stupid horse! I said stand still!" The furious yell was followed by the snap of a whip.

Susan followed the sound. She heard another crack of the whip, and a high squeal of pain and terror. Picking up her skirts, she broke into a run.

She rounded the corner of one of the barns just in time to see a large, overweight man with dark hair and a bushy beard lift his arm to deliver another blow. Without taking time to consider the consequences, Susan sprinted forward and grabbed his arm before he could lower it again.

Catching the man by surprise, she ripped the whip from his hand. "What are you doing?" she asked furiously.

The man wheeled on her, his eyes widening with surprise when he saw his attacker was a woman. "What are *you* doing, little lady?" he snapped.

"Keeping you from abusing a helpless animal," Susan retorted, anger making her heart pound against her ribs. She couldn't remember ever being so angry. The mare the man had been beating was snorting and rearing against her tie-down rope, her eyes rolling with terror and pain. Susan's anger flared into fury when she saw the deep gouges in the mare's flesh.

"Give me that whip," the man snarled, advancing with his hand out. "I'll do whatever I want to my horse. Stupid mare ain't worth nothing anyway."

"You will not touch her again," Susan vowed, pulling the whip out of his reach.

The man stared at her with disbelief. "You ain't nothing but a woman. How do you think you're going to stop me?" He stepped closer; his eyes narrowed as they fixated on the whip.

Susan was aware she had stepped into danger, but her fury outweighed her fear. "Perhaps you would like to know how this whip feels," she replied, somehow managing to sound calm and in control. She lifted her hand and pulled the whip back, taking a measure of comfort from the heavy weight.

The man jolted to a stop. "Are you crazy? What's wrong with you, woman?"

"What's wrong with me is that I refuse to see a defenseless animal beaten," Susan countered. Her mind raced. If she left this mare, the man would only beat her again when there was no one to stop him.

"How much do you want for her?" Susan asked, surprising herself with the question.

"What?" The angry man now looked equally puzzled.

"I'll buy her from you," Susan said, suddenly certain she was making the right decision.

"You ain't got no use for this pointless piece of horse flesh," the man spat.

"Then neither do you," Susan retorted, not letting her arm lower from its position. She was quite certain the only thing protecting her from attack was the threat of the whip. "How much?" she repeated. "I'm not leaving here without this mare."

The man's beady eyes bored into her. Finally, he shrugged. "What do I care? You're obviously crazy. If you're crazy enough to want this horse, you can have her for one hundred dollars."

The price was far higher than what the mare was worth, but now that Susan had resolved to save her, it didn't really matter. She would figure out what she would do with the horse later. Right now, the only thing that mattered was that she rescue her.

"Fine." Susan reached into the pocket of her dress that still carried funds from the earlier auction. She counted out one hundred dollars and shoved it at the man.

The man snatched it, his eyes fixed on the whip still cocked in her hand.

"The price includes the whip," Susan snapped. "It's mine now."

The man opened his mouth to argue, looked at the one hundred dollars in his hands, shrugged and turned to stalk away. "You're one plum crazy woman," he muttered as he disappeared back into the barn.

Convinced he was gone, Susan coiled the whip and stuffed it into a nearby barrel. Then she approached the mare slowly. "Hello, girl," she murmured. "That horrible man will never touch you again. I promise."

The mare continued to roll her eyes and snort, pulling hard against the rope. In addition to the welts and cuts on her side, her head was raw where the halter had bit into it during her panicked struggles.

Susan stopped her approach but continued to talk quietly. "It's all right. I understand that you're afraid. If I were you, I would be afraid, too." Standing still, she continued to murmur quietly. It didn't matter what she said; the frightened horse just needed to hear a calm voice.

Susan didn't know how long she stood there before the mare finally calmed. She gave a final snort and then lowered her head in exhausted defeat. Tears sprang to Susan's eyes as she examined the streaks of blood on the mare's sides. "I'm so sorry, girl. I'm going to fix you up and take you to a place where no one can ever hurt you again."

Rose called good-bye to all her students and then closed the door against the biting wind blowing in from the north. "*Brr*...early November is not usually so cold in Virginia."

Phoebe shrugged. "You've gotten soft living in the South again," she teased. "Surely you remember hold cold it was in Oberlin during November?"

"Oh, I remember," Rose replied with a grin. "It was one of the reasons I was eager to return home." She walked closer to the roaring pot-bellied stove in the middle of the room and held out her hands. "I'm not looking forward to winter."

"Soft," Phoebe scoffed with a wink, and then walked to a window to gaze outside.

Rose went to join her, watching as Amber and Angel walked down the trail through the woods. She knew one of Moses' men would watch them from a distance until they arrived at Cromwell Stables, but they also respected the girl's need for a feeling of independence.

"What is Angel's story?" Phoebe asked. "She struggles to learn, and she seems so sad." She continued to watch the girls until they disappeared around the curve. "She's also missed a lot of school since I've been here. Does she have an illness I don't know about?"

Rose shook her head. "She's not sick, but Angel has every right to be sad. I've tried to help her, but most of the time she just looks at me with a blank expression. Her father has assured me she is actually quite intelligent. She just doesn't have the courage to respond to me."

"Why?" Phoebe demanded. "What happened to her?"

Rose walked over and claimed a chair near the stove. "You'll want to sit down for this story."

Phoebe followed, leaning forward expectantly.

"Angel's father, Daniel Blue, works for Moses," Rose began. "He came to the plantation from North Carolina a few months ago after the Klan killed his pregnant wife and four of his five children. They thought he was dead from the gunshot wound they inflicted, and they didn't know Angel was in the back bedroom. She sleeps so soundly that she never heard a thing. She didn't come out during the attack."

Phoebe gasped, her eyes wide with disbelief. "Why were they attacked?" she whispered.

"Daniel was going to testify in court against a Klan member he saw beat another black man. Friends warned him it was a bad idea, but he was determined to do the right thing."

"Except the Klan wasn't going to let that happen," Phoebe said angrily.

"No," Rose responded, feeling her own anger all over again. "There's more to the story, though. Right before the last Klansman walked out, he lit a pine torch and tossed it into the house. The house started to burn quickly. Somehow, Daniel managed to crawl to the bedroom and wake Angel. They climbed out the back window and escaped. It wasn't until the next morning that Angel discovered everyone else had been murdered."

Phoebe shuddered. "Where did they go?"

"To a neighbor's house. Even though the neighbors were scared to take them in because of what the Klan would do if they found out, they did anyway. The woman nursed Daniel back to health and took care of Angel. Once Daniel was well again, they walked here to Virginia."

"They *walked* here?" Phoebe asked incredulously. "From North Carolina? How long did it take?"

"He said about a month. Daniel and Angel lived with Franklin and Chooli until recently. They just moved into a newly finished cabin where the old slave quarters used to be."

Phoebe's eyes softened with sympathy. "Angel is consumed by the trauma," she said softly. "That poor baby."

"Yes," Rose agreed, her heart twisting with pain for the anguished girl. "I've done everything I can to reach her, but I can't break through."

Fourteen-year-old Amber looked over at Angel as they walked through the woods. Though they were the same age, Angel seemed much younger. Not all the time, though. Sometimes she seemed much older. Like today.

"What are you looking at?" Angel asked. "Do I have something on my face?"

"No," Amber assured her.

"You're still staring at me," Angel complained a few moments later.

"Sorry," Amber said quickly. She had learned early on that Angel wasn't willing to talk about whatever had put so much sadness in her eyes. Her attempts had done nothing but upset her friend, so she had quit trying. Her mother had assured her that if Angel was ever ready to talk about her sadness, she would. Amber suspected her mother knew why her friend was so sad , but she hadn't told her. "I was just thinking. I didn't mean to look at you while I was thinking." It was a lame excuse, but it would have to do. She changed the subject quickly. "Do you want to go riding today?" Riding was the only thing Angel ever got excited about.

Angel nodded eagerly, her narrow face holding the glimmer of a smile.

Amber had never seen Angel actually smile, but even the hint of one was something to consider a victory. Her mama had told her that helping Angel was like helping a horse that was afraid - you had to take it slow and easy. She thought back to when she had helped Robert through hard times. She prayed she could do the same for Angel.

"Who do you want to ride?"

Angel considered the question. "How about Maple? Mrs. Samuels said I could ride her."

"That will be good. Maple needs some exercise. Rose has been too busy to ride her much."

Angel cocked her head. "How come you call her Rose? I thought we had to call her Mrs. Samuels?"

"I call her that at school," Amber said, "but Rose is part of our family. She asked me to call her that a long time ago. My daddy was the one who took Robert in when Moses brought him to us after a big battle during the war."

"Robert?"

Amber felt a wave of sadness. "Robert was Carrie's first husband. We were very close." The memories made her take a deep breath. "He was like another father to me. He gave me All My Heart." Her heart constricted at the memory of that special day.

"What happened to him?"

"The Klan killed him," Amber said flatly. "They came here one night to attack the plantation. They tried to shoot me, but Robert jumped in front of me and they shot him instead." Sorrow clogged her throat.

"The *Klan*?" Frantic terror filled Angel's eyes. "They came here to the plantation?" She looked around wildly. "Daddy said we would be safe here!"

Amber pushed away her sorrow when she realized how frightened her friend was. "You *are* safe here," she said quickly. "That was three years ago, Angel. The Klan hasn't been back." She decided it wasn't necessary to mention the thwarted attacks she had overheard her parents talking about.

"But they been here," Angel whispered, fear radiating from her. "They'll come back." Her voice faltered. "They always come back."

Amber frowned. She didn't know what had happened to her friend, but it was obvious it had something to do with the terrible Ku Klux Klan.

"Hello!"

Amber and Angel whirled around at the same time.

Susan and Harold were riding down the driveway leading a string of five horses.

"Can you girls give us a hand?" Susan called.

Amber hesitated, hoping she should continue the conversation with Angel.

"We're coming," Angel called.

Amber followed. She knew their conversation was finished, at least for now.

"We're just coming back from a buying trip," Susan said when she got close enough.

Amber had been aware of the purpose of her trip. She examined the mares with delight, thinking of the beautiful colts and fillies they would produce. She frowned, though, when her eyes rested on the last one in the string. The dull-coated mare was skinny and staring at them with a mixture of terror and defiance. Amber lifted her face to meet Susan's eyes.

"It's a long story," Susan said quietly. "This little girl has been through more than any horse should ever have to go through."

Amber nodded quickly, knowing she would get answers later. "Where do you want her to go?"

"How about next to Granite? I think he'll be a calming influence."

Amber started forward to untie her from the string.

"Can I take her?" Angel asked tentatively, her eyes fixed on the frightened mare.

Susan hesitated. "Do you believe you can handle her?"

Angel ignored her question and moved forward with an outstretched hand. "Hello, girl," she cooed gently. "It's all right. You and I are going to be friends, aren't we?"

The mare had raised her head in alarm, but suddenly her eyes softened. Instead of rearing back, she relaxed and stood quietly.

"That's a girl," Angel said softly. "I'm going to take you inside that nice, big barn. There's food waiting for you and a thick bed of straw you can lie down on." She slowly reached up and untied the mare's rope. Holding the rope firmly, she stepped next to the mare's head.

The horse threw up her head in protest, but relaxed again immediately.

Amber realized Susan and Harold were watching with the same astonishment she was.

"What's her name?" Angel asked as she laid a gentle hand on the mare's neck.

"I don't know," Susan replied. "Would you like to give her one?"

Angel looked at the horse thoughtfully. "Friday," she announced. "I'm going to name her Friday because today is Friday. It's the day her new life begins." She turned and led Friday into the barn.

Susan watched her go and then turned to Amber. "Can you help her with Friday?"

"Yes," Amber assured her. "I'll make time." She looked toward the barn. "I've never seen so much life in Angel's eyes," she murmured.

"They'll be good for each other," Susan assured her.

"Do you know why Angel is like she is?"

Susan met her eyes evenly. "That's a story for Angel to tell, Amber."

Amber sighed and turned toward the barn. Perhaps someday she would know the story. For now, she had work to do.

Rose looked up with a welcoming smile when Harold and Susan walked in the door and settled down at the dining room table. "To what do we owe this honor?"

"Annie's chicken and dumplings are better than Susan's," Harold replied with a teasing glint in his eyes.

"And I'm not one bit offended," Susan responded. "Any night when we can eat Annie's cooking is a treat. Of course, I want to mention that Harold's chicken and dumplings aren't one bit better than mine. We each tried once before we gave up and decided it would simply stay off our menu unless we were here. Miles told us it was being served tonight..."

Harold's eyes were dancing with fun. "I never knew anyone could make such a mess of chicken and dumplings, but we certainly did."

Annie pushed through the door, holding a huge bowl of steaming food. "The two of you are both smart people," she scolded. "How can you mess up somethin' so simple?"

"It's easy," Susan assured her as she took an appreciative sniff. "I can promise you nothing we have created has ever smelled this good."

"Lazy," Annie scoffed. "The two of you are just plain lazy cooks."

"I reckon we are," Harold said cheerfully. "Which makes us appreciate you all the more, Annie."

"You just butterin' me up," Annie said as she rolled her eyes.

"Is it working?" Harold asked hopefully.

"Sit down and eat that before I change my mind about serving it," Annie replied, chuckling as she put down the bowl and headed back into the kitchen. "I'll be right out to join you," she called. "I'm just checking on the apple cobbler I got in the stove."

Susan sank down in her chair. "Chicken and dumplings *and* apple cobbler?" She lifted a brow as she looked at her husband. "Perhaps we should consider moving back into the plantation house."

"Since we all know you two almost-newlyweds aren't going to do that," Rose said, "why don't you tell us what you're really doing here."

Susan feigned shock. "You don't believe we came for the chicken and dumplings?"

Annie walked from the kitchen and settled into her chair at the table. "I'm with my daughter-in-law. Most nights, you scurry out of here to go back to your home where that man of yours is writing. What you two doing here?"

Susan smiled. "I can't get away with anything around here." Then she grew serious as she looked at Rose. "I want to talk to you about Angel."

Rose was immediately alert. "Is something wrong with her?"

"No," Susan assured her. "Something happened today that I wanted to talk to you about."

Rose listened closely as Susan told her about rescuing the mare from the auction, and how eager Angel was to work with the horse.

"She named her Friday," Susan finished. "Because today is Friday, and Friday is the day the mare's new life begins."

Rose smiled, excited by what she had heard. "And perhaps the day Angel's new life begins." She opened her mouth to say more, but John interrupted her.

"Why was the man mean to Friday?" he asked indignantly.

Susan shook her head. "I don't know, John. Sometimes people just aren't very nice. The important thing, though, is that Friday will never be treated badly again."

"That's good," John said fervently.

Rose watched her son and then exchanged a hopeful glance with Moses. This was the most interest he'd shown in horses since the flood that had killed Rascal. They'd been trying for almost six weeks to get him back to the barn, but he had steadfastly refused.

Rose turned her attention back to Susan. "Why are you asking me about this?"

"I talked to Angel's father this afternoon. He told me Angel is struggling in school because she doesn't care anything about learning."

Rose nodded but remained silent. She wanted to understand everything Susan was thinking before she responded.

"You told Amber she could train the horses, but only if her schoolwork didn't suffer," Susan continued. "She's worked hard at school because she doesn't want to lose the privilege."

Rose smiled. "That's true. Amber has done extremely well."

Susan took a breath. "I'm wondering if the same conditions would work for Angel." She hesitated for a long moment. "I don't want to add pressure to her life, though. She already has so much to deal with."

Rose considered the proposition carefully. Amber was a bright, intelligent girl who simply thought horses were much more important than schoolwork. It had been easy to force the issue by threatening the withdrawal of some barn privileges. Angel, on the other hand, was still deeply impacted by the trauma she had experienced. From what Susan was saying, the girl had developed a bond with the abused mare, but Rose was all too aware that Angel was fragile. Pushing her too hard could cause more damage.

"Why not have her read to Friday?"

Rose turned startled eyes to Felicia. "What?"

"Have Angel read to Friday," Felicia said. "She won't think it's schoolwork. I don't know if it would help the horse or not..." Her voice trailed off uncertainly.

Rose grinned at her daughter. "It's a fabulous idea, Felicia!"

"I agree," Phoebe said enthusiastically. "Anything that will get Angel reading will be a positive thing."

Susan thumped her fist on the table, a wide smile on her face. "It's a brilliant idea, Felicia. I know it will do good things for Angel, but it's also a wonderful idea to help Friday. Angel reading to her will keep her calm, and also strengthen the bond she has with Angel. After all Friday has been through, it's going to be extremely hard for her to trust."

Rose was watching Felicia as Susan spoke to her. She didn't miss the flash of vulnerability in her daughter's eyes when Susan talked about Friday's ability to trust. Shooting a quick look at Moses, she realized he'd seen the same thing. Rose had found no more painful poetry since her earlier discovery, but Felicia remained withdrawn and distant. She was helping at the school, but she no longer had the same enthusiasm. All of Rose's attempts to get Felicia to open up and talk had been met with an insistence that she was fine.

Rose returned to the conversation at hand. "The only stipulation I insist upon is that Angel come to school. We won't demand anything, but I want her there. Isolation won't help her."

"It might be what she needs sometimes," Felicia said quietly, looking as if she regretted speaking as soon as the words came out.

"What do you mean, dear?" Abby asked, her gray eyes soft with compassion.

Felicia took a deep breath. "Just that sometimes you need time alone...to come to grips with things that have happened to you."

Rose thought of all the time Felicia was spending alone in the library. Her daughter's desire to study and learn was far from unusual, but there had been many times she had walked in to discover her daughter doing nothing but staring out the window.

"Daniel told me that Angel has already asked if she can sleep in the barn with Friday tonight," Susan said.

"Let her," Felicia's voice was tight with intensity.

Rose realized that Felicia must have overheard the talk at some point about what had happened to Daniel and his young daughter. She clearly understood what Angel was feeling. "What did Daniel think?" she asked Susan.

"He said anything that will help Angel is fine with him."

"You let that girl stay in the barn," Annie declared. "Me and Miles will keep an eye on her. We just be upstairs in our room if she needs anythin'."

"You'll make sure she goes to school in the morning?" Rose asked. She appreciated that Angel might need time for solitude, but her education was still important.

"I will," Annie promised. "I'll bring her food from the house and make sure she makes it to school every day. Amber is there bright and early every mornin', anyway. Those two girls have become right good friends. Angel and Amber can walk over to school together each day."

Rose already knew what her decision would be, but she looked to Abby for confirmation before she nodded. "All right. I'll take a book over to her after dinner."

"I'll take it," Susan offered. "I think I can convince her how beneficial it will be for Friday."

"Meaning the explanation wouldn't be the same coming from her teacher?" Rose asked with amusement.

"Would it be?" Moses asked.

Rose shook her head, easily acknowledging the truth of their observation. "Daniel says she's a good reader. I think she would enjoy *Little Women*. If not, we can try a book called *Alice's Adventures in Wonderland.*"

Susan cocked her head. "That's one I haven't heard of. What's it about?"

Phoebe smiled. "It's a wonderful book," she said eagerly, "but the story behind it is almost as wonderful. It was written five years ago by an English author named Charles Lutwidge Dodgson under the pseudonym Lewis Carroll. Originally, it was a story he made up to keep Henry Liddell's daughters occupied during a rowboat excursion."

"Henry Liddell?" Felicia asked. "I've heard that name, but I can't place it."

"Henry Liddell is Vice-Chancellor of Oxford University," Phoebe responded, and then returned to the story. "While they were rowing, Dodgson told the girls a story that featured a bored little girl named Alice who goes looking for an adventure and falls through a rabbit hole into a fantasy world with wonderful animals. Alice was the name of Liddell's ten-year-old daughter. The girls loved it and asked him to write it down. He started to work on it, but a month later he made another boat trip with the girls. When he told the story this time, after they begged him to repeat it, he elaborated the plot quite a bit. When he got home from that trip, he began working on the manuscript in earnest." Phoebe paused and took a drink of her hot tea. "In 1864 he gave Alice the handwritten manuscript of *Alice's Adventures Under Ground* as a Christmas gift. It wasn't the complete book, however. He added more to it after that, and then published it the next year as *Alice's Adventures In Wonderland*."

"How wonderful to know the background of the book," Abby said with a smile. "I read it to Hope and John. They both loved it."

Rose looked toward John for confirmation, but he was already sound asleep, his head resting on his father's arm.

She smiled tenderly. "We have a little boy that needs to go to bed."

Moses grinned down at his son's sleeping head before standing to scoop him up in his arms. "I'm taking this one upstairs." Once John was secured in his powerful arms, he added. "For what it's worth, I think Angel should read *Alice's Adventures in Wonderland.* *Little Women* is a great book, but I believe she had benefit from some fantasy."

Rose nodded. "I think you're right. *Alice's Adventures In Wonderland*, it is." She retrieved it from the library and handed it to Susan. "I hope this will help Angel."

Chapter Thirteen

Rose stepped out onto the porch, confused as to why she had felt compelled to climb out of her bed on such a frigid night. The sky was luminous with glowing stars, but they certainly offered no warmth. She pulled her coat around her tightly, but it had no effect on the freezing cold air buffeting her. Plumes of steam released from her mouth were quickly pulled away by the wind. She thought longingly of her soft, warm bed, but tightened her red wool scarf around her face and walked toward the barn.

She wasn't alarmed, merely curious. She had felt the premonition of danger before, but she didn't believe the plantation was in jeopardy. Something different was pulling her forward.

Rose heard Angel even before she reached the barn. The words, spoken lightly and easily, seemed to swirl in the air around her before being carried away with the wind.

"All right, Friday. We've already read this book once, but we both love it, so I'm going to read it again."

Rose smiled. In the last three weeks, Angel had begun to come to life. There was still a fearful glaze to her eyes, and she still steered clear of everyone except Amber, but the haunted look had lessened, and she was actually paying attention in school. She had never raised her hand to answer a question, but Rose didn't care. She was glad for any small amount of progress.

She thought back to Felicia's arrival on the plantation. The young girl had also been traumatized. It had been a long time before she could trust enough to accept their love. The thought made her frown. While Angel seemed to be slowly softening, Felicia seemed to solidify the hard shell around her a little more each day. Neither Rose nor Moses understood what was going on. All of them were slathering the girl with love, but they couldn't see that it was making a difference. Abby continued to encourage them that it was, and that they needed to give Felicia time. There was really no other choice.

As she silently entered the barn, she could barely make out Angel's lithe form outlined in the light of a lantern secured on a platform in Friday's stall. Clint had built the little platform so Angel would have light to read by, while ensuring there was no danger of fire. Friday was standing close, her head dropped to the little girl's level as if she were listening intently.

"Chapter one. Down The Rabbit Hole.

Alice was beginning to get very tired of sitting by her sister on the bank, and of having nothing to do: once or twice she had peeped into the book her sister was reading, but it had no pictures or conversations in it, 'and what is the use of a book,' thought Alice, 'without pictures or conversations?'

So she was considering in her own mind, (as well as she could, for the hot day made her feel very sleepy and stupid) whether the pleasure of making a daisy-chain was worth the trouble of getting up and picking the daisies, when suddenly a white rabbit with pink eyes ran close by her.

There was nothing so very remarkable in that; nor did Alice think it so very much out of the way to hear the Rabbit say to itself, 'Oh dear! Oh dear! I shall be too late!' (when she thought it over afterwards, it occurred to her that she ought to have wondered at this, but at the time it all seemed

quite natural); but when the Rabbit actually took a watch
out of its waistcoat-pocket, *looked at it, and then hurried
on, Alice started to her feet, for it flashed across her mind
that she had never before seen a rabbit with either a
waistcoat-pocket, or a watch to take out of it, and, burning
with curiosity, she ran across the field after it, and was just
in time to see it pop down a large rabbit-hole under the
hedge.*

*In another moment down went Alice after it, never once
considering how in the world she was to get out again.*

*The rabbit-hole went straight on like a tunnel for some
way, and then dipped suddenly down, so suddenly that
Alice had not a moment to think about stopping herself
before she found herself falling down what seemed to be a
very...deep...well..."*

Angel stopped reading, her voice trailing off gradually.

Rose stepped forward soundlessly, content to listen
and watch.

Friday snuffled out a soft breath and reached her
muzzle down to nudge Angel's shoulder.

"I know that Alice is dropping down into a new world,"
Angel said, her words sounding as if she was on the edge
of tears. "I wish I could do the same thing, Friday. You've
kind of done that by coming here, though. I guess I
have...but everything is still all messed up. I can't stop
being afraid." Tears muffled her words. "And I can't quit
missing my mama. And my brother and sisters."

Friday nickered as if in response.

Rose felt tears tighten her throat. Angel carried so
much pain. So did Friday. While the mare allowed Angel
to sleep in her stall, she wouldn't let anyone else near her.
Friday would let Angel groom her, but if Angel moved too

quickly, she still shied away in terror. She had learned the lesson of the whip far too well.

Susan wasn't sure the mare would ever be normal, but no one was giving up yet. Certainly not Angel.

"Friday, I hate that I don't even know what happened that night. I remember my mama tucking me into bed and kissing me goodnight. It was a real cold night and my quilt felt real good, even if I did share it with my three sisters. Mama sang us some songs and then told us to go to sleep. I had spent the day carrying in a lot of firewood, so I was real tired. Mama had made cornbread and buttermilk for supper that night. I ate every bite of mine 'cause it was so good..."

Angel's voice trailed off.

Rose envisioned the homey scene Angel was depicting. Somehow, it made it worse to know Angel had been so well loved and cared for. To have it all ripped away had been perhaps more devastating than if she had never known it. Rose scolded herself as soon as the thought popped into her head. However violently her family had been taken from her, Angel had the foundation of a loving home. Surely that reality, and her father's love, would carry her through.

"I feel real bad 'cause I never heard a thing, Friday. I never heard the gunshots. I never heard those men. I never heard my father yell. Never heard my mother scream..." Angel's voice faltered. "I never heard my three sisters run into the main room. I never heard my little brother get up. I just laid there like a log and slept." Her voice was full of loathing and self-contempt. "Almost my whole family got killed and I never *heard* it!"

Rose knew it was the only reason Angel was still alive, but it was easy to see it from the girl's perspective. Why had she been the one to survive?

"Why wasn't I killed?" Angel demanded, echoing Rose's thoughts. "There isn't anything special about me. Why am I still alive?"

Rose understood the question too well. Hundreds of thousands had died during the war. Blacks were being murdered all over the South. Why was she alive? Why was Moses still alive? Why were any of them still living when so many had died? She was aware it was a question to which she would never have a true answer.

Her mama's voice, as if summoned by her thoughts, rang through her head. *"Rose, girl, you ain't gonna get the answer to eber question you gots rollin' in that head of yorn. There be some things that only God eber gonna know. I figur' if I still be livin', when so many folks be dyin', that dere be a reason. I gots to look for all the ways I can do good. I gots to look for all the ways I can love folks around me. I reckon someday I might get me an answer, but I figure I gots to be dead to get that answer. I ain't in no real hurry for it."*

Rose breathed in the comfort of her mama's presence and firm voice. She wished she could take Angel to her. Her mama would have known how to help the girl get past her grief.

Rose wrestled her attention back to Angel as the girl continued her story to the attentive mare.

"When those bad men from the KKK thought they had killed all of us, they set our house on fire. My daddy had been shot, but he managed to crawl back to me. He knew I was somehow still alive. He woke me up just in time for us to crawl out the window. I could feel the heat of the fire on my legs when we were climbing out."

Rose sucked in her breath, feeling the fear vibrating in Angel's voice.

"We ran into the dark woods. I didn't know right then that the KKK could be after us, but my daddy did. He wouldn't let me say a word. We stumbled around a whole lot. I was trying to help my daddy 'cause he was hurt so bad, but it was too dark to see. We fell a bunch of times. I kept getting up because I knew my daddy needed help." Her voice caught. "Friday, I didn't know right then that everyone else was dead. My daddy didn't tell me until the next morning. I didn't know where everyone else was, and I didn't know why we were crawling out the window, but I never imagined it was because everyone was *dead*." This time her words were swallowed by a sob.

"Everyone died, Friday. My whole family is dead!"

Rose started forward as sobs wracked Angel's body but stopped when Friday lowered her head and moved closer.

"They're dead," Angel wailed. "They're all *dead!*"

Rose heard Annie coming down the stairs from her room but raised a hand to stop her. "Wait," she mouthed silently.

Friday stepped all the way up to Angel and nudged her shoulder. When she got no response, the mare butted Angel gently with her head.

Finally, Angel registered what the mare was doing. "Friday!" she cried, throwing her arms around the mare's neck and burying herself against the horse's warm body. "Why are they all dead?" Her words seemed to spiral up and swirl in the air above the stall.

Rose watched in amazement. Friday didn't shy away or toss her head in protest. The mare nickered and rested her head against Angel's back, seeming to pull her closer into an embrace.

Angel sank into the horse, her entire body heaving with sobs.

Rose watched silently, recognizing the healing that was taking place. She remembered the nights she had spent with her mama, her head buried in the wise woman's lap as she cried out her pain and misery.

She knew she had also witnessed a miracle with Friday. A little girl's love, and then a little girl's pain, had helped the mare move beyond her own fear and pain to return the love she had been so freely given.

"Will you look at that?"

Annie's whisper sounded in Rose's ear. Rose nodded but kept her eyes on the miracle in front of her. She reached down and took Annie's hand.

The two women watched until Angel finally sank down into the straw, obviously too exhausted to stand any longer.

Rose's mouth dropped open when Friday carefully lowered herself to her knees, folded her back legs beneath her, and laid down. Angel, her eyes swollen with tears, cuddled into the horse, pulled several blankets close, and laid her head on Friday's side. Moments later, she was sound asleep.

Friday looked through the darkness, met Rose's eyes for a long moment, and then rested her head on Angel's back.

Four days later, Susan, Rose, Abby, Amber, Felicia, Annie and Phoebe were waiting for Angel when she emerged from Friday's stall in time to prepare for school.

Angel blinked her eyes sleepily before they widened with alarm. "What's wrong?" she cried. "Did something happen?"

Friday stuck her head over the door of the stall, her eyes wide with concern. Granite's head popped over his stall door next. Soon, the entire barn was ringing with questioning neighs and whinnies.

"Heavens!" Annie said. "I don't believe we asked none of you horses for your opinion!"

The other women chuckled, as Susan stepped forward to put her arm around Angel's shoulder.

Rose noticed with satisfaction that Angel didn't pull away; she merely looked up with a question. "All of you are laughing. Does that mean everything is alright?"

"Everything is fine," Susan assured her. "In fact, it's more than fine. I'd say this is a very special morning."

"It is?" Angel's eyes were wide in her face again. "Why? Did I miss something? Is it someone's birthday?" As she asked the question, her voice faltered. "It's..."

"Yes," Susan said gently. "It *is* someone's birthday. Your father told me it's *yours*. Today is December seventh, 1870. You turn fourteen today."

Angel looked around at the women. "I guess it is," she said in wonder. "I didn't remember."

"I think you're always going to remember this one," Amber said brightly.

"I am?" Angel continued to look around. "Why?"

Amber grinned. "Because you're about to get a present you're never going to forget!"

Susan smiled down at Angel when the girl peered up at her. "Angel, we've watched a miracle happen in the last month. You've taken a terrified, abused mare and turned her into a gentle animal that anyone is safe around."

Angel glanced over her shoulder. "Friday is the best horse in the world," she said fervently. "She's even starting to put on some weight. Pretty soon, she'll look as good as any other horse here. *Better* than most," she boasted.

Susan wasn't sure that was true, but the filter of Angel's love had transformed Friday into a gorgeous animal in her eyes. That made what she was getting ready to do even sweeter. "Then I take it you'll be proud to be her owner?"

Angel sucked in her breath. "What did you say?"

Susan's smile broadened. "I asked if you would be proud to be Friday's new owner."

Angel's mouth dropped open as she stared at the assembled women and then turned around to gaze at Friday again. "Friday's *owner*?" Her voice faltered and she swallowed hard. "You're giving...Friday to...me?" she asked, the disbelief dripping from her words. "For my birthday present?" Her voice started to shake. "Friday is *mine*?"

"I figure she's covered all the angles," Rose said with delight.

Amber rushed over to wrap Angel in a huge hug. "Happy birthday!" she cried. "Friday is your very own horse now!"

Angel stared around again before her face dissolved into tears.

Amber looked back at everyone uncertainly. "Did I say something wrong?"

Abby shook her head, a tender smile on her lips. "No, my dear. I believe those are happy tears."

Amber turned back to her friend. "Is she right? Are those happy tears?"

Angel managed to nod. After several minutes the tears finally slowed. She laughed suddenly and threw her arms around Friday's neck. "Did you hear them, girl? You're mine. You're all mine!"

Her face was glowing when she turned back to the group. "Thank you!" she cried. "Thank you!"

Rose stared at the girl with wonder. For this moment, at least, the pain that had engulfed Angel since she had arrived on the plantation had abated. Just like the ocean tide came and went, there would be moments of painful remembrance when Angel's agony would roll back in to swallow her, but Rose was also confident the tide would roll out again, giving Angel hope for a brighter future with each change of the tide.

Friday would see her through every tide change.

Moses, Harold, Franklin and Daniel Blue stood next to the tobacco drying barn that was starting to rise from the ground once again. With the original barn washed away by the flood, the men had worked hard to rebuild. Within a few weeks, every structure on the plantation that had been destroyed would be rebuilt.

"The men are feeling good about things," Franklin said. "There's not a one of them that doesn't understand farming is risky, but they sure appreciated everything you said after the flood, Moses. Even without their profit bonus from the harvest, they're paid better than farmhands anywhere around. They have their eyes on next year."

"They're working hard," Moses agreed. Coming up with the funds to have everything rebuilt had definitely put a dent in the plantation reserves, but they had developed those reserves for times just like this. Hours spent pouring over the books with Thomas had convinced him everything would be fine. He was determined they would be ready for next year.

"My crew is about done clearin' out that field along the river," Daniel reported. "It will take time for all that timber to dry out enough to cut for firewood, but we'll take care of it when it's ready. Once we're done, we's gonna seed it for the cover crop." He paused. "That flood took a lot, but I reckon it gave a lot, too," he mused. "The mud and silt coverin' the fields be some of the finest dirt I've ever seen during all my farmin' years. It's gonna grow a mighty fine crop next year."

"I believe you're right," Moses agreed. The flood had been devastating, but no one had lost their life, and the plantation would recover.

One of the unexpected benefits had been how his men had drawn even closer together. The men who had started with him right after the war—the ones who had received land from Thomas—were helping the newer workers. Everyone had been assured they would have food through the winter. In the last week, the greenhouse had been rebuilt and expanded, and more vegetables planted.

"What am I doing here?" Daniel asked suddenly. "I don't see any other team leaders here, and I reckon y'all already know that the field is about clear. So, what am I really doing here?"

Moses looked at Harold.

"Since the KKK murdered your family, I thought you would want to know about what's going on down in North Carolina," Harold said frankly.

Daniel nodded grimly, his eyes sparkling with both anger and pain. "I been hangin' onto hope that Governor Holden gonna make things right down there. I know he's been trying right hard."

Harold shook his head. "That won't happen, Daniel. Governor Holden is being impeached."

"Impeached?" Confusion flooded Daniel's face. "What's that?"

"It's no surprise you don't know," Harold replied. "His impeachment is the first in the nation's history." He scowled. "It shouldn't happen. Holden is a good man, and he's been a fine governor."

"But what is impeachment?" Daniel repeated. "I don't know what it means, but it don't sound good."

"It's *not* good," Moses said. "Governor Holden's war against the KKK over the summer ended most of the violence, at least for now, but their terror tactics achieved their goal," he said grimly.

"The election in North Carolina happened in August," Harold added, "right in the middle of the militia campaign to squelch the KKK. The conservative press reported unfairly and inaccurately."

"You mean they lied about what was really goin' on," Daniel said angrily.

"Yes," Harold agreed. "The barrage of newspaper articles from the conservative press shifted voting. People believed what they read, even though it wasn't true. When the election was over, the Conservative Democrats were once more in charge of North Carolina."

Daniel gritted his teeth. "What does that mean?"

Harold scowled. "When the new General Assembly met for the first time in November, they wasted little time initiating impeachment proceedings against Holden. A few days ago, Representative Frederick Strudwick introduced an impeachment resolution to the House of Representatives, and they approved it. The whole thing has to go to trial, but everyone knows what the result will be."

Daniel shook his head with frustration. "I'm sorry, but I still don't understand what impeachment is."

"It means the Democrats in North Carolina are going to kick Governor Holden out of office and probably put him in jail," Moses said bluntly.

Daniel swung around to stare at Moses and then looked back at Harold. "Is he right?"

"I'm afraid so."

"That ain't right," Daniel protested. "He's a good man. His tryin' to fight the KKK is what gave me the courage to say I would testify at that trial." His eyes darkened as his face tightened. "The governor is getting kicked out of office. My family was murdered." He clenched his fists angrily. "Does that mean the Klan just gonna take over things in North Carolina?"

A somber silence fell on the four men as they stared out over the fields in the distance.

"It means they're in a position to do just that," Harold admitted.

"I thought all the Reconstruction policies were put in place to keep that from happening." Franklin protested. "What went wrong?"

Harold narrowed his eyes. "As far as I'm concerned, the Klan and its conservative supporters are traitors to the

United States. Nothing has changed since they joined the Confederacy. They lost the war, but now we're learning how much influence the former Confederates still hold in the state," he said bitterly.

Franklin shook his head. "But why isn't the Federal Government enforcing the provisions of the amendments they passed? The Fourteenth and Fifteenth Amendments mean this stuff shouldn't be happening."

Harold met his eyes evenly. "That's true, and Governor Holden advocated for federal intervention for months. They refused."

"But why?" Daniel demanded.

Harold's frustration was evident in his eyes. "Politics are difficult to understand."

"Seems they ain't nothing but wrong if things like this are allowed to happen," Daniel said flatly.

"I agree with you," Harold responded. "Unfortunately, ours are not the voices that are being heard."

"The Klan be makin' sure no black folks at all be heard from," Daniel replied. "At least not in North Carolina. Is it that bad here in Virginia?"

"Not yet," Moses said grimly. "A lot of people are working to make sure things like this don't happen."

Franklin frowned. "Democrats are taking back power all over the state, Moses."

Moses met his eyes, wishing he could refute his words. "Yes," he said heavily. He shook his head. "I wish I could predict the future, but I can't."

Daniel eyed him. "It don't look so good, though, do it?"

Moses slowly shook his head. "No, I'm afraid it doesn't." He hated saying the words, but they were the truth.

"You don't think the government will do *anything* to stop the KKK and all the other groups who are killing and terrorizing black folks, and all the white folks who are helping us?" Franklin demanded.

"There are people in Congress right now who are trying to push through more enforcement acts to stop the Ku Klux Klan and other similar groups," Harold said. "Unfortunately, whatever happens, the actions have come too late to save the Republican Party in North Carolina."

"And now a precedent has been set," Moses stated heavily. "Other states will attempt to follow their lead."

Harold and Moses watched Franklin and Daniel ride away.

"Daniel has every right to be angry and disillusioned," Moses said.

"Along with every person, black or white, who has been a target of the KKK in North Carolina," Harold replied. "Governor Holden tried to do the right thing..."

"But the South has no intention of changing," Moses said heavily.

"We can't assume that for every state," Harold protested.

Moses raised a brow. "You know as well as I do what's going to eventually happen. I can hear it in your voice."

Harold opened his mouth to argue, but his shoulders sagged as he nodded his head. "Our Federal Government couldn't stop a war that destroyed millions of people's lives. I fear they won't be able to stop what's coming to the South, either." He shook his head fiercely. "There are many that are trying to do the right thing, though."

"There are," Moses agreed, the pain of futility squeezing his heart.

Harold stared at him. "We can't give up, Moses."

"No, we can't. I have children who are counting on me to not give up. I won't quit fighting," Moses vowed, his voice coated with bitter sorrow. "When the dark clouds cover this country again, at least I'll know I did everything I could to keep them from taking over."

Harold turned to look over the fields. "Just like the war tried to destroy America, the flood tried to destroy the plantation. Both did a tremendous amount of damage, but good things were also accomplished."

"I can appreciate the value of the silt left behind from the floods, but what possible good did the war bring?"

"Lincoln set over three million slaves free," Harold said quietly. "I would like to think it would have happened anyway, but it was the pressure of the war that made Lincoln take that action. Life is still terribly hard for your people, but at least you'll never be slaves again. You have the ability to fight for equal rights."

"Do we?" Frustration tightened Moses' voice. "Too many of those fighting are being slaughtered by the KKK and other groups. Daniel had most of his family murdered because he was willing to testify at trial. The Federal Government is allowing the Conservative Democrats to take back control of the South. What was the purpose of the war, of all the lives taken, if they're going to let that happen? Why did so many have to die?" Moses gritted his teeth. "We may be free, but as long as we aren't free to have a voice, what difference does it make?"

Janie looked up from her book when a knock sounded at the door. She had been completely absorbed in her studies since returning to Philadelphia several weeks ago. It had been difficult to return to school after so long away, but she was determined to finish her degree. "Are we expecting someone?"

"No," Matthew replied as Annabelle, roused from her nap, began to cry. "Keep studying," he urged. "I'll find out who is at the door." He scooped his daughter up into his arms, tucked the blanket around her to protect her from cold air at the door, and strode over to answer it.

"Telegram delivery."

Janie pushed back from her desk, all concentration lost as the delivery boy's voice rang through the house. Who had sent them a telegram? The few she had received in her life had always contained bad news. She braced herself for what was to come.

"Thank you," Matthew responded, stepping back in to close the door.

"Go ahead and read it," Janie urged as she reached for their daughter. Robert, sound asleep upstairs, hadn't heard the knock. Annabelle had stopped crying and was merely looking around with interest. "That's my girl," she cooed.

Matthew opened the telegram envelope carefully. A moment later he looked up with a smile and began to read.

Safe in Paris. Staying with father's friend, Foreign Minister Washburne. Both working at American Hospital. Home when possible.

Florence

"Florence is safe!" Janie exclaimed. "What wonderful news!" Then she paused. "How long ago was that telegram sent?" Her friend may have been safe when she sent it, but the situation could have changed.

Matthew scanned the telegram. "It was sent two days ago, but that doesn't mean it was written two days ago." He frowned. "Peter told me almost all communications have been cut off from the city. The only messages getting out are being transported by hot air balloon. The only communications *reaching* Paris are being sent by carrier pigeon."

Janie stared at him in astonishment. "That's certainly something you forgot to tell me."

"I talked to Peter two days ago," Matthew replied. "He's in town for an assignment. I knew you would want all the details, but I wasn't going to distract you from your big test tomorrow. I was going to tell you tomorrow night at supper."

"You might as well tell me now." Janie cradled Annabelle close as she walked over to settle next to the fireplace. She pulled a brightly colored, knitted afghan over them. "I'm as ready for this test as I'm ever going to be. I'm much more interested in hot air balloons and carrier pigeons right now."

Matthew smiled as he joined her. "It's quite fascinating," he began.

The afternoon passed quickly as he told her everything Peter had learned.

"Do you really believe Florence is safe?" Janie pressed.

"I do," Matthew said confidently. "Paris is under siege, but there have been no attacks on the city. So long as Florence and her father are with the minister, I'm sure she'll be safe."

"But Florence and Dr. Robinson are working in a hospital there," Janie reminded him. "What happens if Paris is attacked while they're at work?"

Chapter Fourteen

Carrie laughed with joy when Janie read the telegram from Florence. "That's wonderful!" she cried.

"She could still be in danger," Janie reminded her.

"We could all die at any time," Carrie replied philosophically. "At least we know that Florence has a safe place to live in Paris, and that she and her father are able to make a difference. You know our friend—she would be crazy with worry and boredom if she couldn't stay busy."

Janie smiled. "You're right. I wager she'll come home fluent in French."

"I'm not betting when I'm confident you're one hundred percent correct." Carrie lifted her nose and sniffed. "I'd say Deirdre is about to pull that pot roast out of the oven."

"I'd say you're right. It smells heavenly."

Carrie felt a twinge of sadness. "I can hardly wait to return home to the plantation next week, but I'm going to miss Deirdre and her children. They've become an important part of our family."

"Were you able to get her another job?"

"Yes," Carrie said happily as she pushed her sadness away. "Dr. Wild has decided to hire her. His practice continues to grow, and he's tired of eating out all the time. Deirdre met him, liked him, and is thrilled to have a job waiting for her when we leave."

Janie gazed at her. "Can you believe it's almost all over? After so many years of school and study, can you believe it's all going to be behind you?"

Carrie shook her head. "It doesn't seem real yet. I think back to all the years during the war when it seemed increasingly impossible that I would ever be able to attend medical school. And then so much has happened that slowed it all down." She paused as memories assailed her.

Janie, sympathy filling her eyes, reached out to take her hand.

Carrie summoned a smile, pushing back the desire that Robert could somehow know she was close to reaching her goal. She was gloriously happy, but she knew there would always be a void where he had been. "I'm eager to move into the next phase of my life. I'll always have to study and learn to keep abreast of new developments, but knowing the plantation will be my home again is an amazing feeling."

"Mama!"

Carrie smiled when Frances bounded into the room. "Yes, my dear?"

"Can Minnie stay late tonight and have Daddy take her home?"

"I don't know," Carrie responded. "Can she?"

Frances stared at her. "What do you mean? That's what I just asked *you.*" Suddenly her puzzled expression evaporated. "*May* Minnie stay late, please?"

"Much better," Carrie replied. "Now, why do you want her to stay here after her mother leaves?" She wasn't sure how Anthony would feel about going back out on such a frigid night.

Frances glanced toward the kitchen and lowered her voice to a dramatic whisper. "Minnie is knitting a scarf for her mama for her birthday next week. I taught her how to knit in the last few days, but she needs my help. Don't you think that's a good reason?"

"That's a good reason," Carrie agreed, proud of her daughter for teaching Minnie to knit. "Yes, of course she may stay."

"Thank you!" Frances grinned widely and turned to run from the room.

Janie smiled as she disappeared. "Those two are so close."

"Yes," Carrie agreed. "I'm told they're the first best friends either of the girls have had. They spend hours in Frances' room talking and laughing. Minnie is almost five years younger than Frances, but she is mature beyond her years."

"And Deirdre doesn't mind?"

"No. We've talked about it. She's glad for Minnie to have new experiences. When Deirdre came to Ireland, she wanted a new life for her children. She's determined to give it to them."

Janie raised her brow and changed the subject. "You taught Frances how to knit? I've never seen you knit a stitch in your life."

"Not a chance," Carrie said with a laugh. "My mother forced me to knit when I was a child, but I completely forgot it as soon as I could. Deirdre taught her how to knit."

"Then...?"

"Why didn't Deirdre teach Minnie how to knit? Because her daughter didn't care anything about it until her mother taught *Frances* how to knit. Evidently, my daughter has quite a talent for it."

"That explains it. I was confident it hadn't passed down from you," Janie teased.

"You have every right to be confident," Carrie replied. "My mother eventually threw up her hands and admitted defeat. Anyway, Minnie felt badly about not letting her mother teach her to knit, so she asked Frances to teach her when she suddenly developed a desire. I'm sure the scarf she's knitting is meant to be a surprise—not just for Deirdre's birthday, but also to show her that she learned how."

Deirdre appeared in the doorway, her auburn hair curling around her flushed face, red from the heat of the kitchen. "Your dinner is ready," she announced. "You're having a pot roast, mashed potatoes and green beans that I canned over the summer. Dessert is bread pudding."

Janie grinned. "It sounds wonderful, Deirdre. I always love when we're invited to dinner. I've learned how to cook, but we never eat as well as we do when we're eating your cooking."

Deirdre smiled. "I hope you enjoy it, Janie." Then she turned to Carrie. "Are you sure you don't mind me leaving early?"

"Not a bit," Carrie assured her. "I want you to go home and be with your children. They're sick and need their mama." She glanced at Janie. "Her two daughters have a bad cold."

"Their older brother is watching them," Deirdre explained, and then hesitated. "I'm sure they'll be fine if I stay a little longer. Minnie told me you were going to let her stay late, but it's not right for Anthony to bring her home on such a cold night," she said worriedly.

"It's not a problem," Carrie promised her. "The girls are working on a special project." When Deirdre still hesitated, she added, "I understand someone has a *birthday* next week..." She smiled when Deirdre's eyes widened. "Go be with your other children. Anthony will be happy to bring Minnie home. It won't be too late."

Janie nodded her head toward the library when Deirdre left. "What are our two men doing in there?"

"Solving some problem in the world, I'm sure," Carrie responded, leaning her head against the back of the green brocade sofa. She relished the heat from the roaring fireplace. "I wish Jeremy and Marietta could have joined us tonight."

"They wanted to, but Marietta felt it best if she stays home. She was out back of their house playing with the twins when she stepped into that hole. I imagine it's courtesy of the dog Jeremy brought home for the twins last week."

Carrie frowned. "Did she sprain her ankle badly? Annie is counting on them coming for Christmas. She misses all of them, but she misses the twins especially."

"She'll be able to travel," Janie assured Carrie. "I wrapped her ankle and gave her a supply of arnica. I also gave her my children," she added with a laugh. "When I left them, all the children except Annabelle were on the floor playing with their dog, Midnight. Jeremy assured us it would be all right. Matthew and I have so few nights out now, I decided to accept his offer."

"As you should have," Carrie assured her. "Parenting young children can be exhausting."

Janie smiled, but eyed her closely. "Do you regret not having another baby, Carrie? I know how much you love Francis, but I wonder sometimes how you feel about not having a child of your own?"

"I *do* have a child of my own," Carrie said firmly. "I couldn't love Frances more if I had birthed her myself." She pushed aside memories of Bridget. She had learned to accept the pain, but she knew it would never leave her heart. It had lessened over the years, but it still lingered in her soul. It always would.

"Have you and Anthony decided to not have more children?" Janie asked gently. "I know your position when you married, but has that changed? I've been afraid to ask..."

Carrie didn't mind such a personal question coming from Janie. "We've talked about it. Anthony knew before we married that it could be dangerous for me to get pregnant again. There have been many times when I thought it would be worth the risk, but he keeps telling me that I'm more important than children." She smiled as she thought of how much her husband loved her.

"He's right," Janie said staunchly. "I'm glad he feels that way. I know how much you wanted children, Carrie, but we almost lost you..."

"I know," Carrie replied, "but that doesn't mean I don't dream of holding a baby in my arms." She pushed aside the longing that swelled throughout her.

"Would you consider adopting more?"

Carrie nodded, grateful to leave aside the topic of her inability to have a baby. "We've talked about it," she acknowledged. "Now that I'm almost done with school, and we'll be able to move back to Virginia permanently, it's a possibility. There are so many children who desperately need a home."

"I know Frances came from an orphanage," Janie said. "I don't know much about the system, though."

"The system is failing so many children," Carrie said angrily. "Frances was within a few weeks of either being put to work in a local factory or bound out to a family."

"Bound out?"

"Before I explain that, it's helpful to understand how the system works. Until recently, children were legally considered orphans if their *father* was dead."

"Even if their mother was living?" Janie asked with surprise. "You mean the mother didn't have control of her own child?"

"Unfortunately, that's true," Carrie answered. "It hasn't improved that much in the last twenty years. Mothers still have few legal rights over their children or their property. If the husband has money when he passes away, the courts typically appoint a legal guardian to watch over the children's inheritance."

"As if their mothers don't have the brains to do it?" Janie asked with disgust.

"That pretty much sums it up," Carrie agreed. "The guardian is usually the child's closest male relative. If the mother is alive, the child usually remains in her care, but the guardian controls all the money."

Janie rolled her eyes. "And men wonder why we're so determined to get the vote!" she snapped, and then returned to the topic. "What if the child loses both parents?"

"In that case, the community takes over the care of the orphans. That might also become necessary if the mother is unable to support them. Unfortunately, that has become much more prevalent since the war. Hundreds of thousands of wives lost their husbands, or their husbands came home unable to work because of their wounds. These mothers can't find work to support their family.

There are many towns that have built orphanages especially for the children of soldiers and sailors. I believe most of them try to do their best, but the funding is limited." Her frown deepened. "That makes for some bad situations."

"Like?" Janie asked keenly.

"Children are being hired out to the factories," Carrie replied. "Others are bound out to families. Those families don't actually adopt them. They accept them as servants until they're eighteen."

"A new kind of slavery," Janie said flatly.

Carrie sighed. "That's the way I see it, too, but I honestly don't know what the solution is for the millions of children who don't have a family." She paused. "There are also the orphan trains."

"The orphan trains?" Janie asked quizzically as she raised a brow.

"Yes. In many large cities, there are simply not adequate facilities for all the orphans. Many people believe the children face brighter futures in rural areas across the country. Orphanages put children on the trains and send them off. There are evidently many willing families who show up at the train station. They choose a child, sign a contract saying they will shelter and educate them, and then they take them home."

Janie stared at her. "How well does that work?"

"The orphanages are supposed to track the welfare of each child, but it's not proving practical. There are too many children and not enough people to keep track of them. From the research I've done, it seems some children land in good homes and do extremely well, while others are basically adopted for the labor they can provide. Many of them are treated badly."

Janie shook her head. "The future of America is based on our children. What are we doing to them?"

Carrie shared her frustration but didn't have answers. A burst of laughter from above made her smile. At least one child was safe and loved.

Anthony pulled his hat down tighter on his head and wound his scarf more snuggly around his neck as he settled in to take Minnie home. It was bitterly cold, but the snow that had been threatening all day had held off. He was quite certain the city would awaken to a layer of white in the morning, but at least the roads were clear for now. "Are you okay back there, Minnie?"

"Yes, Mr. Wallington."

Anthony looked back to discern why Minnie's answer was so muffled. He laughed when he saw nothing but a mound of blankets. "Are you sure you can breathe under there?"

"I'm fine," Minnie assured him. "I have a little hole that's letting air in."

Anthony laughed again and lifted the reins to urge the carriage horse forward. "We'll be there in about fifteen minutes."

Anthony gazed around as he drove. Despite the frosty temperatures, Philadelphia was a beautiful city at night. Streets normally thronged with people were almost deserted. The brisk wind rattled through the barren trees, making their limbs clack almost in time with the clop of horse hooves on the cobbled streets. Oil lanterns cast flickering shadows that danced in time with the trees. Dimly lit windows spoke of people snug in their homes.

He frowned as they entered the neighborhood where Minnie lived. The cobblestones gave way to frozen dirt. The lack of oil lanterns made the streets dark, and the sudden absence of lighted windows spoke of the number of immigrants pouring into the city who were going without light and heat on a terribly cold night.

Anthony could feel the trouble before he saw it.

His muscles tightened as his eyes strained to see through the darkness. Moments later, the smell of smoke assaulted his nostrils. "No," he whispered.

Fire was a hazard in every American city, but Philadelphia seemed to have more than its share of disastrous conflagrations.

Anthony sucked in his breath as he rounded the final turn leading to the huge boarding house that Deirdre and her children called home. It was really nothing more than a tall, ramshackle wooden structure that had been carved into tiny units. Identical boarding facilities were stuffed onto tiny lots that gave barely four feet clearance from their neighbor.

Flames licking from a building somewhere in front of him illuminated the road. His horse stopped abruptly and threw her head up with panic. "Okay, girl," he soothed. "We don't have to go any closer." He stared into the smoke beginning to fill the street, trying to determine which building was burning. His gut clenched when he realized it was the same block where Minnie lived.

"Mr. Wallington!"

Minnie's frightened cry sounded from behind him. He turned to comfort her, but he honestly didn't know what to say. He had no idea what was happening on the other side of the thickening smoke.

"What's happening?" Minnie screamed. "Where's my mama? Where are my sisters and brother? What building is burning?"

Anthony knew the only way to answer her questions, as well as his own, was to venture through the wall of smoke. Thinking rapidly, he turned the carriage in the empty road, urged the mare to a fast trot, pulled around the corner, and set the hand brake. He hoped moving them away from the fire would keep Minnie and the horse safe.

"We can't leave!" Minnie wailed, her body twisting as she strained to look back.

"We're not leaving," Anthony promised as he leapt from the driver's seat. "I'm going back to find out what's going on. I want you to stay here."

"No!" Minnie cried. "I gotta know what's happening. What if my home is burning?" Her rich Irish brogue rang through the frosty night as people began to appear on the road, pulled from their homes by the threat of danger.

"I'll do everything I can," Anthony promised. He grabbed her hands. "It will only make it harder for me to help your family if you insist on coming. I need you to stay here."

Minnie stared at him with frightened eyes, but finally gulped and nodded. Her face rigid with fear, she whispered, "Go get my mama."

Anthony turned and ran down the street, pulling his scarf tighter around his mouth before he plunged into the smoke, grateful at least that the fire created enough light to see.

He groaned when he drew close enough to the burning building to identify it as Deirdre's home. He knew dozens of immigrant families, mostly Irish, lived in the boarding house. He strained to hear over the sound of crackling flames, mixed with screams and cries for help, but he couldn't hear bells that would indicate the fire department was on the way. He knew these neighborhoods were farther away from fire stations, and they didn't have the benefit of the fire alarm system. There was no way of knowing if an alarm had been sounded.

He breathed a sigh of relief when he saw people pouring from the front door of the boarding house. He rushed forward to see if he could identify Deirdre and her children. His eyes scanned the frightened people clutching blankets around them to buffer the cold, but he didn't find Minnie's family.

He grabbed one man as he passed. "Do you know Deirdre?"

The man nodded, his eyes wide with fear and resignation. "She and her children live on the fourth floor," he gasped.

The man's wife grabbed his hand as he doubled over in a wracking cough. "We got to get out of here, Seamus!"

Both of them turned and ran.

Anthony craned his neck to look upward. He felt sick with dread when he saw flames licking from some of the fourth and fifth-floor windows. He knew these old, wooden buildings burned quickly, and the hard wind blowing from the north would only fuel the flames. He sucked in his breath as the flames leapt to the next building, the roar of their angry advance blocking out the sounds behind him.

"Help us!" A piteous scream ripped through the night, shrill enough to be heard over the inferno.

"Help us!"

Anthony looked up just as a small windowpane was smashed out above him. He stepped back to avoid the falling glass shards, but another groan ripped from him when he recognized the face of Minnie's son, Jack.

"Help us!" Jack hollered. "Someone help us!" His face was already covered with black soot and his eyes were wide with terror.

Anthony sucked in his breath and ran toward the building.

A man grabbed his arm. "You can't go in there!" he shouted.

"I have to save a family," Anthony yelled as he ripped his arm away.

The man grabbed it again. "You won't be saving anyone on the top floors," he hollered over the noise. "You'll be doing nothing but going to your death." He tightened his grip. "The stairs are already burning."

"Mr. Wallington!"

Anthony stared up as Jack somehow identified him through the smoke. The little boy's voice was shrill enough to be heard over the noise.

"Help us, Mr. Wallington! We're trapped! My mama! My sisters!"

Anthony tensed, ready to punch the man holding him if necessary. Suddenly, a ripping sound from above revealed the roof was collapsing. A shower of sparks, followed by a curtain of flame, shot from the third and fourth-floor windows. The fifth floor was already completely engulfed.

Anthony leapt back, pulling his rescuer with him. They crashed to the ground as the flames shot over their heads.

When he raised himself on his elbow to look back up, Jack had disappeared.

Cries and screams rent the air as the flames continued to devour the building.

"The poor people never had a chance," the man who had stopped him muttered. His bleary eyes registered pain, anger and resigned acceptance. "These buildings go up so fast there ain't no stopping it."

Anthony continued to stare upward. He knew Deirdre and her family couldn't possibly have survived the explosion of flames, but his mind couldn't register what had happened. "They're all gone?"

"Aye. They're all gone," the man replied. "I was coming home from work when I saw the fire start. I was able to get most of the people off the first and second floors, but the steps collapsed before I could go any higher."

"No!"

Anthony whirled as the high scream sounded through the night. He leapt forward to grab Minnie before she could reach the burning building.

"No!" Minnie screamed. "Let me go! I have to get my family!"

Anthony held her tightly but had no idea what to say. How could he tell Minnie that her entire family had just died in the fire?

Minnie struggled for several moments and then went still in his arms. Finally, she lifted her face to reveal tears coursing down her cheeks. "What happened? Where's my family?"

Anthony took a deep breath, but still couldn't force words out. "I'm sorry," he finally said. "I'm so sorry, Minnie." He barely recognized his own voice.

Realization dawned on Minnie's face. "They're dead? Everyone is dead?"

Anthony couldn't bring himself to say the words. Instead, he pulled Minnie close to his body and let his tears join hers.

After several minutes, he picked her up and carried her back through the wall of smoke. The fire department would eventually gain control over the fire.

He had a little girl to take care of.

Carrie was nestled next to the fireplace when she heard Anthony drive up. She placed her book aside and drank the rest of her hot tea. A few minutes later, after the horse was secured in the stable, she heard the back door open, accompanied by a puff of cold wind. She pulled her afghan tighter and looked up with a smile. "Welcome home, dea—"

Pushing the afghan aside, she leapt to her feet. "Minnie!" she cried, rushing forward to inspect the little girl her husband was holding so tenderly. "Are you hurt?"

"No," Anthony said quietly, reaching down to push a stray lock of hair from Minnie's face. "She's not hurt."

Carrie stared from Anthony's face to Minnie's, finally recognizing the shocked look of pain and loss. "What happened?" she murmured. Minnie just stared at her and then shrank back against Anthony's chest as she closed her eyes tightly.

"I'm going to take her upstairs."

"Put her in bed with Frances," Carrie replied. "She needs to be close to someone."

Anthony nodded. "I'll be back once I have her settled."

Carrie watched as Anthony walked slowly back down the stairs, weariness and distress etched on every line of his face. She reached up a hand and pulled him down next to her, but didn't ask any questions. Obviously, he had been through a terrible trauma. He would tell her when he was ready.

"They're gone. They're all gone..."

Carrie's breath caught. She didn't need him to elaborate on what he meant. There could have been only one reason for him to return with Minnie. "What happened?"

"Fire," Anthony answered. He shook his head, his eyes going as blank as Minnie's. "Their whole building... The people on the first and second floors made it out." His voice caught. "No one else..."

Tears flooded Carrie's eyes. *Deirdre. Jack. Margaret. Sally.* Her head spun. "They're all dead?" she asked with disbelief.

"I tried," Anthony whispered. "I tried to go into the building to save them. The stairs..." His head dipped to his chest. "The stairs were collapsed. I couldn't reach them. Jack..." His voice broke with agony. "He called to me. He cried for help." Sobs shook his strong shoulders. "I couldn't reach him... I couldn't reach any of them."

Carrie didn't need to hear anymore. She wrapped her arms around her husband and held him tightly, mingling her own tears with his.

The wood in the fireplace had burned down to embers before Anthony could speak again. "Minnie is all alone," he said sadly. "Her entire family is gone."

The hour that had passed while she and Anthony held each other had given Carrie plenty of time to think. "Her family is gone, but she's not alone, my dear. She has us."

"But what is she going to do? We're leaving next week."

"She's coming home to Virginia with us," Carrie said calmly. "I already know she has no other relatives in America. Deirdre left all her family behind when she left Ireland. Her husband died in the flu epidemic. He was an only child. Minnie has no one to take her in."

Anthony turned questioning eyes to her.

"We've talked about adopting another child," Carrie said. "I've wondered how we could possibly pick one from all the multitudes that need a home. Now we don't have to choose one. We already love Minnie. She's already part of our family. We're taking her home with us."

"We're going to adopt her?"

Carrie paused. "As long as you think it's a good idea."

Anthony glanced toward the stairs and then nodded. "It's the perfect solution," he said. "She and Frances are already like sisters, and Frances will understand her pain like few can."

"We'll fill out the paperwork tomorrow. I'm not sure how optimal it is that adoptions are so easy, but I'm grateful for it in this situation." She glanced toward the stairs. "It will take her time to heal. That poor little girl has been traumatized."

"Yes," Anthony confirmed, "She's going to get a lot of love, though. Not only from us, but everyone on the plantation. She'll have all the time she needs to move beyond this." His eyes lost some of their hopelessness. "She's always going to miss her family, but we'll give her a good life," he vowed.

Chapter Fifteen

Carrie could scarcely contain her excitement when the carriage rolled through the gates at Cromwell Plantation. As she breathed in the frosty air, ignoring the burning cold on her cheeks, she could hardly believe she was home for good. Eleven years ago, at age eighteen, all she wanted was to leave the plantation behind her.

Minnie gazed around in wonder as they rolled down the cedar-lined drive. "This is really all yours?"

"Well, it's partly yours now, too," Frances said excitedly. "Now that you're a Wallington!"

Carrie understood the combination of wonder and pain that flashed in Minnie's eyes. She sat back and wrapped her arm around the slender girl's shoulder. "Welcome to Cromwell Plantation, Minnie."

Minnie continued to gaze around her. "I wish Mama could have seen this," she whispered. "And Jack." Her voice caught. "And Margaret...and Sally."

"I do, too," Carrie said tenderly. "I know they would have loved it."

Minnie bit her lip and gave a small, brave smile. "Mama would be real glad I have a place like this to live in. When we were still in Ireland, she used to describe a place to me that was just like this. I was young, but I remember it because of the smile she always had when she told me."

"She did?" Frances asked. "What did she say?"

"She told me that when we got to America we would live in a big house out in the country. We would never be afraid, and we would never be hungry. She told me it would be beautiful all the time." Minnie's voice faltered. "And that we would all be happy."

Carrie took her gloved hand. "Then I believe your mama would be very happy that you're here."

Minnie nodded, but tears glistened in her eyes. "She said *all* of us would be happy, though. She didn't say anything about just me."

"I know," Carrie said softly. "I know." It had been only a week since Deirdre and the rest of her children had perished in the fire that had claimed an additional seventy-five men, women and children. Minnie still had moments where she forgot her whole family had been lost. She would call out for her mama, or recall something Jack had said to her. At those moments, her eyes would light for a brief second, just before her face would crumple into tears.

Carrie pulled her into her arms, while Frances grabbed Minnie's hand and squeezed tightly.

The carriage continued to roll down the drive.

"I have something to tell you," Frances said to Minnie.

"What?" Minnie managed to ask as she gulped back her tears.

"Your mama was right. It's a *real* big house," Frances told her. "I couldn't believe it the first time I saw it. The house I grew up in was real tiny. We didn't always eat very good, and it was cold a lot."

Minnie nodded, the expression on her face far too old for her years. "I know what that's like."

"Well, you're not ever going to be hungry again," Frances declared. "And you'll never have to live in a cold house."

Minnie's expression revealed she wasn't sure that could be true.

"It's not all easy, though," Frances said solemnly.

Minnie nodded. "I'm figuring I'll have to work while I'm here," she said somberly. "There ain't nothing in life for free. My mama taught me that. So did my daddy before he died."

Frances looked startled, but then compassionate.

Carrie knew Frances was remembering the day she had met Minnie, after the factory accident that ripped part of her scalp off.

"You don't have to work here, Minnie. Sometimes I help Miss Annie in the kitchen," Frances said. "And sometimes I help watch the little children, but that's not what I mean about everything not being easy," she said quickly. "I'm talking about the fact that every word that comes out of your mouth has to go through the 'Rose Filter.'"

Carrie scarcely contained the laugh that threatened to explode from her lips.

"The rose filter?" Minnie asked. "What's that?"

"Mama's best friend is named Rose," Frances said seriously. "She's a schoolteacher. She makes you say every word just right. She says it's because she's concerned about our future."

"Is she real mean about it?" Minnie asked nervously. "I been trying to talk better but I don't always get it right."

"No," Frances assured her. "I heard Miss Annie say one time that there ain't a mean bone in Rose's body. But she'll make you say it right, just the same."

Minnie frowned. "I don't think *ain't* is a word you should use. You just said it."

"Oh, that's just how Miss Annie talks," Frances explained.

"How come Miss Annie gets to talk that way? Why don't Rose make her talk right?"

Carrie put a hand over her mouth to contain her mirth. She could tell by Anthony's shaking shoulders that he had already lost the battle, but at least he didn't have to look at the girls with a straight face.

"Because Miss Annie does whatever she wants," Frances said quickly. "You don't ever want to do anything Miss Annie doesn't want you to. Rose is married to Miss Annie's son, Moses, and he's almost as big as a tree. Miss Annie isn't as tall as him, but she's almost as big around." She paused. "It's more than that, though. Miss Annie cooks all the food on the plantation. She came to live here when the war was over. Moses went and found her. Anyway, she's the best cook in the world."

Minnie's eyes narrowed. "You take that back, Frances. There ain't no better cook than my mama!"

Frances recognized her mistake quickly. "I meant that she's the best cook in the world now that your mama is gone."

Minnie considered that and then nodded. "I guess that's all right."

"I think you should know, too, that Miss Annie comes across real gruff sometimes, but she is real nice. For some reason, she doesn't want people to know that, but I figured it out."

Carrie listened as the girls continued to chat, and Frances prepared Minnie for plantation life the best she could. Carrie was confident Minnie would be happy on the plantation, but she knew it would be a huge adjustment.

A shrill neigh split the winter air.

Minnie bolted forward. "What was that?"

Frances grinned. "That was Granite. He's Mama's horse. He always knows when she's coming, and he always greets her just like that. You'll see him in a second."

Carrie leaned forward as the carriage rounded the last curve. She always wanted to remember the moment she returned home for good. She held her breath as the plantation house came into view. Its white coat gleamed under the weak winter sun. The pillars stood out against the magnolia trees that flanked the porch, while the gray branches of the sheltering oak trees reached for the skies.

Another neigh sounded, accompanied by pounding hoofbeats.

Anthony, without being asked, pulled the carriage to a stop so Carrie could jump out. She heard Frances' voice as she ran to greet her horse.

"Mama always does that. She loves Granite as much as he loves her."

Carrie reached the fence at the exact same moment Granite did. She was bundled up too much against the cold to climb the fence, so she had to content herself with throwing her arms around his neck and burying her head against his solid warmth. "I'm home, boy. We're never going to be apart again. Thank you for waiting for me."

Granite rested his head on her shoulder and gave a contented sigh.

Carrie stood that way for several minutes before she stepped back. "I'll see you again soon. Right now, I have a little girl that needs to be introduced to her new home and family. You can meet her tomorrow." Granite eyed her closely and then bobbed his head as if he understood every word. Tears of joy clouded Carrie's vision. She brushed them away and then ran back to the carriage. "Let's go!"

Carrie wasn't surprised to see everyone lined up on the porch. "They're all waiting to meet you, Minnie," she said softly.

Minnie stared at the assembly on the porch with wide eyes. "All those people live here?"

"Somewhere on the plantation," Carrie responded. "They don't all live right here in the house, but they all wanted to meet you when you arrived."

"Why?"

Carrie bit back her smile at the girl's blunt question. She had always loved Minnie's directness and was glad to see her grief hadn't changed that. "Because you're part of our family now. Family is very important to every person on that porch. That makes *you* very important."

"You're going to love everyone," Frances told her. "I promise."

Minnie nodded hesitantly, and then gazed up at Carrie. "Nobody can replace my family, Miss Carrie. I appreciate what you're doing, and I know my mama would be real glad, but they will always be my family."

"I know they will, Minnie," Carrie said softly. "We're not trying to replace your family. We're giving you an *additional* family while you grow up, just like we did for Frances. We want you to be safe, and we want to give you those opportunities your mama talked about."

Minnie stared up into her eyes for a long moment, and then nodded. "Alright."

Minnie could hardly hold her eyes open when she crawled into bed with Frances. Both Carrie and Anthony were there to tell the girls goodnight.

Minnie gazed around the bedroom, her eyes resting on the lace curtains draped over the huge window. The yellow walls glowed in the firelight.

Anthony piled more wood on the fire.

Minnie watched him with wide eyes. "Is the bedroom going to be warm all night?" she asked with wonder.

"The fire won't last all night," Anthony said, "but it will keep the room warm for several hours. You'll probably be eager to run downstairs to the kitchen when you wake up. There's always a fire going down there. Annie will have cinnamon rolls waiting for you."

Minnie continued to inspect the room, her eyes resting on the ornate mirror situated atop the dresser, and then the towering wardrobe snugged against the far wall. There was a nightstand with a pitcher of water and two glasses. "Are there two glasses because I'm here?"

"That's right," Carrie said gently. "Remember, you're part of our family now. I promise you that we'll take good care of you."

Minnie sighed and sank down onto the feather pillow. "Mama would be real glad I'm here," she murmured.

Moments later, she was sound asleep, strawberry blond lashes resting against her pale cheeks.

Carrie and Anthony hugged Frances warmly.

"You're being a good sister," Anthony said.

Frances shrugged. "Minnie was my best friend first. Having her as a sister isn't any different. She's always been like a sister to me, anyway. I love having her with me all the time." She looked over at the other girl. "Minnie is going to be alright," she said seriously. "It's hard to lose the mama and daddy you were born to, but having you two makes it better." She met their eyes. "I'll always love my mama and daddy, but I love you two just as much. I know I wouldn't have a life like this if you hadn't adopted me."

"We're the lucky ones," Carrie said tenderly. "We love you, Frances."

"I love you, too," Frances murmured. Her lashes dropped, and moments later her even breathing revealed she had also succumbed to sleep.

Abby, Thomas, Rose, Moses and Phoebe were waiting for them in the parlor when they returned downstairs.

Rose held up a steaming cup. "Annie made hot chocolate," she announced. "She said any night as cold as this one deserves hot chocolate."

"I couldn't agree with her more," Anthony said as he sank down into one of the chairs next to the fire and reached for a cup. He smiled when he saw what else was on the tray. "Sugar cookies, too?"

Abby smiled. "She claims she's practicing for Christmas baking."

"As if she needed practicing," Anthony replied with a smile. "Frances is right. Miss Annie is the best cook in the world."

Carrie nodded as she wrapped her hands around the steaming cup, savoring the warmth. "It feels as good as it's going to taste," she said. "Am I imagining that it's colder than normal? I'm used to these temperatures in

Philadelphia, but I didn't think it would be this cold here in Virginia."

"Perhaps you're getting soft," Moses teased.

"That's possible," Carrie agreed easily. "I really don't care how cold it is. I'm just happy to be home." She had taken treats out to Granite in the barn earlier, spending precious moments grooming him, before the cold drove her back inside. Visions of a nighttime ride had vanished with the plummeting temperatures.

"Not as happy as we are to have you," Thomas said.

Carrie returned her father's loving gaze before she took a sip of her drink. She rested her head back against the chair with a sigh. "Home..." she murmured.

"In answer to your question," Thomas continued, "yes, this winter is especially cold. I've been keeping records for many years. It hasn't been this cold since the last year of the war."

Carrie frowned as she remembered the horrible cold that had created such suffering among the soldiers tasked with protecting Richmond during the final siege. The number of amputations from frozen limbs had been appalling. She was glad there were no soldiers suffering, but her thoughts turned to Paris. She hoped Florence was still warm and safe.

A long silence fell on the room as they listened to the wind buffet the house. Windowpanes rattled as the flames roared in their battle to beat back the cold.

"I do believe I'll miss the oil furnaces in Philadelphia," Carrie finally said. "It was nice to wake up to a home that was just as warm in the morning as it was when we went to bed. I know it will be a long time before oil furnaces are available here."

Moses shook his head. "I was right. You're getting soft," he said sadly.

Chuckles sounded around the room before silence descended again.

Carrie reached over to take Anthony's hand, relaxing in the knowledge that she was truly home.

Abby broke the silence again. "Minnie is a delight."

"She's a beautiful little girl," Carrie agreed.

"She's also a lucky little girl," Thomas said.

Anthony shook his head. "We're the lucky ones, Thomas. We've been talking about adopting another child, but the idea of choosing one from the thousands of needy children was overwhelming. To have the opportunity to adopt a little girl we already know and love..."

"And who is already best friends with Frances," Carrie added.

"*We're* the lucky ones," Anthony repeated.

Abby eyed them for a moment. "Do you think you'll adopt more in the future?"

"Who knows what the future holds?" Carrie asked. "I've had so many beliefs about what would happen *in the future*. Very few of them turned out the way I envisioned. I've decided it's best to take one day at a time. I try to make the best decisions for that day and trust that those decisions will create the best future."

"My goodness," Abby said. "You're becoming so wise."

Carrie blushed at the look of admiring love in her mother's eyes. "I have you to thank for much of that," she said softly. "You came into the life of a very confused eighteen-year-old and turned my world around. I wouldn't be who I am today if it weren't for you. To have you marry my father after the war was an added bonus."

Abby returned her smile. "Now you will do the same for Frances and Minnie. Like the Bregdan Principle says, every action we take will have an effect on all of history. What you're doing for these girls is changing their lives, which means it will change the lives of the people they touch."

Carrie smiled her agreement and then turned to Rose. "How is Felicia?"

Rose sighed deeply. "Struggling. Some days she seems happier, but then the anger erupts again. She's so volatile. No matter how hard I try, I can't seem to get through to her...or even understand what she's feeling."

"Have you found any more poetry?" Abby asked.

Rose glanced at Moses. When he nodded, she slipped a paper from her pocket. "Felicia left this in the library two days ago. I can only assume she wanted me to find it." She took a deeply troubled breath and began to read.

Silent screams rip from my mouth.
No one hears.
Silent fury boils in my blood.
No one knows.
Invisible tears roll down my face.
No one sees.
Invisible pain rends my heart.
No one cares.
Blood-filled streets fill my dreams.
Hate steals the life of those I love.
Eyes of hatred peer through the darkness.
They see me.
They hate me.
They are coming for me.
Will it soon be my blood in the streets?

Will hatred steal the lives of those I love?
Dark clouds smother the air.
Dark clouds steal the light.
Dark clouds shatter hope.
I look for light.
There is none.

Rose wiped away her tears when she finished reading. Stark silence filled the room for several moments.

"My God..." Carrie uttered.

"That poor child," Abby whispered.

Thomas shook his head. "I was afraid this would happen," he said sadly.

Startled eyes turned to him.

"What do you mean?" Moses asked, his voice deep with emotion.

"Felicia felt safe when she came to the plantation," Thomas replied. "She had lost her parents, but she came to a place where she felt safe. She was loved. Her insatiable thirst for knowledge, however, led her to more information about what's really happening in our country. Going to college, even to a place as protected as Oberlin, has opened her eyes to more reality. She is too intelligent to not understand the ramifications of all that's happening around her, but still too young to understand how to deal with it."

Abby nodded. "She no longer feels safe," she murmured, her eyes soft with understanding. "I remember feeling that way when my first husband, Charles, died. I had always felt safe in Philadelphia..."

"Until you took over his business," Carrie said.

"Yes. Suddenly, people I trusted were a threat to me. I had to be careful every moment of the day. I never knew who or what might be lurking in the shadows to dissuade me from going against the norm for women." She paused. "I was grown, though. If it was so difficult for me, I can only imagine how difficult this must be for Felicia."

"And every other black person in America right now," Rose said grimly.

"Felicia is remembering her parents' murder," Phoebe added. "I've asked her about it, but she refuses to discuss it." She hesitated. "It's like she turns into a rock when she thinks about it."

"With good reason," Moses said. "Felicia was at home with her parents during the Memphis riots four and a half years ago. I was watching when four white policemen kicked in the door of her little house. Her father came out. I know he hoped he could say something to stop the inevitable, but the whole city had gone mad," Moses said angrily. "One of the policemen yelled that he was going to rape the woman and the child before they killed them all."

"Dear God!" Phoebe's eyes widened with horror.

Rose felt the same sickness she always felt when she envisioned what her daughter had lived through.

"Felicia's father heard what they said and stabbed one of the policemen with a knife. The other policemen shot and killed him. Her mother ran from the house and threw herself down on the ground beside her husband." His voice roughened. "One of the policemen shot her in the head."

Phoebe gasped. "Felicia saw all this?"

"Every bit of it," Moses confirmed. "She came running outside screaming at them for shooting her mama and daddy."

"They didn't shoot *her*?" Phoebe asked.

"They would have," Moses said, "but Matthew and Robert saw what was happening, too. They were hiding behind another building, reporting on what was going on. Anyway, they distracted the policemen and knocked them out with pieces of wood. I was able to get Felicia back to the fort to safety, but her last vision of her parents was them lying in the dirt, in a pool of their own blood."

Phoebe swiped at the tears in her eyes. "Poor Felicia. No wonder she's so angry."

"And scared," Abby added.

"You saved her, Moses," Thomas said thoughtfully. "I think you're the one to talk to her now."

"Me?" Moses looked surprised. "I'll do anything I can, but I thought Felicia needed all the women in her life."

"She does," Abby assured him, "but Thomas is right. You're the only one who knows what she experienced. You were the one to save her and make her feel safe."

Moses considered her words and then nodded. "I'll talk to her tomorrow."

Chapter Sixteen

Moses found Felicia in the library reading one of the newspapers Thomas had delivered to the plantation on a weekly basis. "Good morning. What are you reading?"

Felicia looked up at him with a startled gaze. "*The New York Times*," she admitted reluctantly, obviously uncomfortable with his presence in her sanctuary.

Moses was struck by the simmering anger in her eyes. "What are you reading about?" he asked casually. He didn't really know how to go about talking to Felicia. Rose had assured him he would find the right words, but he didn't share her confidence. What if all he did was make his daughter angrier?

"The Enforcement Act," Felicia responded.

Moses raised a brow. "The one passed in May of this year?"

"Yes, but mostly I'm reading about the push to get it amended so it might actually do some good," Felicia said flatly. "Angel told me about her mother and siblings," she added bitterly. "The Enforcement Act certainly didn't help them."

"I see," Moses said slowly, searching his mind for how to respond.

"They're just going to keep killing black people," Felicia said angrily.

Moses wanted with all his heart to disagree with her - to convince her it wasn't true, but he couldn't. What was he supposed to say? He could see in his daughter's eyes that she was accurately reading his silence. Heaving a sigh, Moses sat down. The only thing he knew to do was go with honesty. "I believe you're right."

Felicia's eyes widened with surprise. "You do?"

Moses nodded. He'd been right that she expected him to deny her conclusion, but he wouldn't insult her intelligence. "Tell me what you've learned," he invited.

Felicia eyed him. "The Enforcement Act passed in May was meant to protect our people's right to vote, to hold office, to serve on juries and to receive equal protection of laws. It was supposed to allow the Federal Government to intervene when states didn't protect those rights." She paused. "Like in North Carolina."

"Where it failed badly," Moses acknowledged.

"Yes," Felicia said bluntly. "The KKK knew the government wasn't going to do anything to stop them. That's why they killed so many people, including Angel's family. Too many North Carolina politicians are either part of the Klan, or they lack the backbone to fight them."

Again, Moses knew she was speaking the truth. He thought about a letter he'd received from Matthew recently. "I understand they're going to revise the act to make it more effective."

"They are," Felicia agreed. "President Grant asked Congress to revise it. After what happened in North Carolina, he decided it was the only way to combat the Ku Klux Klan and other white supremacy organizations. According to what I'm reading"—she lifted the paper and read—"'President Grant is having this done so that he has the power to suppress state disorders on his own initiative, and to suspend the writ of habeas corpus.'"

"Which means that members of the KKK can be held without trial indefinitely," Moses said. "They can be kept from killing people until they can be prosecuted and tried."

"Right. Under the Constitution, the Federal Government can suspend the privilege of the writ of habeas corpus if public safety requires it. Basically, it means they no longer have the right to be released from imprisonment if they do anything that goes against the Enforcement Act. President Lincoln did it the first time during the Civil War, but it became inoperative when the war ended."

"And less than five years later they need it again." Moses felt the slow simmer of his own anger.

"Yes," Felicia said, fury lacing her words. "Nothing is ever going to change, Daddy. White people hate us. They want us all dead!"

"Whoa..." Moses held up a hand, alarmed by her virulence. "Not all white people hate us, Felicia."

"I know that," she said impatiently. "But *most* of them do. Even most of the ones that thought slavery was wrong never thought we should be able to vote or have a say in this country. I don't know what they thought we would do with our supposed freedom, but they certainly didn't think we would ever have equal rights with them." Her eyes flamed. "As long as we know our place, we can be allowed to live in *white society.*"

Moses looked at her, suddenly understanding the impact of bitter anger. He was seeing those repercussions exhibited in his daughter. "What good do you think such anger is going to do, Felicia?"

"And what good does compliance do?" Felicia cried. "Am I supposed to go about my life like a good little girl? Never making waves because I'm *black*?" Her fists clenched. "Am I supposed to be all right with the fact that there are millions of people around me who want me dead if I dare to strive to be more than *they* think I should be?" Her voice rose.

Moses grew alarmed when she began to shake with anger, but this was the first honest conversation Felicia had had since all the anger had started. He wasn't going to shut her down and tell her she shouldn't feel what she was feeling.

"Did I ever tell you how my daddy died?" he asked.

Felicia shook her head, obviously confused by the new turn in the conversation.

"I watched white men hang him from a tree when he tried to run away from our plantation. I was eleven."

Felicia stared at him.

Moses stood and slowly removed his shirt, uncertain he was doing the right thing, but feeling compelled to do it anyway. "There's a reason I always have a shirt on, Felicia." He turned so she could see the mudflat of scars on his back.

"They whipped you," Felicia whispered. Her eyes widened with pain, and then they narrowed with anger. "They did that to you because you're black!" she hissed.

"There was a time in my life when I was as angry as you," Moses continued as he pulled his shirt back on.

"You should *still* be angry!" Felicia cried. "All that stuff is *still* happening. We may not be slaves anymore, but we're still being hanged from trees. We're still being beaten!"

"Yes," Moses said calmly. Somehow, experiencing her blazing anger was working to calm his own. "I learned something about anger, though, Felicia." He paused for a long moment, waiting for her eyes to give him permission to continue. "Anger always comes from pain."

Felicia shook her head. "No, Daddy. Not all anger comes from pain. Sometimes it comes from watching terrible things happen. Susan told me she was angry when she saw Friday being beaten."

"What did she do with that anger?" Moses asked gently, praying with all his heart that he would know what to say.

Felicia hesitated. "What did she *do* with it?"

"Yes, what did she do with it?"

Felicia stared at him, and then her eyes suddenly cleared. "She got even with him! She got back at him!"

Moses continued to gaze at her. "Did she? Did she hit him with the whip? Did she hurt him?" He paused again. "She may have wanted to do all those things, but what did she *do*?"

Felicia stared at him defiantly.

Moses listened to the flames and the tick tock of the clock as he waited her out.

"She bought Friday from him and brought her home," Felicia finally said.

"So, what did Susan *do* with her anger?" Moses knew Felicia needed to come up with the solution herself.

Felicia looked down for what seemed an eternity before she finally looked back up. "She was angry, but she used her anger to find a way to make things better." Her expression made it clear that she didn't like the conclusion she had reached.

Moses was proud of her for seeing the truth. He walked over and held out his hand. "Will you come with me?"

Felicia looked at him suspiciously. "Where are we going?"

"Will you come with me?" Moses repeated tenderly, willing her to take his hand.

Felicia looked up at him, and then slowly reached out.

Moses walked out of the tunnel onto the banks of the James River. Snow covered the banks, but it wasn't deep.

"Daddy!" Felicia gasped. "It's cold out here." Her teeth began to chatter.

"Yep," Moses agreed easily. "You're about to do something to warm you up, though."

"I am?" Felicia eyed him as if there was something wrong with him.

"But first..." Moses prayed again for the right words to say, hoping with all his heart that he wasn't about to do something to make Felicia's life more difficult. He stepped forward and grasped both her hands. "I want you to tell me about seeing your mama and daddy die."

"No!" Felicia stepped back and tried to pull her hands from his. "No, Daddy!"

"I know it's going to be painful," Moses said. "I believe it will help."

"No!" Felicia cried again. Her face twisted with both pain and anger. "I won't do it!"

"Why?" Moses asked gently. "You think about it all the time. It's fueling your anger." He held firm to her hands. "Tell me, honey."

Felicia shook her head, her eyes filling with helplessness. "You were there, Daddy. You saw it."

"I saw what I saw," Moses replied. "I didn't see what *you* saw. I didn't see it in the same way you did."

"I don't want to," Felicia said, her words ending in a whimper.

"I know," Moses answered, reaching out one hand to stroke her cheek. "Please tell me about the day your parents died."

Felicia started to shake her head, but her eyes flared with fury. "They didn't *die*," she said angrily. "They were *murdered!*"

Moses waited quietly.

Felicia turned her head away and stared out over the river. "My daddy was home when I came back from school that morning. You saw me at school. You told me I was brave. You told me it was best if I went home. So I did."

Her sentences were short, and her voice sounded young. Moses squeezed her hand encouragingly but didn't say anything.

"Daddy wasn't usually at home during the day. He had to work all the time. He told me it wasn't safe in the city that day. Mama told me we were going to stay in the house. We were going to play games, and we were going to be safe."

Moses felt sick as he heard the pain coating her words.

Felicia shook her head as if she were trying to banish the memories. "Mama had made biscuits. She had picked strawberries that morning from our garden. Daddy and I had a contest to see how many strawberries we could stuff in our mouths." The ghost of a smile from the memory faded, and she frowned. "We heard a lot of shouting and gunshots. Daddy locked the door the best he could, but I could tell by the look on his face that he didn't think it would stop anyone. Mama looked real scared."

The wind blew harder, whipping up white caps on the river. Felicia stood straight, her face set like stone.

"The yelling got closer, and then someone kicked our door in." Felicia's voice caught with fear. "I heard a man yell for my daddy to come outside. Mama begged him not to. He told her he had to go out there or they would just come inside and hurt all of us. Mama was crying real hard. Daddy went outside." She hesitated. "Before he left, I saw him grab a knife off the kitchen table."

A duck skimmed low over the water, his call rivaling the wind.

"When he went outside, one of the men said he wanted to be with a woman." Felicia shuddered. "He said he was going to rape my mama." Her voice dropped to a whisper. "Then he said he didn't mind the little ones, as well. I wasn't sure what he meant back then. Mama grabbed me and said she would never let someone hurt me. I know now that the policeman was going to rape me, too."

Felicia stopped talking and stared out over the river for a long time.

Moses waited, letting her have the time she needed.

"When Daddy heard them say that, I guess he went a little crazy. I was watching out the window when he pulled the knife out and stabbed one of those policemen." Her voice shook with the memory. "As soon as he did that, the other policemen shot him. They...killed...my daddy."

Felicia shut her eyes against the memory as her voice grew flatter. "Me and my mama started crying real hard. I wanted to go to Daddy. Mama held me back, but she told me she couldn't let my daddy die by himself. She told me to hide in a back room, and then she ran outside to be with him."

Tears coursed down her cheeks, forced past her tightly closed eyes. "I heard the policemen laugh at her. And I...heard...another...gunshot..." Her lips were trembling too hard to force the words out clearly. "I saw the blood... pouring out... of her... head."

Felicia gripped Moses' hand with all her strength. "Mama told me to hide, but I couldn't do it. I couldn't leave them out there like that. I ran out and started yelling at the policemen who had killed them. I probably knew they would kill me, too. What did I care?"

Sobs racked her slender body as she relived the sight of her parents lying in the dirt, bullet holes pouring blood onto the ground. "They killed them. They killed them! Just because they were black!"

Moses stepped forward and pulled Felicia into his strong arms. He held her tightly as sobs continued to make her body convulse. Her breath came in gulps as she fought for air between the sobs. He could feel her wilt into him, just like the day he had rescued her. "I've got you, Felicia," he said softly. "I've got you."

He didn't know how long they stood there. It didn't matter. Felicia had been holding this pain inside for years—pain that was festering like an oozing wound that had never known relief. He understood from the core of his being. He also knew the only way she would find release was to begin to let it all go. She had to face the pain if she was ever going to find healing.

Finally, the sobs abated. Felicia shuddered and fell silent.

Moses continued to hold her, stroking her hair softly.

Snowflakes began to swirl through the air. Moses had known the skies were promising snow when he woke that morning. They were keeping their promise.

Felicia looked up. "It's snowing." She lifted her face to stare into the gray skies as snowflakes landed on her hot cheeks and melted.

"Yes."

"I wish it could snow in my heart, Daddy."

"What do you mean?"

"Snow covers up ugly things," Felicia said, continuing to stare into the sky. "I wish it would snow in my heart so it would cover all the ugly things."

Moses knew it was time. "Perhaps we could get rid of some of the ugly things another way."

"How?"

Moses reached down and picked up several large rocks. He turned and threw one of them into the water. "This is what I wish I could do to the man who shot your father."

He threw another one, grunting with exertion and emotion. "And this is what I wish I could do to the man who shot your mother."

He threw the last one he had picked up. "This one is for the man who accosted you in the train station," he said between gritted teeth.

Moses was suddenly aware just how much anger he was holding himself.

Felicia stared at him. "You're throwing rocks?"

"It helps," Moses assured her. "You have to do something with all the anger and emotion inside you. There's nothing wrong with anger itself; it's what you choose to do with it. When you take your anger out on people who had nothing to do with the reason for your anger, it's wrong because it hurts them."

Felicia cocked her head as she considered his answer. "What if you're taking your anger out on the person who caused it?"

Moses spoke carefully. "I suppose you have to decide if the action you're taking is making the situation better."

"Like Susan did when she brought Friday home?"

"Yes," Moses agreed. "She could have beaten that man with the whip. He deserved it, but it wouldn't have saved

Friday. Susan controlled her anger, and she did the thing that would make the situation better."

"Is that what you do, Daddy?"

"Sometimes," Moses said slowly. "Not always." He was determined to be honest. "There are times I've let my anger make me do things I regret. The people may have deserved it, but it didn't make the situation better." He paused. "My anger only made it worse."

He knew Felicia would analyze what she was feeling from every possible angle. There was time for analyzing later. For now, he wanted her to release the remnants of anger that hadn't been washed away by the torrent of tears. Reaching down, he picked up several rocks from beneath the snow and handed them to her.

Felicia took them reluctantly. She looked down at them nestled in her gloved hands. "I feel silly."

"I felt silly the first time I did it, too." Moses smiled. "Actually, I felt stupid." Thinking back over their conversation, he reached down and selected another rock. He threw it with all his might. "This one is for the men who killed Daniel and Angel's family."

Felicia watched him, and then pulled her arm back. She heaved the rock, tears once more flooding her eyes. "This one is for the man who killed my father."

Suddenly, she threw the other two in her hand. "And this is for him, too. He stole my daddy from me. I hate him!"

Moses remained silent. Her feelings were her own. The hate was real. She needed to release it.

Felicia's face contorted. She began to pluck rocks from the shore of the river, throwing them one by one as hard as she could. "These are for the man who shot my mama in the head!"

"These are for all the people who look at me like there's something wrong with me because I'm black!"

"This is for the man at the train station!"

"And for the woman at the train station!"

"This is for people at school who think I'm not as smart as they are because I'm young!"

Rocks continued to fly; their splashes swallowed by the whitecaps dancing on the river.

"These are for the men who killed Angel's family!"

"And the man who killed Robert while he was protecting Amber!"

Her breath came in gasps.

"This is for the man who killed *your* daddy!"

"And especially the evil people who whipped you when you were a slave!"

Her voice fell silent, but the rocks continued to fly, one at a time, in handfuls...

Moses had stepped back long ago, letting Felicia release the rage within her.

Finally, Felicia's hands were empty. She stood for several minutes, her arms down by her side as she stared out at the water that had swallowed the rocks.

Then she turned and looked at Moses. "The river took my anger," she said, her face a mixture of peace and fatigue.

"For now," Moses said gently. He wanted to prepare her for the process ahead. "Letting go of anger is like peeling an onion, honey. It keeps coming off in layers, one at a time until you reach the core. You have a lot of anger to let go of. It's all right if you feel it bubbling back up. The day will arrive when you realize the anger is gone. The day will come when the pain no longer swallows you, and then you'll be free to truly live your life."

Felicia listened closely, nodded, and then turned to look back over the water. "There are a lot of rocks left on the beach."

Moses smiled, stepped to her side and pulled her close. "Yes, there are a lot of rocks left. I'll come throw them with you anytime you want."

"You didn't throw as many as I did, Daddy."

"That's because I've been throwing them for a lot longer than you have, Felicia." He breathed a prayer of gratitude for the peaceful look on her face. "A whole lot longer."

The snow continued to fall, dissolving into the gray water as it hit.

Moses could hardly believe it was the same river that had destroyed so much of the plantation, taken Rascal from them, and almost snatched John from their life. The same river, now flowing placidly within its banks, had gladly accepted Felicia's anger and had handed her peace.

"I want to go to Memphis, Daddy."

"What?" Moses was sure he hadn't heard his daughter correctly.

"I want to go to Memphis," Felicia repeated in a firm voice.

"Why?"

"I need to go there. I need to see where my first mama and daddy died." Her voice had started out tentative but grew stronger as it continued. "I want to visit their grave."

Moses stiffened. This was something he'd never told Felicia. He hadn't wanted to add to her pain. "Honey..."

"I need to visit their grave, Daddy."

"I know," Moses replied. "But..." He couldn't find the words to continue. He didn't want to say the words that would erase the peace.

Felicia looked up into his face. "But what?"

Moses felt sick. What if his revelation rekindled all the anger? He'd started the day determined to be honest, though. He wasn't going to change that now. "Felicia, I don't know where your parents' grave is."

Felicia shook her head. "Why not? You told me you buried them when the rioting stopped."

"I know I did," Moses replied, bile rising in his throat. He had never dreamed this day would come. "I went back to your house, but someone had already taken your mama and daddy. I tried to find out what happened to them, but none of the neighbors knew." He paused. "Or they were too afraid to tell me." He lifted Felicia's chin so he could look into her eyes. "Honey, I'm so sorry I lied to you. You were so young, so frightened and so sad. I just couldn't add to your pain."

Felicia stared at him. "I'm not angry," she said slowly. "You saved my life. I know the whole city was going crazy. I've read some of the old newspapers about it. I suppose if I were in your place, I would have done the same thing."

"You've read some of the old newspapers?" Moses didn't know she had done that. He was surprised, but mostly grateful she had responded to his confession with such grace. He suspected she wouldn't have responded in the same way before their time here on the riverbank.

"Thomas keeps copies of every article Matthew has written. I think I've read all of them." Felicia's shoulders straightened. "I still want to go back there, Daddy. Will you take me?"

Moses wasn't sure revisiting the place of her trauma was a good idea. "Can you help me understand why you want to go?"

Felicia looked out over the river again, her expression thoughtful. "My whole life changed the day my parents were murdered. We didn't have much, but I knew they loved me. They were determined to create a new life so that my life would be different."

"They would be so proud of you, Felicia."

"I know they would." Her tone turned as beseeching as her eyes. "I know the people who lived around us were too afraid to talk to you back during the riot, but maybe someone would tell us now. Maybe someone is still there who knows what happened to them." Her voice intensified. "Daddy, I have to say good-bye to them. I never had a chance to say *good-bye*. And I have to thank them." Her words ended on a desperate note.

Moses still hesitated. What would Rose think of him taking their daughter back to Memphis? He hadn't kept abreast of things to know if it would be safe, because he never planned to return.

"Daddy, it's all right now." Felicia put a hand on his arm. "I've let go of a lot of the anger. I'm never going to let it build up that way again. You told me if I keep peeling the onion, then one day I'll reach the core and be free to truly live my life." She took a deep breath. "I want that, Daddy. I don't understand why I have to return to Memphis, but I do. I think about it almost every day. Will you take me?" she repeated.

As she talked, Moses had a vivid memory of the times he'd wished he could go back to the place where his own daddy had died. He'd wondered what had been done with his body when it had been cut down from the tree he'd dangled from. Moses didn't know if it would have actually helped, but he had always thought it would.

He took a deep breath. "Yes, I will take you, but," he added quickly, "there's a condition."

Felicia turned to face him, her eyes alight with hope. "What condition?" Her expression revealed she would do whatever it took.

Moses picked his words carefully. "Are there people you've hurt with your anger?"

Felicia's eyes filled with sadness, but she didn't hesitate. "Yes."

"I want you to send every one of them a letter of apology," Moses said. "I understand why you were angry, but if you want to be free, you have to make it right with the people you hurt."

He decided not to mention the letter from Oberlin saying that what he was asking for would be necessary before Felicia would be allowed to return. The letter had arrived just a few days earlier. The dean had extolled Felicia's academic accomplishments but also revealed just how much she had been lashing out at students and faculty. Moses and Rose had decided to wait to discuss it with her until after the holidays. Now they wouldn't have to. She might not care about returning to Oberlin right now, but he knew the time would come when she would. He would let her desire to go to Memphis prompt her to do the right thing.

Felicia nodded. "I'll do it today," she promised. "I'm sorry I let my anger make me say horrible things to some people at school. I knew when I was saying them that it was wrong, but I couldn't control it. I hate what I did," she said sadly.

Moses hugged her close. "I'm proud of you. All of us do things we regret. The important thing is to do what's necessary to make it right when we can. You have a chance to do that. You're lucky."

"I guess I am," Felicia acknowledged as a light began to glimmer in her eyes. "You'll really take me to Memphis?"

"I will," Moses said firmly. "I want you to think about something else, though. You'd originally thought about going back to Oberlin with Phoebe after the Christmas holiday. I don't want to travel to Memphis until spring, when I know the train tracks will be clear through the mountains. I propose you stay home for another term. You can start back to college next September."

"Next September?"

"Yes," Moses replied, watching Felicia's eyes closely as she absorbed what he was saying. He wasn't surprised when he saw relief bloom. "You forced yourself to grow up very quickly because of everything that happened to you in Memphis." He was glad he and Rose had already discussed this. "Your mama and I think it would be a good idea for you to stay here on the plantation with us for a while longer. You can still study and learn to your heart's content, but you won't have the pressure of college right now. I think it's best for you, and it would make me and your mama very happy."

Felicia hesitated, obviously struggling with the decision her eyes said she wanted to make. "You don't think it will slow me down from making a difference?"

"I believe it will actually speed things up," Moses answered.

"Speed them up? How?"

"Because you'll have all the time you need to throw lots of rocks," Moses said gently. "When you go back to school, you'll be free from anger and pain. That will make everything easier. Instead of using your energy to attempt to control your anger, you can focus it on the things you really want to do."

Felicia nodded slowly. "That makes sense." She looked up at him with wide, suddenly vulnerable eyes. "Do you really believe I can do it, Daddy? Do you believe I can peel the whole onion?"

Moses gently cupped her face with his huge hands as he gazed into her eyes. He thought of the little girl who had stolen his heart back in Memphis. "Nothing in the whole world can stop you from letting go of the past and starting over. That's something you do in your heart, Felicia. No one can ever take control of your heart away from you."

Chapter Seventeen

Carrie breathed in the smells of the barn. Outside, six inches of newly fallen snow were starting to glow with the glorious, rosy color of the clouds catching the first rays of the morning sun. The whole effect was startlingly beautiful. It was a perfect morning for a ride.

"Mornin', Carrie girl."

"Good morning, Miles." Carrie eyed the axe he was carrying. "How often are you having to break up the ice in the water buckets?"

"Every few hours," Miles replied. "I don't believe I ever seen a winter this cold. All the signs said it was gonna be a brutal one, but ain't no one suspecting this."

"Do you have another axe? I can help," Carrie offered.

Miles shook his head. "Ain't no need. Clint gonna be here in a few minutes. We let most of the horses out in the back fields. Clint goin' out there twice a day to break the ice near the bank so they gots enough to drink. We got plenty of hay we're taking out to them, and we built enough lean-tos over the summer for them to all have shelter."

Granite stuck his head over the door of his stall and gave a shrill whinny.

Miles grinned. "His Highness is just fine, no matter what he be tellin' you right now. I'm making sure his water ain't froze and I even made him a hot mash last night."

Carrie walked over and petted Granite on his silky neck. "At least you have a thick coat of fur, boy. You're lucky that Miles is willing to spoil you." She flashed her friend a look of appreciation, and then turned back to talk to her horse. "I know it's brutally cold out here, but would you like to go for an early ride? I couldn't convince Anthony or Frances to join me, but I thought I might be able to persuade you."

Granite snorted and bobbed his head.

"That's my boy!" Carrie said happily.

Miles shook his head. "Ain't nobody in their right mind gonna ride on a day like today," he grumbled.

"You've been telling me since I was a child that I'm not in my right mind," Carrie teased. "Why do you think I would have changed?"

"Some folks grow up, Carrie girl."

"Growing up sounds frightfully boring to me. I've been going for a ride on Christmas Eve morning since I was thirteen... At least when I was on the plantation. I'm not about to change my tradition now."

"I think it's a fine tradition!"

Carrie looked up when she heard another voice. "Phoebe! What are you doing out here?" Then her eyes widened further when she saw the slender black woman, bundled in her father's thick winter coat, standing next to her. "Grace?"

"We came to go for a ride with you, if you don't mind. All those Southerners in there may be afraid of the temperature, but to a true Yankee, this is just a cold snap." Phoebe grinned. "Grace and I decided we were tough enough to join you. She's lived in the South for a while, but her blood is still from Illinois. She's used to cold weather."

"I know I don't ride all that well, but it sounds like fun," Grace said softly.

"I'm so glad you want to," Carrie assured her. "I suppose you couldn't talk Willard out of bed, could you?"

Grace's eyes glittered with amusement. "He grunted something about me being out of my mind, and then rolled back over."

"At least the men on this plantation have some sense," Miles observed.

Grace laughed lightly. "Sense is so boring. At least the *women* on this plantation can handle a little cold in order to honor fine traditions."

Carrie and Phoebe laughed as Miles shook his head and turned away to enter another stall. Moments later they heard the axe breaking up ice in the water pail.

"Besides," Phoebe continued as she looked at Carrie, "I only have a week before I return to Oberlin. I don't want to miss one opportunity to ride on the plantation."

"Two women after my own heart!" Carrie was thrilled to have them join her.

Miles finished breaking up the ice, strode over to another stall and opened the door. "Amber says Cookie Lady needs some exercise." He led a tall chestnut mare from the stall. "I reckon she would be happy for you to ride her, Miss Phoebe."

Phoebe strode forward to take the lead rope. "I would love to ride this beauty. I've seen Amber on her. She seems well behaved."

"She's a gem," Miles assured her. "She be one of the ones that Amber been workin' with real close. A man already bought her for his wife. Paid top dollar. Amber is toppin' off her trainin' until the man comes to get Cookie Lady in April."

Phoebe patted her neck. "Cookie Lady?"

Miles chuckled. "My Annie came out here to the barn back when this one was a filly. Annie just finished bakin' some of her molasses cookies. Cookie Lady got a sniff of one, reached into Annie's pocket and picked it right out. Amber named her on the spot."

Phoebe stroked Cookie Lady's nose. "A woman who knows what she wants. We'll get along just fine."

Carrie led Maple from her stall. Rose's mare was the most gentle and reliable horse on the plantation. "This mare will be perfect for you, Grace."

Grace nodded. "I've ridden Maple before," she revealed. "When Amber and Felicia took me riding one day. I love how gentle and willing she is."

Carrie breathed in the quiet. The snow swallowed the sound of hoof beats and created the perfect backdrop for the plumes of white puffing out of the horse's nostrils. All three of them, even Maple, were prancing lightly to show their delight at being outside.

"You're sure you don't mind us tagging along?" Phoebe asked, her blue eyes peeking out above the scarf tightly wrapped around her face. A thick wool hat hugged her head.

"I'm glad for the company," Carrie assured her. She had taken a genuine liking to the teacher from Oberlin College, and she already loved Grace. "I'll be sad to see you go next week."

"I'll be sad to leave," Phoebe replied. She turned to gaze around the plantation, resplendent under a gleaming coat of snow that sparkled with diamonds created by the sun.

Moments before, it had crested the horizon and was climbing rapidly. "I've never been anywhere this beautiful. I've also never learned so much in a short period of time from a teacher like Rose. It seems like she has some type of magical touch in the classroom. I've seen a lot of teachers at work, but not anyone who can get through to students quite like she can."

"Her students love her."

Phoebe shook her head. "I know they do, but it's more than that. I believe she gets through to them the way she does because she loves *them* so much."

"Does that surprise you?" Carrie asked. "Every living being, human or animal, responds to love."

"That's true," Phoebe agreed readily. "I suppose I've never seen a teacher love *all* her students so equally."

"You mean both black and white students?" Carrie easily interpreted what Phoebe was trying to communicate.

"It's unusual," Phoebe insisted.

Carrie knew there was more to what she was saying. "You mean it's unusual for a black teacher to equally love her white students." It wasn't a question because she already knew the answer.

Phoebe hesitated. "I suppose that *is* what I mean," she said thoughtfully. "Other than ignorance, I have no reason to be prejudiced against black students. That's not true for Rose. She was a slave. She's been mistreated by so many white people. She must fight prejudice every single day. For her to look beyond all that and treat her white students just like she treats her black students is unusual."

Phoebe turned to Grace. "I know you married a white man, Grace, but you've had to deal with so much prejudice. Do you find it difficult to love white people?"

Grace was quiet for a moment. "I find it difficult to love *some* of them," she admitted. "However, I also find it difficult to love some *black* people, Phoebe. People are people. Some of them are wonderful, and some of them aren't. You're right that all of us have to look beyond the circumstances and treat everyone the same."

"Isn't that what we're trying to make happen in America?" Carrie asked, realizing this was something Phoebe had given a great deal of thought.

"Absolutely," Phoebe replied. "I've just never seen it play out so beautifully. Oberlin College is committed to racial equality, but the rest of our country is far from being that way. As I get ready to graduate, I'm more aware that I'm about to leave the Oberlin cocoon." She shook her head. "I'm challenged and inspired every day I'm here. Being with Rose makes me want to be a better teacher." She paused. "She makes me want to be a better person."

Carrie felt warm pride for her best friend. "Nothing could make Rose happier," she assured her. She turned to Grace. "Are you sure you and Willard have to leave today? I wish you could stay for Christmas. Anthony said Willard didn't have to be back at River City Carriages until the day after."

"I wish we could stay," Grace said sadly. "We're not leaving because of Willard. We have to go back because of my job."

"I didn't know you had a job," Carrie said with surprise. She was aware Willard's black wife had experienced difficulty in procuring employment because white Richmond didn't take the idea of interracial marriage very well. Neither did black Richmond for that matter, though the couple had finally been able to make some good friends since Anthony had hired Willard to co-manage the stable with Marcus. His act of acceptance had opened some people's minds.

"I have a job at the Spotswood Hotel," Grace confided. "Cleaning rooms." She paused. "I don't know for sure, but I suspect Abby had a hand in me getting the job. No one has been willing to hire me, but then I got a message saying the hotel wanted me to work."

"I love the Spotswood Hotel," Carrie said warmly, sure that Grace was right about Abby's involvement. Abby had taken a strong liking to Willard's wife and had made some inquiries when she had been in Richmond several weeks ago. "I've never stayed there, but I've eaten in the restaurant many times. It was a favorite of mine and my father's during the war. What's it like to work there?"

Grace shrugged. "It's all right. Willard didn't want me to work," she admitted in a low voice. "He makes good money at River City Carriages, but I felt bad about not contributing. Especially now..."

"Now?" Phoebe asked when Grace's voice trailed off. "Why now?"

Grace ducked her head, but not before Carrie saw her shining eyes. "We're going to have a baby."

"Congratulations!" Carrie and Phoebe cried in unison.

"We just found out," Grace said. "I don't know how long I'll work, but I want to keep at it for now."

"When are you leaving?" Carrie asked.

"As soon as we get back from our ride," Grace answered. "Willard told me to give myself this ride as one of my Christmas gifts." She looked around, delight dancing in her eyes. "I'm so glad I did."

Phoebe pulled Cookie Lady to a stop and gazed around. Two does and a huge buck emerged from the forest to forage beneath the snow. A pair of hawks screeched overhead as they caught an updraft and soared high above. A thickly coated fox stepped from the trees, its red fur creating a dramatic contrast with the snow. "I didn't dream a place like Cromwell Plantation could exist. It actually doesn't seem quite real." She shook her head. "It's not just the beauty, it's everything about this place."

Carrie smiled. "You're not the first to feel that way."

"Is that why people are threatened? Because they can't believe it's quite real?"

Carrie considered the question before she answered. "I suspect other plantation owners are threatened because they *do* believe it's real," she said slowly. "When you don't believe something is possible, you don't have to feel like you should create it yourself. Or perhaps it's just that since the freed slaves working as sharecroppers know it's possible, they're not satisfied with what they're receiving. If you don't want to change, the knowledge of what is possible is threatening." She frowned, not certain she was explaining herself well.

"You're talking about the plantation owners in the South who believe slavery should never have ended, so they're treating their workers as badly as they used to by forcing them into sharecropping," Phoebe said. "Instead of being encouraged by the Cromwell model of profit-sharing, they're threatened because all their workers would rather be here. The freed slaves know what is possible, so they're not satisfied with what the plantation owners are giving them."

Carrie was impressed with how thoroughly Phoebe had thought this through. "Yes. I believe that's exactly true.

Their thinking is so convoluted that it's difficult to even comprehend. You expressed it much more clearly than I did."

"It's why the KKK has attacked the plantation," Phoebe continued, her eyes sparking with anger. "They believe that if they intimidate you enough, or scare you enough, you'll change how you do things."

Carrie felt a flash of her own anger. "They should have figured out by now that we're not going to be intimidated or scared." She didn't know if Phoebe had been told about Robert's murder, but it wasn't something she wanted to talk about.

"It must be exhausting to always have to be on guard," Phoebe said sympathetically.

"It is," Carrie agreed. She didn't see any reason to deny it. "Grace, you must feel it every day."

Grace nodded. "I wish it weren't true, but it is. I don't believe there's a black person in America who isn't always on guard," she said bluntly. "Willard is the same way. Even though he's white, he has a black wife. There's plenty of white men who have threatened him because of it, but he refuses to be intimidated. I worry constantly that they'll move beyond threats, and actually do something to him." Her voice was troubled. "Things have gotten a little easier since he started working for Anthony, but I still see trouble in his eyes some nights. He won't tell me about it, because I know he doesn't want me to be scared, but I see it anyway. We don't really have any choice except to keep living our lives. I suppose the day may come when we decide to return to the North, but there's no guarantee things will be any better there." She shrugged. "For better or worse, I guess Richmond is home."

"I'm so sorry," Phoebe replied. "I hope it changes."

"Thank you," Grace said quietly. "I do, too."

Carrie ached for the lovely black woman who had such a gentle soul. Grace was equal amounts of strength and gentleness. Making the decision to marry the white Confederate soldier she had fallen in love with had taken great courage, but living in Richmond had to be a daily struggle for her.

Phoebe turned to Carrie. "Rose told me the plantation has been safe from attacks ever since you started treating the veterans."

"That's true," Carrie replied. At least, she knew it had been true so far. She couldn't forget the warning, however, that there were forces from the outside who were being called in to handle the *"Cromwell problem."*

She didn't want to think about it on this beautiful Christmas Eve morning, but suddenly it was the only thought in her mind.

Carrie forced away any unpleasant thoughts when she, Phoebe and Grace pushed through the front door into the excited chaos within the house.

Carrie smiled, bemused as Jeremy and Marietta's twins raced past them on their pudgy two-year-old legs.

"I'm going to beat you!" Sarah Rose chortled.

"No, you're not!" Marcus yelled, his little legs pumping faster. He worked hard to not ever be outdone by his twin.

Suddenly, Frances appeared. "I told you all not to run in the house!"

The children skidded to a stop, their faces crestfallen that they'd been caught.

"We was just walking fast," Sarah Rose tried to explain in her most grown-up baby voice.

"No, you weren't," Frances replied, her arms crossed tightly. "And, you *were* just walking fast. Not 'was.'"

Sarah Rose stared at her. "Huh?"

Frances rolled her eyes. "Oh, never mind. Your mama is a teacher. I'll let her teach you how to talk.

Phoebe leaned closer to Carrie. "Is she seriously trying to teach a two-year-old how to speak correctly?"

Carrie chuckled. "She explained to Minnie before we arrived that every word spoken had to go through the 'Rose Filter.' Evidently, the 'Marietta Filter' is just as strict."

"Mama? What are you laughing at?"

Carrie bit back her amusement when she turned to answer her exasperated daughter. "Well..."

"Let's go!" Sarah Rose yelled, and took off running again.

Carrie burst into laughter. "Honey, trying to control those children is going to be a lot like trying to keep the sun from setting every night. As long as you keep them from hurting themselves or destroying anything, I think you're doing a wonderful job. Just have fun with them."

Grace reached for Carrie's hand and grasped it warmly. "Thank you for the wonderful ride. Willard and I are leaving now."

Carrie glanced out the window when she heard a carriage rattle to a stop. "Have a good trip back to Richmond. I hope you have a lot of blankets to keep warm."

Grace smiled. "We'll be fine. There's a mountain of blankets and Annie packed enough food for an army. The last few days have been very special. I said my good-byes to everyone else earlier so I'm going to slip out."

Carrie grabbed her into a fierce hug, somewhat surprised by her own intensity. "Be safe," she urged, and then watched as Grace left.

"I'll be down in a few minutes," Phoebe murmured before she headed upstairs to her room.

Minnie walked into the foyer to join her as Frances headed into the parlor after her young charges. "Those are some wild children," she observed with an irritated expression. "I saw a magazine on the train that said children should be well-behaved and quiet."

Carrie laughed even harder, wondering how it was possible for a statement like that to come out of nine-year-old's mouth. "Let me know how that works for y'all." Then she sobered. "Minnie, you'll learn that we prefer to do things differently than what is expected. I believe children should be happy. I don't think it's possible for two-year-old's to be *quiet and well-behaved*." She lifted the girl's chin so she could gaze into her eyes. "I also don't expect a nine-year-old to always be quiet and well-behaved. I was forced to act like that when I was growing up in this house, and all it did was make me unhappy. I refuse to make any child endure what I did. The twins are well-behaved when they need to be. Right now, it's Christmas Eve. This is a time of celebration and fun. For *everyone*."

Minnie nodded, her irritation dissolving into a yearning expression. "My mama could be real fun, but we didn't have much to celebrate. I wish my family could be *here* for Christmas. They would love it."

Carrie gave her a warm hug. "I know, Minnie. I wish they could be, too."

As she looked around, she knew anyone would love to spend Christmas at Cromwell Plantation. Every window and doorway was adorned with greenery and red ribbons. The men had brought huge armfuls of cedar boughs into the house. Everyone had worked together to transform it. Candles flickered in every windowsill, but the most brilliant glow came from the candles lighting the massive Christmas tree in the parlor. It had been hauled into the house the day before. The children, overseen by Abby, had spent the morning decorating it.

She lifted Minnie's face so their eyes could meet. "Since your family can't be here, I'm going to focus on how happy I am that *you're* here," she said softly.

Minnie's eyes misted with tears, but she managed a small smile. "I'm glad I'm here, too," she replied. "Frances told me what life was like for her in the orphanage. I'm real glad I didn't have to live in one." She paused. "I know I would already be working in one of the factories again."

Carrie knew she was right. "You'll never have to worry about that," she said firmly. "I promise we'll take care of you."

"I believe you." Minnie looked troubled suddenly. "What am I supposed to call you now? Frances calls you Mama, but..."

Carrie put a finger over her lips. She had had this same conversation with Frances, and Rose had talked to Felicia about the same thing when she had first arrived. "Call me Carrie. You have a mama who you loved very much. She will always be your mama. I don't have any expectations at all, Minnie. If you want to call me Mama at some point, then that would be wonderful, but..." She peered into Minnie's eyes to make sure she was listening closely before she continued. "But if you never want to call me anything but Carrie, that will be wonderful, too. It's enough to have you be part of our family, and to know you're my daughter."

Minnie cocked her head. "Your daughter?"

Carrie nodded. "Yes. Daughters aren't just born to you, Minnie. Sometimes they come to you as a gift." She took a deep breath. "Sometimes, they're the only good thing that comes from a tragic situation."

Minnie's troubled expression cleared. "I'm glad I'm your daughter," she said shyly.

"Minnie!" Frances' loud call sounded from the parlor. "Come in here! Grandpa is getting ready to light the yule log."

Minnie looked up with a question in her eyes. "Yule log? What's that?"

"The Yule log is a very special log," Carrie explained. "It's a tradition that goes back over eighteen hundred years to medieval times. We've had one here on the plantation for as long as I've been alive, and long before that."

Minnie's eyes grew wide. "That long?"

Carrie nodded, amused to be considered old. "It's a very large log that will burn until late tomorrow night. When it finally quits burning, we know Christmas is over."

Minnie looked thoughtful. "Mama used to get a big candle every year. Sometimes that was all we had for Christmas, but she said it was real important. She told us it was a tradition in Ireland that she didn't want to lose when we came to America."

Abby walked into the foyer in time to here Minnie's statement. "Then we're going to light a large candle in honor of your mama, and your sisters and brother."

Minnie gaped at her. "Really?"

"Of course," Abby said with a warm smile. "Traditions are important. People have different ones. We want to add any tradition that's important to you."

"Thank you," Minnie whispered, her eyes full of emotion.

"Minnie! Get in here! We're waiting for you!"

"I guess I should go," Minnie said.

"I guess you should." Carrie gave her a gentle push. "We'll find a big candle and be right in there to join you."

The sumptuous meal Annie and Marietta had prepared was a thing of the past. Chairs had been pulled into the parlor so that everyone had a place. The children were nestled on pillows in front of the brightly burning Yule log.

Carrie looked around the room, her heart swelling with happiness as she took inventory of the people she loved so much. Anthony. Her father and Abby. Moses and Rose. Jeremy and Marietta. Annie and Miles. Harold and Susan. Phoebe. And, of course, all the children. She could hardly believe she and Anthony were now the parents of *two* daughters. She could never have anticipated such a wonderful Christmas gift.

Abby laughed softly and pointed toward the fire. "I didn't think they would last long."

Carrie smiled tenderly. John, Hope, Sarah Rose and Marcus were all sound asleep, the glow of the fire reflecting on their peaceful faces. Thomas had been prepared to read a Christmas Eve story to them, but the fun of the day, combined with a full stomach, had worn them out.

"Should we take them upstairs?" Frances asked.

Carrie interpreted the reluctance in her eyes. "No, honey. I appreciate the offer, but you, Minnie and Felicia can stay down here with us. We won't disturb them by talking. We'd like you to stay here."

Frances smiled brightly and settled back down in her chair. Felicia and Minnie followed suit, tucking their legs beneath them as they pulled their afghans tight around their shoulders.

Silence reigned for several minutes. Everyone seemed content to absorb the beauty of the Christmas tree trimmed with the same decorations that generations had enjoyed. The children had made fresh acorn balls, along with bouquets of dried flowers, but the bulk of the garnishment went back many decades.

Carrie rested her eyes on the angel perched atop the tree. She used to sit and stare at it as a child, imagining that it was her own special guardian. "The angel came over from Europe," she told Minnie. Everyone else already knew the story. "My great-great-grandmother brought it over on the boat when they came to America."

"Your family came on a boat, too?" Minnie asked. "Jack and I came to America with Mama and Daddy that way."

"They did," Carrie assured her. "If you're white, your family came over on a boat from Europe. We're all immigrants – it's just that some of us have been here longer."

"Unless you're black, or you're in California," Felicia said. "Almost all the blacks came here from Africa as slaves. They came on boats, too. The difference was that they were in chains."

Carrie saw anger in her eyes, but it wasn't the bitter rage from before. In truth, the way the slaves were brought to America warranted anger.

"What do you mean about California?" Phoebe asked.

"A lot of the people coming to California on the boats are immigrating from China. There's a whole lot of Chinese coming in to work on the railroads." Felicia frowned. "From what I can tell, they don't get treated any better than blacks do."

Minnie frowned. "If everybody came here from somewhere else, what makes some people think they're better than other people?"

"That's a really good question," Thomas answered. "The short answer is that people aren't very kind sometimes. Too many people want to think they're better than others because it makes them feel better about themselves."

Minnie thought about his answer. "That's dumb."

"You're right," Thomas replied. "It's dumb."

Carrie watched Minnie, knowing she had something more on her mind but wasn't sure how to say it.

"My family died because we weren't good enough," Minnie finally muttered.

Carrie stiffened. "What do you mean, honey?"

Minnie shrugged. "Folks around where I lived talked about fire all the time. You and Anthony lived in big brick house. We lived in a real old place made of wood. Everyone knew if it caught fire, it would burn real fast." Her eyes were sad. "It did." Just as quickly as her eyes had turned sad, they became defiant. "The firefighters didn't like to come down to where we lived.. We had some men in the area that helped put out fires, but we were too far away from the fire stations. By the time the wagons got there with water, things had already burned down."

Carrie and Anthony exchanged a look. They knew she was telling the truth. Many tall boarding houses had burned the night her family was killed before the fire could be extinguished. The alarm system that Philadelphia had installed didn't extend to all areas of the city, particularly the immigrant areas.

"It's a problem everywhere," Jeremy said. "Even in areas where they have fire stations, conditions are extremely dangerous. Especially this winter, because it's colder than usual. People are doing everything they can to stay warm. The rooms where Minnie and her family lived didn't have fireplaces, and the man who owned her boarding house didn't want to spend the money to heat it with the coal furnace. People were desperate to keep their children warm. What little money they had was often spent on kerosene for their small heaters. Too often, the heaters are the source of the fire because they malfunction or explode. We'll never know what started the fire that night, but it was more than likely a kerosene heater or a candle."

"It was always cold," Minnie agreed. "We had a little kerosene heater, but you only felt warm if you were right next to it. Mama was scared of it. We wore all our clothes, and mama bought as many blankets as she could." She looked around. "I never spent a winter night warm like this."

Carrie's heart caught at this revelation. She had had no idea Deirdre went home to a brutally cold home every night. They had paid her well, but obviously not well enough to get her family into a safer, warmer home. If they had... She saw Anthony's expression and knew he was thinking the same thought. If they had helped them get out of their boarding house, the whole family might well be alive.

The conversation eventually turned to other topics, but Carrie knew she would carry the truth with her forever.

Chapter Eighteen

Peter Wilcher stifled a yawn as he stepped off the train at the Broad Street Station in Richmond. He pulled his thick coat around him in a futile attempt to hold onto the warmth from the train. "This feels like New York City," he muttered.

"This cold will cut through you like a knife," one of the porters said cheerfully. "You got far to go, mister?"

"No," Peter said gratefully, knowing it was too late to get a carriage. His train had been due to arrive that morning. His plan had been to surprise everyone on the plantation for Christmas Eve, but engine trouble had stalled them on the track for almost ten hours. Thankfully, there had been enough firewood to keep the stove burning on the passenger car. He was stiff and sore, but at least he hadn't been freezing cold all day. He would count what blessings he could. "I'm headed to the Spotswood Hotel."

"You might want to walk fast," the porter said. "This ain't the first train to come in late. I don't know how many rooms they still got."

Peter reached for his bag. He hadn't considered the possibility that the hotel would have reached capacity. He could always go up to Thomas' house, but he wasn't excited about walking that far in the frigid temperatures. "Thank you for the tip," he said gratefully. He reached into his pocket, handed the porter a more concrete representation of his appreciation, and strode into the night.

"Do you have a reservation, sir?"

Peter shook his head. "No, I wasn't expecting to need a room. I'm just in from New York on the train that was delayed."

The man at the counter nodded sympathetically. "I wish I could help you, but every room is full. Unfortunately, you're not the first who found himself in need of lodging for the night."

Peter sighed. "I understand. Thank you for your time." He reached down for his bag, resigned to the necessity of walking to Thomas' house. He didn't look forward to the cold journey, but he knew May would fix him an excellent breakfast in the morning. That knowledge would help to keep him warm.

"Peter Wilcher!"

Peter turned as he heard his name called out. His eyes widened with surprise when he identified a colleague from the *New York Times*. "Abraham Anderson! What are you doing here?"

Abraham, a short, wiry man with gold-rimmed glasses, shrugged. "I'm on my way back to New York. I'm supposed to be on a train right now, but it was delayed for ten hours so they canceled the trip back north. I'm catching a train out tomorrow morning." He reached up to scratch his bald head. "My wife and children were hoping to have me home for Christmas. I sent a telegram earlier to let them know I wouldn't make it." He looked at Peter's satchel. "Are you staying here tonight?"

"No such luck," Peter responded. "All the rooms are full. I just came in on the train that was delayed for those ten hours."

"What are you going to do?"

"Walk to a friend's house up on Church Hill."

"That's quite a walk isn't it?"

"I'll survive."

Abraham frowned. "Why not share my room? I have two beds. I didn't need a double room, but it was all they had left. No sense in letting the extra bed go to waste."

Peter nodded gratefully. "I would appreciate that." He'd been willing to walk through the cold night, but he wanted to head out to Cromwell at first light. Staying at the hotel would make it simpler.

Abraham stifled a yawn. "I hope you're not interested in a long conversation. I can barely keep my eyes open."

Peter smiled wearily. "That suits me perfectly."

Lying in bed, he couldn't stop the memories of other Christmases. There had been a time when he would never have dreamed of accepting a reporting assignment on his wife's favorite holiday. Amanda had loved everything about Christmas. Losing her during the cholera epidemic four years earlier, right after the riots in Memphis and New Orleans, had almost been more than he could bear. He'd taken six months off from work to grieve, but the need to do something to lift him from his grief had brought him back to the newspaper.

He squeezed his eyes tightly shut as he attempted to extinguish the flashes of her smile... her sparkling brown eyes... her ready laugh.

He would get through this Christmas the way he'd gotten through the last four – one minute at a time.

The grandfather clock was striking ten when a loud knock came at the door.

"What in the world?" Thomas muttered.

Carrie's first action was to look out the window toward the barn. She relaxed slightly when she confirmed the barn wasn't on fire, but she still knew it could only be bad news. Everyone on the plantation, if they weren't standing guard, was hunkered down with their family for the night.

Moses made it to the door first and pulled it open.

"Y'all are in danger!"

Carrie jolted forward when she recognized the voice. "Hank!" She hurried to the foyer and pulled him into the warmth. "What's happening?"

Everyone stood and walked over to hear his answer.

Carrie glanced over to make sure the children were still sleeping. She didn't want them frightened. It was bad enough that Frances, Minnie and Felicia had to hear what Hank had come to say. She already knew that if he was out on Christmas Eve in such bitter cold, it wasn't anything that was going to add to the Christmas spirit.

"There's an attack planned on the plantation tonight," Hank said bluntly, his eyes darting from face to face.

"How do you know?" Moses demanded.

Hank had never met Moses, though both men knew of the other. The look on Hank's face said he was slightly awed by Moses' size, but the smaller man didn't hesitate.

"The news came down the grapevine. There's a group of vigilantes from down in North Carolina that were sent up here to solve what they see as problems here on the plantation."

Abby had heard enough. She turned away and motioned to the older girls. "Help me wake the children," she said quietly. "I don't want them frightened, though."

Hank frowned as he looked over at the children sleeping peacefully. "Just get them as far from any windows as you can."

Carrie knew they were going to do much more than that, but no one outside the house could know about the tunnel. She had planned to reveal the tunnel to Minnie as a New Year's Day surprise, but that revelation was going to come earlier than planned. She hated that she wouldn't be the one to share the secret with her, but that couldn't be helped.

"I don't think anyone's gonna get near the house," Hank said as he glanced around, his eyes widening as he took in the warm beauty surrounding him.

Moses nodded. "We've got men guarding the plantation."

"I know. I met them on my way in. Me and Jeb talked." Hank frowned. "There weren't enough of them out there, but I reckon there are now," he said confidently.

Carrie raised a brow. "What do you mean, Hank?"

Hank turned to her, his cheeks flushed with the cold. "I told you that me and the fellas you're helping wouldn't never let anyone hurt you or the plantation. We can't stop this from happening, but we can help make sure no one gets close." He paused. "Every one of them veterans you're keeping from pain is stationed around the plantation right now. Them, plus Alvin and a bunch of the men who have children in Mrs. Samuel's school. They weren't real keen about them fella's coming up here to try to destroy things. Jeb rounded up the rest of your men, Moses."

Carrie stared at him with amazement. "All that has been done?" While they'd been celebrating around the fire, action had been taken to avert disaster.

"Yep," Hank replied. "I don't think anybody gonna get close to the house, but I figured you should know about it."

The men were already reaching for their coats. "We're coming," they said in unison.

Hank eyed them. "I figured." He looked at Carrie again. "The rest of y'all oughta go where the children are going."

Carrie smiled tightly. "Every woman standing here is a good shot, Hank. It's not the first time we've had to protect the plantation. If they get close to the house, they'll be sorry."

Hank smiled with surprised admiration. "Well, all right then." He stepped back out onto the porch. "I'm heading back to my position by the gate."

"When are the vigilantes supposed to get here?" Thomas asked, his voice a mix of frustration and anger.

"Round about midnight," Hank said. "Least, that's what I heard. I figure it could be earlier or later. Ain't no one going anywhere 'til the sun comes up, though. We ain't gonna take no chances."

Abby stepped forward and grasped his gloved hand. "Thank you, Hank. We've never had a chance to meet. I'm Thomas' wife, Abby Cromwell. I appreciate what you're doing to protect us."

Hank nodded and then smiled at Carrie. "And we appreciate what Doc Wallington and Mrs. Samuels are doing to help all of us. They don't have to do that. I figure if everyone just takes care of each other, we might actually have a state we can all live in." He scowled. "Those fellas from North Carolina ain't got no right coming up here.

We're gonna make sure they don't ever think it's a good idea again."

"If anyone gets hurt, Hank, I want you to bring them here. We'll take care of them."

Hank shook his head. "I'm sorry, Doc, but I ain't bringing no Klansmen into your home. That's not a good idea."

Carrie knew he had a point, but she pressed on. "No one is going to be hurt and have to suffer on a night like this, Hank."

"We'll take any wounded to the clinic," Moses said. "It will be more than they deserve, but I know it's the right thing to do."

Hank eyed them as if he thought they had taken leave of their senses, and shook his head. "I reckon I should have known you'd feel that way, Doc. I suppose it's the only reason me and the others got taken care of. You sure didn't have no other reason. We'll make sure those men get better than they deserve," he promised, before he strode across the porch, mounted and rode off into the night.

Carrie and the other women watched as the men finished putting on their thick coats, gloves and hats, and then crossed the yard to the barn. Five minutes later, they all rode out at a gallop.

Carrie looked over to see all the younger children sitting up, looks of sleepy confusion on their faces.

"Is it Christmas already?" John asked as he rubbed his eyes.

"How come we're not in our nightclothes?" Hope gazed around as she tried to make sense of things.

"It's not Christmas," Rose said with a chuckle. "But we've got a special Christmas Eve surprise for you."

"You do?" Hope said excitedly as the sleep disappeared from her eyes. "We already celebrated my birthday today. Is something else going to happen?"

Annie bustled into the parlor. "You done had all the birthdayin' you're going to get, granddaughter of mine, but we sho'nuff do have a special Christmas Eve surprise for you, children. You're gonna come with me."

John eyed the big basket clutched in her arms. "I'm still full from supper, Grandma."

"I'm sho' you are, child. This here just in case anyone gets hungry before the surprise is over."

John looked suspicious. "What's the surprise?"

Rose eyed him with amusement. "Since when did you become so curious about surprises, young man?"

John looked at her somberly. "Since I found out that things you *think* are going to be real fun sometimes turn out to be real bad."

Rose took his hand, her eyes full of understanding. "I promise you nothing bad is about to happen, John." She turned to look at the group of women. "Annie, Phoebe and I will take the children."

Carrie walked over to Minnie. "Honey, you're about to learn about a very big Cromwell family secret. I was going to share it with you myself on New Year's Day, but it turns out we're going to need it sooner than we thought."

Minnie stared at her with frightened eyes. "Is something bad about to happen, Carrie?"

"No," Carrie said firmly. She was confident all the men guarding the plantation would take care of things, but she wasn't willing to take any risks. She searched for the right words.

Frances took care of it for her. "I've wanted to share the secret with you since the first day you got here, Minnie. I know Mama wanted to do it, but I think it's right that I get to share it with my sister and my best friend." She pointed up the stairs. "We have to go to Mama and Daddy's room to discover what it is." She moved toward the children. "I'll take Marcus. You get Sarah Rose."

Minnie looked mystified, but readily followed the orders.

Within less than a minute, Carrie was left with Abby, Marietta and Susan. They all locked eyes and nodded in unison. No one needed instruction because they'd all been in this position before.

Five minutes later they were stationed at their window posts with rifles and a box of shells.

Anthony dismounted and tied his gelding to a tree, and then took the position Moses had pointed out to him. They'd talked through the plan on the way over. Their biggest benefit was the element of surprise. The Klansmen had chosen Christmas Eve because they believed the plantation would be unprotected. Their hoped-for surprise attack was actually going to end up as an attack on them.

There were fifty men ready to protect Cromwell Plantation. Hank didn't know how many Klansmen had assembled for the attack, but he was certain it wasn't the number the vigilantes had hoped for. Most of the local men they'd approached had declined to be part of their plan, despite the pressure they had applied. Many of the veterans were Carrie's patients; others had their children in Rose's school. Anthony knew there might be repercussions for the men who had declined, but Hank had assured them that none of the men cared. Their first loyalty was to Carrie and Rose.

A warm flush of love swept through him as he thought of his wife. Most people would have turned away the grizzled, angry veterans who had needed help—especially once some of them admitted they'd taken part in the attack that killed Carrie's first husband. She had dealt with her anger and grief, and then done the right thing for her patients. Because she had been willing to do so, the men she had helped were now stepping forward to help Carrie and those she loved.

Anthony shivered as the temperature dipped lower. The thermometer posted in the barn had revealed it was only ten degrees above zero. A northerly wind made it feel much colder, and Anthony knew the temperature would continue to drop. He was grateful the wind wasn't blowing hard enough to cover the sound of approaching hoofbeats on the frozen ground, and a half-moon illuminated the night enough to make easy targets of the attackers.

He burrowed into his thick coat, tugged his hat down, wrapped his thick scarf around his face and settled in to wait. As he waited, he thought of the special evening that had been interrupted. The house had been so full of joy and love. Now they were waiting for an attack from foes determined to destroy their home. They wouldn't allow that to happen, but the very thought of shooting one of the vigilantes made him weary. When would the killing stop?

Minnie watched with confusion as Rose pulled the handle on Carrie's ornate mirror. "What...? Oh my!" She stepped forward and stared into the black hole gaping in front of them. "What is it?"

Phoebe followed her example. "Oh my, indeed. I've been in Carrie's room several times. I never dreamed this was here." Her voice was full of awe.

Rose smiled as she lit the lantern she was holding and then lit everyone else's. Despite the seriousness of what had driven them into the tunnel on Christmas Eve, it was easy to know what Minnie and Phoebe were feeling. She could still remember the first time she had seen the Cromwells' family secret. She had lived in the house since she was six years old, but had no idea it existed until after the war.

"It's a tunnel!" Frances said excitedly. "Mama's great-great-grandfather had it built a very long time ago. He wanted to make sure his family was safe from Indian attacks." She almost danced into the corridor now brightly illuminated by the glowing lanterns.

Minnie continued to gaze around, her head swiveling on her shoulders. "Where does it go?"

"All the way to the river!" Frances gushed. She lowered her voice. "It's a *secret*," she said importantly as she looked at Minnie and Phoebe. "Only family and very important friends know anything about it."

Minnie nodded solemnly. "I will keep the secret," she vowed.

"I will, too," Phoebe promised.

"How long will we be in here?" Minnie asked.

"Until the bad men are gone," Hope said. "They want us to think we're in here for a surprise, but I know the truth." Her lips were quivering when she turned to Rose. "Mama, do you think we'll be in our beds when Christmas comes? Now that I'm six, you can tell me the truth."

Rose's heart caught at the look of sadness in her sweet daughter's eyes. She hated that the children had to feel even one moment of fear on Christmas Eve – she especially hated that Hope was having her birthday disrupted with violence. "You'll be in your bed," she promised. She hoped she wasn't telling a lie.

Rose busied herself helping Annie create makeshift beds on the tunnel floor. Once all the children had a place to lie down, Rose sat down on the tunnel floor with her back against the wall. She would stay awake until Moses came for them.

"Mama, will you sing to us?" Hope asked, the first tinge of fear in her voice.

Rose edged closer, stroked her daughter's head gently, and began to sing.

> *Silent night, holy night,*
> *All is calm, all is bright,*
> *Round yon Virgin Mother and Child.*
> *Holy infant, so tender and mild,*
> *Sleep in heavenly peace,*
> *Sleep in heavenly peace.*

Felicia joined in, her sweet soprano blending beautifully. The words echoed off the walls of the tunnel, wrapping a cocoon of peace around them.

> *Silent night, holy night,*
> *Shepherds quake at the sight;*
> *Glories stream from heaven afar,*
> *Heavenly hosts sing Al-le-lu-ia!*

> *Christ the Savior is born,*
> *Christ the Savior is born!*

By the time Rose got to the last stanza, Annie, Phoebe and the rest of the children had joined in. She closed her eyes and imagined they were still in the parlor, singing along with Abby on the piano as the Yule log burned brightly.

> *Silent night, holy night,*
> *Son of God, oh, love's pure light;*
> *Radiant beams from thy holy face*
> *With the dawn of redeeming grace,*
> *Jesus, Lord, at thy birth,*
> *Jesus, Lord, at thy birth.*

A sweet silence descended upon the tunnel as the song came to an end.

"Merry Christmas, Mama," Felicia said softly.

"Merry Christmas," everyone murmured sleepily.

Rose and Annie locked eyes, hoping that whatever was happening outside the house was not going to rip away every possibility of a merry Christmas.

Carrie scowled as she kept her eyes trained for any sudden movement outside the plantation or barn. She knew Miles was standing guard inside the stables, but if there was a full-fledged attack, one man would be hard-pressed to offer any true defense.

She struggled to control her emotions. While she was grateful Hank had not only kept his promise to warn them of imminent attack, but was also helping them mount a defense, she was tired to the bone of the situation that made it necessary.

She thought of Rose and Annie sequestered in the tunnel, waiting for news while they kept the children safe. Then her thoughts turned to Abby, Marietta and Susan. None of them had anticipated spending Christmas Eve with a rifle in their arms. Instead of a peaceful, loving evening, they were preparing to protect their home from people with hate-filled hearts.

Weariness that went straight to the bone gripped her. She was glad to be home to help, but how long would this go on? Would there ever be a time when they didn't have to be afraid? When men didn't have to stand guard all night long, shivering in the cold, because someone wanted to destroy what they'd all worked so hard to create?

Carrie gritted her teeth as she once again realized no one could give her an answer to that question.

Moses felt the trouble, even before he could hear hoofbeats coming down the road. It was as if something in the air shifted to warn of impending danger. He steadied his breath at the same time he steadied his rifle. There was a chance the noise was being created by travelers, but the odds were extremely slim that someone would happen to be out past midnight on Christmas Eve.

Christmas Day.

The realization that midnight had come and gone made him grit his teeth with frustration. He should have been able to carry John and Hope up to bed, tuck them in, and snuggle into bed with Rose in anticipation of Christmas morning. Instead, he was once again hunkered down in the woods waiting for men who were threatened by what they were doing on Cromwell Plantation. He had no doubt they would thwart this latest attack, but *when* would it all stop?

Would it *ever*?

Moses pushed the pointless frustration aside. None of it would help him focus and do what needed to be done.

The sound of hoofbeats reached him and grew louder. Clouds that had obscured the moon for a time were blown away as the first horsemen rounded the curve. Rifles were held in their arms as they approached at a slow trot, trying to make as little noise as possible, even though the frozen road made a silent approach impossible.

Moses counted twenty-three men—a larger number than he had anticipated, but not one that caused a problem. He and the other defenders were well-hidden, they would be firing on men illuminated by moonlight, and they had the element of surprise.

Moses waited, confident every man watching would do the same thing. The orders had been clear. Don't make a noise, and don't fire a shot until the men turned into the gates at Cromwell, and you heard the order to fire. He smiled grimly as he thought of the panic the vigilantes would experience when the sound of fifty guns firing in unison erupted into the quiet night. He knew there were men stationed around the school and clinic, as well. Whatever the Klansmen's plans, they were going to be defeated.

Moses cocked his trigger as he sighted along the barrel.

The approaching men came to a stop when they reached the entrance to the plantation. There was a discussion for several minutes. Raised voices carried on the breeze revealed that the men were arguing.

Moses waited patiently. Evidently, there was discord in the ranks. He would shoot anyone who stepped a foot onto the plantation, but he harbored a vague hope that they would decide the attack wasn't worth it, and ride on. He was tired of the killing and hate. His heart sank when the first horseman raised an arm defiantly and rode in through the gate.

There would be no reprieve.

He waited until all twenty-three men, clustered closely together, had passed through the brick pillars.

"Fire!" Moses roared.

Fifty guns exploded, their sharp reports creating instant chaos among the Klansmen.

Moses watched grimly as ten of the men slumped off their horses. Five more screamed as they grabbed a part of their body and turned their horses.

"It's a trap!" one of the Klansmen yelled, fear lacing his words. "Retreat! Retreat!"

"Fire!" Moses roared again. Their only hope that these attacks would ever stop was if word spread that any attempt was useless and would only end in death or injury.

The guns roared again in response.

More screams erupted from the Klansmen. The remaining men had already turned their horses and were trying to gallop away, but couldn't outrun the swift attack. Five more slumped forward in their saddles but managed to hang on as their horses galloped down the road, past the reach of the Cromwell guns.

Moses watched as they ran away. As far as he could determine, only three of them had been unscathed. He remained in position, watching the ten figures that had fallen from their horses. Knowing the marksmanship ability of his men, he doubted they were still alive, but he'd promised Carrie he would bring any wounded to the clinic if he thought they had a chance for survival.

Hank had been told explicitly to not let any of the veterans allow themselves to be seen. The surviving Klansmen might suspect who had leaked news of the attack, but Moses wouldn't allow them to have any more evidence that would put Hank and his friends in jeopardy. They had done a tremendous thing for them tonight.

Just then, the subject of his thoughts rode up to him. "I think they're all dead. There was more of them than I thought, but they never had a chance," Hank said heavily.

Moses gazed at him, not able to read his expression in the dark. Hank had done the right thing, but he had also sent fellow Confederate veterans to their death. There couldn't be anything easy about that. "Thank you."

Hank turned to look at him. "You're welcome." His voice was sad. "They're not all bad men."

Moses remained silent. Those men lying out on the road had come here with the intent to destroy his family and home. As far as he was concerned, they were bad men.

"They're not all bad men," Hank said again. "They're stupid and they're wrong, but…" He shook his head. "This whole country has gone crazy. It's making men do crazy things."

"Yes." That was all Moses could agree to. He looked down the road. "Do you think they'll come back?"

Hank shook his head. "I doubt it. They should come back to see if any of their friends are alive, but they're all cowards so I don't reckon they will. They're not going to be willing to find out if you're still waiting for them. Plus, they know the cold will kill those men quickly, if they're not already dead."

Moses nodded. "You're probably right." He stared at the human-shaped mounds on the plantation drive. "I don't get it. Why would they leave their families to come up here on Christmas just to destroy the plantation?"

"Because the war destroyed all they had," Hank replied. "Those men probably don't have homes anymore. They lost everything, so they figure they don't have anything left to lose. All they know how to do is strike back against the thing they believe caused all their loss."

Moses still couldn't make sense of it. "They came a long way. How could those men believe we had anything to do with their lives? You said they're from North Carolina."

"They are," Hank agreed. "But they figure they lost everything because of black folks, and because of the white folks that help them. They're lashing out at whatever they think they can. If they have to come up from North Carolina, they don't really care. Somebody told them this was what needed to be done. The only thing that makes sense to them right now is joining up with other men who hate as much as they do."

Moses stared at him, wishing he could read more of Hank's expression. "You understand them well."

"I do," Hank agreed readily. "I was just like them until Dr. Wallington decided to help me and my friends. She didn't have to do that. Especially once she found out I was part of that raid that killed her husband. She should have hated me for life." He grew quiet for several moments. "What she did showed me that hate doesn't make any sense. It only hurts everybody. I don't know how to keep other men from hating, but I know I've had enough of it. I hated to be part of killing those men, but what they were doing was wrong. I couldn't let them hurt Dr. Wallington or the plantation."

Moses listened carefully. He and the rest of the men hiding in the woods had done what they had to that night, but no one could make them hate. Just like he had told Felicia, he would feel the anger, but he would use it to try to make things different.

Reaching that conclusion, he knew what he had to do. He mounted Champ and rode out into the open. "Men," he called, "I'd appreciate it if you watch my back. I have to check on those men we shot." If any of the vigilantes were close enough to hear him, they would think twice about getting close enough to shoot him. He doubted they wanted to join their friends on the drive.

Moses took a deep breath as he rolled over the first victim. Sightless eyes stared up at him from a narrow, bearded face that belonged to a man who hardly looked to be more than a boy.

Moving quickly from man to man, he checked to see if any of them were alive and needed care. As suspected, the ten vigilantes sprawled on the drive were all dead.

Sick at heart, Moses mounted and rode back down the drive.

It was time to go home.

Rose looked up hopefully when she heard the tunnel door open, but she remained motionless. No one had ever discovered the tunnel, but her first thought was to keep the children safe.

"Rose?"

Rose sagged against the wall when she heard her husband's voice. "Moses!"

Moses strode down the tunnel and pulled her into his arms. "Everything is safe. No one from Cromwell was hurt. We can all go to bed."

Rose heard the deep weariness and heartache in her husband's voice. She would wait until morning to ask questions. For tonight, it was enough to know Christmas morning would not bring fresh grief to the families that called Cromwell Planation home.

She watched as Moses carefully lifted John. The ease with which he did it made her smile. Only a man his size could carry his rapidly growing son.

Jeremy and Harold walked in next.

Jeremy stooped down and lifted Marcus, resting his son's head on his shoulder.

Harold followed suit with Sarah Rose, smiling tenderly as he looked down into her sleeping face.

Felicia, Frances and Minnie silently walked out behind them, obviously too tired to form words or ask questions.

"Merry Christmas, Rose," Phoebe said softly, covering her yawn with her hand.

Rose managed a smile. "Merry Christmas, Phoebe." Then she turned to Annie. "Everyone is exhausted. You don't have to be in the kitchen early. We can bypass Christmas breakfast and just have lunch."

Annie snorted. "Those children been sleepin' real peaceful since we done got into this tunnel. Y'all may be real tired, but they's gonna be rarin' to go about the same time they do ever' Christmas morning. I ain't gonna mess up any more of their Christmas than has already been messed up." She started down the tunnel. "Christmas breakfast gonna be served just like it's always been. I suspect you best go get some sleep, Rose. You ain't gonna get too much before my grandbabies gonna be making sure their mama and daddy wake up to celebrate Christmas."

Rose, however much she longed to deny it, knew she was speaking the truth.

Chapter Nineteen

"It's only five degrees out there!"

Grace looked up from folding laundry. "It's cold," she agreed calmly. "I'm grateful to be working inside a warm building." She eyed the woman who had spoken to her. "You're Mrs. Gordon, aren't you?

"I am," the woman agreed distantly.

Grace smiled. "It's a pleasure to meet you." She decided to ignore the fact that the head housekeeper had not asked her identity. "What's it like to live here?" She continued to fold as she talked.

Mrs. Gordon shrugged. "It's home. I have a room in the most luxurious hotel in Richmond, and I get paid to do my job." Her eyes darkened. "My husband was killed during the first year of the war. I thought my life had ended, until I got this job. Being a housekeeper can be tedious at times, but it's an honest way to make a living." Her eyes swept over Grace. "You're brand new."

"I am," Grace agreed, not certain how to read the housekeeper's expression.

"How did you get a job here?"

Grace didn't miss the hard edge in the woman's voice. "I applied for it," she said simply. She was careful to keep her voice casual. It had taken a long time to finally get a job. She wasn't looking for trouble.

"You and dozens of others," Mrs. Gordon said snidely.

"I guess I was lucky," Grace said amiably. She wasn't interested in conflict with the woman in charge of housekeeping, but she was beginning to suspect it couldn't be avoided. She thought back to the wonderful ride with Carrie and Phoebe earlier that day, and to the fun she had had with Willard during the cold ride back to Richmond. She touched her stomach tenderly, thinking of the new life blooming inside her. She had so much to be grateful for.

"I guess you were," Mrs. Gordon muttered.

The woman's eyes were still calculating, but they'd lost some of their hardness. Grace forced herself to relax. It was easy to suspect everyone was judging her because she was married to a white man, but there was no reason the housekeeper should be aware of that. It was just as likely that a close friend who had also applied for a position had been turned down. "What time will the steward start waking guests who are catching the first southbound train?" Rather than speculate on what she couldn't know, she would focus on doing her job. As soon as the train passengers departed the hotel, she would move into their rooms to prepare for the next guests.

"Soon," Mrs. Gordon said briskly. "He is to begin waking them a little after two o'clock. Their train leaves early." She turned away, suddenly all business.

Grace was happy to focus on work. Her shift had started at ten o'clock on Christmas Eve. The elegant, five-story, brick hotel located on the corner of Main and Eighth Street was resonating with music, light and laughter when she arrived. Gaily clad women swayed in the arms of dashing gentlemen as a band played in the ballroom. The last guests had retired to bed only an hour earlier, laughing and talking as they'd made their way down the corridors to their rooms.

Grace turned back to folding laundry. She almost had her housekeeping cart full of the supplies she would need.

Willard would be waiting for her at home when she completed her shift at eight o'clock. He had insisted on having a Christmas breakfast prepared for her when she arrived. She suspected most of the food would come from the heavy basket Annie had sent home with them, which meant it was sure to be delicious.

Grace smiled as she thought of the day ahead, but stiffened when she heard an odd sound below. She cocked her head as she struggled to determine what the noise was.

Peter jolted awake, dreams of Amanda fading immediately. For a moment he wasn't sure where he was, but then it all came rushing back. A train delay had landed him in Abraham Anderson's room at the Spotswood Hotel. Eager to get on the road, he reached for his watch to determine the time, but it was too dark in the room to read it. He reached for the lantern by his bedside, but then stopped. He didn't want to wake Abraham.

He pushed back the covers, walked across the room, and opened the door quietly, grateful when it didn't make a squeaking noise. He had stayed in more than his share of cheap, rundown hotels around the country. The luxury of the Spotswood was a welcome change.

Slipping out into the corridor, he lifted his pocket watch. If it was close to dawn, he was going to get ready and make his way to River City to hire a carriage. He hoped there would be someone there on Christmas Day. The thought that it might be closed for the holiday made him frown. His frown deepened as he looked down at his watch illuminated by the oil lanterns lining the hallway.

"Two fifteen," he muttered. "What the devil?" There was nothing he could do at that time of day except return to bed and attempt to get more sleep. As he turned to re-enter the room, he paused. There was a noise coming from below that sounded like someone breaking kindling wood. He kept his hand on the doorknob but continued to listen closely. The noise steadily grew, but there seemed to be no other sign of alarm that would indicate it was a problem.

Still...

Suddenly Peter's eyes widened as a thought burst through his sleep-deprived brain. He pushed open the room door and rushed to the window. When he looked out, his heart leapt into his throat.

"Abraham! Wake up!"

Abraham groaned and shifted in the bed, but he didn't wake.

"Wake up!" Peter shouted. "The hotel is on fire!"

The dreaded word created the desired result. A moment later, Abraham was up and standing beside him at the window. "Where is it burning?"

"On the second floor," Peter said tersely. "It seems to be right below us." As he talked, he shoved his shoes onto his feet. "I'm going to sound the alarm on our floor."

"I'll take the fourth floor," Abraham announced. Not bothering to put on his shoes, he ran out the door.

Moments later, Peter heard his friend running up the stairs. Within seconds, he was pounding on the door of the room next to him. "The hotel is on fire! Get up!" He pounded for several moments and then dashed to the next room. "Fire! Get out!"

Willard was sleeping soundly when a distant noise disturbed him. Nighttime noise in Richmond was hardly unusual, but he lay quietly and tried to determine what had roused him.

Seconds later the muted sound of a clanging bell caused him to leap from his bed.

It was a fire engine!

As he threw on his clothes, his mind raced. Richmond was a large city. There was no reason to think Grace could be in danger, especially in a brick hotel, but after hearing the story of how Minnie had lost her family, he wasn't going to take any chances.

Tugging on his hat and gloves, he tore from his small house on the outskirts of town and started running.

When he saw the glow of flames in the distance, he ran faster.

Grace gasped and looked around wildly as the first call of *Fire!* rang through the halls. She watched as a short, bald man dashed up the stairs in his bare feet and began pounding on doors.

"The hotel is on fire!" he yelled. "Get out!"

Paralyzed with indecision, the story of Minnie's family still emblazoned on her mind, Grace couldn't decide what to do.

The man looked up and saw her. "Get out of the hotel!" he hollered. "It's on fire!"

He turned and started pounding on another door. "Fire! The hotel is on fire! Get out!"

The hallway began to fill with panicked people. Men and women stumbled from their rooms, their eyes bleary from a lack of sleep after a night of celebrating Christmas.

"Get out!" the man continued to yell. "You don't have much time!"

Those words jolted Grace from her fearful trance. Not much time? Thoughts of Willard filled her mind as she joined the stream of people headed to the stairway.

"I have to get some clothes on," a woman wailed. She was dressed scantily in nothing but a sheer nightgown.

"Get out!" the man roared.

Grace suddenly understood what she was seeing in the man's face. He had experienced fire before. He'd seen what it could do. Wanting to do nothing but escape, she knew she needed to help. She turned and ran to the opposite end of the hallway from where he had started. She pounded on the last door with all her might. "Fire!" she screamed. "Get out! The hotel is on fire!" She pounded again, and then turned and dashed to the next door.

One by one, until she was looking into the eyes of the man who had first sounded the alarm, Grace pounded on doors.

"Thank you," the man said breathlessly. He turned toward the stairs. "We have to get out of here now. We've done all we can do!"

Grace felt fear tighten her throat as smoke began to waft up the stairway.

"Hurry!" the man urged.

Grace turned to flee, certain she had done her best to give everyone a chance at survival.

"Help me!"

Grace whirled around as she heard the voice of the housekeeper she had talked with earlier.

"Help me!" Mrs. Gordon stood in the door of a room, waving her arm wildly.

"We have to go!" Grace called. "There's no time!"

"No!" the housekeeper screamed. "You must help me!"

The man hesitated in his dash to the staircase. "Is there something wrong with her?"

Grace paused in confusion. "I don't think so." But what if she was wrong?

The man read the confusion on her face, cursed beneath his breath, and sprinted down the hallway toward the housekeeper.

Grace followed.

"Help me with my trunk!" Mrs. Gordon yelled as soon as they arrived at her door.

"What?" Anger flashed across the man's face. "You called us back into danger for a trunk?" He clenched his fists. "Do you not understand the hotel is on fire?" He gave her a look of disgust and turned away.

"You don't understand!" Mrs. Gordon wailed. "It's all I have left." Her voice caught. "It's all I have left of my husband!"

The man paused but shook his head. "You won't care about that when you're dead," he snapped through gritted teeth. He reached out for Grace's hand. "Hurry!"

Grace longed to take his hand, but she couldn't ignore the desperate plea in Mrs. Gordon's eyes. What if Willard had died and she was about to lose everything she had left of him? "You go," she urged him. "I will help her."

The man stared at her as if she had taken leave of her senses, growled something under his breath, and then turned and plunged into the housekeeper's room. "Where is the trunk?" he shouted.

"There!" Mrs. Gordon directed him to a small trunk in the far corner of her room.

Grace ventured close to one of the windows, her heart almost stopping when she saw flames shooting out of the windows on the floors below them. Three fire engines were outside, and throngs of people were on the street staring up at the building.

"We have to go!" the man yelled. He hoisted the trunk to his shoulder and turned to run down the hallway.

Grace and Mrs. Gordon picked up the hems of their dresses and dashed after him.

Grace stiffened when she realized the man had stopped at the top of the stairs. Why wasn't he running down?

A moment later, she had her answer. When she reached the landing, she could see the flames devouring the staircase. Moments later, with a shrieking wrench, the stairs collapsed, flames shooting up into the hallway.

Grace screamed, and then turned and ran.

Peter, wearing nothing but his nightclothes and shoes, stared up at the burning hotel. He'd managed to wake everyone on the third floor. He didn't know if everyone had escaped, but he'd done all he could. His eyes scanned the crowd as he searched desperately for Abraham. There was no use in calling out. He knew he wouldn't be heard above the screams and cries of the spectators, combined with the growing roar of the flames as they devoured the wooden structure beneath the bricks.

He gazed at white-faced women standing in bare feet on the snow-covered ground. Bystanders, called from their homes by the sound of the clanging fire engines, rushed forward to put coats around the survivor's trembling bodies.

Surely Abraham had gotten out.

"He saved us!" a man yelled. "I was sound asleep when he started pounding on our door. If it weren't for him, I would have burned to death."

Peter grabbed the man's arm. "Who? Who saved you?"

The man shook his head. "I don't know. He was small and bald."

Abraham!

"Where is he?" Peter demanded. "He's my friend. Where is he?"

The man shook his head regretfully. "I don't know. He was still pounding on doors when my wife and I ran downstairs. He and that woman."

"Woman? What woman?"

The man shook his head again. "I don't know. She was a black woman who seemed to work there. Perhaps one of the housekeepers?"

Peter knew he could get nothing else useful from the man, so he continued to walk down the road, peering into every face he saw.

Willard felt sick to the core of his being when he realized it was the Spotswood Hotel that was lighting the night with orange flames. The noise grew louder as the flames fed their hunger by consuming the wooden structure, along with everything that was in the hotel.

His heart leapt with hope when he saw the throng of people milling outside the burning structure. He saw a slender form in the distance. *Grace!* He raced forward, his heart plummeting when the woman turned. She wasn't Grace, but her uniform confirmed she worked at the hotel.

"Have you seen my wife?" Willard implored. "Her name is Grace. She's in housekeeping."

The woman shook her head. "I'm sorry, sir. I don't know any Grace."

Willard continued to race up and down the line of people.

"Willard!"

Willard stopped abruptly when he heard his name. His eyes widened when he turned to identify the caller. "Peter?" He stared at his friend in surprise. "What are you doing here?"

"It's a long story," Peter replied quickly. "I stayed here last night." His eyes narrowed. "What are *you* doing here?"

"Grace," Willard gasped. "Grace works here. She's working tonight." He felt a moment of hope, but the question died on his lips before he asked it. If Peter had seen Grace, he would have known why he was here. He still had to ask, though. "Have you seen her?"

"No," Peter admitted. "But so many have gotten out. I'm sure she is out here somewhere. I'm looking for a friend of mine who was helping me get people out of the hotel. We'll look together."

Willard nodded, but a sick knowing was building in his gut.

"Look!"

Willard looked up in the direction the woman was pointing. "What the...?"

The whole crowd fell silent as a man stuck his head out a window on the third floor.

"Help!" the man yelled.

"Why aren't the engines pouring water on the fire?" Willard demanded.

Peter shook his head with frustration. "It's too cold. The water in the engines is frozen. They're trying to thaw it out."

Willard stared at him with disbelief. "So it's just going to burn? Aren't they going to help that man, at least?"

As if in response to his question, one of the firemen ran forward with a ladder.

Another fireman shook his head. "It won't do any good. The ladders don't go up that high."

Peter whirled toward the fireman. "You're telling me you have five-story buildings in this town, and you don't have ladders that will reach to the top floors? What are you going to do about that man up there?"

The fireman shook his head, his eyes glazed with pity as he stared up.

Moments later, the man leapt from the third-floor window.

Peter knew it was a desperate attempt at life. He also knew there was no way the man had survived the fall.

Grace dashed into the housekeeper's room. She sensed it was a futile effort, but at least she was as far from the fire as she could get.

Mrs. Gordon ran in after her. "What are we going to do?" she cried. Tears rolled down her cheeks. "I'm so sorry I asked you to help me with the trunk!"

At the mention of the trunk, Grace looked around for the man who had helped save so many of the guests. He was nowhere in sight. She sent up a prayer for him, and then rushed to the window. She tugged with all her might and was able to force it open.

Mrs. Gordon rushed to join her. Together, they stuck their heads out the window to gulp in fresh air.

"Help!" Mrs. Gordon screamed. "Help!"

Down below, Grace saw a crowd of faces turn to stare up at them.

"Grace! Grace!"

Grace sucked in her breath when she heard Willard.

"Willard!" she screamed. "Willard!"

Just as she cried out, a gust of wind fed the inferno with more oxygen. Flames leapt from the windows below her, forcing her to duck back inside to escape them.

Willard sprinted toward the hotel when Grace disappeared from the window.

"Stop!"

Willard felt two men grab his arms and wrestle him back. "Let me go!" he yelled, exerting all his strength to break away from them.

"You can't go in there!" one man yelled. "It's a death trap."

Willard recognized the uniform of a Richmond policeman. "My wife is in there," he yelled. "I have to get to her! I have to help her!"

The two men didn't release their grips. "You can't get to her, buddy," one of them said, sympathy softening his stern voice.

Peter saw the policemen grab Willard, and then turned back to stare at the window where Grace had disappeared. He willed her to appear again.

As he watched, he saw several people climb from their windows and lower themselves by sheets and blankets they had knotted together. One person let go with a scream when fire exploded from a window they were passing, but more of them made it. If Grace would only look out again, he could tell her what to do.

"Look out," he muttered. "Look outside, Grace!"

Peter stiffened as another figure climbed from a fourth-floor window, gripping tightly to a windowsill and cornice. He peered through the smoke, recognizing the slight figure of a man. "Abraham," he whispered.

Abraham stretched out a foot until it touched a cornice, and then slid down the face of the hotel. Once he was standing on the cornice, he peered over the edge, identified the next one, and continued his treacherous descent down the building.

Peter knew that if Abraham's hands slipped, his friend would fall to his death. "Come on, Abraham. You can do this."

"You can do it!" another man yelled out.

All around him, people began to yell encouragement to the man who was descending the face of the burning hotel like a squirrel. Flames shooting out the windows all around him threatened to dislodge his desperate grip, but Abraham somehow held on, even when the nightclothes he was wearing caught fire.

Abraham reached the bottom and dropped into the arms of two firemen. They quickly extinguished the flames by wrapping a blanket around him, but Peter knew his friend must be horribly burned.

Grace stared around the room frantically. Willard couldn't watch her die. There had to be a way out of the burning hotel.

"What are we going to do?" Mrs. Gordon screamed, panic contorting her face.

Somehow, her panic helped Grace analyze their situation calmly. She opened the doorway and looked down the hall. It was already consumed with flames that were licking their way toward them rapidly. She slammed the door shut. There was no hope of escape down the hallway.

Grace turned back to the window. A shift in the wind had forced the flames away from the opening. Hope burgeoning in her heart, she ran toward the window and poked her head out again.

"Grace!"

Grace stared down, momentarily shocked at the sight of Peter Wilcher. It didn't matter how he had gotten there. A second later, Willard appeared next to him.

"Willard!" Grace cried.

Peter's voice boomed through the noise. "Tie some bedsheets together and let yourself down!"

Grace stared at him, and then watched with disbelief as she saw two other people doing just what he suggested.

"Do it!" Willard yelled. "Do it!"

Grace whirled away from the window. "Pull the bedsheets and blankets off the bed." She was ripping down floor length curtains as she gave the order. "We'll tie them together and climb down."

"We don't have time," Mrs. Gordon cried, her eyes brimming with hopelessness.

Grace rushed to push her aside and rip the bedding off. She might be about to die, but she was going to fight for life with every breath she had left. She began to knot the sheets together as quickly as she could, coughing as smoke crept in under the door. She could tell by the orange glow around the frame that the fire was just outside the room.

Grace continued to knot the sheets together, praying she would soon have enough to reach the ground. Her hands trembled as tiny flickers of fire appeared through the wooden door.

"The fire is here!" Mrs. Gordon screamed.

Grace felt hopelessness engulf her as she realized the knotted sheets weren't long enough to reach the ground. She also knew she couldn't climb out the window and leave Mrs. Gordon alone. She touched her stomach tenderly, and then closed her eyes to emblazon Willard's image on her heart.

She doubled over with coughs when a cloud of hot smoke exploded into the room, followed by a flash of searing flames. Reaching forward, she grasped Mrs. Gordon's hand and led her to the open window.

Willard stared up at the window, grasping onto hope that Grace would soon appear and begin to climb down the front of the hotel. "Come on!" he yelled. "Where are you, Grace? Where are you?" He was sure his heart was going to explode from his chest.

After what seemed an eternity, he finally saw Grace's face at the window.

Another woman appeared next to her, tears streaming down her face.

Why weren't they climbing out? Where was the rope of bed sheets?

Grace met his eyes, a tender look of love on her face. He saw the terror in her eyes, but they also held pity. "I'm sorry," she mouthed. "I love you."

"No!" Willard yelled. "No!"

Moments later an explosion of flames illuminated the window where the two women had stood just seconds earlier.

Chapter Twenty

Carrie had just finished giving Granite his Christmas treat of an apple when she heard the distant sound of a carriage rolling down the drive. She hugged her horse and then walked toward the door to discover who their visitor was.

"Hold on, Carrie Girl." Miles materialized from the tack room and took hold of her arm. "After all the trouble last night, you ain't just gonna go waltzing out there."

Carrie stopped with an exasperated sigh. She knew he was right, but she hated that his warning was necessary. It wasn't likely that the vigilantes were going to just ride up to the house, especially after the loss they'd experienced the night before. However, if they'd been crazy enough to attempt an attack in the first place, there was really no telling what they would do. She edged to the door to peer out.

The door to the house opened at the same time. Moses and Anthony stepped out, rifles cradled in their arms as they peered down the road. They made impressive-looking figures as they stood silhouetted against the late afternoon light.

As Annie had predicted, the children had woken early that morning, excited about Christmas Day. Despite all that had transpired during the night, and despite lingering fatigue, it had been a day full of joy and laughter. It had also been a day filled with great appreciation that the vigilantes had been stopped at the gate before they could do any damage, and that not one person involved in the protection of the plantation had been harmed.

Jeb had come right after breakfast to tell Moses that the bodies of the dead vigilantes had all been removed during the night. He had watched the KKK members return, but had informed all the men still standing guard to let them collect their friends and leave. Moses had been clear that there would be no more death unless absolutely necessary.

After dinner had been served and enjoyed, Annie had filled a basket to overflowing and asked Jeb deliver it to Hank's decrepit cabin in the woods. Everyone was keenly aware of how much they owed him for his willingness to betray the vigilantes.

Carrie stiffened as the carriage rounded the last curve. "Who...?" Her eyes widened as she identified the driver. "Peter? What a pleasant surprise!" Then her eyes narrowed. "Who's with him?" It was impossible to tell beneath the mounds of blankets piled around his passengers.

"Only one way to tell," Miles said laconically.

Carrie gave him a smile and then hurried to the house, arriving just as the carriage pulled to a stop. "Hello, Peter! What..." One look at his face made her heart sink. What had caused the hollow look of grief in his eyes?

When the blankets were tossed aside, she took a step back in surprise.

Thomas and Moses strode down the porch steps as Marcus helped Hannah from the carriage, but all eyes were on Willard. The same vibrant, laughing man who had departed early the morning before now looked like a mere shadow of himself. He stared back at them silently.

Carrie held a hand to her mouth. Grace wasn't with them. It could mean only one thing, but she couldn't begin to wrap her mind around what Grace's absence was saying.

Carrie tore her eyes from Willard. "What happened?" she asked Peter quietly.

Peter shook his head. "I think it's best if we all go inside."

Thomas stepped onto the carriage, helped Willard to his feet, and then assisted him as he shakily climbed down. Once Willard's feet hit the ground, it took all of Thomas' strength to hold him up.

Marcus sprang to Willard's other side. "I've got you," he said gently.

Carrie fought back the tears flooding her eyes. She understood the grief Willard was feeling all too well. The details would be revealed in time. The only thing that mattered right now was taking care of a brokenhearted man.

Annie and Abby had taken over as soon as Willard stepped into the house. They got him settled into a bed, wrapped him with blankets to still his shaking body, and sat with him until he fell asleep from sheer exhaustion.

Not one word had been spoken.

Now they were all seated around the fire in the parlor. Felicia, Frances and Minnie were upstairs with the younger children.

"Tell us what happened," Thomas said.

Peter opened his mouth, but no words came out.

Everyone waited quietly, giving him time to say what no one really wanted to hear.

"There was a fire at the Spotswood Hotel," Peter finally managed. His voice choked. "Grace…"

Marcus came to his rescue. "Grace didn't make it out," he said quietly.

The whole room stared at him in stunned silence. They had already assumed the worst, but the full truth was more than they could bear.

"Grace died…in the fire?" Rose whispered. "She's…gone?"

Hannah swiped at the tears rolling down her face. "She was on the fourth floor. She didn't make it out."

Marcus took a deep breath. "Peter and his friend Abraham were responsible for getting most of the people off those floors. Grace helped Abraham clear the fourth floor… It was too late for her to make it out.

Carrie didn't know why Peter had been at the Spotswood Hotel, but it hardly mattered. Grace was gone, along with her unborn child. Carrie's heart broke as she fully comprehended the depth of Willard's agony.

Peter finally found his voice. "Willard saw it happen," he said hoarsely.

"Saw it happen?" Thomas echoed in a stunned voice. "What do you mean?"

Peter swallowed. "We were standing together when Grace leaned out the window and called for help." He shook his head as if wanting to deny what was coming from his mouth. "We tried to get her to tie sheets together to climb down the sides of the hotel. It was too late…We saw the fire take her. We heard…" His face twisted with pain as he fell silent.

Carrie didn't try to stop her sobs. She thought of Grace's bright face on their ride together the morning before. She remembered the look of utter joy in her eyes when she had informed them she was pregnant.

"How many more?" Abby said angrily. "How many more lives will fire take?"

Carrie was jolted from her grief by Abby's anger. Eddie and Opal's children had died in a fire in Philadelphia years earlier. They'd lost Deirdre and her children just two weeks ago. And now Grace. Carrie felt her own anger swell, but it was quickly doused by the memory of the total devastation on Willard's face. There was no room for anger in the face of such grief.

"Where were the firemen?" Anthony demanded. "There are new alarms. New fire engines." He shook his head. "How much of the hotel burned?"

"All of it," Peter said heavily. "Five other business burned as well, but they were empty." He looked down at his shaking hands for a moment. "The alarms sounded, and the fire engines came, but they were encased in ice and the water was frozen. The building was almost consumed before the water thawed enough to use it." His voice turned bitter. "There were people on the top floors that could have been saved, but the ladders weren't long enough to reach them."

"No," Abby said in an agonized whisper. "How is it possible that their ladders weren't long enough? How is that possible?"

Carrie closed her eyes as she thought of Grace waiting for help that wasn't able to arrive.

"How many?" Anthony asked.

"The last I heard, there are seven dead, but there could be more," Peter reported. "The guest register was burned.

All they know is that there are several unidentified trunks that haven't been claimed. It's assumed their owners were in the hotel."

"Who is Abraham?" Jeremy asked.

Carrie wasn't surprised by the dull shock in Jeremy's voice. He and Marietta were the first that Willard and Grace had told when they learned they were expecting a child. The four had spent hours talking about what it would be like to raise a mulatto child in Richmond. Jeremy had told her after they left that Willard and Grace were considering a move north, just like they had made, to provide a better life for their child.

Peter flinched. "A friend who is a reporter for the *New York Times.* I was sharing a room with him. I was going to surprise you yesterday, but my train was delayed. I stayed at the Spotswood instead..."

The room remained silent as he fought for control.

"Abraham went up to the fourth floor to wake up guests. I woke everyone on the third floor." He swallowed. "He managed to get out, though. He climbed down the side of the hotel. Without ropes or bedsheets..."

Carrie gasped with surprise. "From the fourth floor?"

"No one knows how he did it. He was determined to get home to his family for Christmas..."

Marcus finished his words. "He made it down to the ground, but Abraham was badly burned. He's at the hospital now."

Carrie watched him, knowing that what Marcus *wasn't* saying was more important than the words coming from his mouth. Abraham must be terribly burned. They would have no way of knowing if he had lived through the day.

"I sent his family a telegram," Peter said. "Then I found Marcus and Hannah so we could bring Willard out here."

Now that he'd gotten through the worst of the story, his voice was a little stronger. "He didn't need to be in his house alone. He could have stayed with Marcus and Hannah, but we all thought it would be better if he was back here."

"You were absolutely right to bring him here," Abby said. "We're his family."

Carrie understood the deep grief in her mother's eyes. Everyone loved Grace, but Abby had taken an instant liking to the young woman and had taken on a motherly role in her life. She had also been the one responsible for helping Grace get the job at the hotel. Carrie could imagine what she was feeling now. There was no reason to feel guilty, but it wouldn't keep her from feeling it, just the same.

"Has Willard said anything?" Carrie asked.

Peter shook his head. "He screamed Grace's name when she disappeared in the fire." His voice tightened with pain. "Then he collapsed in my arms. He hasn't said a word since."

Carrie stood. "I'm going up to sit with him. He shouldn't be alone when he wakes."

Everyone nodded. Only someone who had experienced the grief Willard was feeling should be there when he was forced to face reality again. All of them had suffered loss, but Carrie's was most recent, and the death was equally senseless.

The room was shrouded in darkness. The only light was created by flickering flames in the fireplace, their shadows dancing across the walls. Even though Carrie was exhausted from lack of sleep, memories kept her awake. Robert's laugh… his twinkling blue eyes… his constant encouragement for her to become a doctor. Ripped apart by the war many times, they'd always found their way back into each other's arms. She had slipped into his arms for the last time just a few minutes before he closed his eyes for good, ending the dreams they'd shared.

Most of the time, the memories stayed in a back room of her mind, kept at bay by the joy of her new life, but sitting here in this room with Willard had brought them all roaring back. Any death was a cause for grief, but senseless deaths in the prime of life were almost impossible to bear.

Somehow, she had made it through. Willard would do the same.

Carrie became aware of a shift of energy in the room. Looking over at the bed, she saw Willard watching her, an inscrutable look on his face.

"Hello," she said softly.

As anticipated, Willard remained silent.

Carrie knew there was absolutely nothing she could say that would ease the pain waking had caused, though she suspected his sleep had been nothing but nightmares of the fire. She stood, moved her chair closer to him, and reached over to take his hand. "I'm here," was all she said.

Willard stiffened and started to draw away, but then stopped, a vulnerable look suffusing his eyes. He gripped her hand and closed his eyes.

Carrie knew the grief was still too raw for the anger to have settled in. She continued to hold his hand, not moving when his labored breathing finally relaxed into sleep again.

Carrie and Anthony were still in bed the next morning when Frances and Minnie slipped through the door.

"Mama?"

Carrie opened an eye. "Mmm?"

"Mama, why is Willard still in his room?" Frances asked in a small voice. "Peter won't tell us. Neither will Marcus or Hannah."

Carrie yawned, hoping the oxygen to her brain would wake her enough for this conversation.

Anthony patted the space between them. "Come on up, girls."

Frances and Minnie clambered onto the bed, their faces full of worry.

"Is Mr. Willard all right?" Minnie asked. "I saw him out the window when they rode up in the carriage. He didn't look very good."

"No," Carrie agreed. "He didn't look very good." She prayed for the right words that wouldn't make Minnie's recent catastrophic loss even worse.

"What happened?" Frances asked. "And where is Grace? Why couldn't she come with him? Did she have to work at the hotel?"

Mention of the hotel made Carrie wince. "There was an accident last night," she said slowly. Was it possible to explain what had happened without mentioning the fire?

"Is Miss Grace hurt?" Minnie asked sharply. "I like her a whole lot. She taught me more knitting stitches when she was here. She's real nice."

Carrie took a deep breath. Both the girls had experienced tremendous loss in their lives. If it were possible, she would protect them from any more pain for the rest of their lives, but she owed them the truth. She reached out and gripped their hands tightly. "Girls, Grace is dead." It didn't matter that she said the words gently - they still hung in the room like a dark cloud.

The girls blinked once and then twice but remained silent.

"There was an accident last night," Carrie said softly. "Grace didn't survive." Saying the words made her want to scream with frustration. Willard's lovely wife should be laughing and planning the birth of her baby.

"She's *dead?*" Minnie said slowly, her eyes dull with confusion.

Carrie gripped her hand more tightly. "Yes."

"How?" Frances demanded. "She was just here yesterday morning. She was fine. How could she have died?"

Carrie looked at Anthony helplessly. She couldn't bring herself to say the words.

"Girls," Anthony said and then fell silent. He, too, was struggling for the right words. "Grace died in a fire last night while she was working." The look in his eyes revealed he could hardly believe what he was saying. He'd seen Minnie's family perish in a fire just two weeks earlier. Now he was explaining that the same thing had taken another friend.

Minnie gasped and recoiled away from them. "A fire?" Her blue eyes went from sad and confused to wildly turbulent "Grace died in a *fire?*" She started shaking her head frantically. "That can't be!"

Carrie tried to pull her into her arms, but Minnie drew back.

"A *fire?*" Minnie's whole body was shaking uncontrollably. "How?"

Anthony looked at Carrie with alarm but answered in a calm, easy voice. "There was a fire last night at the hotel where Grace worked, sweetie. She didn't make it out."

Carrie was glad the girls would never need to know the details of how Willard had watched his wife be consumed by the flames.

"It's my fault!" Minnie cried.

"What?" Carrie grabbed her hands again, jolted from her own thoughts. "Minnie, no! It's not your fault." How could the little girl possibly think that?

Minnie continued to shake, tears pouring down her face. "Me and Grace became friends... She's dead because of me," she insisted.

It took a minute for Carrie to realize what Minnie was really feeling. The little girl had cried inconsolably the night her family died, but she had been stoic since then. She had talked about her sadness and about missing her family, but she hadn't shown more of her emotion.

Carrie had thought that Minnie was incredibly resilient, but now she realized it had been nothing more than burying emotions she couldn't bear to face. "Come here, honey." This time, when Minnie resisted her efforts to pull her into her arms, Carrie hugged her close anyway.

"Minnie, it's not your fault that your family died," Carrie said. "It was a horrible accident."

Minnie continued to sob. "I should have been there. If I hadn't been making Mama a birthday gift, I would have been there, too. I would have died with my family..." She fought for breath. "I should be dead, too," she wailed.

Carrie understood her daughter's pain. She had seen so many soldiers deal with the struggle of surviving a battle when their friends had died all around them. Part of them was glad to have survived, but an equal part believed they weren't worthy to be the one left living. It didn't matter that their belief wasn't logical; it was *their* belief.

She thought back to the long conversations she had had with the soldiers under her care. It didn't help to tell them they shouldn't feel guilty, because they were going to feel it anyway. It also didn't help for them to feel relief and appreciation for having survived, because they felt guilt and shame for having those very feelings when others hadn't been as lucky.

Carrie prayed silently as she held Minnie in her arms. She had seen the guilt resolve itself over time in many people. Robert had battled it. Moses had battled it. Every soldier she had treated had battled it. Not everyone was successful, though. She was convinced it was the reason many veterans were now fighting a losing battle with alcohol and drugs. They were the only way to escape the pain.

"Honey, I don't believe your mama would have wanted you there that night, but I understand why you feel guilty."

Minnie gulped back her tears and peered up through watery blue eyes. "You...do?" she stuttered.

"Yes. I'm also sure that everyone who didn't die in the fire that night feels the same way you do. They're all wondering why they lived when so many others died."

Minnie nodded. "It feels real bad."

"I know," Carrie said sympathetically. "It's okay to cry about losing your family, sweetie. I want you to cry any time you need to."

Minnie stared up at her again, her eyes glittering with uncertainty. "I don't want you to think I don't appreciate your taking me in."

Carrie hugged her more closely. "Honey, you can feel grief and gratitude at the same time. When my first husband died, I cried for a very long time. Just when I thought it was getting better, something would remind me of him, and I would start crying all over again."

"I cry in bed at night," she admitted.

Carrie tipped her head up so their eyes could meet. "It's all right if you need to cry at night, but it's also all right if you cry during the day. Doesn't it help a little bit for me to be holding you when you cry?"

Minnie sniffed but nodded again. "Yes," she whispered.

"There's also nothing wrong with being glad you lived," Carrie said gently. "Being glad you're alive doesn't mean you're not terribly sad that your family died."

Minnie was silent for a long moment as she absorbed that thought. "I still don't know why I wasn't there that night, Carrie. I don't know why I didn't die."

"Neither do I," Carrie admitted. "I've never figured out why some people die while others live." She gritted her teeth as she thought of Grace trapped in a burning building when so many others had lived.

"Do you think I should have died?" Minnie asked in a small voice.

"No," Carrie said firmly as she pulled her close again. "I'm so very glad you lived, Minnie. I may not know why some people die and other people live, but I can promise you that you're alive for a reason."

"I am?" Minnie pushed back and looked up into her face. "What's the reason?"

Carrie brushed back the hair from the little girl's face tenderly. She wanted to give Minnie the solid answer she was looking for, but she couldn't. There were still days she asked the same thing herself. "I can't tell you all the reasons, but I can tell you that as you grow up, you should look for every way possible to create something good from the second chance at life you've been given."

"That's what I'm doing," Frances said as she took one of Minnie's hands. "I don't know why I lived and everyone else in my family died, but I finally decided it's not bad to be glad I'm alive."

Minnie considered her words. "How long did it take to be glad?"

Carrie stroked the little girl's cheek. She understood her impatience all too well. "That's going to be different for everyone, Minnie. The important thing is that we're here to help you with the grief *and* with the questions. You're not alone with them."

Minnie fell silent for several moments and then looked back up, a hopeful question in her eyes. "So... I'm not selfish? It's not bad to be glad I'm still alive?"

"I promise you it's not a bad thing," Carrie replied. "Every moment that you can be glad you're still alive is a good thing. It means you appreciate the gift you were given."

"A gift..." Minnie murmured the words quietly, her face reflecting the struggle to accept the idea of her survival being a gift.

Carrie had one more thing to add. "Do you think your mama would want you to feel bad about living?"

Minnie stiffened and turned her head, but didn't pull away. "No," she finally admitted softly. "Mama used to tell me almost every night that she wanted me to have a happy life. She was real sad that she couldn't give that to me, but she wanted it for me more than anything." She shook her head. "She wanted it for Jack and Margaret and Sally, too," she said sadly. "I guess, though, that she had be real happy one of us got it."

Chapter Twenty-One
New Year's Day, 1871

Carrie was grateful for the silence as the Cromwell women walked from the tunnel and onto the shore of the James River. Maintaining silence until the sun rose on the new year was tradition, but she needed it especially this year. So much had happened to change her life dramatically in the year that had just ended. She already knew the coming year was going to create the same type of massive transformation.

Gazing across the circle of logs that the Cromwell men had created for them, she locked eyes with Rose. She thought back to all the times she had shared the beginning of a new year with her best friend. Each year had brought surprises and unexpected situations. Neither of them had ever dreamed they would still be here on the plantation—professional women, wives and mothers. And still best friends.

Carrie felt herself relax a little. No matter how many things in life might change, there were always things that were a constant. While she had a plan for 1871, she already suspected that when she reached the end of the twelve months looming ahead of her, the reality would be quite different than that plan. As she got older, that became easier to accept.

Her eyes settled on Frances lovingly. Her oldest daughter had her eyes fixed on the horizon, waiting for the first hint of the sunrise. She thought about how Frances had bloomed in Philadelphia, finding her passion in helping children trapped in the factories. Matthew had sent a framed copy of the first article she had written, and then had published in the *Philadelphia Inquirer*. Carrie would never forget the look of pride on Frances' face when she opened it on Christmas morning.

Minnie huddled next to her sister, wrapped securely in the thick quilt she had carried through the tunnel. Her narrow face revealed equal parts of sadness and hope. Carrie knew her daughter's thoughts were wrapped around the family she had lost so recently, while also wishing with all her heart that the new year would be easier.

Minnie, after their long talk when Grace died, was more willing to share her sadness. There had been many times in the last week when she had allowed Carrie or Anthony to hold her while she cried. Each time, the tears seemed to end just a little bit faster, and the eventual smile would appear just a tad sooner. There was much healing still to be done, but the little girl was taking a new step every single day.

Carrie allowed her eyes to roam around the circle. Abby, Marietta, Susan, Polly, Frances, Minnie, Felicia, Amber, Annie, Phoebe, Hannah and Angel were all snuggled into cozy quilts, their breath forming plumes of smoke as they waited, each silent with their own thoughts.

Carrie loved having all their daughters with them. She was sure that as the girls grew, they would carry on the tradition of welcoming in the new year with the women in their lives.

Her heart caught when she remembered Grace's joy at being part of the tradition the year before. It was inconceivable that the sweet, loving woman had died in the Spotswood Hotel fire.

Eight people had died that night. Abraham Anderson was still fighting for his life in the City Hospital in Richmond, but the doctors' confidence in his eventual recovery was high. His body would never be the same because of the terrible burns, but having his wife arrive from New York had lifted his spirits tremendously. Peter had visited with his friend before catching the train for New York the day before.

The knot in her heart tightened as she realized that any one of the beloved women she was looking at now might not be with them in twelve months.

A gasp from Minnie pulled her from her somber thoughts. Carrie smiled as her daughter, her eyes fixed on the glowing horizon, bounced on her log.

The silence held, all eyes fixed on the golden orb as it peeked over the edge of the earth and then slowly ascended, kissing the clouds with pink, orange and purple as it rose.

Carrie held her breath. Last year's sunrise had been swallowed by snow clouds that had delivered on their promise before they left the beach that morning. While it had still been a memorable time, this year's glorious daybreak spoke of new beginnings and the promise of light shining through the dark clouds that had threatened so many of their lives.

Carrie watched Minnie. She could see hope illuminated in the little girl's eyes as the sun landed on her uplifted face. When Minnie turned back, she saw peace for the first time since the fire had claimed her family.

When the sun had fully loosed itself from the horizon, Minnie looked at her. "Now?" she mouthed silently.

Carrie smiled and looked at Rose. When she grinned and nodded, they pushed aside their quilts and leapt to their feet, every other woman followed their lead.

"Happy New Year! Happy New Year!"

Laughing and yelling with joy and celebration, the women danced on the snowy bank, their arms lifted in the air. They hugged each other with exuberance, and then went back to dancing. The sun continued to climb, casting its bright light on them until they finally collapsed back onto their logs.

When everyone had caught their breath, Carrie nodded at Abby.

Abby stood, her warm smile sweeping over everyone. "Happy 1871!"

The women cheered again and then fell silent, watching her expectantly.

"1870 has been a year full of joyous happenings, but also times of great loss," Abby said. "As I look back over my life, I believe every single year has been that way. While we might think this year was unique, every year offers joy and loss." She let her words sink in for a moment before she continued. "We had new life enter the world when Annabelle was born."

Carrie smiled tenderly when she thought of Janie's adorable daughter.

"We had miraculous occurrences that saved lives we thought would be lost."

Carrie's throat tightened when she thought of how close the Capitol collapse had come to taking Anthony, her father and Matthew from them. Her heart swelled with gratitude that all of the men had survived.

Abby's voice grew somber. "And we've lost people who will forever be part of our hearts and our memories." She gazed at Angel. "Honey, you will always miss your mama, your brother and your sisters, but this year is going to bring amazing things into your life. You have become part of the Bregdan Women. We are here for you."

Murmurs of agreement sounded around the circle as Amber and Polly took her hands. Angel smiled, her eyes full of wonder.

Abby's eyes turned to Minnie next. "Minnie, your loss is so new. I know it hurts to breathe sometimes and you wonder why you're the one who is still alive."

Minnie brushed away tears as she nodded.

Abby gazed at her lovingly. "The pain will never completely go away, but it will become a little more bearable with each day that passes." She walked over and reached down for Minnie's gloved hand, clasping it tightly with both of hers. "As each day and year passes, you'll understand a little more why you're still here. You're surrounded by Bregdan Women who all promise to help you have the best life possible. We love you, and we're here for you." She knelt down and hugged her. "I'm so very glad you're my granddaughter now," she whispered.

Carrie blinked back tears as her mother stood again.

"All of us are going to miss Grace," Abby said quietly, her eyes reflecting the pain of her personal loss.

Carrie's thoughts flew to Willard. It had been a week since Grace had died. Yesterday, for the first time, he'd been willing to eat some of the soup Annie had sent up to him, just as she had three times a day since he'd arrived. He still hadn't spoken Grace's name except when he was tossing at night, consumed with nightmares. Everyone had taken turns sitting with him to make sure he wasn't ever alone. Marcus and Hannah would return to Richmond tomorrow, but Willard would stay on the plantation until he was certain he could face returning to the city that had stolen his dreams.

"It's easy to focus on the losses of life," Abby continued. "I have found it much more helpful to focus on the things I'm grateful for. Every year of my life has delivered a loss, but every year of my life has also created so many things that are a reason for gratitude. There is a place for grief, but there should also be plenty of room for joy. I find it's a choice I must make every single day. Sometimes every single *moment* when things are especially hard."

Abby's eyes misted over. "I loved Grace very much. She was quite special to me, and she was a remarkable woman full of bravery and conviction. She died because she felt compassion for a woman who had lost her husband and couldn't face the thought of losing the only memories she had of him. There is nothing that could make her horrific death make sense, but I know that if Grace could sit with us today, she would tell us to make the most of every day of life we have." She took a deep breath. "I don't know why I'm alive today. I don't know why each of you is alive today, but we all are. Every day of life that we're given is a gift we should cherish. It's also a day that we should do something to make our country a better place...to make our world a better place."

Carrie listened closely. This was already a belief she held close to her heart, but on the cusp of starting a medical clinic in Richmond, it struck home even harder. All the years of school and study were behind her. She realized that what had seemed like such a long time was minimal compared to the years that stretched before her. She agreed with Abby that it was impossible to make sense of all the losses that had come in the past year, or all the years before for that matter.

The simple fact was that she was alive.

What she did with that fact was up to her.

"I'm going to stop fires from happening!" Minnie said defiantly, her eyes snapping with determination.

Abby smiled at her encouragingly. "I believe you'll do just that."

Carrie agreed. Minnie had all the motivation needed to help change things in the country so that fewer people lost their lives in fires. It would take people with great passion and determination to make the changes.

"I'm going to be a doctor just like Mama," Frances said. "If she hadn't helped Mr. Hank and his friends, they wouldn't have helped us on Christmas Eve. I want to care about people as much as she does!"

Carrie reached over to take both her daughters' hands, amazed she had the privilege of being a part of these girls' lives. "Thank you," she said warmly.

"What are you going to do with *your* life, Mama?" Frances asked.

Carrie met her eyes. The easy answer was that she would be the best doctor she could be, but she could feel something compelling her to search deeper. She remained silent for a long moment and then smiled. "I'm going to be the best doctor I can be, but..." She took a deep breath as she suddenly understood. "But...I believe the most important thing I'll do is help as many children as possible become all they can be."

Speaking the words solidified what had been growing in her heart since the day she had adopted Frances. It had intensified when Minnie had become her and Anthony's daughter. She and Anthony had avoided adopting another child after Frances because they couldn't envision walking into an orphanage and having to choose what child they would leave with.

What would happen if they simply opened their life to whatever child was brought to them?

Carrie looked up and saw Abby and Rose watching her closely, their faces glowing with understanding and approval.

"I'm going to do whatever it takes to become as good a teacher as Rose," Phoebe said, breaking the silence that followed Carrie's statement.

Carrie was grateful when Abby and Rose stopped staring at her so intently and switched their attention to Phoebe. She was certain of her decision, but she needed some time to absorb it.

"You're already a wonderful teacher," Rose replied. "Teaching with you has been a joy."

Phoebe took a deep breath, her eyes shining with nervous excitement. "Enough of a joy to accept me as your co-teacher when I graduate this spring?"

Rose grinned. "I can't think of anything that would make me happier!"

Phoebe clapped her hands, jumped up, spun in a circle, and then sat back down, her eyes glittering with excitement. "Thank you," she breathed.

"Of course," Susan said dryly, "the question is whether you're returning for your students or the Cromwell horses." Her eyes were dancing.

Phoebe laughed. "Let's just say there are several things that make me want to return to the South."

Laughter flowed around the circle.

Carrie listened as the rest of the assembly shared what they intended to do with the life they'd been given, but her mind continued to race through her sudden decision.

Actually, while it may have felt sudden, she was aware this decision had been building for a long time. Though part of her had held onto the hope that she could have a child of her own someday, she had slowly come to realize that her life, just the way it was, was far too precious to risk. She already knew any attempt to have another child could kill her, but it was more than that. She had grown to understand that she couldn't possibly love a biological child any more than the two children who had been given to her through tragic circumstances.

Everyone had finished Annie's New Year's Day feast. The older children were putting together a puzzle, the men were playing cards in the parlor, and Hope, Marcus and Sarah had settled down for a nap.

"What am I going to do, Mama?" John asked.

Rose raised a brow, wishing that John was clamoring to go out to the barn. It broke her heart that he still refused to even look in that direction. "What would you like to do, son?"

John sighed heavily and looked down. "I don't know."

Rose frowned. When he wasn't at school, John seemed lost. Rascal had been his whole life. When he wasn't riding, he had spent every minute helping his grandfather in the stables. He refused to ride the fields with Moses, becoming hysterical if they pressed, so they'd learned not to. He pretended not to care when Hope would ride off with her daddy on her little pony, Patches, but Rose could read the pain in his eyes.

Miles walked in the house just then, whistling cheerfully. "Where's my favorite grandson?"

John managed a chuckle. "I'm your *only* grandson, Grandpa."

"Which makes you more special," Miles answered. "That must be why I got you a New Year's gift."

Rose looked at him with raised brows. He hadn't told her anything about a surprise. Moses hadn't mentioned it either.

John jumped up from the table, his boredom forgotten. "What is it, Grandpa?"

"I reckon you're gonna have to come outside to find out," Miles said mysteriously.

John frowned and hesitated. "I'm not coming to the barn, Grandpa."

His face was set in the stubborn lines that Rose knew so well. He looked just like his daddy when he got that expression.

"I don't remember sayin' nothin' about the barn," Miles responded. "I just said it was outside."

John still hesitated.

Rose knew Miles had done everything within his power to get John back to the barn after Rascal died, but nothing had worked for him either.

Miles stood quietly, waiting for John to decide.

John's curiosity finally won out over his reluctance. He nodded and headed for the door.

"Put your winter clothes on," Rose called.

"I'm just going outside," John replied in a dismissive voice.

Miles stepped in front of the door. "Do what your mama says, young man."

John sighed but quickly put on his coat, hat and gloves. "I'm ready," he announced.

Rose walked to the window so she could see outside. What she saw made her gasp with surprise. Moments later, Carrie, Abby, Annie and Phoebe were crowded next to her, peering over her shoulder.

Rose turned to Annie. "Did you know about this?"

Annie shook her head, her eyes as big as Rose's. "Nope. My Miles didn't say a word to me."

Rose turned her attention back to the porch, thankful she could hear everything through the glass.

John stepped outside and froze, his whole body stiffened in rigid defiance. "What's that?"

"It looks like a horse to me," Miles answered.

"What's it doing here?" John demanded.

"*It* is actually named Cafi," Miles said calmly.

"He's exquisite," Rose whispered, not wanting to alert John to their presence at the window. Though not quite as tall as Rascal, Cafi was still plenty big enough to carry John when he grew to his full height. Since he was certain to be as big or bigger than his father, the size of the horse was important. Still, was it possible for Miles to find another horse that had Rascal's temperament?

"What kind of name is Cafi?" John asked, not moving any closer but also not stepping back into the house as he stared at the beautiful chestnut gelding standing quietly at the hitching post.

"My question exactly," Carrie said. "I'm so glad he asked. Cafi sounds like you're saying coffee, but with a very bad cold."

Rose smiled, but held up her hand so they could hear Miles' answer.

"Cafi is a word from a country in Africa called Somalia. It's where my family came from before we were slaves."

"What does it mean?" For the first time, John sounded genuinely curious.

Miles knelt to look into John's eyes before he answered. "It means forgiveness," he said gently. "John, it's time for you to forgive yourself." When John started to shake his head, Miles held up his hand. "Can I tell you a story?"

"I guess," John said grudgingly as he looked back at the front door. His expression made it clear that he wanted to escape back to the warm confines of the house.

Moses appeared behind Rose. "What's going on?"

Rose turned and held a finger to her lips. "Just watch and listen."

"Once upon a time," Miles began, "there was a horse who belonged to a boy just about your age. The horse and the boy loved each other a whole lot. They were together every day."

Even without seeing John's face, Rose knew he was thinking about Rascal. Part of her wanted to run out and stop Miles. What if John wasn't ready, and his grandfather's insistence only strengthened his determination to never be around horses again?

Carrie, reading her mind, spoke softly. "Trust Miles," she murmured.

Rose gazed at Miles' compassionate face and nodded slowly.

"Then came the day when the little boy got real sick with pneumonia," Miles continued. "That horse missed his little boy somethin' fierce. He would hang his head out of the stall every day, calling for his boy to come get him. He couldn't understand that the little boy was too sick to get out of bed."

"What happened?" John asked.

Miles shook his head sadly. "The little boy died, John. He died saying his horse's name. Of course, all the horse knew was that the little boy didn't come to see him anymore."

"He must have been so sad," John said.

Rose knew John was feeling his own sadness. Her heart ached for her little boy who had been forced to pay such a high price for a mistake.

"He was real sad," Miles agreed. "Finally, the boy's father decided he had to sell him because the horse didn't want anyone but his boy to come around. That horse just couldn't seem to forgive the world for takin' his boy away."

"But selling him would make the horse even sadder!" John burst out. "The father shouldn't have done that. Maybe the horse just needed more time."

"That could be," Miles agreed. "It might also be that the horse just needed another boy."

John thought about that for a few moments and then nodded. "Did the horse find another boy?"

Rose knew how much John loved stories. For at least the moment, he was more intent on the story than he was on refusing to be interested in Cafi.

"I don't know," Miles said.

"You don't know the ending to the story?" John looked confused. "How can you not know the end to the story?"

Miles shrugged. "There ain't an end yet." He turned and looked at Cafi. "I'm hopin' maybe you can give me an end to the story."

John stared at him. "What do you mean?" His voice was bewildered.

Miles stood and walked down the stairs to stand next to the gelding. "John, Cafi is the horse that needs another boy."

John gasped. "This is the horse in the story?"

Miles nodded.

"The little boy who used to own him died?"

"Just last month," Miles said. "The owner told me Cafi hasn't eaten hardly anything since then."

Rose looked at the horse more closely, recognizing Cafi's thinness for the first time. He was still beautiful, but you could see the beginning of his ribs. She felt Moses' hand tighten on her shoulder.

"He won't eat?" John's voice was full of compassion.

"Nope." Miles walked back onto the porch and knelt again. "I reckon his name is just right. Cafi needs to forgive the world for takin' his boy away from him." He reached out a hand and put it on John's shoulder. "And you need to forgive yourself for makin' a mistake, John. I know you loved Rascal with all your heart, but there is another horse right here that needs you to love him, too."

John didn't say anything, but he also didn't turn away.

Rose prayed he would let his compassion conquer his guilt. "Please, John," she whispered. "Do it..."

"A friend of mine done told me about Cafi a few days ago. As soon as I heard about him, I figured you would be the one who could save him."

John took a step toward the edge of the porch. "You think *I* can save him?" he asked with wonder. "Even after what...happened?"

"You got a natural way with horses, John. That Rascal loved you somethin' fierce. You know, I think he would like it if you were to love another horse like you loved him."

John stared at his grandfather. "Why do you think that? Wouldn't loving another horse make Rascal feel bad?"

Rose suddenly had another piece to the puzzle of why John had refused to be around another horse. He thought it would make him disloyal to Rascal.

"Nope. I don't reckon horses are like people. They don't get jealous like we do. Rascal would be real happy if you were to help another horse the way you helped him. He's in a real good place now, but Cafi..." His voice trailed off. "Cafi needs a boy to love him."

John still hesitated. "What if Cafi doesn't want me to be his little boy?" His voice was a mixture of yearning and uncertainty.

"Well, I reckon that's possible," Miles conceded, "but I got a feelin'."

John took another step forward. "Cafi," he said softly.

Rose held her breath.

The gelding turned his eyes and locked them on John. They stared at each other for several minutes, John instinctively knowing not to approach the horse too quickly. Finally, after what seemed an eternity, Cafi nickered gently and lowered his head.

John walked down the stairs slowly, right past his grandfather who merely stepped aside.

"Cafi," John said again. This time he walked up to the horse's head and laid a hand on his muzzle. "Hello, boy."

Rose watched in amazement as Cafi dipped his head lower and stood quietly.

The horse and boy stood that way for several minutes before John stepped forward and untied the gelding's lead rope. "Grandpa, I need to get Cafi some food. He's hungry."

Rose swiped at her tears, while a huge smile bloomed on her face.

"I reckon he is," Miles answered. "He's in the first stall to the right. I reckon if you'll stay with him, he might eat some of that grain and hay I put in last night."

"I'll stay with him," John vowed.

"Will you look at that," Moses said gruffly. He hugged Rose tightly from behind.

"I'm going to bake that man of mine some of the chocolate cake he loves so much," Annie said fiercely. "He just did a right wonderful thing."

"Yes, he did," Rose agreed as she watched John disappear into the barn with Cafi. Her little boy had finally found forgiveness.

Carrie waited until she and Anthony were cuddled in bed before she brought up the subject she had wanted to talk with him about all day. "I had something very interesting happen this morning."

Anthony gazed down at her. "Whenever you get that tone of voice, I know something very big is about to happen."

"Tone of voice?" Carrie was both amused and mystified.

"Trust me," Anthony replied. "You get a tone of voice. However, that's not what is important right now. What's important is to know *why* you have that tone of voice."

Carrie shared the revelation she had had that morning during the New Year's sunrise, choosing her words carefully. She wanted to reveal her passion while attempting to not be persuasive. It was important that both of them feel the same way on their own.

Anthony was silent as he mulled over her words.

Carrie was fine with the silence because she knew he was thinking hard. She had had all day to ponder what she had just told him. The least she could do was give him time.

"Are you certain you're all right with not having a child?"

Carrie nodded, surprised at just *how* certain she was now that she had made the decision. Despite her conversation with Janie in the fall, she hadn't entirely given up hope that she could still conceive a child. As a doctor, she was keenly aware of the risk to herself and her child if she were to become pregnant, but the hope for a child had been more powerful than her fear.

"I am," she said quietly. "There are so many children who need our love and what we have to give them. When I think of the risk of a pregnancy, I'm certain I'm not willing to risk leaving you or the life we're building with Frances and Minnie. Our life is so rich. A child of our own could not possibly make it any richer." She paused. "It's important, though, how you feel about it. I'm not trying to convince you."

"How do *I* feel about? I'm thrilled," Anthony replied.

Carrie pushed back so she could look up into his face. "Do you mean that?"

"With all my heart," Anthony said. "I fathered a child that I lost. I lost my wife at the same time. I never want to experience that kind of pain again. I was given a second chance at life when you fell in love with me. I love you with all my heart, Carrie. I can't imagine life without you." He gathered her close in his arms. "I love Frances and Minnie, too. I'm their father, and they are my daughters. It doesn't matter that they were born to someone else. They've been given to us now."

"They are our gifts," Carrie murmured, her heart exploding with appreciation for the amazing man who was her husband. She snuggled back into his side.

"Yes," Anthony agreed. "I also agree there are other children out there who will need our family. We may walk into an orphanage and find the right ones, or they may come to us like Minnie did. Only time will tell."

"How many do you want?" Carrie asked tentatively. She wasn't at all certain how she would answer the question herself.

Anthony fell silent for a moment. "I don't know. We don't need a number tonight, do we?"

Carrie laughed. "No. I'm happy to wait and see what happens."

Anthony nodded. "You already have a very full year planned. We'll know when the next child we're supposed to open our hearts to comes along."

Carrie looked up at him tenderly. "I'm really very lucky, you know."

Anthony eyed her and grinned. "Just how lucky are you?"

Carrie smiled slowly. "How about if I show you...?"

Chapter Twenty-Two

Florence stepped closer to the woodstove in the middle of the tent to warm her hands. While the source of heat made the tent a toasty fifty-five degrees compared to the twenty-five degrees outside, she wanted her hands to be warm and nimble before her next surgery. She ignored the pervasive fatigue, knowing she was living a life of ease compared to the vast majority of Parisians.

Everywhere she looked there was intense suffering. The hospital tents were full of soldiers who had been wounded during the last futile attempt to drive back the Prussian forces a month earlier. Within the confines of the American hospital, their misery was like the suffering of any soldier during war.

Their suffering was somehow easier to accept than the agony of the hollow-eyed women and children who went hungry on a daily basis, and who had no heat to provide respite from the chilling cold of a Paris winter. There were daily pilgrimages to the local cemetery to lay to rest those who had succumbed to starvation and disease. As always, the children most often paid the price of war.

What had begun as a shortage of food was now, for many people, complete nonexistence of anything to eat. More and more often people were turning to dogs and cats to keep their children from starving. It turned Florence's stomach to think of eating animals who had so recently been pets, but she understood the desperation of mothers who were watching their children slowly waste away.

When it was available, rations consisted of little more than hard bread they had to wait for in long lines.

Florence was heartbroken every time she walked from Minister Washburne's home to the hospital. She was also besieged with guilt, certain that every person who looked at her wondered why she looked so well-fed and healthy. She knew she and her father needed their strength to care for the wounded soldiers, but every bite she put in her mouth made her aware of how many were starving.

"A penny for your thoughts."

Florence looked up as Dr. Silas Amberton appeared at her side. "I'm afraid they're rather depressing," she admitted.

"I would wonder at your compassion if they weren't." His dark eyes held nothing but understanding.

Florence smiled, grateful for the easy friendship she had developed with him. "Thank you, Silas."

"How many surgeries do you have today?"

"Five," Florence answered. "Unless someone decides that another battle they have no hope of winning is a good idea." She had been appalled at the number of injured soldiers that had poured into the city after General Trochu launched an attack at the end of November. He had hoped for a victory that would raise the morale of the dispirited Parisians. All it had done was refill the hospitals in a city that already had no room for more wounded men. His effort to raise morale had only sent people's spirits plummeting to the depths.

"Or until Prussia decides this long siege is costing too much," Silas said grimly. "At some point, I suspect the cost of the siege will prompt a different action."

Florence tensed. "You believe they'll attack Paris?" It wasn't that she hadn't thought of it already, or that she hadn't discussed it at length with her father, but hearing it come from Silas' mouth somehow made it more dire.

Silas shrugged. "I'm not sure they'll have a choice. I've heard reports that the Prussian Army is also suffering. Disease is breaking out in their troops. They may be winning the battles, but they're still losing a lot of their soldiers."

"Minister Washburne says there is grumbling in Germany because the long siege is putting a strain on their economy," Florence said. "The Prussians are also afraid that an extended siege could convince the new French government that they could still be beaten, which means the war could drag on."

Silas nodded thoughtfully. "Most European countries have remained neutral about the war. If the siege continues, it could allow France time to rebuild a new army and convince those countries to enter the war."

"And so, just like in America, decisions are being made that are destroying the lives of innocent people and children, all because of men's greed." She thought of the small caskets she had seen carried through the city on her way to the hospital that morning. "Because Prussia and Germany want to increase the size of their kingdoms, thousands are dying." Anger flared as she thought of all the unnecessary suffering.

Silas put a hand on her shoulder. "I wish I could disagree with you, but your assessment is far too correct."

Florence fought the urge to close her eyes with pleasure as Silas touched her. No one had been more surprised than her when she had started thinking of him outside the hospital. She had always imagined she was immune to men's charms...until she met Silas. Suddenly, there was something as important as medicine to think about. Her father had asked her about her distant expression a few times during their walks home, but so far she had been able to give him elusive answers that wouldn't reveal her inner struggle.

"Florence?"

Florence suddenly realized Silas must have asked her a question. She flushed, searching for an excuse that would hide the real reason for her distraction. "I'm sorry. I didn't hear your question. I'm afraid my mind is already on the next surgery."

Silas regarded her thoughtfully for a long moment before he nodded. "I'll let you get back to work."

Florence gazed after him when he walked away, unsure of what to say or do. She had always been completely focused on medicine, shunning the idea that courtship and marriage should be important to her. Tall and angular, she had never fit the criteria of a beautiful woman in America. It had never really bothered her before, but now she found herself wishing there were something about her that would make her appealing to the American doctor with kind brown eyes and a ready smile.

"Dr. Robinson?"

Florence turned when a nurse approached her from behind. "Yes? Is my patient ready?"

"He is."

Florence walked over to the sink basin and washed her hands thoroughly, and then covered her clothing with a gown. The soldier she was performing surgery on had arrived at the hospital with a severely wounded leg. Despite their best efforts to save it, an infection had set in that was causing the leg to become gangrenous. He was going to die if they didn't remove it.

The soldier looked up at her with pain-shrouded eyes as she approached. "Je n'ai pas de chance aujourd'hui."

Florence smiled sympathetically. "No, I'm afraid you're not going to be lucky today, Pierre. Except," she added firmly, "we *are* going to save your life. You're going to lose your leg, but your wife is going to keep her husband, and your children are going to keep their father. That seems very lucky to me."

"C'est la vie," the man said as he forced a smile.

Florence had fallen in love with the French. Despite all the suffering and hardships, their spirits remained indomitable. During Pierre's long hospitalization, he had taught her much about the people of France. He insisted the resistance in Paris would remain strong because the Frenchmen of today were the sons of those Gauls for whom battle was a holiday. She would never share his opinion of battle, but she loved his attitude.

"You are working on your French?" Pierre asked as he eyed her keenly.

Florence knew he was trying to delay the surgery, but who could blame him for not being eager to lose his leg? Besides, she owed him for all the time he'd taken to help her with the language of the city where she found herself captive. "Mais, oui." She laid a hand on his forehead to make sure his fever hadn't gone higher. "Pratiquez-vous votre anglais?"

Pierre rolled his eyes. "Yes, I am practicing my English, Dr. Robinson." He spoke the words carefully.

Florence smiled. They were both trying to improve their grasp of the other's language. Usually, if they spoke slowly enough and used hand signs, they could understand each other. She had met his wife and children and had liked all of them. When they visited, the ward rang with laughter.

She encouraged their visits because it raised the spirits of all her patients. "It's time," she said gently.

Pierre nodded bravely.

Florence was exhausted when she left the hospital in the late afternoon. When she exited her tent, the bright sunshine she had hoped for was actually a heavy layer of gray clouds.

"How did your surgeries go?"

Florence looked up with surprise when Silas fell into step beside her. "They were fine." The day had been so full that she could hardly remember what had happened. Her brain was completely exhausted.

"Pierre?"

One of the things she liked about Silas was that he went out of his way to remember patients' names, and he seemed to always be aware of their condition. "His surgery went well. I checked on him just before I left." She felt sad for the young man who would never run and play with his children again. A prosthetic would give him mobility, but it wouldn't be the same.

"You saved his life," Silas reminded her.

"I know," Florence acknowledged. "It's just that he'll never have the life he had before." She shook her head. "Is war ever anything but a waste?"

Silas eyed her. "I've learned to not be too philosophical about war. It can tend to drive a person mad. I find I handle it better if I focus on saving lives."

Florence shook her head. "I wish I could do that, but..."

"It's difficult."

"Yes." Florence looked up as they passed under a flag, similar to many others on the long boulevard they were walking down. "I can focus on caring for my patients when I'm in the American Ambulance, but then I come out here and see all of this!" She waved her hand at the red flag with the white cross that fluttered from many buildings. "Just how many homes and apartments are serving as hospitals in Paris?"

Silas scowled. "Far too many. I've never seen a city with such chaotic medical care. Parisians have done so much to make their city beautiful, but they seem to have totally forgotten about setting up a system that will care for their citizens in case of a health crisis or war."

"When I first heard about the Red Cross, I thought it was such a wonderful thing. I loved that groups of people from many countries were caring for the wounded, until I realized how inadequate the care is," Florence said angrily. "The mortality rates are staggering. People accept soldiers into their homes just so they don't have to fight in the war. I can understand that reasoning, but what I can't understand is how they can then simply neglect them and not give them the care they need."

"I agree. If it's not enough that it will keep them from fighting, the Red Cross flag flying on their home will protect them if Prussia invades the city," Silas added.

Florence seethed with anger as she thought of the needless suffering going on behind hundreds of doors in the city. "Minister Washburne said the Geneva Convention that was signed in 1864 is a good thing, but they neglected to take human nature into account. He suspects they will add many conditions after this war is over that will ensure the care is better."

"But not before thousands of men will die." Silas clenched his fists in frustration.

Florence took comfort in the fact that he was as upset as she was. "What will you do after the war is over, Silas?"

Silas shrugged. "I don't know yet. Before the siege began, my sister wrote me about returning to America."

"How long have you been in France?"

"Four years. I came over during the International Exhibition with Dr. Evans. At the time, I was worn out from treating soldiers during our own war. It seemed like a grand adventure, but I hadn't expected to fall in love with Paris." He smiled. "I wish you could have been here before the war, Florence. Paris is a city like no other. I had nothing to return to in America, so I decided to stay."

Florence listened closely. She wanted to ask him why he had nothing to return to, but it seemed too personal a question. While they were becoming friends, their banter and camaraderie had been focused on the hospital and their patients. She wasn't sure how to change that. "What were you doing here?" she asked instead.

"As little as possible," Silas admitted. His eyes darkened. "I saw so many men die in America. I treated so many severe wounds. When our war was over, I needed time to do nothing."

Again, questions sprang to Florence's mind that she didn't feel free to ask. *How was he able to do nothing for four years?*

"You're wondering how I was able to not work for four years."

Florence flushed when she realized he'd been able to read her expression. "I'm sorry. It's none of my business."

"I don't mind telling you," Silas replied. "My father was a successful businessman in Massachusetts. He was also an extraordinary father. My mother passed away when I was just a boy. He never remarried, so he was everything to us." He paused and cleared his throat. "He encouraged both my sister and me to become doctors. He told us we could do anything we wanted to. He used to tell my sister all the time to not let men's ignorance keep her from achieving all that she wanted."

Florence smiled. "He sounds like my father."

"They would have liked each other immensely," Silas agreed. "Anyway, my father was taken from us by the flu shortly after the war. I'd like to think either my sister or I could have saved him, but by the time we received notice he was sick, it was too late. He was dead when I arrived home."

"I'm so sorry."

Silas smiled slightly. "Thank you. Anyway, the war and then my father's death seemed to suck the life right out of me. When my father died, he left me enough money to make it possible for me to escape to Paris." He shrugged. "So here I am."

"I'm glad you had that option," Florence said softly. While she was caught up in the story, she was more intrigued by the emotion he was so comfortable showing. That, more than anything, told her what kind of man his father must have been. "What has working here in the hospital been like? You left America to get away from war and death, yet here you are again."

"Yes," Silas said heavily. "When Dr. Evans asked me to work at the hospital right after the siege began, I couldn't say no." He looked toward the horizon. "It's going to snow again."

Florence sighed. "I don't mind for myself, but all the people without heat are going to be even more miserable."

She realized Silas was struggling as much as she was about the wounded soldiers they were treating. She cast about in her mind for another topic, but he saved her having to come up with one.

"What do you like best about working in the hospital?"

Florence swallowed the words that first came to mind. *Working with you.* Clearly, he was only interested in her as a friend and colleague. At least, it seemed that way to her. She wasn't sure how she had reached that conclusion since she had no previous experience with men, but she had reached it just the same.

She considered his question carefully. As much as she cared about her patients, she hated that she was back in the midst of wartime medicine. Suddenly, she knew the answer. "It's keeping me from going mad."

Silas laughed.

"I mean it," Florence insisted. "I know the correct answer is that I want to make a difference. That's certainly true, but if you hadn't made a place for us in the hospital, I would have slowly been going crazy in Minister Washburne's house."

Silas laughed again. "One of the things I love about you is your honesty."

Florence stared at him. He *loved* something about her? Her mind spun as she tried to discern what that meant.

Silas stopped laughing. "I'm sorry. I didn't mean to make you uncomfortable."

"No," Florence said quickly. "I was just surprised. My mother has told me endless numbers of times that my honesty is very off-putting to men. I find I can't be any other way, however."

"You shouldn't be," Silas said firmly. "I suppose growing up with my sister taught me that women should be able to speak their mind." He chuckled. "Harriet certainly did."

Florence smiled as she thought of the outspoken woman who had been one of her instructors. "That doesn't surprise me. Dr. Amberton was an inspiration to me." Her mind was still trying to sort through his statement that her honesty was just *one* of the things he loved about her.

"I wish things were different."

Florence raised a brow. "How do you mean?"

"I wish the city weren't under siege. I would have liked to take you out to eat at one of the city's fine restaurants. *Before* they replaced their menu with horsemeat," he said ruefully.

"You would have?" Florence asked in amazement. He wanted to take her out to eat?

Silas turned to her when they reached the gated entrance to Minister Washburne's house. "Yes," he assured her. "Do you mind?" He looked suddenly uncertain.

"No." Since her honesty was one of the things he loved, she saw no reason to be coy. "I don't mind at all. I would have liked that, too." She was astonished when Silas looked relieved. She would never have guessed that he too might be insecure.

Silas looked at the house. "Are you expected home now?"

"No. There are many nights when I arrive home late from the hospital. Father left two hours before I did, so no one is expecting me."

"Would you care for a walk in the park?" Silas asked, and then hesitated. "I realize you're tired. It's been a long day."

Suddenly, Florence wasn't tired at all. She smiled brightly and boldly tucked her hand through his offered arm. "I would love to go for a walk."

The next two hours passed more quickly than she dreamed was possible. Now that Silas had said he wanted to spend time with her, she felt free to ask the questions swarming in her mind for the last three months. He answered her freely and asked many questions of his own.

Finally, when the cold had her shivering almost uncontrollably, Silas escorted her back to the house and stopped at the gate. It was only then that he noticed her trembling. "You should have told me you are freezing!"

Florence shook her head. "I didn't want to miss one moment of our walk together."

Silas stared at her. "You really are quite amazing," he murmured. "Smart. Talented. Honest. Pretty."

Florence caught her breath. Not once had anyone told her she was pretty. Her father, of course, but he hardly counted. She had given up hope that she would ever hear those words from a man.

"Go inside and get warm," Silas urged. Without warning, he leaned forward, kissed her forehead softly, and walked quickly away.

Florence stared after him, the cold completely forgotten as warm emotion swept through her. She had never been kissed before that moment. The day that had started out so normally had handed her many firsts in her life. She watched until Silas' broad shoulders disappeared into the encroaching darkness.

At that very moment, the snow began to fall. Despite the hardship it would bring to most Parisians, she couldn't help but feel it was the perfect ending to the afternoon. Tilting her face up for a moment, she allowed the flakes to fall on her warm cheeks. This was a day she would always remember.

Her father met her in the foyer, a worried expression on his face when she finally let herself in the house.

"Florence! I was getting quite worried. Being out so late at night is not such a good idea, my dear. Paris is a rather volatile city right now." Dr. Robinson looked at her closely. "Is everything all right at the hospital?"

"Yes," Florence assured him. "I just had some last-minute things tie me up." She wasn't ready to talk about her new feelings for Silas, and she certainly wasn't ready to discuss that he obviously felt the same way.

"I was concerned that you were feeling quite sad today."

Florence looked at her father with surprise. "Why would I feel sad?"

It was Dr. Robinson's turn to look startled. "This is the day Carrie, Janie and Elizabeth open the clinic," he reminded her. "Without you."

Florence stared at him, shocked that she had totally forgotten. When she had left America, the culmination of all she had worked toward waited for her in Richmond, Virginia. Somehow, that now seemed a lifetime away. "I've had to push it to the back of my mind," she managed, and then faked a yawn. "I'm going to go up to bed."

"You don't want supper? The cook set something aside for you in the kitchen."

Florence's stomach was growling, but all she wanted was to go to bed and ponder every moment of the magical time she had spent with Silas. "I'm not hungry," she lied as she leaned forward to kiss her father's cheek, remembering the feel of Silas' lips on her forehead. "Goodnight, Father."

"Florence."

Florence stopped short at the bottom of the staircase, alerted by something in her father's voice. She turned and looked at him closely. She had thought the troubled look in his eyes had been solely because of worry for her, but now she realized it was something else. "What's wrong, Father?"

When her father hesitated, she tightened with a flash of impatience. "Father, just tell me. All of Paris is in trouble right now. I'd much rather know what's going on. I certainly don't need protecting."

"You're right," her father agreed. "Washburne brought me news tonight. You know about the shelling the Prussians have been doing on the military outposts of the city, but they've moved their guns into a new position." His eyes glittered with something she realized was fear.

"They're going to bomb Paris?" Florence asked with disbelief.

"He suspects so," her father said heavily. "The siege has gone on for too long. Instead of breaking the Parisian spirit, it seems to be strengthening it."

Florence thought of the hopeless expressions she had seen on the faces of all the women and children she had passed on the way home that day. "Not everyone," she said crisply. "Of course, as far as I can tell, the men of the

National Guard still in the city who are eager to continue the fight, are finding a way to eat and continue drinking their wine." Her stomach tightened with anger as she thought of the drunken guardsmen she and Silas had seen laughing in the street on their way back to the house. "The women and children who are starving and losing hope would tell you a different story."

"I know," her father agreed. "It's a terrible situation." He paused. "Washburne suggested we stay close to the house until we know what's going to happen." He held up a hand when Florence opened her mouth to object. "I already told him that wasn't going to happen. Our patients need us."

"More will need us if fighting breaks out again," Florence said through gritted teeth. She shook her head. "I'm going to bed now. If we're to be bombed, I would at least like to be rested."

As she trudged up the stairs, she lamented how quickly the starry-eyed feeling from her time with Silas had dissipated. Instead of dreaming about his kiss, she was going to be listening for the first bombs to fall on the city.

Chapter Twenty-Three

May gazed around with satisfaction as she carried out platters of food. "This is the way this house is meant to be," she announced. "Full of people."

Carrie looked around the table as she took servings from every dish that was passed to her. Matthew and Janie had arrived two days earlier and were now situated in the East Wing of her father's Richmond home. Robert and Anabelle were in the room right next to them.

Elizabeth Gilbert had arrived the day before. Her dark eyes flashed as she laughed loudly at something Micah leaned down to tell her. When she looked up and saw the inquisitive eyes watching her, she laughed harder. "Micah was just warning me that Southerners don't seem to like Italians any more than they like black folks."

"What you go and tell her somethin' like that for?" May scolded. "You wantin' to run her out of town before she's even been here a day?"

Micah shook his head, but he didn't look repentant. "It's best folks know what they're walking into," he said staunchly. "Dr. Gilbert seems to be a real fine woman. It can take a while to toughen up when people treat you bad."

Carrie joined Elizabeth and Janie in the laughter that greeted his statement.

Micah stared at all of them as if they'd taken leave of their senses.

"Micah," Janie said fervently, "if any of us let what people think bother us, none of us would be doctors. All of us have been yelled at..."

"Told we're a disgrace to women," Elizabeth added.

"And we've all been spit on," Carrie said cheerfully.

"Spit on?" May raised a brow. "That ain't true!"

"Completely true," Carrie assured her. "Becoming a woman doctor is not for the faint of heart."

Micah shook his head. "All that happened up in Philadelphia? I heard that was a right good city to live in."

"Any city is a good city to live in if you follow their rules and do things their way," Elizabeth responded ruefully. "I don't really know any place in America that feels women should do a job that has always been the private sanctum of men. There are women who are doing it anyway, but it's certainly never easy."

"What are you women gonna do in *Richmond*? If Philadelphia gave you a bad time, what do you think all these white Southerners are gonna do?" May demanded. "Miss Carrie, I've heard the stories about what you went through during the war when you was treating all the black patients. Am I going to have to send my Spencer with you everywhere you go?"

Carrie smiled, but the memories of the threats and barely averted violence during the war were still painful to her. Truth be told, there were many times she had been afraid. "I don't believe I'll be putting Spencer in any more danger," she said lightly. "This is a different time."

"Hmph!" May was clearly not impressed with her attempt to sound unconcerned.

"Who y'all planning on treatin'?" Micah asked.

"Sick people," Janie responded blithely.

Micah scowled at her. "I know what you women are doing. You're trying to convince us that you ain't worried about what you're gettin' ready to face, but this old butler knows better than that. I reckon if you women are smart enough to become doctors, then you're smart enough to know you're getting ready to step into a hive of angry bees down here."

Carrie raised a hand to stop Janie's reply, knowing she was about to crack a joke about angry bees. It was time to face this head on. "You're right, Micah. We know we're about to step into a hive of angry bees, but we believe we're doing the right thing. There are people—especially women—in Richmond who need us to help them. We talked about it at length and decided we're not willing to let some angry bees stop us from doing the right thing."

Micah shook his head. "I know that look, Miss Carrie. I seen it a whole bunch of times."

"Yep," May said solemnly. "That's the look that say I'm gonna do what I believe is the right thing, no matter what happens. From what my man Spencer has told me, that look got you in a whole heap of trouble during the war."

Spencer walked in, his dark eyes bubbling with amusement. "I heard just enough of that to know Miss Carrie and these other women know what they want to do, and they's gonna do it. I also got to tell you that Miss Carrie knows how to take care of herself." His face split with a grin. "There was one time back during the war when me and her were coming back out from the black hospital late at night. We didn't like to do that, but somebody was real sick so she wouldn't leave. I tried to talk her into leaving sooner, but she got that *look* y'all were talking about."

Everyone chuckled as they leaned forward to hear the rest of the story.

"Anyway, we was coming back out when we got stopped by a group of angry white men intent on starting trouble."

Elizabeth's eyes widened. "What did you do?"

"I didn't do nothing. Miss Carrie knew that if I made a move, they wouldn't have thought twice about stringing me up. I wasn't going to be able to stop them. Miss Carrie, though…" His voice trailed away as he remembered. "Miss Carrie pulled out a whip she had on the back seat with her. She cracked it right at them. 'Bout the same time, she pulled out a pistol and asked which ones of them wanted to die. She admitted she couldn't kill them all. Then she asked them again which ones wanted to move first, because those would be the dead ones."

"What happened?" Elizabeth breathed.

Spencer grinned. "They weren't none too happy, but ain't a one of them that wanted to die that night. They stepped back and told us to move on. I moved on all right."

Elizabeth stared at Carrie. "Weren't you frightened?"

Carrie considered giving a light response, but the knowledge that they might find themselves in a similar situation sometime in the near future made her answer honestly. She was glad Frances and Minnie weren't there to hear the story of that night. She didn't want them worrying about her every time she came to Richmond. Most times they would join her, but they'd decided to stay on the plantation since school had just started back up. "I was scared half to death," she admitted. Then she shrugged. "I'd already decided I wouldn't let fear stop me from doing the right thing. I can tell you, though, that I promised Spencer we would never get caught out at night like that again. I don't know for certain that they would have hurt me, since Father was so well known in the city, but they wouldn't have hesitated to do harm to Spencer." She scowled. "I hated that I'd put him in that situation. I certainly wasn't ever going to do it again."

"And she didn't," Spencer added solemnly. "Mr. Thomas had asked me to drive her around the city so I could keep her safe. I was ready to die protecting her that night 'cause she was doing a real good thing for black folks, but I'm glad I didn't have to."

"Me too," May said fervently. "I've gotten real used to having my husband around. I hate to think I wouldn't have gotten the chance!"

Micah eyed her keenly. "That's a real good story, Miss Carrie, but you still didn't answer my question."

"Janie told you the truth, Micah. We're going to treat sick people. It doesn't matter if they're male or female."

"Or black or white," Elizabeth added.

"Or poor or rich," Janie said firmly.

"And you figure white people gonna come to the same place where a bunch of white women be treatin' black folk?" Micah looked skeptical.

"Probably not at first," Carrie admitted readily. She wasn't offended by Micah's questions and skepticism because she knew he wanted them to succeed. He wasn't asking anything they hadn't already asked themselves. "When the time comes, though, that they realize no other doctor can help them, I believe they'll swallow their prejudice and come."

May raised a brow. "I wouldn't be so sure about that. There be a lot of white folk that ain't gonna step foot in a place where black people be, no matter what's going on with them. I figure they're willing to die first."

Carrie shrugged. "That will be their loss. I experienced the same thing out at the plantation clinic. White people said they would never come see me. First, I was a woman doctor. Second, I was treating black people. It took a while, but now people come because they need me. They know I'm going to treat them the same way I treat everyone else."

"When you're a great doctor," Anthony said staunchly, "people are going to come." His eyes swept the table. "These three women are great doctors. When Florence returns from Paris there will be four of them."

"Besides," Janie added, "we've planned for it to be this way. We don't think we're going to waltz into the South and have people suddenly decide to embrace women doctors. None of us are dependent on the money we hope to eventually make. Carrie has her income from the stables and the money Anthony makes, I have Matthew's support as a best-selling author, and Elizabeth has the full support of her father."

"Your daddy all right with you coming down here, Miss Elizabeth?" Micah asked with a raised brow. "He know what you're gettin' yourself into?"

Elizabeth smiled. "My father is a doctor in Boston, Micah. He was the first person to tell me I should become a doctor. My mother was close friends with Biddy Flannagan before she died. The two of them used to talk about how women could turn the world upside down if they just decided to do it. Both of my parents have told me that what we're about to do is going to be quite difficult, but they're cheering me on from home."

"Well then," Micah said slowly. "I reckon y'all know what you're getting' into."

"We do," Carrie assured him, but she was uncomfortably certain they actually had no clue what challenges they were about to face.

Florence smiled up at Silas when she walked outside the house to join him. For the last three days, he'd come to walk with her to the hospital. "Good morning, Silas."

"Good morning, Florence."

Florence gazed at him, not missing the strained look in his eyes. "What's happened?" she asked quietly. She had gotten used to the constant sound of artillery outside the city since the bombing of the forts had started on December twenty-seventh, but she sensed there was something more. "Are the Prussians about to start bombing Paris?"

"The bombing of the forts surrounding the city intensified this morning. The garrison on the plateau d'Avron, east of Paris, has already been abandoned. Fort de Vanves and Fort d'Issy are on the verge of collapse, as well." Silas sighed. "The French are discovering their fortifications aren't adequate to face the latest German cannons. Of course, I doubt there are *American* forts that could withstand the bombardment of Krupp artillery."

"Krupp?" Florence wasn't familiar with the name. It was somehow easier to think about an unfamiliar name, than it was to deal with what he was telling her.

"The Krupp family has formed a dynasty in Germany," Silas explained. "They're famous for their production of steel, artillery and ammunition. The world has never seen the kind of weapons they're developing. This war is the first time they're being used. Quite effectively, I might add. I spoke with a friend of mine who has been to the plateau d'Avron since the bombing began. He says he never imaged the size of the craters created by the projectiles that are being fired. Most of them are fifty-six pounds, but some of them are evidently over one hundred pounds." He shook his head. "War will never again be the same."

Florence closed her eyes as she absorbed the news. She could only imagine the type of damage projectiles of that size could create within the crowded confines of Paris. "How far are the guns capable of reaching?" Silas hadn't actually said the Prussians were planning on attacking the city, but Minister Washburne and her father were simply waiting for what they considered was inevitable. She knew the city of over two million residents was close to forty square miles in size. Surely the German guns couldn't reach to the center where the hospital was located. She suspected Minister Washburne's house in western Paris was far out of the reach of the guns. There was always the possibility the Prussians would eventually surround the entire city with their artillery, but she couldn't bring herself to think about that.

"No one knows for certain, but if the forts fall today, which everyone expects, they will be seven hundred and fifty yards closer. The eastern side of the city will be in grave danger."

Florence frowned. "That's the Belleville area. They're suffering so much already." She knew Belleville, primarily a working-class area, had been hit especially hard by the siege. Soaring prices had taken so much out of their reach almost as soon as the blockade began. Many of the men had been assigned to the National Guard as part of the city defenses, meaning the women and children were left on their own to go cold and hungry.

Florence had stepped outside the hospital for a break when she heard an explosion that sounded much nearer than the ones she had grown used to. She jumped in fear and looked around to see if there was anything on the horizon that would indicate what had happened.

Moments later, Silas stepped from the tent. "What was that?" he asked sharply.

"I don't know," Florence said shakily, "but I suspect the bombardment of Paris has begun."

Silas' answer was to step closer and wrap a strong arm around her waist.

Florence shivered, wondering how stark fear and total joy could fill her soul at the same time.

"Ils bombardent la ville!"

Florence watched as a wild-eyed man raced down the street yelling out the news. The bombardment of the city had begun. She longed to stop him and ask questions, but he'd appeared so quickly there was no way he could have been close to the location of the explosion. The plume of smoke on the horizon appeared to be several miles away. She knew he could provide no answers. She looked up at Silas. "Would you like to come to dinner tonight? Minister Washburne will have information."

"I would love to," Silas replied, his eyes focused on the smoke.

"We eat at seven o'clock," Florence said, thrilled with the prospect of spending the evening with him.

Florence's appetite for vegetable soup and bread evaporated as Minister Washburne delivered the news in a grim, sorrowful voice.

"The first shell burst in the Rue Lalane on the Left Bank. It killed a baby asleep in its cradle. The ones that followed landed in the Montparnasse Cemetery. The good news is that they could cause the occupants no harm, despite the damage." There was a faint glimmer of amusement before sadness swallowed it again. "A little girl on her way home from school near Jardin du Luxembourg was sliced in half by one of the shells. She died instantly."

Florence pushed her bowl of soup away from her as she battled with nausea.

Minister Washburne continued. "Two children were killed when a mortar exploded on their home. Six women died while they were standing in a food queue." He shook his head. "Others were killed, as well." He stopped and gazed around the table. "This is only the beginning, I'm afraid. The Prussians' goal is to finally extinguish the Parisian spirit."

"Starvation and disease aren't enough?" Florence asked angrily.

"Not to the Prussians," Washburne replied. "They won't stop until Paris has surrendered."

Silence met his words.

Dr. Robinson finally cleared his throat. "What is Trochu's position on all this?"

Washburne scowled. "It hardly matters. Governor Trochu is proving himself to be the weakest and most incompetent man ever entrusted with such great affairs. The man is too weak to be any good at all for this great city!" He shook his head. "I have no idea why the Government of National Defense gave him that position when Napoleon was captured. Every battle waged since the siege began has been caused by public pressure, instead of careful strategy for military effectiveness. It's hard to believe the man spent most of his career in the military and advanced to be a general." His voice grew more frustrated. "If the city weren't suffering so much because of his decisions, I might actually have compassion that he was thrust into a position he obviously has no idea how to handle."

"Do you believe he'll retaliate for the bombing?" Silas pressed.

Washburne considered the question. "I believe it's too late for an effective campaign, but that doesn't mean he won't bow to public pressure again. The question is how many men will die the next time."

Florence's stomach tightened. She had never heard Washburne be so negative and pessimistic, but she understood the reasons for it.

"Is the hospital in danger?" Dr. Robinson asked.

Washburne spread his hands. "Are any of us safe? I've been astonished at how far the projectiles have come. I've never experienced artillery like the ones they're using. And if they manage to get the guns closer..." His voice trailed off.

"Will Paris surrender?" Silas asked.

"I don't know," Washburne admitted. "Governor Trochu has declared he will never capitulate."

"He'll continue to let the people of Paris suffer?" Florence burst out. "How many more have to starve or freeze to death? Or be killed in the street by bombs?"

Washburne met her eyes. "I understand your anger, but in all fairness, no one knows what will happen if Prussia is victorious. The result could be even more suffering than what the people are experiencing now."

"Hasn't your connection with the Prussian government given you *some* idea of what to expect?" Florence asked.

Washburne shook his head. "I would like to think so, and I would also like to think Prussia would honor this great city, but emotions are volatile on both sides." He sighed. "I simply don't know.

"It's a good thing we like our new office," Elizabeth said wryly.

"We've been open for more than two weeks, and no one has been in to see it except us." Janie eyed Carrie. "Not even anyone from the Black Quarters has come in. Is everyone down there just amazingly healthy right now?"

Carrie shook her head, gazing around at the cozy office a few blocks off Main Street. They had optimistically signed a year's lease on the bottom half of a building, planning to expand to the top half as their practice grew. Their office included a private room for each of them to see patients, an operating suite that had been equipped with the newest surgical equipment, and a cheerfully decorated waiting room. She gazed into the flames blazing in the fireplace as she struggled with the conclusion she had reached. "I don't think so."

"Then why aren't they coming?" Janie asked. "You've treated many of them before."

"Yes," Carrie agreed, "but I've always treated them where they felt safe." She hesitated, hating the words she was about to say. "I believe they're frightened to come here." She shook her head. "I'm afraid I may not have adequately taken that into consideration."

"They're frightened?" Elizabeth asked. "Why?"

"Because there are a lot of white Richmonders that are willing to endure their presence if the blacks stay in their part of town, but they don't want them coming into what they consider the *white* part of town," Janie said bluntly. "They tolerate them coming here to work, but they don't want them to think they can come for any other reason."

Elizabeth stared at her. "What are the Blacks afraid will happen if they come?"

Carrie sighed. "Welcome to the South. It wasn't that long ago that the Black Code was still in place. Even though blacks now have the right to vote and are legally considered equal citizens in America, it's going to be a long time before people actually feel that way. There are far too many Richmonders who would have no qualms hitting or beating a black person who is in the wrong part of town to do business. They would also not hesitate to make sure they lose their job," she said grimly. "Too many white people expect blacks to know their place."

"Black people won't come because they're afraid," Elizabeth said slowly. "White people won't come because we're women doctors. What are we going to do?"

The three friends and colleagues stared at each other. The only sound was the crackling of flames.

"We'll hold seminars!" Janie exclaimed after a long silence. "I've heard they do that in Philadelphia and New York. It seems to be effective."

"Seminars about what?" Elizabeth asked.

"We'll start with seminars for women," Janie said excitedly. "Women will be the first ones who are likely to come see us—perhaps the only ones. Instead of waiting for them to come to us as patients, we'll teach them about things they want to know for free. Then, when they need a doctor, they're more likely to trust us and take the risk to come."

Carrie nodded, her mind working rapidly. "It's a wonderful idea," she said enthusiastically.

"I agree," Elizabeth responded, "but what exactly are we going to teach them?"

"That male doctors don't understand women," Carrie replied. "Too many doctors have been able to convince women that their only acceptable role is in the home as wives and mothers. To think of doing anything else is wrong."

Elizabeth hesitated. "It seems like most women in the South feel that way already. Of course, most women in the North believe that, too. It's just that it's a little easier there to go against the norm."

Carrie nodded. "Many Southern women have been convinced that it's the only way to live, but there are plenty of others who simply go along with it because they don't see another option." She smiled. "Do I need to remind you that both Janie and I are Southern women?"

Elizabeth laughed. "I know that's true, but I don't see either of you that way."

"There are many Southern women who want to live a different life than the one they're forced into" Carrie replied. "They don't have fathers or husbands that encourage them to pursue something out of the norm, but that doesn't mean they don't dream of it."

Elizabeth raised a brow. "Are we talking about medicine? Or are we talking about launching a revolution?"

Janie laughed heartily. "Probably a little of both. It's going to require revolutionary thinking for women to come see us as their doctors, but the only way they're going to receive adequate health care is if they have the courage to do it."

"Look at it this way," Carrie added. "The worst thing that can happen is that we'll fail and have to close our practice. You and Janie can return to the North where you'll be more readily accepted, and I'll keep running my clinic on the plantation. Either way, at least we'll know we tried everything we could to help women in Richmond."

Elizabeth regarded her for a long moment. "You're trying to sound very casual, but I know you. There's something you're not saying."

Carrie sighed, wishing her friend wasn't always so perceptive, but she didn't dodge the question. "It's a little daunting to think of the consequences of mounting what most men will probably see as a revolution." There hadn't been enough years between then and the years of the war to erase the memories of what she had encountered by starting the Black Hospital. She wanted to believe tensions had eased since the end of the conflict, but she knew that wasn't true. If anything, freedom for the slaves had probably increased it. While she had no regrets about her actions during the war, she wasn't exactly looking forward to repeating what had happened as a consequence.

"We didn't let it stop us then," Janie reminded her. "We can't let it stop us now."

"I agree," Carrie said firmly, pushing the memories as far back as she could.

Elizabeth looked between the two of them and finally nodded. "Where do we start?"

Anthony and Matthew looked at each other after the women laid out their plans that night.

Carrie knew what was going through their minds, but she waited for them to speak.

"That's taking a big risk," Anthony finally said, his eyes revealing the depth of his concern. "It's only been two weeks since you opened the clinic. Might you need to give it some more time?"

"He's right that it might just take more time," Matthew added. "If patients are unwilling to come to the clinic for care, would they be willing to come to a seminar?"

"I would have," Carrie said quietly.

"You were unusual," Anthony observed.

"There are far more women like me than you would think," Carrie answered, certain she was right. The three of them had talked extensively about the risk they would be taking if they followed through with their plan, but they'd all agreed it would be worth it.

"We can give it all the time we want," Janie said, "but short of an epidemic, I doubt anyone is going to walk through our doors. Women need education regarding what the medical profession is doing to them."

"We're alright with failing," Elizabeth added. "We're *not* all right with failing if we don't believe we've done everything we can to help women in Richmond."

Anthony and Matthew exchanged another glance and then both shrugged at the same time.

"I didn't really imagine that anything I say could change your mind," Anthony said wryly. "Quite honestly, I think it's a wonderful idea. Knowing that doesn't do anything to alleviate my concern, but I support your decision to do it."

Matthew nodded but remained silent.

"Matthew?" Janie asked. "What are you thinking?"

Carrie could read the worry in his eyes. She was confident he would support them, but she wanted to know what her clear-headed, journalist friend was thinking.

"Are you familiar with Anthony Comstock?" Matthew asked.

All three women shook their heads.

"I'm afraid you're going to know who he is soon," Matthew said grimly. "Let me ask you one more question. It's none of my business what you're going to talk about in your Women's Hygiene Seminar, but I imagine it might include birth control and contraceptives?"

"It might," Janie said evasively, neither denying nor confirming.

"Peter has been asked to do a series of articles on contraceptives and birth control," Matthew said, obviously not offended by her evasiveness. "In doing his research, he learned about Anthony Comstock. We talked about it a few weeks ago when he stopped in Philadelphia on his way back to New York City. Comstock was a Union soldier during the war, but he was stationed in a relatively peaceful area of Florida. He saw no fighting action, so he launched private battles of his own."

"Such as?" Elizabeth asked.

"He decided to improve the morals of the troops by fighting their use of tobacco, alcohol, gambling and atheism. He did this by becoming a part of the Christian Commission."

"I think I read something about that," Elizabeth said. "Wasn't it formed by the Young Men's Christian Association, the YMCA, to send ministers to the battlefields during the war?"

"Yes."

"I've heard many good things about that," Elizabeth responded.

"They achieved a lot of good," Matthew confirmed. "They were aware that publishers were providing soldiers with obscene books and pictures. They believed it was compromising the morality of the soldiers, so they created a provision in the 1865 Post Office Bill that made it a misdemeanor to send any obscene, vulgar or indecent books or images through the mail."

Carrie was listening closely. "So far, I don't see any reason to do anything but thank Anthony Comstock."

"I don't always agree with his methods," Matthew replied, "but I certainly agree with the principle. However, in the last few years he's come to believe that any drug, medicine or device to be used for the prevention of contraception should also be banned from the mail service. He's pushing for that to happen." He paused. "He has quite a lot of influence and support in Congress."

Carrie stiffened. "Excuse me? He believes women shouldn't have the freedom to use contraceptives?"

Matthew looked uncomfortable. "This isn't something I normally discuss, but since your seminar could be taking you into risky territory, I thought I should at least make you aware of potential issues."

Carrie shook her head, trying to understand what she was hearing. "He believes women shouldn't have the right to control the number of children they have?" In truth, she didn't know why she was surprised – most men seemed determined to control every aspect of a woman's life.

"He believes abstinence or controlling when you have sex are the only dignified or ethical means for family limitation," Matthew said carefully. He held up his hands in self-defense. "Don't look at me like that. I didn't say I believe it. I'm merely making you aware of what's going on in the country. If you're going to take a bold stand, it's best to know what you could be up against in the near future."

Carrie forced a smile. This wasn't a conversation she was comfortable continuing with Matthew, but she and Anthony had talked at length about how to make certain she would not become pregnant. They were acutely aware of how dangerous a pregnancy could be for her, as well as for any baby that was conceived. Abstinence in their marriage was a ludicrous concept, and she knew of far too many of her patients who had come to her pregnant after trying to time when they had intercourse.

"Thank you for the warning," Elizabeth said quietly.

Carrie could tell by the concerned gleam in her eyes that her friend knew how much this conversation was disturbing her.

"Carrie, I didn't mean to upset you," Matthew said contritely. "I'm sorry."

"I know that," Carrie said sincerely. "This issue just hits a little close to home." That was all she was willing to say.

Matthew nodded. "Having said all that, I agree with Anthony that your seminars are a wonderful idea, but I'm wondering if you would be willing to take some precautions."

"Such as?" Janie asked.

"Such as having some men at the clinic during the workshops." He held up his hand to stop Janie from interrupting him. "They obviously don't have to be in the seminar, but I think it would be helpful to have them there to deter anyone from thinking they should disrupt it. Anthony and I could watch the entrance from upstairs. If we suspected trouble, we could take care of it."

Carrie nodded slowly, glad to think about something else. "I believe it's a good idea. It will serve several purposes." She held up her fingers as she talked. "One, it will show the women that not all men think they're an inferior species that only belongs in the home. Two, it will provide the women with a sense of security while they're in the seminar. Three, it will protect us and give our husbands peace of mind."

Janie considered her words and then smiled. "When you put it that way, there's nothing to say no to."

Chapter Twenty-Four

Florence was fighting to not give in to discouragement, but the struggle intensified with each passing day. The endless pounding of the bombardment showed no evidence of stopping. For the last ten days, three to four hundred shells had fallen on the city each night. After the initial daytime bombing, the Prussians' strategy had changed to terrorizing the citizens of Paris every night for four to five hours. No one knew when a shell might come blasting into their home. While no shells came close to Minister Washburne's residence, the ceaseless noise had made sleep impossible. Awareness that it was part of the Prussian strategy to exhaust the citizens of Paris made it no easier to deal with the pervasive fatigue.

Daily reports of the bombing targets made it clear the enemy was entirely focused on destroying the spirit and the morale of the Parisians. The domes of the Panthéon and les Invalides, Paris' hospital and home for retired veterans, became favorite targets. The amount of destruction around them was horrifying. While none of the bombs had reached their designated targets, the suffering of those unfortunate enough to live close by was staggering, and the residents of les Invalides lived in constant fear.

Florence's own morale had sunk lower when she discovered the Salpêtrière Hospital had been hit repeatedly. She could imagine the terror of the two thousand elderly women, and the one thousand lunatics who called it home. It seemed that almost every night a different part of the building was hit.

Every day, the number of deaths increased, as did the number of wounded seeking help in Paris hospitals. As with the wounded soldiers, most of them received completely inadequate care.

"Dr. Amberton is here," the butler announced.

Florence pushed aside her gloomy thoughts. As she wrapped her thick coat around her, she was reminded of the fact that they were experiencing the coldest winter in Paris history. There seemed to be no end to the way that Parisians were being forced to suffer.

Silas was waiting in the foyer when she walked out of the parlor. His cheeks were red with the cold, but his eyes glowed with appreciation as they landed on her.

Florence caught her breath. How was it possible that amid starvation and bombs she had found the man who could bring light into the darkness? The smile that bloomed on her face dispelled the depressing thoughts that had threatened to consume her. "Good morning, Silas."

"Good morning, Florence."

Florence loved the deep timbre of his voice. In truth, there wasn't anything she didn't love about him. Somehow, during the last two weeks, she had quit pretending she was not in love with this incredible man. No words had been spoken, but the truth grew in her heart on a daily basis. She tucked her gloved hand through his elbow and exited the house.

The brutal cold stole her breath. "Today is even colder than yesterday! What are people going to do?"

"Before I answer that question, I would like to do something else."

Florence couldn't interpret the look in his eyes. "What would you like to do?"

"This." Silas turned and pulled her into his arms just before they reached the gate. "I want to hold you."

Florence, for one of the few moments in her life, was speechless. Following instinct, she wrapped her arms around his waist and squeezed him back as tightly as he was squeezing her. The sheer wonder of the moment stole the remainder of her breath.

Silas held her for several minutes before he stepped back.

Florence felt the loss the moment she was no longer pressed against him. Uncertain of what to say, she merely looked at him.

"I hope I didn't offend you."

Florence laughed with disbelief. "Far from it, Silas. I've never experienced anything quite so wonderful."

"I love you, you know."

Florence was once again speechless. Though she was aware her mouth was gaping open, she was incapable of forming words.

"I keep waiting for something to happen that would make it an appropriate time to tell you," Silas said. "Between the bombs and the cold and the hunger..." He shrugged his massive shoulders. "I finally decided the appropriate moment might not appear for quite some time, and I ran out of patience."

Florence found her voice. She reached up and put her hands on Silas' cheeks. "I understand Paris is called the City of Love, as well as the City of Light."

"That's true," Silas said huskily, his already dark eyes even darker with emotion.

"Which is exactly why it's so easy to tell you that I love you, too," Florence said softly. Ignoring how appalled American society would be at what she was going to do, she leaned forward and kissed Silas gently.

As she started to pull away, Silas grabbed her again and pulled her into a more ardent kiss. Suddenly, the cold completely disappeared as heat coursed through her body. Florence wrapped her arms around his neck and returned the kiss with all the passion inside her. If a bomb were to drop on them right now, he would at least know the truth about the depth of her love for him.

"Excuse me."

Florence pulled back when she heard her father's startled voice behind them. Any embarrassment was overridden by the wonder of the kiss. "Hello, Father," she said, surprised to find her voice completely normal.

Dr. Robinson recovered quickly and smiled "Hello, dear." Then he turned to Silas. "Good morning, Dr. Amberton." His eyes were twinkling.

Silas grinned. "Good morning, Dr. Robinson. It's a beautiful day, isn't it?"

"Any day you find love is a beautiful day," Dr. Robinson agreed. "Washburne warned me Paris is the City of Love. He was obviously correct." He reached out and shook Silas' hand. "If it matters at all, I want the two of you to know that I'm thrilled."

Silas shook her father's hand firmly. "It matters a great deal," he assured him.

Florence flung her arms around her father. "Thank you," she whispered. She knew they would talk more later, but for now it was enough to know he approved.

The three of them fell into step on their way to the hospital.

"Washburne lost the rest of his backyard fences last night," her father said ruefully.

Florence nodded. Desperate people did what they must. "What else are those poor people going to do? Oil has been gone since November, coal is no longer available, and wood is running out." She knew fences all over the city were being ripped down for use as firewood. "I talked with the wife of one of the soldiers at the hospital yesterday. She told me that in order to keep her home warm for their children, she needs one hundred kilograms of wood per day. She's entitled to only seventy-five kilograms a week, when it's available at all. They all wear everything they own, but they're still cold."

She'd noticed that even Minister Washburne's home was no longer warm and toasty, but it was definitely not cold. Having to wear a light coat indoors was hardly anything to complain about in the current situation. They were far better off than most other Parisians. While their meals were no longer extravagant, she had not gone hungry a single time. On the nights that horsemeat was served, Florence chose to dine on vegetables and bread.

Dr. Robinson nodded. "I suppose the bombing has made their raids much easier. No one heard a thing over the noise of the bombs last night."

"Now that the trees are gone," Silas commented, "they have no choice but to scavenge any source of wood they can."

Florence gazed down the broad avenue they were walking along. "I'm glad I saw Paris before the siege," she said wistfully. "I understand why people have cut down every tree, but it's still hard to see these beautiful streets stripped naked." Every street, every park, and every public place were slowly being denuded. It would be years before blooms and colorful fall leaves decorated the city with their magic again.

Silas nodded. "It will take a long time for Paris to regain its former beauty when this is all done. I was walking through a different part of town yesterday to take care of an errand. Several enormous trees had been felled sometime recently. All the large limbs were gone, but there was a swarm of children hacking away at the trunk with their puny hatchets. They gathered the chips into their shirts or coats to carry them home."

Florence frowned, wondering how many were attacked for their precious cargo on the way back to where they lived. "Yesterday, I saw a group of old women down in the massive hole left from a tree being toppled. They were digging out as much of the root as they could."

"All that effort for such a small amount of heat. Still," Silas said thoughtfully, "I suppose even an hour or so of not shivering is a welcome respite."

"Hunger is making the cold even harder to endure," Florence said. She turned to her father. "Is it true that the government has now reduced the ration of bread to just half a pound per adult per day? And half that amount for children?" She shook her head. "Not that what they're eating should be called bread" she said with disgust. The combination of flour, oatmeal, peas, beans and rice created a black heavy loaf that was almost impossible to eat.

"It's quite horrible," her father agreed. "I understand the quality is so poor that many children are dying from enteritis. Their small intestines are becoming terribly inflamed."

"But their mothers have no choice but to feed it to them," Florence said sadly. "Having to choose between possible death from enteritis and certain death from starvation is beyond horrible."

Florence's sorrow deepened when a gaggle of children hurried past them going in the opposite direction. She could hear their hoarse coughing long after they passed by. "The number of pneumonia cases is increasing."

"Along with smallpox." Dr. Robinson said grimly.

"Not to mention typhoid," Silas added. "The siege has forced Paris to draw most of her drinking water unfiltered from the Seine River."

Florence shuddered. "The river has become so foul, it's no wonder disease is spreading. Deaths have increased dramatically since the beginning of January. Most of them are the result of pneumonia."

"Dr. Robinson, has Washburne mentioned what effect the bombing is having on the city? How much longer can this possibly go on?" Silas asked.

Dr. Robinson scowled. "Washburne is privy to information others don't have. We talked last night. Though the bombing has caused a lot of damage, at this point only ninety-seven people have been killed. Two hundred and seventy-eight have been wounded. In comparison, the Prussians have lost over three hundred gunners to French counter-battery fire, not to mention the ones that have died when their artillery has exploded during firing."

"Is that is supposed to be good news?" Florence demanded.

"Certainly not," her father said quickly. "However, despite everything the people are going through, so far it's not had the effect of hastening a surrender. It seems to be making the people more determined to resist."

Florence gazed at the hollow-eyed women and children they were passing. "I wonder if the government has adequately consulted the children who are suffering, and the mothers who are burying them."

Carrie, by a drawing of straws, had been selected to start the first seminar.

The three women waited with bated breath to see if anyone would attend. They'd advertised in the *Richmond Dispatch* and distributed flyers through some of the neighborhoods. They knew, though, that coming to the seminar would require a great act of bravery on any participant's part.

They had decided to simply name the seminar, *Women's Hygiene*. The description had stated that the seminar would cover the best ways for women to remain healthy. They decided to keep it deliberately vague in hopes of arousing curiosity.

Carrie was thrilled when ten women eventually walked through the door. All of them looked uncomfortable, and all of them had peered furtively over their shoulders when they entered the office, but they'd come. Five of them looked to be between twenty and thirty; the other five were older.

Once the attendees had been greeted by all three of them, and they'd settled into their chairs with expectant looks, Carrie gave them a warm smile. "I'm so glad all of you are here. I recognize the courage it took you to attend."

All the women shifted in their seats as they cast sideways looks at the others. Several gave her a tentative smile in return.

"We realize that a women's medical practice in Richmond is rather unusual."

"*Rather* unusual? Let's call it what it really is—unheard of."

Carrie laughed, immediately liking the red-haired young woman with the direct style of communication and sense of humor. "It's Darlene, right?" She waited for Darlene's nod before she continued. "You're correct that it's unheard of."

"Are y'all Yankees from up north who've come down here to cause trouble?"

Carrie kept her warm smile, though she was immediately suspicious that the woman asking the question might be the one interested in causing trouble. When she looked closer, however, she saw the fear shimmering in the woman's eyes. "No, Matilda," she said calmly, glad she'd made the effort to memorize their names when she met them. "Actually, I was born and raised on a plantation a few hours from here. My father served in the Confederate government during the war." She wasn't surprised by the startled looks that came with her revelation.

"And I was born in Raleigh, North Carolina," Janie added. "I worked with Dr. Wallington at Chimborazo Hospital as a nurse during the war. When the war ended, I decided to become a doctor."

Matilda swung her eyes to Elizabeth. "And you?"

Elizabeth grinned. "I'm the Italian Yankee you're referring to, but I can assure you I'm not down here to cause trouble."

Carrie was grateful when a chuckle rumbled through the room. It was obvious their willingness to answer questions and not be offended by humor was being well accepted.

"So what are we going to hear about today?" Darlene asked. "I've never been to anything like this."

"That's up to you," Carrie answered. "The other doctors and I decided that we want this seminar, and any that follow, to be about what you're interested in." She reached down to pick up slips of paper and sharpened pencils. "I'd like each of you to write a question on this slip of paper. To make sure no one feels uncomfortable, I want all of you to write *something*, even if you just write a line about the weather. When you're done, I'll collect them and choose one randomly."

"That seems a rather odd way to do it," a tired-looking woman with defiant eyes said.

"Would you like to suggest a better way, Ruth?" Carrie asked. It was obvious the woman was uncomfortable with the suggestion. She was struggling to remember everything Rose had taught her about teaching. She knew arguing or being defensive would only make the women more resistant, so she was doing her best to stay open.

"No," Ruth said reluctantly. "I suppose this is as good a way as any."

"I understand your hesitancy," Carrie said gently. "You thought you were coming to a seminar where you would sit and listen to someone talk."

"Well, yes. Isn't that usually how it's done?"

"I'm sure it is," Carrie replied. "We decided, however, that the women who attended today weren't going to be normal women."

"You did?" Darlene asked in a startled voice. "Why is that?"

"Because most women don't choose to be brave," Carrie said bluntly. "Coming here today took a lot of courage. All women have the *ability* to be brave, but too many choose to live with fear. All of you made a different choice." She smiled. "We believe we should honor that bravery by giving you the choice to talk about what *you* care about, not what *we* think you should care about." Her eyes swept the room, looking for more resistance. When she didn't see any, she handed out the paper and pencils.

Carrie was eager to see what was written on every single piece of paper, but she forced herself to place all of them into a basket. She handed it to Elizabeth, who stirred them around and handed her one.

Carrie accepted the folded sheet of paper and then looked at the women. Every one of them was staring at her with intense anticipation. "Don't be concerned if I didn't pick your question," she said. "Now that we know women will come, we'll do more of these. We'll keep the questions you've written and answer another one in the next seminar."

Darlene eyed her. "Well, we came this time, but if we don't like your answer we probably won't be back." Her expression was a combination of humor and challenge.

The rest of the women looked at Darlene with shocked expressions, but Carrie merely laughed. "I would do the same thing," she assured them. She unfolded the sheet of paper. "Let's see how we do with this question."

I have eight children already. I'm not even thirty years old, but I'm told I have kidney and heart disease. I don't want any more children. I don't know how to stop it from happening. Can you help?

Carrie smiled, wondering which of these women looking at her had written the question. "I believe we can. The first thing I want you to understand is that you're not alone. You may not know that in 1800, the birth rate in the United States was the highest in the world. The average mother had eight children. Things are changing, though. The number, seventy years later, is much lower. At least for *most* women." She was aware that fact didn't apply to the woman who had written the question.

"Why?" Darlene asked, her face avid with interest. "I don't have eight children, but I've got more than I know what to do with, and my husband doesn't seem to care. I know I don't really have a say in it, but I guess I believe I should."

"I agree with you," Carrie said firmly, deciding to take a risk and tell some of her personal story. "My first child was stillborn, and I came very close to dying. Right before I went into labor, my husband was murdered. When I somehow survived, my doctor made it very clear that if I were to become pregnant again, I most likely wouldn't live through it."

"Oh my," one of the women murmured.

Looks of sympathy softened every face in the room.

"When I got married again," Carrie continued, "I was very clear with my husband about the risks. We decided, together, that we would take the steps to ensure I didn't get pregnant."

"How?"

Carrie had been confident she could count on Darlene to ask the question every woman there was thinking. "There are many ways to keep from getting pregnant. One is abstinence, but I love my husband far too much for either of us to choose that method," she said with a smile.

One of the women who looked to be close to forty shifted in her seat uncomfortably. "Isn't this a rather delicate subject to discuss?"

"I know it is for many women," Carrie agreed, "but that's also the reason too many women are having children they would rather not have. Now," she added quickly, "being a mother is one of the greatest things in the world. I have two adopted children who mean the world to me. Making the choice to not have children, or to not have more than you can care for and support, while also taking care of yourself, doesn't mean you don't value motherhood. It means that you value yourself, as well."

She let the women absorb her words for a few moments.

"So, abstinence is out," Darlene said. "Even if the woman is happy to never have sex again, I don't know a man alive who's going to go along with *that* plan. What else is there?"

"Have you ever heard of timing when you have intercourse?" Janie asked. "With this method, you avoid sex on your most fertile days by being aware of your menstrual cycle."

One of the women snorted with disdain. "I don't mind saying I'm the one who asked the question you're answering. I used *timing* for the last four pregnancies," she said sarcastically. "My mother-in-law told me it would work, but it's sure not working for me."

"You're not the only one," Janie said reassuringly. "It can be an effective method, but it's far too easy to miscalculate your menstrual cycle and end up pregnant."

"I'm proof of that," the woman said ruefully.

"Abstinence is out and trying to get the timing right is out," Darlene said. "Is there anything that *works*?"

"I have to caution you that there's nothing that's guaranteed to work one hundred percent of the time," Carrie answered. "However, the methods I'm about to share have kept most women from getting pregnant."

"Start talking," Matilda demanded.

Carrie smiled. "Have any of you heard of the book by Dr. James Ashton called *The Book of Nature*?" Blank faces staring back at her was her answer. "The book came out ten years ago. Dr. Ashton believes there is no sin nor ethical dilemma in a married couple trying to limit family size." She mentioned that first because she knew many women battled that belief.

"I tried to talk to my doctor about it," Matilda admitted, her eyes sparkling with anger. "He told me I should put my focus on being a good wife and mother. He said if my husband wanted sex, it was my role to provide it. When I told him trying to time intercourse wasn't working, he told me I should try harder. After four more children!" she snapped. Her anger deflated as her face sagged in defeat. "Even after he diagnosed my health problems, he refused to provide any methods to help me. I suppose he was fine with me dying, as long as I provided what my husband wanted while I was alive."

Carrie knew just how true that was. She exchanged a look with her friends. Their expressions revealed all of them were more certain than ever that the women of Richmond needed them.

"Not every doctor feels that way," Elizabeth replied.

"Every doctor in *this* city," Darlene retorted as she looked around the room. "I daresay that if any other woman in this room talked to their doctor about this, they were told the same thing."

Several women nodded their affirmation.

"There are now doctors in Richmond that don't believe what you've been told," Elizabeth said. "You're looking at them. Unfortunately, men aren't always the best doctors for women. They don't understand our bodies, nor..." Her voice trailed off.

Darlene looked at her sharply. "We're having an honest conversation aren't we, Dr. Gilbert? You might as well say what you were going to say."

Elizabeth hesitated, and then finished her thought. "My experience has been that male doctors are using their perceived authority to control women when it comes to their health. They seem to be more concerned with their societal agenda than they are with actually caring for their patients."

Carrie leapt into the conversation. "Men are threatened by the new demands women are making. The medical profession is being used far too often to exert control over women by insisting they only belong in the roles *they* mandate to be appropriate." She thought of Alice's horrific experience in the insane asylum, simply because two male doctors, prodded by her husband, deemed her insane without ever laying eyes on her. Now, if Matthew was correct, there was an increased drive to keep women from using methods of birth control that would be effective.

"I just want to control the number of children I have," Matilda said, her face showing how uncomfortable she was. "I like being a wife and mother. I don't want anything else."

"Then that's all you should ever do," Janie replied firmly. "Do you have daughters among your eight children, Matilda?"

"Five of them," Matilda said proudly. "The oldest is twelve."

"Do all of them want to be wives and mothers?"

Matilda started to nod, but then stopped. "Well..." she said hesitantly.

"Go on and tell us," Darlene urged.

Matilda squirmed and took a deep breath before she answered. "My oldest says she wants to be a lawyer. I have no idea where she got a crazy idea like that. I've told her it's ridiculous."

"Why?" Janie asked gently.

Matilda shook her head, her lips set in a stubborn line. "Women don't become lawyers."

"Women aren't supposed to be doctors, either," Janie said.

"I'm not sure you *should* be," Matilda retorted.

Carrie knew she was responding so defensively because Matilda was afraid of what life might hold for her daughter. She was intrigued to see how this was going to play out.

"Why not?" Janie asked quietly, her tone conversational.

Carrie was impressed with Janie's ability to ask piercing questions without sounding like she was attacking Matilda.

Matilda was silent for so long, however, Carrie wasn't sure she was going to answer.

Finally, Matilda cleared her throat. "My doctor told me what would happen." Her voice bordered on hysteria.

"What would happen if your daughter became a lawyer?" Janie asked.

"Yes." Matilda's voice was a mixture of defiance and sadness. "He explained that women aren't meant to take on roles that belong to men. He told me that if she decided to become a lawyer, she wouldn't be able to bear children."

Janie raised a brow. "Did he say why not?"

"He said the energy she would use to apply her brain for law school would have to come from the energy her body has to produce children. There wasn't enough energy in her to do both, so if she went to law school, she could never have children."

"That's not true," Carrie said firmly, appalled by what she was hearing.

Matilda stared at her. "You lost *your* baby," she said bluntly.

Carrie took a deep breath to dispel the pain that came from her statement and forced a smile. Responding with defensiveness would never give Matilda a chance to change her mind. She would simply dig in her heels to protect her position. "Yes, that's true," she said calmly, "but my mother almost died having me, and she was never able to have more. It is much more likely that it was something passed down from her that makes childbirth so difficult for me."

"You don't know that for sure, though, do you?" Matilda demanded.

Janie came to her rescue. "I'm a doctor, Matilda. I have two beautiful children. Robert is almost two. Annabelle was born this past September. I can assure you that using my brain to go to medical school didn't destroy my chance to have children."

Matilda looked thoughtful, but her posture remained rigid.

"All of this is very interesting," Darlene said, "but we still haven't found out how to not have more children."

"You're right," Carrie said quickly. They'd given Matilda something to think about. She also knew every other woman in the room would ponder what they'd heard. That was enough for now. "Women keep from having more children by understanding that if they block their husband's sperm from their egg, they can't get pregnant."

"*How*?" Darlene asked impatiently.

Carrie smiled at Darlene. "I promise I'm going to tell you. A lot of methods and ingredients have been used over the centuries, but the basics are the same." The three doctors had decided they were going to talk frankly with any women who came to the seminar. "You have to either put up a barrier to keep the sperm out, wash it out, or try to kill it before it reaches your egg." She held back her smile this time when she saw the expressions on some of the women's faces. They were most certainly not used to such direct communication.

"Many women start by buying a high quality sponge at any drugstore here in town. You want to cut off a piece about the size of a walnut. Then make a fine silk string by twisting together some threads of sewing silk. You tie one end of the string to the piece of sponge and then wet it in a weak solution of sulphate of iron. You can get that at the drugstore, as well. Before having sex, you want to insert it far into your vagina. You can push it out of the way of intercourse by using a smooth stick. The string will hang out, but it doesn't create a problem. When you're done, you withdraw the string."

"Does it work?" Darlene asked.

"Many women have had great success," Carrie assured her. "Another very popular method is the womb veil."

Matilda laughed. "The *what*?"

Carrie joined the laughter, glad to see Matilda had put her earlier pique behind her. "I agree that it sounds odd, but it's remarkably effective. The womb veil is a device inserted into the vagina to block the sperm's access to your eggs. Another word for it is a pessary. Some form of them has been around for centuries, but the womb veil, invented just seven years ago, is made of rubber. It's more effective and quite inexpensive. One of the things women like most about it is that you can order it through the mail. Once it's inserted, the man has no idea it's there unless you tell him."

Matilda's eyes widened. "I can protect myself and my husband would never know?"

"That's right," Carrie told her. She decided to not mention that Anthony Comstock was working hard to make their availability through the mail illegal.

Darlene was watching her closely. "Which of those methods do *you* use, Dr. Wallington?"

"None of them," Carrie said honestly.

"Then why are you telling us about them?" Ruth looked confused.

"Because they're the most accepted methods of birth control in America right now," Carrie replied. "I wanted to tell you about the ones you'll be most comfortable with."

"I'd rather use the one that works best," Ruth retorted.

Carrie nodded, happy to see how engaged the women had become. In truth, she was eager to tell the women how she prevented pregnancy, but she'd been determined to share all their options before she did. She had not discussed douches yet, but that was another one she didn't use because it wasn't always effective.

"When I first decided to become a doctor, I attended the Women's Medical College in Philadelphia. I learned a tremendous amount, but when the cholera epidemic swept through the country several years ago, it became very obvious that medicine couldn't help the tens of thousands who were dying. In my desperation to help people, I learned about homeopathy. Suddenly, people who would have died were being saved. I left the Medical College and got my degree in homeopathy. Janie and I are both homeopathic physicians, but I'm also a certified surgeon. I find combining the two fields enables me to help more patients." She paused. "I'm also a very strong believer in herbal medicine. During the war, when drugs were unavailable because of the blockade, we treated many soldiers at Chimborazo Hospital with medicinal herbs. There was a whole team of women who went out into the woods to gather plants." She smiled. "I treat patients at my country clinic with them on a regular basis."

"You use herbs to keep from getting pregnant?" Darlene asked with surprise.

"Queen Anne's lace to be exact," Carrie replied.

Matilda gasped. "The plant that seems to grow all over Virginia? The one with the lacy white flowers?"

"That's the one. Queen Anne's lace has been used as an effective form of birth control for thousands of years," Carrie told them. "The seeds are harvested in the fall. I take them orally every day." She shrugged. "So far, I haven't become pregnant. I don't believe I will."

"Did you find out about Queen Anne's lace in school?" Darlene asked.

"We talked about it, but I first learned about it from one of my father's slaves when I was growing up. We called her Old Sarah. She was a fountain of wisdom and knowledge when it came to herbal medicine. She taught me more than anyone has since. I remembered what she told me about Queen Anne's lace after I almost died in childbirth. I started using the seeds as soon as I married again."

"How do you get the seeds?" Matilda asked eagerly. She held up a hand before Carrie could answer. "Don't tell me I can collect the seeds this fall. I'm not waiting for nine months and then tramping around in the country to find the seeds. Surely there is a way to buy them."

"There is," Carrie confirmed. She turned to open the door of the large cabinet on the wall. "We have a supply of them here, and I also have a supply at my clinic outside the city."

Suddenly, all the women, even the ones who hadn't spoken at all, looked excited.

"I want some," Darlene said.

"Me, too," Ruth and Matilda said at the same time.

"I have a question," another woman asked. "What happens if I decide I want more children in the future? Will taking these seeds keep that from happening?"

Every woman in the room suddenly hesitated. Clearly, they hadn't thought of that possibility.

"That's an excellent question, Vivian," Carrie said warmly. "The answer is that you can certainly have children again. When you decide you want to be pregnant, quit taking the seeds. It usually takes about a month to clear from your system, but I've had women become pregnant in as little as two weeks." She held up her hand.

"I want to warn you that anything, even the Queen Anne's lace, is only as effective as your consistency in using it. I take the seeds every day because I don't want to risk being pregnant. You'll have to do the same thing."

"Well, we have our first patients," Carrie said happily as they watched the women depart down the sidewalk, all of them laughing and talking among themselves. It was hard to believe they were the same women who had entered so fearfully just two hours earlier.

"All of them set up appointments to see us," Elizabeth said in a stunned voice. "*All* of them. I can hardly believe it."

"It's a beginning," Janie agreed. "And all of them promised to bring someone with them to the next seminar."

"We may have to expand upstairs sooner than we thought," Elizabeth said excitedly. "I can't wait to write home and tell Mother and Father."

"I have a feeling I'll be hiring a lot of the plantation children to collect Queen Anne's lace seeds this fall," Carrie predicted.

"I'd say you're right," Janie agreed as she looked up. "I suppose we should let Anthony and Matthew downstairs now."

Carrie laughed. "I forgot about them!"

"A comment like that can make a husband feel very insecure."

Carrie whirled around as Anthony walked into the room. She was relieved to see a broad smile on his face.

"We figured it was safe to come down when we saw the last woman leave," Anthony said.

"So you heard how well it went?" Elizabeth asked.

"We did," Matthew replied. "Congratulations. I'd say you had a very successful day. And we didn't even have to step in to provide security."

"Perhaps Richmond is more ready for a women's medical practice than we believed," Elizabeth said thoughtfully.

"Perhaps," Carrie agreed.

Janie gazed at her. "What aren't you telling us?"

"Nothing," Carrie protested, not wanting to give voice to her thoughts after such a successful event.

Janie continued to look at her. "Carrie..." she warned.

Carrie shook her head. "I know this city. I've seen what happens when people go against the norms of what they believe is acceptable behavior."

"You're thinking about the factory," Anthony observed.

"How can I not? Father and Abby dared to employ both blacks and whites in the factory. People in the city put up with it for a while, but in the end, someone burned it down. Father almost died."

"But he didn't die," Janie pointed out.

"You're right," Carrie acknowledged. "But it's also true that more than one hundred people lost their jobs. Anthony has hired some of them for the carriage company, but the rest have had to take jobs that pay far less."

Elizabeth took her hand. "Are you afraid?"

"I'd be a fool not to be afraid," Carrie said honestly. "I have no intention of letting my fear stop me from coming here and working at our practice when I'm not on the plantation, but..." She paused as she looked at Janie and Elizabeth. "I'm afraid for the two of you, as well. I'll be coming back and forth from the plantation, but y'all will be here all the time."

"We're going to be careful," Janie assured her as she took her other hand.

"Promise me you'll be *very* careful," Carrie urged. "Anthony and I are going back to the plantation tomorrow. As much as I want to go home, I'm worried about my partners."

"We'll be careful," Janie assured her. "I don't believe you have anything to worry about, though. People may think we're quacks and a poor representation of the female gender, but that doesn't mean they want to harm us."

Elizabeth nodded. "I agree. Besides, I want to celebrate what we accomplished today." Her eyes sparkled. "Do you think May will make us some Irish oatmeal cookies for tonight?"

Carrie laughed despite her worry. "Do you always celebrate with food?"

"I'm Italian," Elizabeth retorted. "Of course I celebrate with food! If I can't have some of my mother's spaghetti and meatballs, I'll settle for Irish oatmeal cookies."

Laughing and talking, the five of them headed home.

It was time to celebrate.

They were only a block from the office when a disheveled looking man walked up to Carrie, stopping just in front of her. "Are you Doc Wallington?"

Anthony started toward him, but Carrie held up her hand, never letting her eyes leave the man's face. She knew that look all too well. "I am. How can I help you?"

The man hesitated, but then blurted, "You the doc who's helping veterans who got hurt in the war?"

"I am," she assured him. "What is your name, sir?"

"Milner," the man said gruffly, his expression revealing he was not accustomed to being called *sir*. "Davis Milner."

"It's a pleasure to meet you. I was just leaving my office, but I'll go back if you'd like to tell me what you need. I would schedule you for tomorrow, but I'm leaving town for two weeks."

"Two weeks?" Milner looked alarmed. "I would be grateful if you could see me now, ma'am," he blurted. "Have you got some of that medicine here that helped Hank?"

Carrie smiled. "You're a friend of Hank's?"

"We served together," Milner confirmed. "I haven't seen him since we both got hurt in the war. At least, not until last week," he amended. "He came into Richmond to buy some supplies, and I ran into him. He told me about that stuff you give him that took away his pain. He told me you were setting up an office here, and I saw your flyer and decided to come by. Hank told me what you looked like. That's why I stopped you."

Carrie nodded and looked at everyone. "All of you go talk May into those cookies. I'll take care of Mr. Milner before I come home."

"I'll wait for you," Anthony said quickly.

Carrie knew Anthony and Matthew were going to have to get over their need to provide protection all the time, but she was honest enough to admit it would be nice to have Anthony there.

"I'll make sure there are Irish oatmeal cookies," Elizabeth promised.

Carrie watched her friends depart and turned to the veteran. "Come with us."

Mr. Milner fell into step with them. "Do you really think you can help me, Doc Wallington?"

"I believe so," Carrie responded. "The Hypericum doesn't work for one hundred percent of my patients, but it helps almost all of them. Even if it doesn't completely take away your pain, you'll feel much better than you do now."

Mr. Milner looked startled. "You can tell I'm hurting?"

"It's all over your face," Carrie said gently. "How long ago were you hurt?" She'd planned to wait until they got to the office to talk with him, but he was obviously comfortable talking about it with Anthony there, so there was no reason to wait.

"The last battle of the war," he said ruefully. "I thought I'd been real lucky, but then we got to Appomattox Courthouse."

Carrie fought the desire to close her eyes to block out the memory of how close Robert had come to dying at Appomattox Courthouse. It had been pneumonia rather than a bullet that had almost taken him, but a bullet would have been kinder. His body, weakened by the stresses of the last battles of the war, had taken months to heal. His mind and spirit had taken longer.

She forced herself to focus. "What happened?"

Mr. Milner shrugged. "I got shot, just like lots of other fellas before the surrender. I thought I'd get out of the war with all my limbs, but obviously my leg got left behind in a hospital tent."

Carrie was amazed by how matter-of-factly he was reporting what had happened. "You left your leg behind, but you weren't able to leave the pain behind."

"That's the truth of it," he acknowledged. "I'd give just about anything for a few minutes with no pain."

Carrie turned up the walkway when they reached the office. "I believe we can do much better than a few minutes."

"Does it ever stop feeling like a miracle?" Anthony asked as they walked the few blocks to River City Carriages. Because they had sent the rest home in their carriage, they needed another one...unless they wanted a long, cold walk home. The vote to get a carriage had been unanimous.

"No," Carrie replied, still glowing from the look of warm gratitude in Mr. Milner's eyes when she had handed him the bottle of hypericum. He would check in with Janie in a week, and then return again to see her when she came back to the city. "Every single person I'm able to help seems like a new miracle." She looked up at him. "I dreamed of being a doctor for so long, but the reality of it is so much more than I ever could have imagined."

"I'm proud of you," Anthony told her, his green eyes glowing with pride and love.

"Thank you," Carrie replied. "I can't wait until Florence gets here. Besides the fact that she's going to be thrilled by what's happening, we're going to need her!"

Chapter Twenty-Five

Florence smiled at Silas wearily. "Are you as tired as I am?" She had just finished a long surgery. She stretched and flexed her hands and fingers, drawing in deep breaths of fresh air as she did.

"Undoubtedly," Silas responded. "I wish we could go someplace warm and cozy for a delicious meal."

Florence groaned. "Talking like that does not make things easier. I spend far too much of my time already trying not to think about the foods I left behind in America."

"In *America*?" Silas gave her a look of astonishment. "How I wish you had found the City of Light before its grand restaurants ran out of food. The finest restaurants in the world are right here in Paris."

Florence raised a brow. "I suppose I'm forced to accept your word on that. Father and I did have a few wonderful meals before the siege, but I've also had spectacular meals in Philadelphia, Boston and New York City."

Silas waved his hand nonchalantly. "If I had the chance, I could change your mind in a matter of weeks."

Florence gazed at him thoughtfully. They had professed their love for each other, but not one word had been spoken regarding the future. The uncertainty of the situation they found themselves in made that completely understandable, but it didn't quiet the questions in her mind.

Her father talked at length about when they would be able to leave Paris and return to America. She knew her mother must be frantic, and her father's thriving medical practice was surely missing his presence. Their intention to be home by early December had certainly evaporated. If they lived through the end of the war, there was no way to know when they would be free to leave the city. All steamer traffic into France had stopped shortly after the war began. There would be a rush of people eager to cross the ocean when ships once more sailed into French ports.

"What are you thinking?"

Florence pushed aside her thoughts and forced a smile. "I'm thinking that I'm grateful for the warmer temperatures." She could tell by the expression on Silas' face that he didn't believe her, but he didn't press. In truth, she'd been thrilled to walk outside into a warm, southerly breeze that morning.

"It's going to turn Paris into a sea of mud," Silas commented.

Florence shrugged. "Mud is easier to deal with than freezing to death."

"I suppose you have a point," Silas teased.

Florence knew he was trying to lighten the mood again. He must be confused as to how a comment about Paris restaurants could so alter her mood. She sighed as she realized continued honesty was the only way to navigate their relationship. "I'm sorry," she said contritely. "Your comment about the restaurants illuminated the fact that we've never discussed the future. I'm not expecting us to," Florence said quickly. "There's far too much going on right now that is more important. It's just that I've always had very clear goals and plans for my life. It feels odd to not know what's going to happen in the future."

"What would you like to happen?" Silas asked gently.

Florence took a deep breath. "I don't know." Despite her fear of saying the wrong thing, she was determined to be forthright. "I love you. I want to be with you. The problem is that I don't know what that means."

Silas regarded her steadily. "I love you and want to be with you, as well."

"What does that *mean*?" Florence asked.

Silas sighed. "I wish things were simple, but I'm afraid they're not. You plan on returning to America to work at the clinic in Richmond."

"And you?" During all their long discussions, Florence had never heard Silas talk about his future plans. He was happy to talk about the past and the present, but he carefully avoided any discussion of the future. It was time to ask him directly.

"I wish I knew," Silas said quietly. "I've thought about what it would mean to return to America. I can't quite imagine it," he admitted. "There are many painful memories for me back there."

Florence swallowed her question about whether a new life with her would create enough good memories to erase the bad. She wanted to hear his thoughts.

"When I think about staying in Paris, I can't feel good about that either," he continued. "Even once the siege is over, the city is going to remain in turmoil for a long time. It's going to be an even longer time before it's once more the city I fell in love with. Part of me feels guilty for wanting to leave, but it doesn't change the fact that I feel that way."

Florence fixed her gaze on his face, listening intently while he talked through his feelings.

Silas paused. "Aren't you going to say anything?"

"Why? If I love you, I want you to be happy. Only you can know what that means for you."

Silas stared at her. "Extraordinary," he murmured. "You are truly extraordinary."

Florence smiled, but she hoped that being extraordinary wasn't going to mean she would also be lonely and heartbroken.

"What made you decide to move to the South to start your practice?" Silas asked suddenly.

Florence blinked with surprise and carefully considered her answer. "I suppose because I wanted to work with Carrie, Janie and Elizabeth. We all went through so much together to earn our medical degrees." She'd already told him about the period of time when their divergent opinions on medicine had almost destroyed their relationship. "We're good friends, but most importantly, our interests in medicine complement each other." She paused. "It also seemed like a rather grand adventure."

Silas raised a brow. "How much time have you spent in the South?"

"None," Florence said slowly, uncertain as to why the confession made her uneasy. "Why?"

"You have no idea what you'll walk into," Silas said bluntly. "You're a strong-minded, independent woman, Florence."

Florence listened closely. She knew that was true, and she also knew it had become truer since she'd arrived in Paris. The doctors at the American hospital had embraced her as an equal from the beginning. "Yes," she said, "but so is Carrie. And Janie and Elizabeth." She forced herself to think about what had compelled her decision in the beginning. "Carrie invited me to join the practice because she believes Southern women are ready for something different." She met his eyes. "I agree with her."

"Without ever stepping a foot in the South?"

Florence tensed momentarily but forced herself to relax. He was simply asking her questions. There was nothing attacking or derisive about either his voice or what he was asking. It was uncomfortable to acknowledge she had based her decision on so little personal knowledge, but it didn't change the reality. "Do you believe I'm making a mistake?"

"It's not my place to say," Silas responded. "I agree with your earlier statement. If I love you, I want you to be happy. Only you know what that means."

Florence stared off into the distance. What had started off as a discussion about their future *together*, had somehow become a discussion about the decisions she had made about her future in America. "Working here at the hospital has been wonderful," she began. "It astonished me in the beginning that I was accepted so readily as an equal, but..." She thought hard about what she was about to say. "But I don't believe I would ever be able to accept not being seen that way in the future. I know Carrie and the rest would see me that way, but I wonder what it would be like to work within a medical system that shuns us." She knew that, at least in the beginning, the South wouldn't open the doors of medicine to her and her colleagues.

Carrie had warned her about the challenges they would face when she'd issued the invitation. The problem was that what had been acceptable when she left America had become repugnant to her now.

She appreciated Silas' silence as she worked through her thoughts. "I had accepted that thought before I came to Paris," she said slowly.

"And now?"

Florence sighed. "And now I find the thought intolerable." The realization was both calming and terrifying. Closing the door on one possibility without another to walk through was frightening.

Silas read her expression accurately. "What if there were another option?"

Florence took a deep breath. "Such as?"

Silas looked nervous, but gazed at her steadily as he answered her question. "What if we were to start a practice of our own here in Paris? You already know how poor the French medical system is. We would provide a huge service to our patients."

Florence raised a brow. "Just a few minutes ago you said you didn't feel good about staying in Paris because the city will remain in turmoil after the siege ends. You said it would be a long time before the city is what it used to be."

"Those things are true," Silas agreed.

"Then why the abrupt change?"

"I can be happy any place where you are, my love," Silas said warmly. "It's really as simple as that. When I thought you were returning to America, Paris lost its appeal. I wasn't happy about being in America again... at least not right now," he amended quickly, "but I couldn't imagine being separated from you."

Florence caught her breath as she thought about his suggestion, as well as his statement that he couldn't imagine being separated from her. *Start a practice in Paris with Silas?*

What would her father think? What about her mother? Could she stand being so far away from her family? What would Carrie and the rest think if she were to tell them she wasn't returning? The questions tumbled through her head with lightning speed.

Silas took her hand. "I know this is a lot to consider, Florence."

Florence nodded silently. Part of her wanted to throw herself into his arms and scream *yes*. Another part couldn't imagine not returning to America.

Once again, Silas read her expression. "We could return to America every year. You'll want to be with your family, and I'll want to see my sister," he added persuasively. "Choosing to stay here for now doesn't mean forever. We may decide to return to America in the future."

"And we may not," Florence commented, determined to examine his request with unflinching honesty. "I have to consider what it would mean to never return home for good." She gazed around her. Silas had shown her pictures of what Paris had been like before the war. She was certain it was a city she could fall in love with. In most ways, she was far better suited to a life in Paris than she would ever be to life in Richmond, Virginia.

"I realize you need time," Silas said calmly.

As Florence looked into his steady brown eyes, the confusion suddenly floated away. She loved him. She couldn't imagine life without him. She was being offered a chance to partner with him in a medical practice. France was a country in turmoil, but so was America. She could remain and be a part of the solution that would rebuild the most wonderful city in Europe.

Florence threw back her head and laughed.

"Florence?"

Florence laughed harder at the alarmed expression on Silas' face. "I've not lost my mind," she assured him. "I've suddenly realized how simple this is." Unmindful of anyone that might be around, she threw her arms around him. "Yes, Silas Amberton. Yes!"

Silas laughed loudly and then sobered as he leaned back to gaze into her eyes. "You do realize I'm asking you to be my wife, don't you?"

Florence stopped laughing and smiled calmly. "I would certainly hope so, Dr. Amberton. The answer to that is yes, as well."

Silas stared at her for a long moment and then grinned widely. "I love you, Florence," he whispered, just before he claimed her lips in a long kiss.

Florence could feel the tension in the house as soon as she and Silas entered. Her father was waiting for them in the entrance. "Father? What's wrong?" Without him saying a word, she knew she and Silas were going to delay the announcement of their engagement.

"Washburne is waiting for us."

Florence exchanged a somber look with Silas, took the hand he offered, and entered the dining room. Washburne nodded pleasantly and waved them to their seats, but she could see the lines of strain on his face.

They all took their seats and waited for him to speak.

He wasted no time in getting to the point. "Paris is going to launch another assault against the Prussians," he announced. "The whole situation within the city has become completely untenable. Instead of being able to focus on the enemy, the French government is obliged to fight two enemies at once."

"The Prussians and the Reds," Dr. Robinson said.

"Yes. The Reds within Paris continue to look for every way possible to destroy the new government. There has been talk of surrender, but Trochu and the rest of the government doubt the Reds would permit it to happen."

"They could stop a surrender?" Florence asked with astonishment. "Who is actually running the government?"

Washburne scowled. "My question, precisely. I find it unfathomable that the government has not taken action against the Reds long before this. While their leader Gustave Flourens is in prison a second time for his revolutionary politics, his followers have only intensified their attacks in the papers and in the clubs they frequent around the city. In truth, the outcome of the war was decided in September at the Battle of Sedan when Napoleon was captured, but the French weren't willing to capitulate." He shrugged. "Even though the consequences of that decision have been disastrous, I can't know for sure, if I were in their position, whether I wouldn't have made the same decision. Anyway, the difficulties of the siege have only increased the Red's fervor. They're now calling for the National Guard to be sent out to vanquish the Prussians once and for all."

"How can they still want to go to battle after all they've endured?" Silas asked.

"They're French," Washburne said, as if that explained everything, and then clarified. "They can't conceive of bowing to the Prussians. They believe they haven't yet *shed enough blood* for their nation, and they're demanding they have the chance to go into battle. They are supremely confident they can vanquish the Prussians."

"Trochu is going to let them?" Silas demanded. "He's sending them to their death."

Washburne nodded wearily. "Trochu knows they don't stand a chance at victory, but with the Reds pining for a fight, he fears he's risking open rebellion if he doesn't allow it to happen."

"You said he knows there's no chance of victory," Florence said. "How can he be willing to send so many to their death?"

Washburne shook his head. "I've heard that a member of the government made a statement that the refusal to surrender would die down if ten thousand of the National Guard were lying on the ground."

Florence stared at him speechlessly.

"They're going to get their wish," Dr. Robinson said angrily. "And what then? How will the deaths of ten thousand or more help Paris? When they lose, they'll still be forced into surrender. Only now there will be many more who are grieving and angry."

"You know that, and I know that," Washburne said, "but emotion is not usually reasonable. When it comes to the French, that truth is even more so."

A heavy pall fell over the room. The only sounds were the whistling wind and the rattle of window glass.

"When will the battle begin?" Silas finally asked.

"In two days, on the nineteenth."

Florence waited at the hospital with the rest of the staff for the first load of wounded soldiers to be brought in by the hospital ambulances.

News filtered in slowly.

The battle had been set to commence at dawn, but one of the three columns, led by General Ducrot, didn't arrive at the scheduled time. They were said to have been impeded by mud and fog. Governor Trochu delayed the attack for as long as he could, but when Ducrot still failed to appear, he was afraid of losing what little tactical advantage he had.

He ordered the battle to begin without Ducrot's column.

To everyone's amazement, the attack caught the Prussians by surprise, driving them back from two of their positions surrounding the city. Unfortunately, the National Guard, which only the day before had boasted about its military prowess, fought horribly. They inflicted almost as many casualties on each other as the enemy. There were some that fought well, but the massive numbers of inept soldiers made advancement impossible.

By the time General Ducrot managed to arrive on the battlefield, he couldn't compel his soldiers to advance. Frozen with fear of certain death, they simply ignored his orders and stayed where they were.

As the news rolled in, so too did the ambulances begin to roll in full of the wounded from the muddy and bloody battlefield.

"The first ambulance is here," Silas announced grimly.

Florence nodded, gritted her teeth, and went to work. She already knew there would be no real rest for days to come.

The battle resumed the next morning, but within hours, Trochu, realizing there was no hope of victory, had ordered a withdrawal.

It was over.

Three days later, Paris was in even more turmoil than it had been previously. Whatever morale and resistance that had remained was now destroyed. The only difference was that there were more bodies being piled into the mass burial site.

Trochu had been relieved of duty. Commander Vinoy took over the military reins, but everyone understood it was too late for any kind of resistance.

Vice President Favre had been given the job of negotiating an armistice with Prussia.

Though the National Guard had insisted on being allowed to fight, that reality seemed to have been forgotten as they dealt with the futile slaughter of so many of their own.

Rage grew in Paris by the hour.

Florence could barely keep her eyes open as she walked slowly down rue de Rivoli, thinking only of how good it would feel to fall in bed when she arrived at the minister's house. She'd slept on a cot in the hospital for the last three nights, grabbing a few minutes of sleep between surgeries whenever she could. Silas was still there, but he'd insisted she would be no good to her patients if she didn't get some rest. Recognizing the wisdom of his logic, she had kissed him good-bye and departed.

She sighed when she drew near the Hotel de Ville. As usual, protestors were lined up outside the gates, yelling for the destruction of the Government of Defense. While she understood their anger, she also realized they were largely to blame for the death of so many of their comrades. Hopeless and heartbroken, they could only think of casting blame on someone else.

Florence had passed protests at the hotel many times. Stepping to the far side of the road, she continued her steady walk. Her eyes narrowed when she heard the tromp of boots coming toward her. There was something unusually ominous about the sound. Not certain what to do, she stopped and slipped into a narrow opening between two buildings. She hated the feeling of being trapped between the two stone facades, but instinct told her it was safer than being out on the road.

One of the other doctors had warned hospital staff that the National Guard was intent on revenge. The afternoon before, a band of armed guardsmen had appeared at the gates of the Mazas Prison and demanded the release of Flourens and the other Red leaders that had been arrested in the fall. Remarkably, the prison commander had turned them over, merely asking for a receipt for their bodies. The guardsmen had then marched on to the administrative offices of the twentieth arrondissement, pillaged all the food and wine stored there, and set up their headquarters.

Florence was suddenly certain she was about to experience the next development in their plan for revenge. Her heart hammered in her chest as she pondered making a run for it, but the crowd was so volatile she didn't know what would happen. At least she was mostly out of sight. She would stay where she was until the demonstration had ended.

As she watched, her fatigue forgotten, she saw a man walk out from the hotel. She couldn't hear what he was saying, but from the way he was waving his arms and pointing his finger, she figured out he was warning the protestors that there were armed men behind the hotel windows.

It was evident General Vinoy was not going to take the same passive approach that General Trochu had about the Reds faction in the city. As the government official walked back inside, the men belonging to the boots she had heard materialized.

Florence stiffened when she realized they were all armed to the teeth, their thin faces pinched tight with anger and determination. She watched as they took up a position in front of the hotel. The thought of running entered her mind again, but was just as quickly banished. Now was not the time to appear in the open. She prayed as she pressed back against the rough stone behind her. She had no idea what might happen if she were discovered, but she had no interest in finding out.

A shot suddenly rang out in the cold air.

Florence strained to determine who had fired it, but from her confined position it was impossible to tell.

Stark silence followed the lone shot for several moments but was quickly followed by a shout. "Ils nous tirent dessus"

Florence easily translated the panicked French. *They're firing on us!*

Florence watched as terrified expressions filled almost every face. What had started as a protest had suddenly become something much more menacing.

The armed men who had just arrived lowered to one knee and fired a volley into the Hotel de Ville.

"No," Florence cried. She knew no one would hear her over the explosion of the guns. "No!" Even before the response came, she knew the outcome was going to be horrific.

She saw a uniformed man fall just inside the gates and then a devastating fusillade crackled out of every window of the hotel.

The crowd began to scream and run in all directions as they stampeded to escape the deadly bullets. People were falling everywhere as the shots found their marks.

The Reds who had not been shot found positions behind overturned omnibuses and continued firing.

Florence felt sick as she realized that for the first time during the long war and siege, it was Frenchmen firing on other Frenchmen. Their countrymen had now become their enemy.

The firing seemed to go on forever.

Any attempt to escape now would be suicidal. She prayed for the building to somehow swallow her, but the cold stone scraping her skin through her coat was the only answer.

Suddenly, she saw a large group of soldiers appear in the distance. Reinforcements had been called in. She took a shaky breath of relief as the National Guardsmen turned and ran, overturning more omnibuses to cover their retreat.

When the guns in the hotel finally fell silent, Florence did the only thing she could. She ran toward the twenty-three people left lying on the ground. Bile rose in her throat when she realized there were women and children in the mix. She had no idea if there were any survivors, but she had to help if possible.

One of the newly arrived soldiers stepped forward. "*Arrêtez!*"

Florence slowed when he yelled at her to stop, but she called out loudly: "*Je suis médicin!*"

Upon hearing she was a doctor, the soldier waved her onward.

Florence dropped to her knees beside one of the children. Tears sprang to her eyes when she saw the massive bullet wound in the girl's abdomen. She pulled the jacket off one of the dead guardsmen and ripped it into pieces. She quickly tied a thick piece of the cloth over the wound, hoping she could at least slow the bleeding. The girl needed surgery soon if she was to live.

She beckoned the soldier who had tried to stop her. "*Elle a besoin d'un docteur,*" she said urgently.

The soldier looked at her closely. "You are American," he said in clear English.

"Yes!" Florence was relieved to not have to practice her French just then. "She is badly wounded. She needs to go to the American hospital."

The soldier frowned and started to shake his head.

"She's nothing but a child," Florence implored. "She was brought here by her parents. Surely she should not have to die for their actions."

The soldier hesitated again, but then gave a curt nod.

Florence didn't care that there was no enthusiasm on his face. She kept pressure on the wound while he beckoned to a fellow soldier.

"This child is to go to the American hospital." When the man he was giving orders to hesitated, his voice sharpened. "Now!"

Grumbling, the man picked up the young girl.

"It is only a few blocks to the hospital. You will carry her there quickly," the soldier ordered.

The man scowled but obeyed.

"Please tell him to ask for Dr. Amberton, and to tell him Dr. Robinson sent the child."

She waited until the soldier translated the message and then turned to the next patient. She knew Silas would make sure the girl received care. Moving from person to person, she did the best she could to help. With no supplies, she was quite limited. At that moment, fifteen of the twenty-three were still alive.

"Florence!"

Florence looked up with relief when she heard Silas' voice. She managed a weary smile when she saw six of their colleagues with him.

"Are you all right?" Silas demanded as he knelt next to her. "You're hurt!"

Only then did Florence realize she was covered with blood. "I'm fine," she assured him. "This isn't my blood. I'll give you all the details later. Right now, we have to help these people."

Later that evening, Washburne joined them at the dining room table. Florence seemed to have reached a point beyond exhaustion. As tired as she was, she knew sleep would elude her until she had some answers.

"It was awful," she said with a shudder when she concluded her telling of the afternoon events. "The French were firing on *each other.* I know there has been much turmoil, but I never suspected it would come to that."

"How could you not?" Washburne asked gently. "Not so long ago, it was Americans firing upon Americans. How quickly we can forget what passion enables us to do."

"Passion, or the inability to think clearly?" Florence demanded.

"Both," Washburne said immediately. "Regardless of the reasons, Paris is on the brink of its own civil war," he predicted grimly.

Florence looked across the table at Silas. A civil war? After having lived through one in America, she couldn't fathom living through another one.

"I'm told Favre is going to request an immediate audience with Bismarck, the Prussian commander," Washburne added.

"Do you believe Prussia will negotiate an armistice?" Silas asked.

"Yes," Washburne answered immediately, "My sources reveal they are more than willing to end the war, but they know they hold the upper hand in the negotiations. They're definitely coming from a position of strength," he said somberly. "However, they are perhaps just as eager to end this war as France is."

Five days later, on January twenty-seventh, the guns fell silent.

The City of Light had capitulated.

Twenty years of uninterrupted prosperity had ended. The city that had called itself the vanguard of civilization had been starved and bombed into submission.

Florence stood just inside the gates to Washburne's house, not certain what to do with the quiet night. Though the city streets created their own noise, it was nothing compared to the constant boom of the guns.

Dr. Robinson appeared next to her. "Why aren't you inside getting ready?"

"I'm trying to feel the city," Florence admitted. "The siege is over. The Prussians will start sending food in immediately, but the needs are going to continue for a long time. It's going to take time to eradicate the diseases and bring people back to health."

"Sounds like a good place for two excellent doctors to set up practice."

Florence peered into her father's face. "You're really all right with this?"

Her father gazed back at her. "With leaving my daughter in a foreign country that is just emerging from war? It would be stretching it to say I feel good about it, and I'm going to miss you terribly, but I believe you and Silas are meant to stay here for now."

"You do?" Florence gasped. Her father had not once said anything negative about her engagement, and he'd appeared to be delighted, but she knew there was more boiling under the surface of his placid demeanor that he hadn't been willing to say.

"I do," he said firmly. "The two of you are meant to be together. Paris needs both of you. Silas has promised he'll bring you home every year, and I'm going to do my best to convince your mother to get on a ship with me."

"Good luck," Florence commented. "After sailing straight into a war with our last trip, I'm not sure you'll ever convince her it's safe."

"Perhaps," her father replied, "but it's amazing what a mother's love can conquer. Especially if you and Silas have children. Your mother will want to see as much of her grandchildren as possible."

Florence laughed a little helplessly. "Children? Aren't you getting ahead of things? I'm not even married yet."

"True," her father conceded. "When the time comes, however, you'll be a wonderful mother." His eyes misted with emotion.

Florence hugged him tightly. "You're really leaving next week?" She had found out just that morning.

Her father nodded. "Washburne was able to use his connections to get me on the first steamer out of France. I'm not too proud to take advantage of his influence."

"I'm glad you're getting to go home to Mother," Florence said softly, tears pooling in her eyes as she thought of saying good-bye to her father. She thought of the long letter she'd already written for him to take home. "I do hope you can convince her to come back soon."

"No tears," he chided gently, using his finger to wipe them away. "A bride shouldn't be crying on her wedding night."

Florence stared at him. "I'm really getting married tonight," she whispered.

"You are if you go inside and get ready." Her father raised a brow. "Unless you're planning on getting married in what you wore to the hospital this morning."

Florence laughed. "Not a chance."

Florence had no idea how Minister Washburne had procured a pianist and a minister on such short notice, but music was floating softly up the stairway as she exited her room.

Her father, dressed in one of the suits he had carried with him from America, waited at the top of the stairs. His eyes were full of love as he smiled at her. "I'm glad to see the money we spent on Paris fashion at the beginning of our trip won't be wasted."

Florence returned his smile. The cream-colored gown that had fit perfectly in September was now loose, but she knew it still flattered her tall figure. The silky material seemed to float to the ground, and a blue sash pulled it snugly into her waist.

One of Washburne's assistants had eagerly volunteered to do her hair. Usually pulled back carelessly, it was now piled elegantly on her head, soft ringlets framing her blue eyes.

"You're beautiful," her father said reverently. "Silas Amberton is a very lucky man."

"And I'm a very lucky woman," Florence said. "I love him, Father."

"I know you do," her father assured her. "I also know he loves you. If I didn't believe that with every fiber of my being, I wouldn't leave Paris without you."

The music floating up the staircase changed from a soft melody to the opening chords of the wedding march.

"Dr. Robinson, it's time for you to get married."

Florence caught her breath with wonder. "I'm ready, Dr. Robinson."

As Florence walked down the stairs with her father, she was amazed at the turns her life had taken. What had begun as a fun graduation trip, had turned into a life or death situation. The Paris Siege had stretched her beyond anything she could have imagined. It had matured her, and it had given her the love of her life that she never believed she would find.

She'd learned so much. She had discovered the greatest beauty of life was its mystery. She had learned to embrace the inability to know what course her life would take. At the same time, she had realized she could impact the final form of her life by being open to constant discovery, and committed to determined effort. Once unable to move forward without guarantees of certainty, Florence had learned to welcome the fact that accepting the unknown and the unknowable would eliminate regret.

When her father walked her toward the front of the room, her friends and colleagues from the hospital rose, warm smiles on every face. She glanced at them and returned the smiles. Then she focused her attention entirely on the man waiting for her.

Silas Amberton had been a complete and utter surprise.

She could hardly wait to spend the rest of her life embracing the unknown and the unknowable with him.

Chapter Twenty-Six

"Good morning!" Carrie called as she entered the medical office they had recently named Bregdan Medical Clinic, in honor of Biddy Flannagan. She opened her mouth to comment on the beautiful spring day but closed it when she saw the expression on her partners' faces. "What's wrong?"

Janie held up a telegram. "I'm not sure I would say it's *wrong*, but it certainly changes things."

Carrie walked over and took the telegram from her.

Not coming back to America. Married Dr. Silas Amberton. Starting practice together in Paris. Father will bring letter with all the details. Sorry to disappoint but I've never been happier.

Carrie's mouth dropped open as she read it once, twice and then several times more as she tried to absorb what she was reading. "Well..." she finally murmured.

"I know I should be thrilled for her," Janie said. "And I *am*, but I was so looking forward to having her be part of the practice."

Carrie looked back at the telegram. The news had come through from Peter days ago that the Franco-Prussian War was over, and Paris was no longer under siege. The three of them had been counting the days until Florence returned to the shores of America and sent them a telegram saying she was on her way to Richmond. Now, that telegram would never arrive.

"It must be quite the story," Elizabeth said. "I never thought Florence would marry. She was so focused on her career that I didn't think it was possible for her to fall in love." Her voice was bemused. "To fall in love in the middle of a city under siege is quite a feat."

"It's not as difficult as you might think," Carrie said with amusement, remembering how the horrors of the war had not kept her from falling in love with Robert. "It sometimes intensifies what's already there because you're in constant fear of losing each other."

"He's a doctor," Janie commented. "They must have worked together."

"And now they're continuing to work together," Carrie replied. "Oh, come on girls, we should be wildly happy for her. It's so romantic to sail to Paris, get trapped by a war, and fall in love with a doctor who steals your heart."

Janie looked abashed. "When you put it like that, I feel horribly selfish for feeling a moment of anything but happiness for her."

"Besides," Elizabeth added with a smirk, "now we won't have to share our patients."

Carrie laughed. "Since I just got back into the city last night, perhaps you can tell me what's going on around here. We won't know the full story on Florence until we receive the letter she wrote."

"Always the practical one," Janie grumbled.

Carrie laughed harder. "This may be the only time in the history of the world when you tell me I'm the more practical one of the two of us. I'm going to savor this moment because I'm quite sure it will never happen again!"

Janie scowled at her and then joined in the laughter.

"If you two can stop laughing long enough to hear my report, I'll be happy to give it," Elizabeth said primly.

The sound of their vibrant Italian friend being prim and proper sent Carrie and Janie into peals of laughter again.

Carrie was gasping for air by the time she could control her mirth. "Mercy!" she pleaded. "Please don't anyone make me laugh again."

Elizabeth chuckled. "If any of our patients walked in right now, they would probably walk right back out, convinced we're crazy."

"On the other hand," Janie pointed out, "they would probably be thrilled to have doctors that know how to have fun."

"True," Elizabeth conceded. "I have no idea why most doctors seem to be so dour and serious."

"It makes them look more authoritative when they're trying to control women's choices and rights," Carrie retorted. The truth of her statement was instantly sobering. "So what's happened in the last two weeks?"

Elizabeth grinned. "We've gained eight new patients," she said triumphantly. "Our last three seminars have helped spread the word. We're selling a lot of Queen Anne's lace…" Her voice trailed away. "By the way, did you bring a new supply?"

"I did," Carrie assured her. "I'm keeping my fingers crossed that I'll have enough to last through the fall. I've already set up a team of Rose's students who are eager to earn some extra income. When the mothers found out about it, they asked if they could help, too. They're as excited about the extra income as they are about learning how effective it is."

"Good!" Elizabeth continued with her report. "While most of our patients have come looking for contraceptive help, we're also helping them with many other issues." She frowned suddenly. "The only time the surgical room is in use, though, is when you're here. We had one of our patients bring in her son who had broken his leg. We had to send her elsewhere." Her frown deepened. "We'd counted on Florence filling that gaping hole."

"Losing Florence is hard," Carrie agreed, "but I have to believe that someone else is waiting for us to make an offer to them. Florence isn't the only wonderful surgeon coming out of medical college. We'll find the right person."

"When?" Elizabeth demanded.

"At just the right time," Carrie replied evenly.

Elizabeth regarded her with exasperation. "You do realize your constant optimism can be wearing, don't you?"

"Perhaps," Carrie said calmly, "but it works better for me than your constant worry seems to work for you." She raised a brow. "Isn't it exhausting?"

"It's unnatural to be happy all the time!" Elizabeth retorted. "Don't you ever get pessimistic or angry?"

Carrie and Janie looked at each other and started laughing all over again.

When they regained control, Carrie answered the question. "Of course I do! There have been so many times in my life when I've been pessimistic and angry." She paused as she considered her next words. "I suppose I've discovered that it takes far less energy to be optimistic and hopeful. From my experience, it never helps to worry about anything. It just makes me tired, and it makes it harder to focus on finding a solution. There are certainly times when I fall back into my old ways, but it's easier to come out of them now."

Elizabeth stared at her. "You're not even thirty years old, Carrie. It's unnatural to have so much wisdom at your age."

Carrie smiled. "I'm only a month away from turning thirty." The realization was sobering. "I've lost my mother, been shot while escaping the plantation, gone through a war as a doctor—when my city was under siege for far too long—and had my husband murdered on the same day I lost my daughter. I suppose all of those things have forced me to be old before my time." She pushed away the sadness her words brought. She would have been happy to give up the lessons she had learned from any, or all, of those experiences. Since that wasn't an option, she chose gratitude for the things she'd learned.

Elizabeth sighed dramatically. "Fine. I suppose I'll have to accept that I'm a spoiled, childish Yankee."

"Every practice needs one," Janie assured her.

Elizabeth's eyes widened with disbelief. When she looked more closely at Janie, though, she saw the laughter dancing in her eyes. "You're a terrible person," she accused.

"Perhaps," Janie said serenely. "But you're a spoiled, childish Yankee."

The good-natured sparring sent Carrie into side-holding laughter again. "I certainly don't have this much fun at the plantation office!"

"Which means you need to spend more time here," Elizabeth observed when she got her own hysteria under control.

"Um, is this a bad time?"

Carrie started at the sound of another voice in the room. A quick look toward the door confirmed it was Davis Milner. "Of course not," she said, doing her best to make her voice sound professional, though her lips continued to twitch. "Please come in, Mr.Milner."

The veteran entered, his face lively with curiosity. "Y'all sure were laughing hard when I came up the sidewalk."

"Are you sure that was us?" Janie asked innocently.

Mr. Milner appraised her closely. "Unless you have three other people in this building that sound like cats caterwauling."

Carrie tried to control the laughter from bubbling over again, but it was impossible. The room erupted once more, only this time Mr. Milner joined them.

When the laughter finally stopped, he spoke again. "You mind telling me what we're laughing about?"

"The list is long," Carrie answered. She reached for his chart. "Let's go into my office for your checkup."

When they were settled, she turned to him eagerly. "Your face says you're doing much better."

"Yep. The hypericum started working right away, but it's taken most of these two months for almost all the pain to go away. I ain't complaining, though. I figured I would have to spend the rest of my life hurting." He paused. "I got a new job yesterday. I didn't believe I would ever work again, but now that I don't spend every moment of the day in pain, I realized I could. I got a job in an office where I don't have to stand on my fake leg all day."

Carrie was thrilled. "I'm so happy to hear that."

Mr. Milner turned to look out her window for a moment. Spring had caused an explosion of color from the brilliant azaleas and hundreds of daffodils they'd planted outside the clinic. "When the war ended, I figured my life was over. I didn't die like so many of my friends, but I might as well have. I didn't have anything to come back to. I couldn't work. I didn't figure a woman would ever want me."

"And now?" Carrie asked softly.

"And now...and now I have hope."

Moses could feel Felicia trembling as they stepped off the train onto the station platform in Memphis. He grasped his daughter's hand more tightly but didn't say anything. He knew Felicia needed to experience the return to Memphis in her own way.

Moses grabbed their bags and led them toward a carriage. He'd made reservations for them at a small hotel close to the neighborhood where Felicia had lived with her parents. He hoped being so close to her old home wouldn't make her trip even more traumatic, but she'd assured him she wanted to stay there.

"Are you alright?" Moses asked quietly.

Felicia gazed up at him. "I think so," she said unsteadily.

As the carriage wound its way through the streets, Moses battled his own emotions. It had been almost five years since he, Robert, Matthew and Peter had traveled to Memphis to help Matthew commemorate the *Sultana* tragedy that had claimed so many lives at the end of the war. He had never expected to be caught up in the violent race riot that had killed Felicia's parents.

Every corner created flashes of memory - scared faces, bloodied bodies, burning buildings...

"Daddy?"

Moses pushed his memories away as he looked down. "Yes, Felicia?"

"Can we go by my school first?"

Moses leaned forward and spoke to the driver. "Will you take us by the school at the corner of South and Causey?"

The driver looked back at him. "Why you want to go there?"

"My daughter attended school there when she was young. She would like to see it again."

The driver cast a sympathetic look at Felicia before his eyes hardened. "The school ain't there no more."

Felicia gasped. "What happened to it?"

The driver hesitated. "You know about what happened the first days of May, back five years ago?"

Moses nodded. "We were here."

The man looked at him sharply. "The school got burned," he said gruffly. "'Course, that was a right bad time. By the time it all ended, there were ninety-one homes that got torched. They destroyed four churches and eight schools at the same time." He shook his head. "I'm real sorry 'bout your school, miss."

"Thank you," Felicia said weakly.

Moses could hear the tears in her voice, but her eyes were dry. "How well do you remember seeing me at your school that morning?"

"I remember all of it," Felicia replied. "I went to school that day, like I always did. Our teacher, Mr. Rankin, told us that we were being incredibly brave, but that he wanted us to go home because it was too dangerous." She managed a smile. "I'd met you the day before, when you came to tell us stories. I told Mr. Rankin about the men who burned down Mama's school back in Virginia. You had told us everyone was real scared, but that they came back for school the next day." She lifted her chin. "I told Mr. Rankin I wanted to be brave like those students, and that I wanted to be in school."

Moses swallowed past the lump in his throat. "I had never seen anyone so brave." He'd also been terrified for her.

"You told me there was a time for bravery, and there was a time when it was wise to be careful. You told me to go back home and to stay inside with my mama and daddy."

"I remember." Moses could feel the driver's questioning eyes on him, but he wasn't in the mood to explain his relationship with Felicia just then.

Felicia hesitated before she looked him in the eye. "I asked you what would happen if the men who were doing bad things came to our house." Her voice quavered, sounding too much like the little girl she had been five years ago. "You told me that wouldn't happen."

"I know," Moses said gruffly. "I knew at the time that I might be lying to you, but I didn't know what else to say. I'm sorry."

Felicia nodded and took a deep breath. Then she looked at the driver. "How many people died that day?"

Moses stiffened but didn't say anything. If Felicia wanted to understand what had happened, then she needed the facts.

The driver answered. "There were forty-six of us killed, miss. Seventy-five others got hurt bad."

"How many women were raped?"

"Felicia..." Moses couldn't help the protest that rolled from his lips.

"I need to know, Daddy. The policeman who killed my mama said he was going to rape her and me first. I want to know."

Moses wasn't sure the information was good for her, but he was afraid denying it would make what she was trying to accomplish even harder. He nodded slowly to the driver who was waiting for his direction.

"We know for sure that five women was raped," he said sorrowfully. "There mighta been more, but we didn't know. I 'magine there were some that didn't want to talk about it."

Felicia turned her eyes to stare at the road they were riding down.

Moses watched her closely, uncertain how to help her deal with being in Memphis again.

"I want to go by the house," Felicia stated quietly.

Moses started to shake his head, thought better of it, and stopped. Perhaps he could present her a better option. "Honey, I thought we would check into our hotel first. We're both tired after being on the train for two days. We can eat dinner and then go tomorrow."

Felicia turned to him, her lips set in a determined line. "I want to go now, Daddy." She gazed at him with eyes full of wounded vulnerability. "Please."

Moses relented. He gave the driver the closest cross streets he could remember. So much of that day had been a blur. As they rumbled down the street, he desperately tried to figure out what Felicia would need from him when they got to her old house.

"What happened to the men? The ones who killed my parents? And all the other ones that killed and hurt people?"

Moses grimaced. He knew the answer, but he'd hoped he wouldn't have to say it. Dealing with her grief and pain was going to be hard enough. Felicia didn't need even more to be angry about.

Felicia turned to him. "Daddy? What happened to them? Do you know?"

"I do," Moses admitted. He took a deep breath and told her the truth. "Nothing, Felicia. Nothing happened to them."

Felicia turned astonished eyes to him. "*Nothing*? What do you mean?"

Moses' throat tightened so badly he couldn't force the words out. He knew the rage that had engulfed him when he learned the truth from Matthew. How would Felicia handle it?

The driver saved him from answering. "He means nothing happened to them. Not a one of those men paid for what they did. Not even one got charged."

Felicia stared at him wildly and then turned to Moses. "Is that true?"

Moses' silence and anguished expression was her answer.

"How is that possible?" she cried.

"It happens, miss," the driver said gruffly. "It ain't just happenin' in Memphis. I figure it be happenin' everywhere."

Moses could feel the tension and anger radiating from his daughter. He didn't blame her; he just didn't know how to help her. He reached over and took her ice-cold hand, but he didn't say anything as the driver continued forward.

When the driver pulled to a stop, Moses had a thought. "Would you wait for us until we return? I'll most certainly pay you for your time."

"I can do that," the driver agreed readily. "What you lookin' for?"

"Where my parents lived," Felicia told him, her face set in hard lines. "They both were murdered during the riot."

"I'm real sorry, miss."

"My name is Felicia. This is Moses. He's my daddy now. My mama, Rose, is back home in Virginia. Moses saved me and took me home with him after my parents were killed."

The driver dipped his head in acknowledgement. "I'm Gus. It's a pleasure to meet you both." He chose his next words carefully. "Miss Felicia, don't be too disappointed if you don't find that house. Lots of houses been deserted. They either fall down after a while, or they get tore down."

"Why are they being deserted?" Felicia asked. "What are the people doing?"

"They're leaving," Gus said bluntly. "Back before the war there weren't no more than three thousand blacks here in Memphis. I was one of the ones that came during the war when we got our freedom. I fought for the Union for the last two years, and then I came right back here. By the end of the war, there was close to twenty thousand of us. When we first started coming, the folks here were real glad to have us." He grimaced. "When the war ended and all the soldiers came home lookin' for work, it was real hard for everyone. They figured we was takin' their jobs. That was too much for some of the white folks, so they figured they would make us want to leave. They wanted us to go back out to the plantations to work cotton again. I reckon it worked. After that riot, over five thousand black folks left the city. Don't know how many are workin' the fields again, but they's gone. Ain't no new ones comin' in. Can't say as how I blame 'em."

"Where did they go?" Moses asked.

Gus shrugged. "Lots of places. Didn't matter much as long as they could get out of Memphis. There's still a bunch of us left, but we be a whole lot more careful now."

"Why haven't you left?" Felicia asked.

Gus shrugged again. "Where would I go? I don't reckon there's any place in this country that be what I think of as safe for black folk. Even though there weren't nobody that paid for what they done back durin' the riots, the whole country paid for it in a different way."

"How?"

Gus turned to Moses. "I remember them journalist fellas you were with, Moses. Weren't one of them named Matthew?"

"Yes."

"I talked to Matthew a couple days after it all happened. He promised me that him and the other fellas he was with were gonna tell the story in every newspaper in America."

"They did," Moses assured him.

Gus nodded. "I figured they must have. I heard that the riot here, and the one down in New Orleans round about the same time, was what got the government all riled up to give us the right to vote. They was able to push out the Democrats, includin' that President Johnson fella. I know they's tryin' to do the right thing now." He sighed. "I reckon it's gonna take a long time, though."

"Aren't you angry?" Felicia burst out.

Gus turned to look at her. "I don't know as how I'm the one you should be askin' that question to, Miss Felicia. You seem to be right angry yourself."

"How could I not be?" Felicia said rigidly.

"I reckon you got a right to be angry, sho 'nuff."

"But what?"

Gus raised a brow. "I didn't say nothing with a 'but' in it."

"I could hear it in your voice," Felicia said impatiently. "You told me I have a right to be angry, but what you were actually thinking was that I have a right to be angry, *but...*"

Gus held her gaze for a long moment. "But what you be doin' with that anger, Miss Felicia?"

Moses wanted to cheer when the question came out of their driver's mouth, but he knew it was best to remain silent.

"What am I *doing* with it?"

Moses didn't miss the look Felicia shot him. His daughter was wondering if he was somehow in cahoots with the driver to say essentially the same thing he'd told her on the banks of the James River. She had come a long way in dealing with the anger that had gotten her removed from Oberlin College, but he wasn't surprised that being back in Memphis had reignited it. Perhaps the only way to be rid of it for good was to allow it to flame up and burn out.

"Yes," Gus answered. "What you be doing with it? You seem like a real smart young lady, Miss Felicia. I seen anger eat a lot of people up."

Felicia stared at him. "Are you saying you're not angry about what happened here five years ago?"

"I didn't say that," Gus said calmly. "I simply asked what *you* be doin' with your anger."

Moses joined him in silence as they both waited for Felicia to respond.

She finally shook her head. "I don't *know* what to do," she admitted in a small voice. "I used to be so certain that I was going to make life better for all blacks in America. Especially black girls and women." She looked at Gus. "I'm a student at Oberlin College in Ohio."

Gus whistled. "That's a fine school." His eyes narrowed. "Ain't you a bit young to be in college, Miss Felicia?"

"I suppose so," Felicia said impatiently, "but I am." She shook her head again. "I used to be real proud of that," she said bitterly. "Now...I suppose I don't see the point."

"The point of what?" Gus asked.

"The point of trying to make a difference. America is never going to let blacks be equal. They're never going to do anything but put us down and wish we didn't exist. No matter what we do, the KKK and other vigilante groups are going to continue to hurt and kill us. It's not just them, though. It was policemen who killed my mama and daddy. It's not going to stop."

Gus eyed her steadily. "I reckon that's true."

Felicia narrowed her eyes. "You believe that, too?"

Gus' gaze never wavered. "I didn't say that, Miss Felicia. I reckon I've learned that if somebody believes somethin' strong enough, then it be true for them. If you done decided to give up, there ain't nothin' I can say that's gonna change that. But me?" he asked. "I ain't never gonna give up. I'm gonna keep right on fightin' for change. It weren't so long ago that I couldn't figure out a way I could ever be free. I grew up on a cotton plantation not too far outside Memphis. I worked from sunup to sundown from the time I be six years old. I figured being a slave was the only life I would ever know." He shrugged. "Then it changed. All of a sudden, I was free. I ain't never gonna give that up. I figure it's gonna take a right long time for things to be right in this country for black folk, but I ain't gonna sit back and just give up."

Moses stared at the carriage driver, wondering what this man could have become if he'd been born free, with opportunity. He had a keen intellect, and his ability to cut through to the heart of an issue was impressive. He hoped someday the doors would open for him to be in politics.

"What do *you* do?" Felicia asked after an extended silence. "To change things?"

Gus peered at her speculatively. "You know Katrina Harper?"

Felicia gasped with surprise. "Katrina Harper? Yes, she's a student at Oberlin. She's a few years ahead of me. Is that the Katrina you're talking about? How do *you* know her?"

Moses watched Gus closely, not certain he was going to answer. In truth, Moses was as curious as Felicia to hear the man's response.

"I'm payin' for her college," Gus revealed. "Her and three others. Two of them be at Fisk University in Nashville. The last be going to Hampton University over there in Virginia where you be from."

Felicia's mouth gaped open. "How are you doing that?"

"I drive this carriage a whole lot," Gus admitted. Suddenly, he reached out and took Felicia's hand. "Miss Felicia, I figure the best thing I can do for black folks is to make sure some young people get a chance to be all they can be. There always gonna be things to be angry about. Blacks ain't the only people who got things to be angry 'bout. I figure if anybody wants things to change, it's up to them to do somethin' about it." He smiled. "Them young people I got in school promised me they gonna work hard to make things better for ever'body else. I believe them. They got things to be angry 'bout, too."

"But they decided to do something about it," Felicia said.

"Yep."

Moses watched as conflicting emotions rolled across his daughter's face. He knew she had unfinished business in Memphis. When she turned to gaze at him, he held out his hand. "You've got a lot to think about," he said gently, "but we still have some things to do."

He turned to Gus, hoping the man could read the gratitude in his eyes. "Will you wait?"

"Long as it takes," Gus assured him.

Claim a *FREE* copy of
The Bregdan Principle!

You'll receive it in high resolution and full color – a file you can print directly on your own printer, or send to have it done. Just join my mailing list!

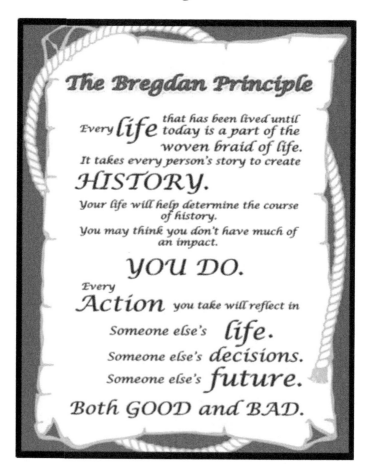

An Invitation

Before you read the last two chapters of Shining Through Dark Clouds, I would like to invite you to join my mailing list so that you're never left wondering what is going to happen next. ☺

I will also GIVE you a free copy of The Bregdan Principle that you can print or your computer, or have printed for you.

Join my Email list so you can:

- Receive notice of all new books & audio releases.
- Be a part of my Launch celebrations. I give away lots of gifts! ☺
- Read my weekly blog while you're waiting for a new book.
- Be part of The Bregdan Chronicles Family!
- Learn about all the other books I write.

Just go to www.BregdanChronicles.net and fill out the form.

I look forward to having you become part of The Bregdan Chronicles Family!

Blessings,
Ginny Dye

Chapter Twenty-Seven

Moses held Felicia's hand securely as they walked into the neighborhood where she had lived with her parents. Her footsteps were steady, but he could feel the trembling in her hands. Not for the first time, he wished Rose had been able to join them. Felicia had insisted that Rose not leave her students, but he suspected she was wishing for her mama right now.

As they rounded the curve and came in sight of the rundown shack, Felicia faltered for the first time. When she stumbled, Moses put his hand under her elbow to steady her.

Felicia took a shuddering breath and continued onward. Her face looked like it had been carved in stone, with the exception of trembling lips.

When they drew closer, Moses could tell the once rundown shack was on the verge of collapse. He suspected it hadn't been lived in since her parents' murder.

When they drew closer, Felicia stopped just before the spot where she had last seen her parents laying in a pool of blood. She was silent but continued to take deep shuddering breaths.

Helpless to know how to alleviate her pain, Moses gripped her hand tightly but remained silent.

Though the blood had long ago been absorbed by the weed-choked ground, it couldn't absorb the feeling of loss and violence that seemed to still be in the air.

Groaning softly, Felicia collapsed to her knees and covered her face. Continuing to groan, she began to rock back and forth.

Moses stepped back in respect for her grief. "Let it go, honey. Let it go," he whispered.

Finally, the sobs came. Shuddering sobs wracked her body.

"Mama... Daddy..." The words seemed ripped from her soul, sounding guttural as they floated into the air.

Moses could feel the eyes of people watching, but no one came outside.

"Mama... Daddy... I'm so sorry... I'm so sorry." Felicia shook her head as she pounded her fist on the hard ground. "I miss you. I'm so sorry." The last words came out in a whisper as the sobs began to subside.

Felicia still knelt on the ground, but her sobs had run their course. She'd never experienced such raw emotion, not even during the day on the James River with her father. Part of her felt achingly, painfully empty. Another part of her felt as if something had finished. Her heart was still too sore to analyze this new feeling, but she felt it just the same.

"Felicia?"

Felicia jerked her head up when she heard someone say her name.

"Felicia? Is that really you?"

Felicia searched her memory bank, but she couldn't put an identity to the round-faced woman staring down at her with kind eyes full of compassion. "Yes. I'm sorry, but I..."

"I'm Roberta Ann, honey. I knew you when you was little."

Felicia felt a spark of hope. "You knew my parents?"

"Yes, honey. We wasn't real close, but me and your mama used to talk while we was puttin' out laundry and workin' in the garden." The woman's eyes devoured her. "You was the apple of her and your daddy's eye."

Felicia felt tears prick the back of her eyes again, but she swallowed them. "Do you know where they're buried, Roberta Ann? Do you know what happened to them?"

Moses stepped forward. "I think I remember you. I talked to you the day after they were murdered."

"Yes," Roberta Ann replied, shame etched on her face. "I was too scared to talk to you back then. I didn't know you..."

"I understand," Moses said soothingly.

"Do you know something?" Felicia asked. She had come here hoping to say good-bye to her mama and daddy. In some ways she felt she had just accomplished that, but... "I want to tell them good-bye. Do you know where they're buried?"

Roberta Ann's eyes were full of pity. "I wouldn't say they was rightly buried, Felicia. All of us were real scared after what happened the day they killed your folks. We was real scared to be out after dark, but your mama and daddy were real kind to folks."

Felicia remembered. Her mama used to fix soups to take to sick neighbors, and she shared any extra that came from their garden. She waited quietly to hear what else the woman had to say.

"That first night, we crept out and pulled your mama and daddy's bodies back into the house. We didn't want nobody from the city comin' down to take them."

"You mean they were in the house the next day when I talked to you?" Moses asked with astonishment.

Felicia gritted her teeth. Moses would have made sure they were buried properly if he'd known. Why hadn't she told him?

"They were," Roberta Ann admitted. She turned to Felicia. "I'm so sorry, Felicia. All of us were terrified. Somebody told another woman who used to live on the other side of your house that the policemen had paid off some black folks to tell them where bodies were." She scowled. "I reckon they didn't want anybody to know the truth about what they done. I knew if the city came and got them, we wouldn't ever know what happened to them."

As much as Felicia hated what she was hearing, she suspected she would have done the same thing if she had been in that situation. "What did you do with them?"

"We buried them at Elmwood Cemetery, honey. Two days after the riot was over. We waited until late one night and then carried them over in a wagon."

"Do you know where they are?" Felicia asked eagerly, feeling hope for the first time.

"I do," Roberta Ann assured her. "I made sure they took me along with 'em. No one knew what happened to you, but I figured if you ever came back, I could at least tell you that much."

Felicia gasped and threw her arms around the woman. "Thank you," she whispered. She hugged her for several moments and then stepped back.

"What *did* happen to you, child? Where you been all this time?"

"Virginia," Felicia responded. She reached back for Moses' hand and pulled him forward. "This is Moses. He saved me that day after I saw my parents killed. He took me back to Virginia. He and his wife, Rose, adopted me.

They're my mama and daddy now. They've been wonderful to me."

"Do tell?" Roberta Ann asked with delight. She eyed Moses carefully. "Now that I don't suspect you're working with the police, you seem like a real fine fella."

Moses smiled. "Thank you. And thank you for taking care of Felicia's parents. We came here hoping to find out what happened to them so that she could say a proper good-bye."

Roberta Ann wasn't done with her questions. She turned back to Felicia. "What are you doin' now?"

"I'm a college student," Felicia responded quietly. She didn't have the energy to explain all that had happened in her life in the last five years.

Roberta Ann stared at her. "Am I not remembering somethin' right? Ain't you just fifteen now?"

Felicia smiled. "I am, but I'm in college."

Roberta Ann threw back her head with a laugh. "Your mama used to tell me every time we talked that you was the smartest little girl she'd ever seen. I thought she was just talking the nonsense all proud mamas talk, but..." She whistled. "I reckon she was tellin' the truth."

Felicia opened her mouth to respond, but Roberta Ann wasn't done. "Your mama used to tell me that you was gonna change the world, Felicia. She told me that *her* little girl weren't gonna have to be a slave. She told me that you was gonna make things better for ever'body cause you were so smart."

Tears began to swim in Felicia's eyes again. She remembered her mama telling her that, but she had no idea she'd told other people. Somehow, it made it mean more. "Thank you for telling me that," she said softly.

Roberta Ann's face filled with soft compassion. "Baby, your mama and daddy are so proud of you. I don't know all the mysteries of death, but I reckon they know just what you're doin'. If they was here right now, your mama would be raising those eyebrows at me and tellin' me just how right she had been."

Felicia and Moses stood next to each other, hands clasped as they stared down at the simple wood cross that designated the place where her parents had been laid to rest together.

Elmwood Cemetery was beautiful. The trees had burst forth with leaves, their vibrant green shouting of new life in the midst of death. Azaleas contributed beautiful red and white blossoms, while dogwoods were on the verge of bursting into bloom.

Felicia held a large bouquet of daffodils picked from Gus' yard.

The day after he had driven them around the city, they had appeared at his house with most of the money they had brought with them on the trip. Felicia had insisted he needed it more than they did. She wanted it to go to the students he was paying for.

His gift to them had been a huge bouquet of flowers for the grave.

"Are you sure you don't want some time alone?" Moses asked.

Felicia shook her head firmly. "No. I want Daddy and Mama to meet you. If Roberta Ann is right that they know what's going on with me, I want to introduce them to the man who saved my life."

Moses' throat tightened as she looked up at him with loving eyes. "I'm honored to meet them," he said gruffly. For the thousandth time, he wished Rose was with them.

Felicia knelt to put the daffodils on the grass around the cross.

When she looked up at Moses, he knelt to join her.

"Hi, Daddy. Hi, Mama," Felicia began softly. "I'm glad I found you. I want you to meet Moses." Her voice caught. "I would have given anything if y'all could have been my parents forever, but that didn't happen. I want you to know that God gave me a new mama and daddy. They've been wonderful to me."

A soft breeze picked up, causing the leaves to rustle and sway above their heads.

"Mama, I want you to know I'm doing what you wanted me to do. I'm in college now. I lost my way for a bit," Felicia admitted. "I was so angry about what happened... and what is still happening... I lost hope for a while." Her voice faltered but then grew strong again. "I know now that anger is only acceptable if I use it to change the things that make me angry. You always told me that you believed I would make things better for black people. I don't know exactly how that's going to happen, but I promise you I'm not ever going to stop trying." She swallowed hard. "Losing you and Daddy was the worst day of my life."

Moses laid a hand on Felicia's shoulder as tears made it impossible for her to continue.

"I wish I'd had the chance to meet you two," he said. "I wish y'all could have raised this extraordinary young woman, but my wife and I love her with all our heart. She's so special because of everything y'all did for her when you were alive. We're going to make sure she has every chance to become what you dreamed she would be. You have my promise on that."

"Moses always keeps his promises," Felicia whispered. "He and Rose, both." She leaned forward and placed her hands on the small, unmarked cross. "Roberta Ann made sure you had a beautiful place to be after you died. She waited for me to come looking for you so I would know how to find you. She showed me where you were yesterday."

Moses' eyes misted over as he thought of Roberta Ann's compassion and sacrifice. She had left Memphis early that morning – catching a train after she came by the hotel to tell them good-bye. She had stayed in the city that held so many terrifying memories just in case Felicia returned. Her two sisters had fled north to Chicago a few days after the riot, but she had refused to join them. Until now…

"I don't know when I'll be back," Felicia said softly, "but I'm glad I got to tell you a real good-bye. I love you both. I always will."

Moses turned and wrapped her tightly in his arms as she cried. The gut-wrenching sobs from before had been replaced by quiet tears that siphoned off the fragile remnants of the pain in her heart.

He knew Felicia would be alright now.

Chapter Twenty-Eight

Carrie, Rose and Abby sank down on the log they had claimed as their own. The calm waters of the James River lapped gently at the shore. Swallows and purple martins swooped and soared over the surface, dining on the bugs that hovered. Dusk announced an end to another day as the sun sat slightly above the horizon.

"How are you doing with Felicia going back to school?" Carrie asked.

"It was time," Rose replied. "We originally thought it was best for her to stay through September, but she came back from Memphis a new person. When she told us she wanted to return and take summer classes to make up for what she missed, we knew she was ready." She stared out over the water before she continued. "I will miss her terribly, but Felicia has a purpose far bigger than anything I can possibly understand."

"Not true," Abby said. "Both you and Carrie are fulfilling that same kind of purpose. It's because you understand it that you were willing to let her go."

Carrie pondered those words as she watched the river flow by. "It's been a hard seven months. There were times I wondered if all of us would make it."

"And yet here we all are," Abby said gently. "In all honesty, if I look back at the last eleven years, each of them has been difficult."

Rose nodded. "There were so many times when I wondered if I would make it through these last months."

"I remember the conversation we had last fall," Carrie said. "We talked about dark clouds that were threatening to swallow our country. We decided then that we were going to be part of the light shining through the dark clouds."

"And on that note..." Rose pulled out a sheet of paper. "Felicia gave this to me right before she got on the train in Richmond yesterday."

I have faced the darkness.
I have revisited the pain.
I have knelt in the blood that stole my life.
I have said good-bye to the love ripped from me.
I have screamed my fury.
I have cried my tears.
And now life begins anew.
Dark clouds almost smothered me.
Dark pain almost swallowed me.
In my fury, I blocked the light,
Afraid of what I would see.
But now I know...
I am the light that shines through the darkness.
I must *be the light that shines through the darkness.*
I must *be the breeze that forces the dark clouds away.*
I am.
I will.
Forever.

To Be Continued...

#16 Coming Early Fall 2019

Would you be so kind as to leave a Review on Amazon?

Go to www.Amazon.com

Put Shining Through Dark Clouds, Ginny Dye into the Search Box.

Leave a Review.

I love hearing from my readers!

Thank you!

The Bregdan Principle

Every life that has been lived until today
is a part of the woven
braid of life.

It takes every person's story to create
history.

Your life will help determine the course of
history.

You may think you don't have much of an
impact.

You do.

Every action you take will reflect in
someone else's life.

Someone else's decisions.

Someone else's future.

Both good and bad.

The Bregdan Chronicles

Storm Clouds Rolling In
1860 – 1861

On To Richmond
1861 – 1862

Spring Will Come
1862 – 1863

Dark Chaos
1863 – 1864

The Long Last Night
1864 – 1865

Carried Forward By Hope
April – December 1865

Glimmers of Change
December – August 1866

Shifted By The Winds
August – December 1866

Always Forward
January – October 1867

Walking Into The Unknown
October 1867 – October 1868

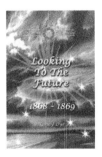

Looking To The Future
October 1868 – June 1869

Horizons Unfolding
November 1869 – March 1870

The Twisted Road of One Writer
The Birth of The Bregdan Chronicles

Misty Shadows of Hope
1870

Shining Through Dark Clouds
1870 - 1871

Many more coming... Go to DiscoverTheBregdanChronicles.com to see how many are available now!

<u>Other Books by Ginny Dye</u>

<u>Pepper Crest High Series - Teen Fiction</u>
Time For A Second Change
It's Really A Matter of Trust
A Lost & Found Friend
Time For A Change of Heart

<u>Fly To Your Dreams Series – Allegorical Fantasy</u>
Dream Dragon
Born To Fly
Little Heart
The Miracle of Chinese Bamboo

All titles by Ginny Dye
www.BregdanPublishing.com

Author Biography

Who am I? Just a normal person who happens to love to write. If I could do it all anonymously, I would. In fact, I did the first go 'round. I wrote under a pen name. On the off chance I would ever become famous - I didn't want to be! I don't like the limelight. I don't like living in a fishbowl. I especially don't like thinking I have to look good everywhere I go, just in case someone recognizes me! I finally decided none of that matters. If you don't like me in overalls and a baseball cap, too bad. If you don't like my haircut or think I should do something different than what I'm doing, too bad. I'll write books that you will hopefully like, and we'll both let that be enough! :) Fair?

But let's see what you might want to know. I spent many years as a Wanderer. My dream when I graduated from college was to experience the United States. I grew up in the South. There are many things I love about it but I wanted to live in other places. So I did. I moved 57 times, traveled extensively in 49 of the 50 states, and had more experiences than I will ever be able to recount. The only state I haven't been in is Alaska, simply because I refuse to visit such a vast, fabulous place until I have at least a month. Along the way I had glorious adventures. I've canoed through the Everglade Swamps, snorkeled in the Florida Keys and windsurfed in the Gulf of Mexico. I've white-water rafted down the New River and Bungee jumped in the Wisconsin Dells. I've visited every National Park (in the off-season when there is more freedom!) and many of the State Parks. I've hiked thousands of miles of mountain trails and biked through Arizona deserts. I've canoed and biked through Upstate New York and Vermont, and polished off as much lobster as possible on the Maine Coast.

I had a glorious time and never thought I would find a place that would hold me until I came to the Pacific Northwest. I'd been here less than 2 weeks, and I knew I would never leave. My heart is so at home here with the towering firs, sparkling waters, soaring mountains and rocky beaches. I love the eagles & whales. In 5 minutes I can be hiking on 150 miles of trails in the mountains around my home, or gliding across the lake in my rowing shell. I love it!

Have you figured out I'm kind of an outdoors gal? If it can be done outdoors, I love it! Hiking, biking, windsurfing, rock-climbing, roller-blading, snow-shoeing, skiing, rowing, canoeing, softball, tennis... the list could go on and on. I love to have fun and I love to stretch my body. This should give you a pretty good idea of what I do in my free time.

When I'm not writing or playing, I'm building Millions For Positive Change - a fabulous organization I founded in 2001 - along with 60 amazing people who poured their lives into creating resources to empower people to make a difference with their lives.

What else? I love to read, cook, sit for hours in solitude on my mountain, and also hang out with friends. I love barbeques and block parties. Basically - I just love LIFE!

I'm so glad you're part of my world!

Ginny

Join my Email List so you can:

- Receive notice of all new books
- Be a part of my Launch Celebrations. I give away lots of Free gifts!
- Read my weekly BLOG while you're waiting for a new book.
- Be part of The Bregdan Chronicles Family!
- Learn about all the other books I write.

Just go to www.BregdanChronicles.net and fill out the form.

Made in the USA
Las Vegas, NV
12 December 2022